ECHOES

Also by Danielle Steel

Danielle Steel

ECHOES

Doubleday Large Print Home Library Edition

Delacorte Press

This Large Print Edition, prepared especially for Doubleday Large Print Home Library, contains the complete, unabridged text of the original Publisher's Edition.

ECHOES
A Delacorte Book / November 2004

Published by Bantam Dell
A Division of Random House, Inc.
New York, New York

Delacorte Press® is a registered trademark of Random House, Inc., and the colophon is a trademark of Random House, Inc. The jacket format and design of this book are protected trade dresses and trademarks of Bantam Dell Publishing, a division of Random House, Inc.

ISBN 0-7394-4733-5

Manufactured in the United States of America

This Large Print Book carries the
Seal of Approval of N.A.V.H.

To my beloved children, who are
so infinitely precious to me, each
of them so special:
Beatrix, Trevor, Todd, Nick, Sam,
Victoria, Vanessa, Maxx, and Zara.
May the echoes of your past, present,
and future always be kind and gentle.

With all my love,
Mommy
d.s.

"It's a wonder I haven't abandoned all my ideals. They seem so absurd and impractical. Yet I cling to them because I still believe, in spite of everything, that people are truly good at heart."

—Anne Frank

"Whoever saves one life, saves a world entire."

—Talmud

ECHOES

1

IT WAS A LAZY SUMMER AFTERNOON AS BEATA Wittgenstein strolled along the shores of Lake Geneva with her parents. The sun was hot and the air still, and as she walked pensively behind them, the birds and insects were making a tremendous racket. Beata and her younger sister Brigitte had come to Geneva with their mother for the summer. Beata had just turned twenty, and her sister was three years younger. It had been thirteen months since the Great War had begun the previous summer, and this year her father had wanted them out of Germany for their holiday. It was late August 1915, and he had just spent a month there with them. Both of her brothers were in the army and had managed to get leave to join them for a week. Horst was twenty-three and a lieutenant at divisional headquarters in Munich. Ulm was a captain in the 105th Infantry Regiment, part of the Thirtieth Division, attached to the Fourth Army. He had just turned twenty-seven during the week he spent with them in Geneva.

It had been nothing short of a miracle to get the entire family together. With the war seeming to devour all the young men in Germany, Beata worried constantly now about her brothers, as did their mother. Her father kept telling her that it would be over soon, but what Beata heard when she listened to her father and brothers talk was very different. The men were far more aware of the bleak times ahead than were the women. Her mother never spoke of the war to her, and Brigitte was far more upset that there were hardly any handsome young men to flirt with. Ever since she had been a little girl, all Brigitte had ever talked about was getting married. She had recently fallen in love with one of Horst's friends from university, and Beata had a strong suspicion that her beautiful younger sister would be getting engaged that winter.

Beata had no such interests or intentions. She had always been the quiet one, studious and far more serious, and she was much more interested in her studies than in finding a young man. Her father always said she was the perfect daughter. Their only moment of dissent had been when she had insisted she wanted to go to university like her brothers, which her father said was foolish. Although he himself was serious and scholarly, he didn't think that that degree of education was necessary for a woman. He told her he felt sure that in a short time she would be married and tending to a husband and children. She didn't need to go to university, and he hadn't allowed it.

Beata's brothers and their friends were a lively lot, and her sister was pretty and flirtatious. Beata had always felt different from them, set apart by her quiet ways and passion for education. In a perfect world, she would have loved to be a teacher, but when she said it, her siblings always laughed at her. Brigitte said that only poor girls became schoolteachers or governesses, and her brothers added that only ugly ones even thought about it. They loved to tease her, although Beata was neither poor nor ugly. Her father owned and ran one of the most important banks in Cologne, where they lived. They had a large handsome house in the Fitzengraben district, and her mother Monika was well known in Cologne, not only for her beauty but for her elegant clothes and jewelry. Like Beata, she was a quiet woman. Monika had married Jacob Wittgenstein when she was seventeen, and had been happy with him in the twenty-eight years since then.

The marriage had been arranged by their respective families, and was a good one. At the time their union had been the merger of two considerable fortunes, and Jacob had enlarged theirs impressively since then. He ran the bank with an iron fist and was almost clairvoyant about the banking business. Not only was their future secure, but so were those of their heirs. Everything about the Wittgensteins was solid. The only unpredictable element in their life now was the same one worrying everyone these days. The war was a great concern to them, particularly to Monika, with two sons in the army. The time they had shared in Switzerland had been a comforting respite, for the parents as well as the children.

Ordinarily, they spent their summers in Germany, at the seashore, but this year Jacob had wanted to get them all out of Germany for July and August. He had even spoken to one of the commanding generals whom he knew well, and gently asked the enormous favor of having both of his sons on leave and able to join them. The general had quietly arranged it. The Wittgensteins were that great rarity, a Jewish family that enjoyed not only great wealth but also enormous power. Beata was aware of it but paid little attention to her family's importance. She was far more interested in her studies. And although Brigitte sometimes fretted over the constraints their orthodoxy put on them, Beata, in her own quiet way, was deeply religious, which pleased her father. As a young man, he had shocked his own family by saying that he wanted to be a rabbi. His father had talked sense into him, and at the appropriate time, he had joined the family bank, along with his father, brothers, uncles, and grandfather before them. Theirs was a family steeped in tradition, and although Jacob's father had a great respect for the rabbinical life, he had no intention of sacrificing his son to it. And like the obedient son he was, Jacob went to work at the bank, and married shortly thereafter. At fifty, he was five years older than Beata's mother.

The entire family agreed that the decision to summer in Switzerland this year had been a good one. The Wittgensteins had many friends here, and Jacob and Monika had attended a number of parties, as had their children. Jacob knew everyone in the Swiss banking community and had gone to Lausanne and Zurich to see friends in those cities as well. Whenever possible, they took the girls with them. While Horst and Ulm were there, they spent as much time as they could enjoying their company. Ulm was leaving for the front when he got back, and Horst was stationed at divisional headquarters in Munich, which he seemed to find vastly amusing. In spite of the serious up-bringing he'd had, Horst was something of a playboy. He and Brigitte had much more in common with each other than either of them did with Beata.

As she fell behind the others, walking slowly along the lake, her oldest brother Ulm hung back and fell into step beside her. He was always protective of her, perhaps because he was seven years older. Beata knew he respected her gentle nature and loving ways.

"What are you thinking about, Bea? You look awfully serious walking along by yourself. Why don't you join us?"

Her mother and sister were far ahead by then, talking about fashion and the men Brigitte had found handsome at the previous week's parties. The men in the family were talking about the only subjects that interested them—which these days were the war and banking. After the war, Ulm was going back to work at the bank again, as he had for four years before. Their father said that Horst was going to have to stop playing, become serious, and join them. Horst had promised that as soon as the war was over, he would. He was only twenty-two when war was declared the year before, and he had assured his father that when the war was over, he'd be ready. And Jacob had said several times recently that it was time for Ulm to get married. The one thing Jacob expected of his children, or anyone in his immediate circle actually, was that they obey him. He expected that of his wife as well, and she had never disappointed him. Nor had his children, with the exception of

Horst, who had been dragging his feet about working when he went into the army. The last thing on Horst's mind at the moment was marriage. In fact, the only one interested in that prospect was Brigitte. Beata hadn't met a man who had swept her off her feet yet. Although she thought that many of her parents' friends' sons were handsome, many of the young ones seemed silly, and the older ones frightened her a bit and often seemed too somber. She was in no hurry to be married. Beata often said that if she married anyone, she hoped he would be a scholar, and not necessarily a banker. There was no way she could say that to her father, although she had confessed it to her mother and sister many times. Brigitte said that sounded boring. The handsome young friend of Horst's she had her eye on was as frivolous as she was, and from an equally important banking family. Jacob was intending to meet with the boy's father in September to discuss it, although Brigitte didn't know that. But so far, no suitor had emerged for Beata, nor did she really want one. She rarely spoke to anyone at parties. She went dutifully with her parents, wearing the dresses her mother chose for her. She was always polite to their hosts, and immensely relieved when it was time to go home. Unlike Brigitte, who had to be dragged away, complaining that it had been far too early to leave the party, and why did her family have to be so dull and boring. Horst was in complete agreement with her, and always had been. Beata and Ulm were the serious ones.

"Have you had fun in Geneva?" Ulm asked Beata quietly. He was the only one who made a serious effort to speak to her, and find out what she was thinking. Horst and Brigitte were far too busy playing and having fun to spend time on more erudite subjects with their sister.

"Yes, I have." Beata smiled shyly up at him. Even though he was her brother, Beata was always dazzled by how handsome he was, and how kind. He was a gentle person, and looked exactly like their father. Ulm was tall and blond and athletic, as Jacob had been in his youth. Ulm had blue eyes and features that often confused people, because he didn't look Jewish. Everyone knew they were, of course, and in the social world of Cologne, they were accepted in even the most aristocratic circles. Several of the

Hohenlohes, and Thurn und Thaxis were childhood friends of their father's. The Wittgensteins were so established and so respected that all doors were open to them. But Jacob had also made it clear to all his children that when the time came for them to marry, the spouses they brought home would be Jewish. It was not even a subject for discussion; nor would any of them even think to question it. They were accepted for who and what they were, and there were many eligible young men and women in their own circles for the Wittgenstein children to choose from. When the time came for them to marry, they would marry one of them.

Ulm and Beata didn't even look remotely related as they walked along the lake. Her brothers and sister looked exactly like their father, they were all tall blondes with blue eyes and fine features. Beata looked like their mother, in total contrast to them. Beata Wittgenstein was a tiny, frail-looking, delicate brunette, with raven-dark hair and skin the color of porcelain. The only feature she shared with the others was enormous blue eyes, although hers were darker than her brothers' or Brigitte's. Her mother's eyes were dark brown, but other than that minor difference, Beata was the image of her mother, which secretly delighted her father. He was still so much in love with his wife after nearly twenty-nine years that just seeing Beata smile at him reminded him of when her mother was the same age in the early years of their marriage, and the similarity never failed to touch his heart. As a result, he had an enormous soft spot for Beata, and Brigitte frequently complained that Beata was his favorite. He let her do whatever she wanted. But what Beata wanted was harmless. Brigitte's plans were considerably racier than her older sister's. Beata was content to stay home and read or study, in fact, she preferred it. The only time her father had actually gotten annoyed with her was on one occasion when Jacob found her reading a King James version of the Bible.

"What is that about?" he asked with a stern expression, as he saw what she was reading. She had been sixteen at the time and was fascinated by it. She had read quite a lot of the Old Testament before that.

"It's interesting, Papa. The stories are wonderful, and so many things in it are exactly what we believe." She preferred the New Testament to the Old. Her father found it less than amusing and had taken it away from her.

He didn't want his daughter reading a Christian Bible, and he had complained about it to her mother, and suggested that Monika keep a closer eye on what she was reading. In fact, Beata read everything she could get her hands on, including Aristotle and Plato. She was a voracious reader and loved the Greek philosophers. Even her father had to admit that if she had been a man, she would have been an extraordinary scholar. What he wanted for her now, as he did for Ulm and even for the other two sometime soon, was for her to get married. He was beginning to fear that she would become spinsterish and too serious if she waited much longer. He had a few ideas he wanted to explore in that vein that winter, but the war had disrupted everything. So many men were serving in the army, and many young people they knew had been killed in the past year. The uncertainty of the future was deeply disturbing.

Her father thought that Beata would do well with a man who was older than she was. He wanted a mature man for Beata, a man who could appreciate her intellect and share her interests. He wasn't opposed to that idea for Brigitte either, who could use a strong hand to control her. Although he loved all his children, he was extremely proud of his oldest daughter. He considered himself a man of wisdom and compassion. He was the kind of person others never hesitated to turn to. Beata had a deep love and respect for him, as she did for her mother, although she secretly admitted to the others that their mother was easier to talk to, and a little less daunting than their father. Their father was as serious as Beata, and often disapproved of his younger daughter's frivolity.

"I wish you didn't have to go back to the war," Beata said sadly, as she chatted with Ulm while they continued walking. The others had turned back, and now she and Ulm were far ahead of them, instead of straggling behind.

"I hate to go back too, but I think it will be over soon." He smiled at her reassuringly. He didn't believe that, but it was the sort of thing one said to women. Or at least he did. "I should be able to get leave again at Christmas." She nodded, thinking that it seemed a lifetime away, and unable to bear the thought of how awful it would be if something happened to him. More than she ever told him, she adored him. She loved Horst too, but he seemed more like a silly younger brother than an older one. He loved to tease her, and he always made her laugh. What she and Ulm shared was different. They continued to chat pleasantly all the way back to the hotel, and that night they shared a final dinner before the boys left the next day. As always, Horst amused them endlessly with his imitations of everyone they'd met, and his outrageous stories about their friends.

All three of the men left the next day, and the three women stayed for the last three weeks of their holiday in Geneva. Jacob wanted them to stay in Switzerland as long as possible, although Brigitte was beginning to get bored. But Beata and her mother were perfectly content to be there. Brigitte and her mother went shopping one afternoon, and Beata said she would stay at the hotel, as she had a headache. In truth, she didn't, but she found it tiresome shopping with them. Brigitte always tried on everything in the shops, ordered dresses, hats, and shoes. Impressed by her good taste and keen fashion sense, their mother always indulged her. And after they exhausted the dressmakers and cobblers and milliners and the shops that made exquisite gloves, they would make the rounds of the jewelers. Beata knew they wouldn't be home until dinner, and she was content to sit in the sun, reading in the garden on her own.

After lunch, she went down to the lake and walked along the same path they had taken every day since they'd been there. It was a trifle cooler than the day before, and she was wearing a white silk dress, a hat to shield her from the sun, and a pale blue shawl the color of her eyes, draped over her shoulders. She was humming to herself as she strolled along. Most of the hotel guests were at lunch, or in town, and she had the path to herself, as she walked with her head down, thinking about her brothers. She heard a sound behind her suddenly, looked up, and was startled when she saw a tall young man who walked briskly past her on the path, and smiled as he did so. He was heading in the same direction, and she was so surprised as he brushed by her that she took a rapid step to the side, stumbled, and turned her ankle. It smarted for a minute but didn't seem serious, as he quickly reached a hand out and caught her before she fell.

"I'm so sorry, I didn't mean to frighten you, and certainly didn't mean to knock you over." He looked instantly apologetic and concerned, and Beata noted that he was astonishingly handsome. Tall, fair, with eyes the color of her own, and long powerful arms and athletic shoulders. He kept a firm grasp on her arm as he spoke to her. She realized her hat was slightly askew from their encounter. She straightened it, while secretly glancing at him. He looked a little bit older than her older brother. He was wearing white slacks and a dark blue blazer, a navy tie, and a very good-looking straw hat that made him look somewhat rakish.

"Thank you, I'm fine. It was silly of me. I didn't hear you in time to get out of your way."

"Or see me, until I nearly knocked you down. I'm afraid it was a deplorable performance on my part. Are you all right? How's your ankle?" He looked sympathetic and kind.

"It's fine. You caught me before I did any real damage to it." He had spoken to her in

French, and she responded in the same language. She had learned French at school and polished it diligently since then. Her father had also insisted that they learn English, and he thought they should speak Italian and Spanish as well. Beata had studied both but never really perfected either. Her English was passable, but her French was fluent.

"Would you like to sit down for a moment?" He pointed to a bench near them, with a peaceful view of the lake, and he seemed reluctant to let go of her arm. He acted as though he was afraid she would fall over if he let go of his firm grip on her, and she smiled at him.

"Really, I'm fine." But the prospect of sitting next to him for a moment appealed to her. It wasn't the sort of thing she normally did, in fact she had never done anything like it, but he was so pleasant and polite and seemed so remorseful over their near-accident that she felt sorry for him. And it appeared harmless to sit and chat with him for a minute before continuing her walk. She had nothing to rush back to the hotel for, she knew that her mother and sister would be gone for hours. She let him lead her to the bench, and he sat down beside her with a respectful distance between them.

"Are you truly all right?" He looked down at her ankle, peering just beneath the hem of her skirt, and was relieved to see that it didn't appear to be swollen.

"I promise." She smiled at him.

"I meant to just slip past you and not disturb you. I should have said something or warned you. I was a million miles away, thinking about this damnable war, it's such an awful thing." He looked troubled as he said it, and sat back against the bench as she watched him. She had never met anyone even remotely like him. He looked like a handsome prince in a fairy tale, and he was remarkably friendly. There seemed to be no airs or pretensions about him. He looked like one of Ulm's friends, although he was far better looking.

"You're not Swiss then?" she asked with interest.

"I'm French," he said simply, and as he said it, she frowned and said nothing. "Is that awful? My grandfather is Swiss actually, my mother's father. That's why I'm here. He died two weeks ago, and I had to come and help settle the estate with my brother and parents. They gave me a leave to do it." He was remarkably easy and open, without being presumptuous or inappropriately familiar. He seemed very well-bred and aristocratic, and extremely polite.

"No, it's not awful at all," she answered honestly, as her eyes looked directly into his. "I'm German." She half-expected him to leap from the bench and tell her he hated Germans. They were enemies in the war after all, and she had no idea how he would react to her confession.

"Do you expect me to blame you for the war?" he asked gently, smiling at her. She was a young girl, and incredibly pretty. He thought her truly beautiful, and as he spoke to her, he was touched by her apologetic expression. She seemed like a remarkable young woman, and he was suddenly glad he had nearly knocked her over. "Did you do this? Is this dreadful war your fault, mademoiselle? Should I be angry at you?" he teased her, and she laughed along with him.

"I hope not," she said, smiling. "Are you in the army?" she inquired. He had mentioned being on leave.

"In the cavalry. I attended the equestrian

academy called Saumur." Beata knew it
was where all the aristocrats became officers of the cavalry, which was a most pres-
tigious unit.

"That must be interesting." She liked
horses and had ridden a lot as a young girl.
She loved riding with her brothers, particularly Ulm. Horst always went wild and drove
his horses into a frenzy, which in turn
spooked hers. "My brothers are in the army,
too."

He looked at her pensively for a long moment, lost in her blue eyes, which were
darker than his own. He had never seen hair
as dark contrasted by skin as white. She
looked like a painting sitting there on the
bench. "Wouldn't it be nice if troubles between nations could be resolved as simply
as this, two people sitting on a bench on a
summer afternoon, looking out at a lake. We
could talk things out, and agree, instead of
the way things are, with young men dying
on battlefields." What he said made her knit
her brows again, he had reminded her of
how vulnerable her brothers were.

"It would be nice. My older brother thinks
it will be over soon."

"I wish I could agree," he said politely. "I

fear that once you put weapons in men's hands, they don't let go of them easily. I think this could go on for years."

"I hope you're wrong," she said quietly.

"So do I," and then he looked embarrassed again. "I've been incredibly rude. I am Antoine de Vallerand." He stood up, bowed, and sat down again. And she smiled as he did.

"I am Beata Wittgenstein." She pronounced the W like a V.

"How is it that you speak such perfect French?" he asked. "Your French is almost flawless, without any accent. In fact, you sound Parisian." He would never have guessed she was German. He was fascinated by her, and it never occurred to him, even once he heard her name, that she was Jewish. Unlike most people of his ilk and milieu, it made no difference to him. He never gave it a thought. All he saw in her was a beautiful intelligent young woman.

"I learned French in school." She smiled at him.

"No, you didn't, or if you did, you are far more clever than I. I learned English in school, or so they say, and I can't speak a word. And my German is absolutely terrible.

I don't have your gift. Most French people don't. We speak French and not much else. We assume the whole world will learn French so they can speak to us, and how fortunate that you did. Do you speak English, too?" He somehow suspected that she did. Although they didn't know each other, and he could tell that she was shy, she looked extremely bright and surprisingly at ease. She was amazed herself by how comfortable she was with him. Even though he was a stranger, she felt safe with him.

"I speak English," she admitted, "though not as well as French."

"Do you go to school?" She looked young to him. He was thirty-two, twelve years older than she.

"No. Not anymore. I finished," she answered shyly. "But I read a great deal. I would have liked to go to university, but my father wouldn't let me."

"Why not?" he asked, and then caught himself with a smile. "He thinks you should get married and have babies. You don't need to go to university. Am I correct?"

"Yes, completely." She beamed at him.

"And you don't want to get married?" He

was beginning to remind her more and more of Ulm. She felt as though she and Antoine were old friends, and he seemed to feel equally at ease with her. She felt able to be completely honest with him, which was rare for her. She was usually extremely shy with men.

"I don't want to get married unless I fall in love with someone," she said simply, and he nodded.

"That sounds sensible. Do your parents agree with that idea?"

"I'm not sure. Their marriage was arranged for them, and they think that's a good thing. They want my brothers to get married, too."

"How old are your brothers?"

"Twenty-three and twenty-seven. One of them is quite serious, and the other just wants to have fun, and is a bit wild." She smiled cautiously at Antoine.

"Sounds like my brother and I."

"How old is he?"

"Five years younger. He is twenty-seven, like your older brother, and I am a very old man of thirty-two. They've given up hope for me." And until that moment, so had he.

"Which one are you?"

"Which one?" He looked blank for a moment and then understood. "Ah yes, he's the wild one. I'm the boring one." And then he caught himself. "Sorry, I didn't mean to suggest that your older brother is boring. Just serious, I imagine. I've always been the responsible one, my brother just isn't. He's too busy having fun to even think about being responsible. Maybe he's right. I'm much quieter than he is."

"And you're not married?" she asked with interest. It was the oddest chance meeting. They were asking each other things they would never have dared to inquire about in a ballroom or a drawing room, or at a dinner party. But here, sitting on a bench, looking out at the lake, it seemed perfectly all right to ask him anything she wanted. She was curious about him. There was a lovely, decent feeling about him, in spite of his striking good looks. For all she knew, he was the rakish one and he was lying to her, but it didn't seem that way. She believed everything he said, and had the feeling he felt the same way about her.

"No, I'm not married," he said with a look of amusement. "I've thought about it once or twice, but I never felt it was the right thing, in spite of a great deal of pressure from my family. Oldest son and all that. I don't want to make a mistake and marry the wrong woman. I'd rather be alone, so I am."

"I agree." She nodded, looking surprisingly determined. At times, she seemed almost childlike to him, and at other times, as she spoke to him, he could see that she had very definite ideas, like about marriage and going to university.

"What would you have studied, if they'd let you go to university?" he asked with interest, and she looked dreamy as she thought about it.

"Philosophy. The ancient Greeks, I think. Religion perhaps, or the philosophy of religion. I read the Bible once from beginning to end." He looked impressed. She was obviously a brilliant girl, as well as being beautiful, and so very easy to talk to.

"And what did you think? I can't say I've read it, except in snips and bits, and mostly at weddings and funerals. I seem to spend most of my time on horses, and helping my father run our property. I have a lifelong romance with the earth." It was hard to convey to her how much his land and his own turf meant to him. It had been bred into him.

"I think a lot of men do," Beata said quietly. "Where is your family's property?" She was enjoying talking to him and didn't want it to end.

"It's in Dordogne. Horse country. It's near Périgord, near Bordeaux, if that means anything." His eyes lit up just speaking of it, and she could see what it meant to him.

"I've never been there, but it must be beautiful if you love it so much."

"It is," he assured her. "And where do you live in Germany?"

"Cologne."

"I've been there," he said, looking pleased. "I like Bavaria very much, too. And I've had some lovely times in Berlin."

"That's where my brother Horst wants to live, in Berlin. He can't, of course. He has to go to work for my father after the war, he thinks it's horrible, but he doesn't have any choice. My grandfather and my father and his brothers, and my brother Ulm all work there. It's a bank. I suppose it isn't much fun, but they all seem to like it well enough. I think it would be interesting," she said, and he smiled at her. She was full of bright intelligent ideas, and interest in the world. Antoine was certain, looking at her, and listening to her, that if she had gone to university, or been able to work at the bank, she would have done well. He was still impressed that she had read the Bible as a young girl.

"What do you like to do?" he asked with interest.

"I love to read," she said simply, "and to learn about things. I'd love to be a writer one day, but of course I can't do that either." No man she would marry would tolerate her doing something like that, she would have to take care of him and their children.

"Maybe you will one day. I suppose it all depends on who you marry, or if you do. Do you have sisters as well, or only brothers?"

"I have a younger sister, Brigitte, she's seventeen. She loves going to parties, and dancing and dressing up, she can hardly wait to get married. She always tells me how boring I am," Beata said with an impish grin, which made him want to reach out and hug her, even though they hadn't been properly introduced. He was suddenly so pleased that he had nearly knocked her down. It was beginning to seem like a stroke of good fortune that he had, and he had the feeling that Beata thought so, too.

"My brother thinks I'm very boring. But I must tell you, I find you anything but boring, Beata. I love talking to you."

"I like talking to you." She smiled shyly at him, wondering if she should go back to the hotel. They had been sitting on the bench together by then for quite a long time. Perhaps longer than they should. They sat in silence for a long moment, admiring the lake, and then he turned to her again.

"Would you like me to walk you back to the hotel? Your family might be worried about you."

"My mother took my sister shopping. I don't think they'll be back till dinnertime, but perhaps I should go back," she said responsibly, although she hated to leave.

They both stood up reluctantly, and he inquired how her ankle felt. He was pleased to hear that it didn't bother her, and he offered her his arm, as they walked slowly back toward the hotel. She tucked her hand into his arm, and they chatted as they strolled, talking about a variety of things. They both agreed that they hated parties generally but loved to dance. He was pleased to hear that she liked horses and had ridden to hounds. They both liked boats and had a passion for the sea. She said she never got seasick, which he found hard to believe. But she confessed that she was afraid of dogs, since she'd been bitten as a small child. And they both agreed that they loved Italy, although he said that he was extremely fond of Germany, too, which wasn't something he could admit openly at the moment. The war, and the fact that their respective countries were currently enemies, seemed of no importance to either of them as they got to know each other. Antoine looked seriously disappointed as they got back to the hotel. He hated leaving her, although he had plans to meet his family for dinner. He would have liked to spend many more hours with her and was clearly lingering, as they stood in front of the hotel, looking at each other.

"Would you like to have tea?" he suggested, and her eyes lit up at the idea.

"That would be very nice, thank you." He led her to the terrace where they were serving tea, and elegant women were sitting together and chatting, or prosperous-looking couples were eating little sandwiches and speaking in hushed tones in French, German, Italian, and English.

They shared a very proper high tea, and finally, unable to drag it out any longer, he walked her into the lobby, and stood looking down at her. She seemed tiny and appeared fragile to him, but in fact after hours of talking to her, he knew that she was spirited and more than capable of defending her ideas. She had strong opinions about many things, and so far he agreed with most of them. And the ones he didn't agree with amused him. There was nothing boring about her. He found her incredibly exciting and breathtakingly beautiful. All he knew was that he had to see her again.

"Do you suppose your mother would allow you to have lunch with me tomorrow?" He looked hopeful, as he longed to touch her hand but didn't dare. Even more, he would have loved to touch her face. She had exquisite skin.

"I'm not sure," Beata said honestly. It was going to be difficult to explain how they met, and the fact that they had spent so much time together, chatting, without a chaperone. But nothing untoward had happened, and he was unfailingly polite and obviously well-born. There was nothing they could object to, except the fact that he was French, which was admittedly inconvenient at the moment. But this was Switzerland, after all. It wasn't like meeting him at home. And just because their countries were enemies didn't mean he was a bad man. But she wasn't sure her mother would see it that way, in fact she was almost positive she wouldn't, since her brothers were participating in a war against the French and could be killed by them at any moment. Her parents were rigidly patriotic and not necessarily famous for their open minds, as she knew well, and Antoine feared. Beata was also aware that if he presented himself as a suitor, her family would consider him ineligible because he was obviously not Jewish. But worrying about that seemed premature.

"Perhaps your mother and sister would join us for lunch, too?" he asked hopefully. He had no intention of giving up. A war seemed like a small obstacle to him at this point. Beata was too wonderful and magical to lose over something like that.

"I'll ask them," Beata said quietly. She was going to do more than ask, she had every intention of fighting like a tiger to see him again, and she was afraid she might have to. Beata knew that in her mother's eyes, he would have two major strikes against him, his nationality and his faith.

"Should I call your mother and ask her myself?" He looked concerned.

"No, I'll do it," she said, shaking her head. They were suddenly allies in an unspoken conspiracy, the continuation of their friendship, or whatever this was. Beata didn't think he was flirting with her and only hoped that they could be friends. She didn't dare imagine more.

"May I call you tonight?" he asked, looking nervous, and she gave him her room number. She was sharing the room with Brigitte.

"We're eating at the hotel tonight." For once.

"So are we," he said with a look of surprise. "Maybe we'll see each other, and I can introduce myself to your mother and sister." And then he looked worried. "How shall we say we met?" Their chance meeting had been fortuitous, but not entirely decorous. And their long conversation had been unusual, to say the least. Beata laughed at the question. "I'll just say you knocked me down, and then picked me up."

"I'm sure she'll be impressed by that. Will you say I pushed you into the mud, or just that I dropped you into the lake to clean you up after you fell?" Beata laughed like a child at his suggestions, and Antoine looked happier than he had in years. "You really are very silly. You could at least tell her that I caught your arm and kept you from falling, even though I did try to knock you over as I rushed past." But he no longer regretted it. The minor mishap had served him well. "And you could have the decency to tell your mother that I properly introduced myself."

"Maybe I will." For a moment, Beata looked genuinely worried as she looked up at him, somewhat embarrassed by what she was about to suggest. "Do you suppose it would be terrible to tell her you're Swiss?"

He hesitated and then nodded. He could see that his nationality was a problem for her, or she feared it would be for her mother. What was going to be a much bigger problem was that he was a French nobleman and not Jewish, but Beata would never have said that to him. She was cherishing the illusion that since they were just friends, her mother wouldn't mind that much. What harm was there in making friends with a Christian? Several of her parents' friends were. It was an argument she planned to use if her mother objected to Beata having lunch with him.

"I am a quarter Swiss, after all. I'll just have to remember not to count in front of your mother, or I might say *soixante-dix* instead of *septante.* That would be a bit of a giveaway. But I don't mind if it's easier for you to say I'm Swiss. It's a shame that has to be an issue for any of us these days." The truth was that his own family would be horrified that he was making friends with a German girl and, worse than that, was totally smitten by her. There was no love lost these days between the Germans and the French. But he didn't see why he and Beata should pay a price for it. "Don't worry, we'll work it out," he said gently to her, as she looked up at him with her enormous blue eyes. "It's all right, Beata. I promise. One way or another, we will see each other tomorrow." He was not going to let anything stand between them, and she felt totally protected as she stood looking up at Antoine. They were nearly strangers to each other, and yet she knew that she already trusted him. Something remarkable and wonderful had happened between them that afternoon. "I'll call you tonight," he said softly, as she stepped into the elevator, and turned to smile at him as the elevator operator closed the doors. He was still standing, looking at her, as the doors closed, and she rode upstairs, knowing that in a single afternoon her whole life had changed. And Antoine was smiling to himself as he left the hotel.

2

Much to her chagrin, Beata was not prepared for the reaction of her mother, when she casually suggested lunch with Antoine to her when they got home. Beata said that they had met at the hotel at teatime, had spoken for a short while, and Antoine had suggested they all have lunch the following day. She didn't have the courage to suggest to her mother that she and Antoine have lunch alone. Her mother looked horrified at the suggestion, as it was.

"With a total stranger? Beata, have you taken leave of your senses? You don't know this man. What were you doing that he invited you to lunch?" Her mother looked highly suspicious, she had only left Beata alone for a few hours, and it wasn't like her to have a conversation with a strange man. He was obviously some sort of masher, trying to prey on young girls, and loitering around the hotel. Monika Wittgenstein was not as innocent as her daughter, and she was incensed that this man had made advances to her, and even worse, that Beata seemed to find it appealing. It only proved to her mother that she was desperately naïve and still a child. And she assumed only the worst of Antoine.

"I was just having tea on the terrace," Beata said, looking upset. This had not gone well, and she didn't know what to say to Antoine. "We started speaking, about nothing in particular. He was very polite."

"How old is he? And what's he doing here instead of in the war?"

"He's Swiss," Beata said primly. That was something at least. She never lied to her mother, although Brigitte did frequently, and this was a first for her. But somehow seeing Antoine seemed worth any risk she had to take or any breach it involved. In a single afternoon he had won not only her loyalty but her heart.

"Why wasn't he working? What's he doing

loitering around a hotel?" As far as Monika was concerned, respectable men worked. They did not have time to hang around hotels at teatime, picking up young girls.

"He's visiting, just as we are. He's here to see his family, because his grandfather just died."

"I'm sorry to hear it," Monika said tersely, "and he may be a perfectly nice man, but he is a total stranger. We have not been properly introduced to him by anyone who knows us or him, and we are not going to have lunch with him." And then as an afterthought, a few minutes later, "What's his name?"

"Antoine de Vallerand." Her mother's eyes met hers and held them in a viselike grip for a long time. She wondered if Beata had met him before, but there was nothing duplicitous about the girl. She was just young and foolish and naïve.

"He's a nobleman," her mother said quietly, her words full of reproach. And as such, he was not a suitable option for either of her daughters, no matter who he was. There were some lines one didn't cross, and that was one of them. Beata knew what she was thinking, her mother didn't have to spell it out. They were Jewish. He wasn't.

"Is that a crime, being noble?" Beata said a little tartly, but as she looked at her mother, her eyes were sad, which worried her mother even more.

"Have you ever met this man before?" In answer, Beata shook her head, as Brigitte bounced into the room with armloads of her purchases. She had had a wonderful time in the shops, although she thought they were better in Cologne. But at least here in Switzerland they had none of the obvious shortages of war. It was nice to get a break from all that.

"What does he look like?" Brigitte asked, holding up a new black suede handbag and a beautiful pair of long white kid gloves. "Is he handsome?"

"That's not the point," Beata snapped at both of them. "He just seems like a very nice man, and he invited all three of us to lunch, which was very polite and kind."

"And why do you suppose he did that?" her mother asked with a look of disapproval. "Because he is dying to meet me and Brigitte? Of course not. He obviously wants to spend time with you. How old is this man?" All her suspicions were on high alert.

"I don't know. Maybe around Ulm's age." In fact, he was five years older, as she knew. It was the third lie she had told to protect him and their budding friendship. Spending time with Antoine seemed worth it to her. She wanted to see him again, even if it was with her mother and sister, if that was all she could do. She just wanted to spend a little more time with him. Who knew when and if they would meet again.

"He's too old for you," her mother said bluntly, when in fact her objections to him were in an entirely different vein. But she didn't want to voice them to Beata.

She didn't want to give enough credence to this man's invitation to state what her real objections were, but Beata knew anyway. Other than being a total stranger, Antoine wasn't Jewish. Monika was not going to expose her daughters to handsome young men of the Christian faith. Jacob would have had her head for it, and she agreed unreservedly with him. There was no point letting this new acquaintance of Beata's go any further. She was not going to do anything to encourage a Swiss Christian nobleman to pursue one of her daughters. Even the thought of it was insane. Some of their own friends certainly were Christian, but she would never have introduced their sons to her daughters. There was no point putting the girls in harm's way, or tempting them with something they could never have. And however beautiful her daughters were, none of her Christian friends had ever suggested introducing them to their sons. In this case, as in all cases, the adults knew better. And Monika remained intransigent and firm. Jacob would have killed her, and rightly so, if she weren't.

"I don't understand what you think is going to happen at lunch. He's not a murderer, after all," Beata said plaintively.

"How do you know?" her mother asked in a stern voice. She was definitely not amused, particularly as this was so unlike Beata. Although it was not unlike her to fight for something she believed in and wanted desperately. This was just stubbornness on her part, since she didn't even know the man. And as long as Monika was there to see to it, she never would. It was better to stop this kind of thing before it could start. She knew full well what Jacob expected of her as their mother. What it did point out to her, however, was that it was time to find Beata a husband. If suddenly young noblemen were beginning to circle around her like vultures, it was time for her to settle down, before something unpleasant happened.

Beata was far too liberal in her ideas, although normally she was obedient and well behaved and a credit to her parents. Monika decided then to talk to Jacob about it when they got back. She knew he had several respectable, substantial men in mind, including one who owned a rival bank. He was nearly old enough to be Beata's father, but Monika agreed with her husband, as she did in all things, that an older man of intellect and substance would suit her very well. Although still young, she was a very serious girl, and a young man wouldn't suit her nearly as well. But whatever else he had to have in his favor, the most important factor in her parents' eyes was that he had to be of the same faith. Anything other than that was out of the question. And clearly the young nobleman who had invited them to lunch was in that realm. He was obviously Christian, and more than likely Catholic, with a name like Antoine de Vallerand. At least he was Swiss, and not French. Monika had developed a powerful hatred for the French in the last year, ever since war had been declared. The French were out there in the trenches trying to kill her sons.

Beata did not argue with her mother further, in fact she said not a word as she and Brigitte dressed for dinner.

"So what really happened with that man today?" Brigitte asked, looking mischievous, in peach satin underwear trimmed in cream lace, which her mother had bought her that day. Monika had found it a bit racy, but there was no harm in indulging her. No one was going to see it except her sister and her mother anyway. "Did he kiss you?"

"Are you insane?" Beata said, looking angry and upset. "What do you think I am? Besides, he's a gentleman. He actually caught my arm and kept me from falling when he nearly knocked me down."

"That's how you met?" Brigitte looked enchanted at the idea. "How romantic! Why didn't you tell Mama that? She might have been grateful that he kept you from falling and getting hurt."

"I don't think so," Beata said quietly. She knew her mother better, and gauged her better than Brigitte, who was still given to childish tantrums and making scenes, which wasn't Beata's style, to say the least. "I thought it sounded more respectable to say we met over tea."

"Maybe. Did you fall in the dirt? That would have been embarrassing," Brigitte said, as she slipped on a white linen dress and combed out her long golden curls, as Beata looked at her with envy. Brigitte was so beautiful she almost looked angelic. Beata always felt like a mouse next to her, and hated her dark hair. She didn't resent Brigitte for it, she just wished she could look more like her. And her figure was far more voluptuous than Beata's. Next to her younger sister, she looked like a little girl. And Brigitte seemed far wiser in the ways of men. She talked to them far more often than Beata did, and loved teasing them and driving them insane. Beata was far more comfortable and at ease in the company of women. Brigitte was fearlessly flirtatious, and painfully adept at torturing men.

"I didn't fall in the dirt," Beata explained. "I told you, he kept me from falling down."

"That was nice of him. What else did he do?"

"Nothing. We just talked," Beata said, as she put on a red silk dress, which set off the sharp contrast of her hair and complexion. Beata looked glum. She was going to have to tell Antoine that she couldn't see him when he called. She knew with total certainty that there was no way she could talk her mother into lunch as a group, and surely not alone.

"What did you talk about?"

"Philosophy, the Bible, his land, going to university, nothing important. He's very nice."

"Oh my God, Beata," Brigitte looked at her with unbridled seventeen-year-old excitement, "are you in love?"

"Of course not. I don't even know him. He was just nice to talk to."

"You shouldn't talk to men about things like that. They don't like it. They'll think you're strange," she warned her older sister with the best of intentions, which only depressed Beata more.

"I guess I am strange. I'm not interested in . . ." She struggled to find the right words, so as not to offend Brigitte. "I'm not interested in 'lighter' things. I like serious subjects, like the ancient Greeks."

"I wish you'd talk about something else. Like parties and fashion and jewels. That's what men want to hear. Otherwise, they'll think you're smarter than they are, and you'll scare them off." Brigitte was wise for her years, based on instinct if not experience.

"I probably will." She wasn't even sure she cared. Most of the young men she met at parties seemed ridiculous to her.

Beata adored her brother, but she would rather have died than marry a man like Horst. She could have tolerated a man like Ulm, but the prospect of marriage to anyone in her world didn't appeal to her much, or at all. They all seemed dreary and boring and more often than not foolish and superficial to her. Antoine had seemed very different. Earnest, and deeper than most of the men she met, protective and sincere. She had never felt about anyone after a few hours as she did about him. Not that it would go anywhere. And she had no idea how he felt about her. She had none of Brigitte's instincts or artful ways with men. Brigitte could have told her in an instant that Antoine was crazy about her, but she hadn't seen them together. Although it sounded good to her. And the invitation to lunch was a sign that there was some interest there, but she didn't say anything to Beata. Her older sister was clearly not in the mood to discuss the matter further.

Beata was still silent as they rode the elevator downstairs for dinner, and as it was a warm night, their mother asked for a table on the terrace. She was wearing a very elegant navy blue silk dress, with a sapphire necklace, and matching navy silk shoes and bag. And she was wearing sapphire and diamond earrings that matched the necklace. They were three very beautiful women as the headwaiter seated them at their table. Beata was still quiet after they had ordered their meal, while Brigitte and their mother chatted about the shopping they'd done that afternoon. Monika told Beata that they had seen several dresses that would look well on her, but Beata showed no interest.

"It's a shame you can't wear books," Brigitte teased her. "You'd have much more fun in the shops."

"I'd rather make my clothes myself," Beata said simply, as her sister rolled her eyes.

"Why go to all that trouble when you can buy them in shops?"

"Because then I can have what I want." She had in fact made the pretty red silk dress she had on, which fit her to perfection, and hung on her slim body in clean, simple lines.

She was a gifted seamstress and had loved sewing since she was a child. Their governess had taught her, although Monika always told her that she didn't have to do that. But Beata preferred it. She had made some of her own evening gowns too, copied them from magazines, and drawings she saw of Paris collections, which were no longer available to them now anyway. She liked modifying them, and simplifying them to suit her tastes. She had made a beautiful green satin evening gown for her mother once as a gift, and Monika had been stunned by how expertly made it was. She would have done it for Brigitte, but she always said she hated homemade clothes. They seemed pathetic to her. Instead, sometimes Beata made her sister the satin and lace underwear that she loved, in a rainbow of colors. Brigitte loved those.

They had just finished their soup course

when Beata saw her mother look up and just past her older daughter's shoulder with a stunned expression. Beata had no idea what it was, and turned, to find Antoine standing just behind her, with a warm smile that took in the entire group.

"Madame Wittgenstein?" he asked politely, ignoring both her daughters, including the one who had captivated him that afternoon. He appeared to be riveted by their mother. "I must apologize for interrupting you, but I wanted to introduce myself and apologize as well for inviting your daughter to tea this afternoon without a chaperone. She had a little stumble on a walk near the lake, and I believe her ankle was hurting her. I thought the tea would do her good. Please forgive me."

"No, I . . . not at all . . . of course . . . how kind of you . . ." Her gaze darted to Beata and then back to him as he introduced himself, bowed politely, and kissed her hand. Quite correctly, he had not made the same gesture to Beata, as she was unmarried, and hand kissing was a courtesy properly only proffered to married women. Beata had gotten only the bow, as was proper. In Germany, young men like him and her brothers bowed as he had, and clicked their heels together. But neither the Swiss nor the French did that, nor did he now. "I didn't realize she'd gotten hurt." Monika looked momentarily confused, as Antoine turned to look at Beata, and nearly caught his breath when he saw her in the red dress. She had lit up like a starburst when he saw her from across the room, and had excused himself from his own mother to come to meet hers.

He made no attempt to introduce the two mothers as he knew he would be in deep waters, since Beata wanted him to claim to be Swiss. So he couldn't introduce Monika to his mother, and was content to meet her himself, and the striking Brigitte, who was staring at him in disbelief. He barely looked at her, treating her like the child she was, and not the woman she was longing to be, which won Monika's approval. Antoine had impeccable manners, and was obviously a man of breeding, and not a masher, as she had feared.

"How is your ankle, mademoiselle?" he asked with concern.

"It's fine, thank you very much, monsieur. You were very kind." Beata blushed as she said it.

"Not at all. *C'était la moindre des choses . . .* it was the least I could do." He turned his attention back to her mother then, and reiterated his luncheon invitation, which for once actually flustered her mother. He was so polite, so properly solicitous, so ingenuous, and so warm and kind that even Monika didn't have the heart to rebuff him, and in spite of herself she accepted, and they agreed to meet on the terrace at one o'clock the next day for lunch. As soon as that arrangement was made, he bowed again, kissed Mrs. Wittgenstein's hand again, and left to rejoin his own family, without a single longing look at Beata. He was entirely correct and pleasant. And once he was gone, Monika looked at her daughter with uncomfortable amazement.

"I can see why you like him. He is a very nice young man. He reminds me of Ulm." It was an enormous compliment coming from her.

"He did me, too." Only infinitely better looking, but she didn't say that as she quietly cut her meat, and prayed that no one could hear her heart pounding. He had pulled it off to perfection, not that it mattered. Whatever they felt for each other could go nowhere, but at least she could see him. Once more anyway. It was a happy memory she could take with her. The handsome young man she had met in Geneva. She was sure that everyone she met after that would compare unfavorably with him for years. She was already resigned to it, and imagined herself as a spinster for the rest of her life as she ate her dinner. His most unforgivable sin was that he wasn't Jewish. Not to mention the fact that he wasn't Swiss either. It was hopeless.

"Why didn't you tell me you hurt your ankle this afternoon?" her mother asked, sounding concerned after he left.

"It was nothing. He bumped into me as I came up to the terrace at teatime, after my walk at the lake. I think he felt sorry for me. I just turned it a little."

"In that case, it was nice of him to invite you to tea. And us to lunch tomorrow." She could see that her mother was momentarily under his spell, too. It was hard not to be. He was so handsome and so nice to everyone, and Beata was secretly pleased that he had ignored Brigitte. All the other men Beata knew nearly fainted at her sister's feet. But he seemed unimpressed. He was dazzled by Beata, although he hadn't shown that either. He had seemed perfectly normal and friendly, quite like Ulm, which was why Monika had accepted his invitation to lunch. He was definitely not a masher, as she had feared, but entirely respectable and agreeable to talk to. Beata said nothing more about it as the three of them finished their dinner. She didn't even glance his way as they left the terrace, and he made no effort to speak to them again. It was not at all what Monika had suspected or feared. Even Jacob couldn't disapprove. The chance meeting had obviously been harmless.

Only Brigitte was far more clever than either of them when the two girls finally reached their room, after saying goodnight to their mother.

"Oh my God, Beata, he's gorgeous!" she whispered to her older sister in wild-eyed admiration. "And he's crazy about you. The two of you totally fooled Mama." Brigitte thought it was terrific and could imagine clandestine lovers' meetings at midnight.

"Don't be stupid," Beata said as she took off the red dress and tossed it on a chair, wishing now that she had worn something more glamorous. As she thought of him, the dress seemed so plain. And she thought she was, too. "He's not crazy about me. He doesn't even know me. And we did not fool Mama. He invited us to lunch, and she accepted. That's all, just lunch, for heaven's sake. He's just being friendly."

"Now you're being stupid. Men like that don't invite you to lunch unless they're mad about you. He didn't even look at you when he came to the table, or barely, and that says everything."

"What on earth do you mean?" Beata looked amused.

"Oh, Beata"—her sister laughed at her— "you know absolutely nothing about men. When they act like you mean nothing to them, it means they are madly in love with you. And when they make a big fuss over you and look wild with love, they're usually lying." Beata laughed at her sister's worldly wise analysis of the situation. But she was far more sophisticated in the ways of the world, and men, than Beata. She had good instincts. Better than her shy, serious sister.

"That's ridiculous." Beata laughed with her, but she was secretly pleased. "So you are telling me that all the men who ignore me, like everyone in the restaurant tonight, are actually madly in love with me. How wonderful! And I'll certainly have to watch out for the ones who appear to love me, if they're all lying. Good Lord, how confusing!"

"Yes, it is," Brigitte agreed, "but that's usually the way it works. The ones who make a fuss are just playing. It's the others, the ones like him, who mean it."

"Mean what?" Beata looked at her younger sister, lying elegantly across the bed in her satin underwear, looking like a very glamorous young woman.

"Men like him. That they love you. I'm sure he's fallen in love with you."

"Well, it won't do him much good. We're going back to Cologne in three weeks," Beata said matter-of-factly, as she took off her slip and put on her nightgown, which made her look like a child compared to her sister. She always made herself white cotton nightgowns that were the same ones she had worn since she was a little girl. They were comfortable, and she liked them.

"A lot can happen in three weeks," Brigitte said mysteriously, as Beata shook her head, looking serious again. She knew better.

"No, it can't. He's not Jewish. All we can ever be is friends."

That sobered even Brigitte, as they both thought of their father. "That's true," Brigitte said sadly, "but at least you can flirt with him. You need the practice."

"Yes," Beata said thoughtfully as she walked into the bathroom to wash her face and brush her teeth. "I suppose I do." Neither of them mentioned Antoine again that night, but as Beata lay in bed, thinking of him for hours before she fell asleep, she thought with regret of the miserable luck that the first man she had ever been absolutely enchanted by wasn't Jewish. And nearly as bad, he was French. Nothing could ever come of it, but at least she could enjoy his company for the next three weeks. It was nearly four o'clock in the morning, when she finally fell asleep.

3

THEIR LUNCH WITH ANTOINE THE NEXT DAY WAS everything it should have been, and everything Beata had wished. Polite, pleasant, cordial, totally respectable. He was extremely respectful to her mother, treated Brigitte like a silly little girl, and made them all laugh when he teased her. He was intelligent, charming, kind, funny, and wonderful to be with. Not to mention the fact that he was gorgeous. He told them funny stories about his family, and described his family's property as a nightmare to run and keep, although it was obvious that he loved it. He never slipped and let on that it was in France not Switzerland. By the end of lunch, Monika adored him, and saw nothing

wrong with his taking a walk with Beata after lunch. He had made no romantic over-
tures during lunch, and there was nothing
sleazy or sneaky about him. As far as
Beata's mother was concerned, he was just
a very nice person, enjoying three new
friends. Beata's mother had absolutely no
qualms or concerns about him. It was a
huge relief to both Antoine and Beata when
they were finally alone, and walked for miles
along the lake. This time when they finally
stopped to sit and talk, they did so on a narrow rim of beach, and sat on the sand with
their feet in the water, talking about a thousand things. They seemed to share similar
tastes and opinions on almost everything.

"Thank you for taking us to lunch, you
were so nice to my mother and Brigitte."

"Don't be silly. They were very nice to me.
Although your sister is going to be a terror
and break men's hearts. I hope they marry
her off soon."

"They will," Beata said with a quiet smile.
She had particularly appreciated the way he
had reacted to Brigitte. He kept her in her
place, teased her like the child she was, and
had no romantic interest in her whatsoever.
Beata felt unkind for it, but she was

pleased. Brigitte was a lot for her to live with. "She's more or less in love with one of Horst's friends, and my father is going to talk to his father soon. I'm sure she'll be engaged by the end of the year."

"And what about you?" Antoine asked, looking concerned, although Beata didn't see it. "Are they going to settle on someone for you?"

"I hope not. I won't do that. I don't think I'll ever marry," she said quietly, and she sounded as though she meant it.

"Why not?"

"Because I can't imagine wanting someone they pick out for me. The thought of it makes me feel ill. I don't want a husband I don't love, or know, or want. I'd rather be alone, forever." There was real vehemence in her voice, as he watched her, feeling both relieved and sad for her.

"Forever is a long time, Beata. You'll want to have children, and you should. Maybe you'll meet someone you'll fall in love with one day. I'm sure you will. You're only twenty, you have your whole life ahead of you." He sounded sad as he said it, and as she looked at him, their eyes met and held for a long time before she answered him.

"So do you."

"I have a war to fight. Who knows which of us will survive it? Men are dropping like flies on the battlefields." And then as he said it, he thought of her brothers, and was sorry to have said what he did. "I'm sure we'll all come out of it in the end, but it makes it hard to think about the future. I've always thought I would stay single, too. I don't think I've ever been in love," he said honestly, looking at her, and his next words stunned her almost as much as he stunned himself, "until I met you." There was an endless silence after he spoke, and she had no idea what to answer, except that she knew she was in love with him, too, and they had just met. It was a crazy thing for him to say, and for either of them to feel, but they did, and there was nothing they would ever be able to do about it. It was impossible and they both knew it, but he had said it anyway.

"I'm Jewish," she blurted out. "I can never marry you," she said as tears filled her eyes, and he took her hand in his.

"Stranger things have happened, Beata. People do marry outside their faith." He had been fantasizing about marrying her all day. It was a crazy dream for both of them, but he couldn't deny what he felt. It had taken him thirty-two years to find her, and he didn't want to lose her yet. Or ever, if he could help it. But there were certainly obstacles in their path. It would be difficult at best. His own family would be incensed. He was the Comte de Vallerand, a count, and he hadn't even told her that yet. He was sure it would make no difference to her. What they were drawn to in each other was far deeper than faith or titles or position or birth. He loved everything about her, what she said and how she felt, how she viewed the world, and she loved the same things about him. They were drawn to each other for the right reasons, but their faith and their nationalities and allegiances and families would conspire to keep them apart. The trick would be not to let them win, if they could do it. That remained to be seen.

"My family would never allow it. My father would kill me. They would disown me," she said in response to his comment about people marrying outside their faith. In her family, it was unheard of.

"Maybe not, if we went to them one day. Mine would be upset, too. They'd have to have time to get used to the idea. And we have a war to fight first. If we decide to do this, we have a long road ahead of us. This is only the beginning, but I want you to know that I love you. I've never said that to anyone before." There were tears in her eyes as she nodded and looked at him. They sat next to each other on the beach, holding hands, and her voice was only a whisper when she spoke.

"I love you, too." He turned and smiled at her, and without saying a word, he leaned over and kissed her and held her for a long time. They didn't do anything they shouldn't, he was just happy to be with her.

"I wanted you to know that I love you, in case something happens to me when I go back. I want you to know that this man loves you, and will love you till the day he dies." It was a huge statement to make after knowing her for two days. But he meant it. She felt that way, too.

"That better not be for a very long time," she said solemnly, referring to "loving her till the day he died."

"It won't be," he said. They sat there for an hour, and he kissed her again before they went back. He didn't want to do anything to jeopardize or hurt her. All he wanted to do was protect and love her, but the very fact that they cared about each other put them both in a difficult spot. Theirs was not going to be an easy path, but it seemed like their destiny to each of them. They both felt that, as they walked back toward the hotel hand in hand.

They worked out a plan to see each other later that night. She said that Brigitte slept like a rock and wouldn't hear her leave. They were going to meet in the garden at midnight, just to talk. It was a risky prospect if her mother found out about it, but Beata said that if she or Brigitte were still up, she wouldn't come. He urged her to be cautious and wise, although what they were doing was anything but. By some miracle, she managed to get out, and every night after that. For three weeks they took walks, had tea together, and met late at night. All they did was kiss and talk. And by the time he left Geneva, shortly before she did, they were deeply in love, and had vowed to spend the rest of their lives together, some way, somehow. They were going to speak to their families after the war, whenever that was. In the meantime he would write to her. He had a cousin in Geneva and would mail letters to him, and he would send them on to Beata in Cologne. He had worked it all out. Otherwise it would have been impossible to get letters into Germany from France.

Their last night together was torture, and he held her in his arms for hours. It was nearly dawn when she went back, with tears running down her face, but she knew that if the fates conspired to help them, they would be together one day. He was due to get a leave at Christmas, but he had to go home to Dordogne. There was no way he could come to Germany to see her, as long as the war was on. Her family had no plans to come to Switzerland again. They would have to wait. But there was no doubt in her mind or his that they would. What they had found came once in a lifetime and was worth waiting for. They were both absolutely sure of their feelings for each other.

"Don't forget how much I love you," he whispered, when she left him in the garden. "I'll be thinking of you every moment till I see you again."

"I love you," she whispered between sobs, and then she went back and slipped into her bed in the room she shared with Brigitte. Two hours later, still awake, she saw a letter slide under her door. She got up to get it, and when she carefully opened the door, he was already gone. The note told her what she knew already, how much he loved her, and that she would be his one day. She folded it carefully and put it in the drawer where she kept her gloves. She didn't have the heart to destroy it, although to be safe, she knew she should. But being so much taller than her older sister, Brigitte never wore Beata's gloves, so she knew it was safe. Beata had no idea what would happen now. All she knew was that she loved him, and all she could do now was pray that he stayed alive. Her heart was his.

By some miracle, Beata had managed to keep everything that had happened from Brigitte, and she insisted that she and Antoine were just friends. Brigitte was disappointed to hear it, and at first wasn't inclined to believe her, but in the end, she did. She had no other choice. Beata showed no sign of the love or passion she felt for Antoine, and admitted nothing to her. There was too much at stake. She could trust no one with their future except Antoine himself, just as he trusted her. Her mother thought it nice that she had made a friend, and said she hoped to see him again when they came back someday. With the war on, she knew that Jacob would want to come to Switzerland again, for some peace.

It was stressful going back to Cologne in September, when they did. The war raged on, and it was depressing hearing about people's sons and husbands and brothers being killed. Too many had died already, and Monika was constantly worried about her sons, as was Jacob, but he was worried about his daughters, too. He did what he had promised his wife he would do. In October, he spoke to the father of Horst's friend in Berlin, the young man whom Brigitte found so enchanting, and when he spoke to her, she was over the moon. The young man had agreed, and his family thought that a marriage between the two families was an excellent idea. Jacob gave his younger daughter an enormous dowry, and promised to buy them a handsome house in Berlin. Just as Beata had pre-dicted, Brigitte was engaged at the end of the year, when she turned eighteen.

In peacetime, her parents would have given her an enormous ball to celebrate her engagement, but because of the war, it was

out of the question. Her engagement was
announced, and they gave a large dinner
party for both sets of parents and a number
of their friends. Several generals attended,
the young men who were available and on
leave came in uniform, and Ulm managed to
come, although Horst couldn't get leave.
But it was a proud event. The merging of
two fine families, and two beautiful young
people.

All Brigitte could think of was her wedding
and her dress. She was to be married in
June, which seemed an interminable wait to
her. Beata was happy for her. It was everything Brigitte had dreamed of since she was
a little girl. She wanted a husband and babies, and parties, and pretty dresses and
jewels, and she was going to have all of it.
And with great good fortune, her fiancé was
stationed in Berlin. He was in no imminent
danger, and his father had managed to have
him attached to a general as an aide. His father had been assured he wouldn't be sent
to the front, so Brigitte had nothing to fear.
Her wedding and future were secure.

Beata seemed enormously peaceful about
it, and was happy to see her sister so
happy. She had promised to make all the

underwear for her trousseau and sat constantly sewing pieces of pale satin, as she
trailed bits of lace everywhere. It didn't
seem to bother her at all that her younger
sister was getting married and she wasn't.
She was far more interested in the war. And
once a week, she received a letter from
Antoine via his Swiss cousin, which reassured her that he was alive and well. He was
near Verdun, and she thought of him constantly as she sewed, and reread his letters
a thousand times. Her mother had noticed
one or two letters when they arrived in the
mail, but most of the time Beata got the mail
now before anyone else did, and no one realized how many letters she had gotten, or
how steadily they continued to come. They
were as much in love as ever, and prepared
to wait for a life together until after the war.
She had already vowed to herself, and to
him, that if anything ever happened to him,
she would never marry anyone else. It
seemed reasonable to her. She couldn't
imagine loving anyone as she did him.

Her father had noticed how quiet Beata
was in the past few months, and interpreted
it as great sadness on her part in the face of
Brigitte's joy. Believing her unhappy nearly

broke his heart. It drove him to speak to several men he knew well, and in March, he knew he had found the right one. He would not have been his first choice, but on closer inspection, he knew that the man he had chosen was the best one for her. He was a widower who had no children, from an excellent family, with a large fortune of his own. Jacob had wanted someone older and more stable for Beata than the handsome young man he had secured for Brigitte, who could turn out to be flighty, was still immature and playful, and was definitely spoiled, although Jacob thought him a nice boy. And Brigitte was crazy about him. The husband Jacob had selected for his older daughter was a thoughtful, extremely intelligent man. He wasn't handsome, but he was not unattractive, although he was going bald. He was tall and somewhat portly, and forty-two years old, but Jacob knew he would be respectful of her. The man in question said he would be honored to be betrothed to such a beautiful girl. He had lost his wife five years before, after a long illness, and had had no thought of marrying again. He was a quiet person, who disliked social life as much as she did, and all he wanted was a quiet home.

Jacob and Monika had him to a dinner party at their home and insisted that Beata attend. She didn't want to since Brigitte was staying with her future parents-in-law for a round of parties in Berlin, and Beata didn't want to attend a dinner party without her. But she knew she would have to learn to go to parties without her, after Brigitte moved to Berlin with her husband in June. Her parents absolutely insisted she join them, without telling her why they wanted her there. She appeared in their drawing room looking very regal in a midnight blue velvet dress, with a handsome string of pearls around her neck, and small diamonds at her ears. She paid no attention to the man they hoped she would marry, as she'd never met him before, and seemed unaware of his presence. When they introduced him to her, she shook his hand politely and drifted away a few moments later, thinking he was someone from her father's bank. She sat quietly next to him at dinner, answered his questions courteously, but her mind was full of Antoine's most recent letter, which she had received that afternoon. She could think of nothing else, and ignored her dinner partner for most of the night. She didn't hear a thing he said, which he interpreted as shyness, and found charming. He was utterly enchanted by her, she hardly noticed him, and didn't have the remotest idea that he had been invited for her. She thought she was seated next to him at random, and not by design.

She was worried about Antoine that night, and hadn't heard from him in days until the letter she had just received, which spoke of German forces attacking the French at Verdun. She could hardly think of anything else as she sat through the dinner party, and finally claimed she had a headache, and left just after dessert, without saying goodnight. She thought it more discreet to simply quietly disappear. Afterward her future fiancé asked Jacob when they intended to tell her, and Jacob promised it would be within days. He wanted her to be as happy as Brigitte, and was certain this was the man for her. Her future husband even shared her passion for Greek philosophers, and had tried to discuss them with her at dinner, but she had been distracted and vague, and only nodded at what he said. She hadn't listened to a word he'd said from soup to dessert. It was as though she was hanging somewhere in space, unable to come to earth. Her future fiancé thought her a modest, charmingly discreet young girl.

She was in far better spirits when her father saw her in the hall the next day. She had just gotten another letter from Antoine, and he had reassured her once again that he was well and as madly in love with her as ever. They had had hellish days near Verdun, but he was alive and well, though exhausted and hungry. The conditions he described were nightmarish, but just knowing he was alive was enough to improve her spirits dramatically, and her father was delighted to see her so happy, when he asked her to come into his library to speak to him. He asked how she had enjoyed the dinner party the night before, and she politely said she had had a lovely time. He inquired about her dinner partner, and she barely seemed to remember him, and then said he was very nice and pleasant to talk to, but it was obvious she had no idea what they had in mind for her.

As her father explained it to her, Beata's face went pale. He said that the man she'd sat next to, whom she had barely noticed, and certainly wasn't attracted to, was willing to marry her. In fact, he saw no reason to delay. He would prefer to marry her sooner rather than later, and her father thought a small wedding just after Brigitte's, in July perhaps, would be sensible. Or even before that, if she preferred it, since she was the eldest, perhaps in May. There was no need to wait. With the war on, people were marrying quickly these days. Beata sat and stared at her father with a look of shocked horror on her face, and Jacob didn't fully understand her revulsion at first. She jumped to her feet and strode around the room, looking anxious and panicked, and spoke with such vehemence and outrage that Jacob stared at her in disbelief. This was not the reaction he had expected from her, nor the one he wanted. He had all but assured her widowed suitor that their marriage was a certainty, and had already discussed the terms of her dowry with him. It would be extremely embarrassing if Beata refused to marry him. She had always been a good girl, and obedient to him, and Jacob was sure that she would be once again.

"I don't even know him, Papa," she said, with tears running down her face. "He's old enough to be my father, and I don't want to marry him," she said with a look of desperation. "I don't want to be given to a stranger, like some kind of slave. If you expect me to share a bed with him, I would rather die an old maid." Her father looked embarrassed at her all-too-graphic description of his expectations, and resolved to have her mother talk to her. He made one last attempt to reason with her. He had expected her to be pleased, not enraged.

"You have to trust my judgment on this, Beata. He is the right man for you. At your age, you have romantic illusions about what love is that don't make sense in the real world. What you need is a lifetime companion who shares your interests, will be responsible, and respect you. The rest will come in time, Beata. I promise you. You're far more sensible than your sister, and you need a man who will be just as reasonable and practical as you are. You don't need a silly young boy with a handsome face. You need a man who will protect you and provide for you and your children, a man you can count on and talk to. That's what marriage is about, Beata, not about romance and parties. You don't want that, or need it.

I much prefer a man like this for you," he said almost sternly, as she stood across the room from her father and glared at him.

"Then you sleep with him. I won't let him touch me. I don't love this man, and I won't marry him because you say so. I won't be sold into slavery to a stranger like a herd of cattle, Papa. You can't do that to me."

"I will not tolerate you speaking to me that way," he boomed at her, shaking with rage. "What would you have me do? Allow you to live here as an old maid for the rest of your life? What will happen to you when your mother and I die and you are without protection? This man will take care of you, Beata. That's what you need. You cannot sit here and wait for a handsome prince to find you, and carry you away, a prince who is as intellectual as you are, as serious, as fascinated by books and studies as you are. Perhaps you'd prefer a university professor, but he couldn't afford to support you in the way you're accustomed to and deserve. This man has means comparable to what you grew up with. You owe it to your children to marry someone like him, Beata, not some starving artist or writer who will leave you to die of consumption in a garret somewhere. Beata, this is reality, marrying the man I choose for you. Your mother and I know what we're doing, you're young and foolish and idealistic. Real life is not in the books you read. Real life is right here, and you will do as I say."

"I will die first," she said, her eyes never leaving her father's, and she looked as though she meant it. He had never seen her look as fierce or as determined, and as he saw her, he thought of something that had never crossed his mind, particularly not with her. He asked her a single question, and his voice was shaking as he did so, and for the first time in his life with her, he feared what he might hear.

"Are you in love with someone else?" He couldn't imagine it. She never left the house, but the look in her eyes told him that he needed to ask her, and she hesitated before she spoke. She knew she had to tell him the truth, there was no other way.

"Yes." She stood still and stiff before him as she said the single word.

"Why have you not told me?" He looked both heartbroken and livid all at once, and more than that, he looked betrayed. She had allowed him to go forward with this charade, merely by never telling him that there was someone she cared deeply about. Enough to jeopardize the match he had made, the one he knew was right for her. "Who is it? Do I know him?" He felt a shudder run through him as he asked her, as though someone had walked on his grave.

She shook her head in answer and spoke softly. "No, you don't. I met him in Switzerland last summer." She was determined to be honest with him. She felt she had no other choice. This moment had come sooner than she wanted or expected, and all she could do now was pray that he would be reasonable and fair to her.

"Why didn't you tell me? Does your mother know about this?"

"No. No one knows. Mama and Brigitte met him, but he was just a friend then. I want to marry him when the war is over, Papa. He wants to come and meet you."

"Then let him come." Her father was furious with her, but nonetheless willing to be honorable about the matter, and reasonable with his child, although he was deeply upset with her for this profession of love at the eleventh hour.

"He can't come to see you, Papa. He's at the front."

"Do your brothers know him?" She shook her head again, and said nothing. "What are you not telling me about him, Beata? I sense that there is more here than you're saying." He was right, as he so often was. She felt her whole body shake in terror as she answered him.

"He's from a good family, with a large estate. He's well educated and intelligent. He loves me, Papa, and I love him." There were tears running down her cheeks.

"Then why have you kept this a secret? What are you hiding from me, Beata?" His voice was bellowing, and Monika could hear him from upstairs.

"He is Catholic, and French," Beata said in a whisper, as her father let out a sound like a wounded lion. It was so awful that she took several steps backward as he advanced on her without thinking. He stopped only when he had reached her and grabbed her small frame in both his hands. He shook her so hard by the shoulders that her teeth rattled as he shouted into her face.

"How dare you! How *dare* you do this to us! You will not marry a Christian, Beata.

Never! I will see you dead first. If you do this, you will be dead to us. I will write your name in our family's book of the dead. You will never see this man again. Do you understand me? And you will marry Rolf Hoffman on the day I tell you. I will tell him the deal is done. And you will tell your Catholic Frenchman that you will never see or speak to him again. Is that clear?"

"You can't do that to me, Papa," she said, sobbing, choking for lack of air. She could not give up Antoine, nor marry the man her father had chosen, no matter what her father did to her.

"I can and I will. You will marry Hoffman in one month."

"Papa, no!" She fell to her knees, sobbing, as he stormed out of the library and went upstairs. She knelt there for a long time, crying, until her mother finally came to her in tears. She knelt beside her daughter, heartbroken over what she had just heard.

"Beata, how could you do this? You must forget him . . . I know he's a good man, but you cannot marry a Frenchman, not after this terrible war between us, and you cannot marry a Catholic. Your father will write your name in the book of the dead." Monika was beside herself with anguish, as she saw the look on her daughter's face.

"I will die anyway, Mama, if I don't. I love him. I can't marry that awful man." He wasn't awful, she knew, but he was old in her eyes, and he was not Antoine.

"I'll tell Papa to tell him. But you can never marry Antoine."

"We have promised to marry each other after the war."

"You must tell him you can't. You can't deny all that you are."

"He loves me as I am."

"You are both foolish children. His family will disown him, too. How would you live?"

"I can sew . . . I could be a seamstress, a schoolteacher, whatever I have to be. Papa has no right to do this." But they both knew he did. He could do whatever he wanted, and he had told her that if she married a Christian, she would be dead to them. Monika believed him, and she couldn't bear the thought of never seeing Beata again. It was far too high a price for her to pay for a man she loved.

"I beg you," she implored her daughter, "don't do this. You must do as Papa says."

"I won't," she said, sobbing in her mother's arms.

Jacob was not entirely foolish. He told Rolf Hoffman that afternoon that Beata was young and foolish and appeared to be afraid of the . . . physical obligations . . . of marriage, and he was not sure that his daughter was ready to marry anyone. He didn't want to mislead the man, nor tell him the whole truth. He told him that perhaps after a long courtship, and if they got to know each other, she would feel more comfortable with all that marriage entailed. Hoffman was disappointed, but said he would wait as long as he had to. He was in no hurry, and he understood that she was an innocent young girl. He had been well aware of her shyness the night they met. And even an obedient daughter deserved the opportunity to become acquainted with the man who was going to wed her and take her to his bed. At the end of the conversation, Jacob was grateful to him for his patience, and assured him that Beata would come around in time.

She did not come to dinner that night, and Jacob didn't see her for several days. According to her mother, she had not left her bed. She had written Antoine a letter, telling him what had happened. She said her father would never agree to their marriage, but she was prepared to marry him anyway, either after the war or before that, whatever he thought best. But she no longer felt at ease in her home in Cologne. She knew that her father would continue to try to force her to marry Rolf. She also knew it would be weeks before she had a response from Antoine, but she was prepared to wait.

She did not hear from him for two months. It was May when she finally got a letter from him, and for the entire time she had been terrified that he had been hurt or killed, or that hearing of her father's rage, he had decided to back out and never write to her again. Her first guess had been correct. He had been wounded a month before, and was in a hospital in Yvetot, on the Normandy coast. He had very nearly lost an arm, but said that he would soon be all right. He said that by the time she got his letter, he would be at home in Dordogne, and would speak to his own family about their marriage. He would not be going back to the front, or even to the war. The way he said it made her fear that his injury had been worse than he said. But he repeated several times that he was doing well, and loved her very, very much.

Beata answered his letter quickly, and sent it, as always, via his cousin in Switzerland. All she could do after that was wait. What he had said in his letter was that he hoped that his family would welcome her to their bosom, and they could be married and live on his property in Dordogne. Although, no question, bringing a German woman into France at this point, or even after the war, would be no small thing. Not to mention the religious issues between them, which would be as upsetting to his family as to hers. A count marrying a Jewess in France would be as horrifying to them as her marrying a French Catholic in her world in Cologne. There was no easy road, for either of them. And once she had written to him, Beata spent her days quietly helping her mother around the house, and staying out of her father's way. He had made repeated attempts to get her to spend time with Rolf, and each time she had refused. She said she would never marry him, or even see him again. She had grown so pale she looked like a ghost, and seeing her that way broke her mother's heart. She begged her continuously to do as her father said. There would be no peace for any of them until she did. With the weight of the trauma she had brought into the house, their home felt like a morgue.

Both her brothers had spoken to her, to no avail, when they came home on leave. And Brigitte was so furious she was no longer speaking to her. She had become increasingly full of herself with the excitement of her impending marriage.

"How could you be stupid enough, Beata, to tell Papa?"

"I didn't want to lie to him about it," she said simply. But he had been furious with all of them ever since. He held everyone responsible for Beata's foolishness and betrayal. More than anything, he felt that Beata had betrayed him, as though she had chosen to fall in love with a French Catholic just to spite him. In his eyes, she could have done nothing worse. It was going to take him years to get over it, even if she agreed to give Antoine up, which so far she had not.

"You don't really love him," Brigitte said

with all the self-assuredness of an eighteen-year-old about to marry her handsome prince. She had the world by the tail, and felt sorry for her stupid sister. It seemed ridiculous to her. What had seemed romantic to her for a few days in Geneva no longer made any sense. You didn't put your whole life on the line, and risk your family, for someone from another world. She was utterly enchanted with the match her father had made for her, and it suited her to a tee. "You don't even know him," Brigitte chided her.

"I didn't then, but I do now." They had bared their souls in six months of letters, and even in Geneva, after three weeks, they had both been sure. "It may not make sense to you, but I know that this is right for me."

"Even if Papa writes you in the book of the dead, and never allows you to see any of us again?" The thought of it, and she had thought of nothing else for the past two months, made Beata feel ill.

"I hope he won't do that to me," Beata said in a choked voice. The thought of never seeing her mother again, her brothers, Papa, and even Brigitte was unthinkable. But so was giving up the man she loved.

She couldn't do that either. And even if her father banished her at first, she hoped that he would relent one day. If she lost Antoine, he would be gone forever. She didn't believe you could lose your family.

"And if Papa does do that, and forbids us to see you?" Brigitte persisted, forcing Beata to face yet again the risk she was taking. "What would you do then?"

"I'd wait till he changes his mind," Beata said sadly.

"He won't. Not if you marry a Christian. He'll forgive you for not marrying Rolf eventually. But not if you marry your Frenchman. He's not worth that, Beata. No one is." Brigitte was happy to have her parents' approval, she would never have had the courage and audacity to do what Beata was doing, or threatening to do. "Just don't do something stupid that upsets everyone before my wedding." It was all she could think of, and Beata nodded agreement.

"I won't," she promised.

As it turned out, she heard from Antoine the week before the wedding. His family had had the same reaction as hers. They had told him that if he married a German Jew, he had no choice but to leave. His father had all but banished him, and told him he would take nothing with him. By French law, he could not bar his inheritance, nor his right to the title when his father died, but his father had assured him that if he married Beata, none of them would see him again. Antoine had been so outraged by their reaction that he was already in Switzerland, waiting for her, when he wrote to her. All he could suggest to her was that they sit out the war in Switzerland—if she was still willing to marry him, knowing the isolation from their families that it would mean to both of them. His cousin had said that they could live with him and his wife, and work on their farm. Antoine made no bones about the fact that it would not be easy, and neither of them would have any money, once estranged from their families. His cousins had very little as it was, and he and Beata would have to live on their charity and work for their keep. Antoine was willing, if she was, but it was up to her. He said that he would understand and not hold it against her if she decided that leaving her family for him was too difficult. He said he would love her no matter what her ultimate decision was. He knew that she would be sacrificing everything she loved and cared about and that was familiar to her, if she decided to marry him. He couldn't even imagine asking her to do that for him. The final decision was hers.

What touched Beata was that he had already made the same sacrifice for her. He had already left his family in Dordogne, and been told never to return. He was wounded and alone, at his cousins' farm in Switzerland. And he had done that for her. Their countries were still at war with each other, even if for him the war was over. She wanted to come back to Germany one day, and to her family certainly, if her father would allow it. But until the war ended, there seemed to be no other choice than to wait in Switzerland, and figure out the rest later. Perhaps by then his family would have relented, too. Although in his letter, Antoine said there was no hope of repairing the damage with his family. His departure and the raging battle that had caused it had been too decisive and too bitter. Even his brother Nicolas hadn't spoken to him when he left, and they had always been close. It was a great loss to him.

Beata spent the week before her sister's wedding, looking dazed and feeling tortured. She knew she had to make a decision. She went through the motions at Brigitte's wedding, feeling as though she were in a dream. And the irony of it was that Brigitte and her husband were going to Switzerland for their honeymoon. Jacob had advised them that it was the only safe place in Europe. They were going to spend three weeks in the Alps, above Geneva, not far from where Antoine was waiting for her, if she decided to go. She wanted to, but she had promised Brigitte not to do anything dramatic before her wedding. And she didn't.

The final explosion came two days later, when her father demanded that she assure him Antoine was out of her life forever. Both her brothers had gone back to their companies by then. Brigitte was on her honeymoon. And their father went after Beata with a vengeance. The battle was short and brutal. She refused to promise her father she would never see Antoine again, knowing that he was waiting for her in Switzerland. Her mother was hysterical as she tried to get them both to calm down, but they wouldn't. In the end, her father told her that if she would not give up her Catholic, she should go to him and be gone, but to know that when she left his house, she could never come back again. He told her that he and her mother would sit shiva for her, the vigil they held for the dead. As far as he was concerned, when she left the house, she would be dead to them. He told her she was never to contact any of them again. He was so awful about it and so enraged with her that Beata made her decision.

After hours of fighting with him and begging him to be reasonable and at least be willing to meet Antoine, she finally went to her room, defeated. She packed two small suitcases with all the things she thought she could use on the farm in Switzerland, and put framed photographs of all of them in her suitcase. She was sobbing when she closed her valises, and set them down in the hall, and her mother stood sobbing as she watched her.

"Beata, don't do this . . . he will never let you come home again." She had never seen her husband so enraged, nor would she again. She didn't want to lose her daughter, and there seemed to be nothing she could do to stop this tragedy from happening. "You'll always regret it."

"I know I will," Beata said tragically, "but I will never love any man but him. I don't want to lose him." She didn't want to lose them, either. "Will you write to me, Mama?" she asked, feeling like a child as her mother held her close to her, their tears mingling in a single torrent as their cheeks met. For an eternity, there was no answer from her mother, as Beata realized what this meant. When her father banished her and said she was dead to all of them, her mother felt she had no choice but to obey him. She would not cross the boundaries he was setting for all of them, not even for her. His word was law to her, and to all of them. And he had every intention of declaring her dead. "I'll write to you," Beata said softly, clinging to her mother like the child she still was in many ways. She had just turned twenty-one that spring.

"He won't let me see your letters," she said, holding Beata for as long as she could. Watching her leave was like a living death. "Oh my darling . . . be happy with this man . . . I hope he'll be good to you," she said, sobbing uncontrollably. "I hope he's worth it . . . oh my baby, I'll never see you again." Beata squeezed her eyes shut, holding tightly to her mother, as her father watched them from the top of the stairs.

"You're going then?" he said sternly. He looked like an old man to Beata for the first time. Until then, she had always thought of him as young, but he no longer was. He was about to lose the child he had most favored, the one he had been most proud of, and the last child he had at home.

"Yes, I am," Beata said in a small voice. "I love you, Papa," she said, wanting to approach him, so she could hug him, but the look on his face told her not to try.

"Your mother and I will sit shiva for you tonight. God forgive you for what you're doing." She wouldn't have dared, but she wanted to say the same thing to him.

She kissed her mother one last time, then picked up her bags, and walked slowly down the stairs as they both watched her. She could hear her mother's sobs all the way downstairs and as she opened the front door. There was no sound from her father.

"I love you!" she called upstairs to the hall where they were standing, and there was no answer. There was no sound except her mother's sobs, as she picked up her bags and closed the door behind her.

She walked until she saw a taxi, carrying the two heavy bags, and told the driver to take her to the railroad station. She just sat in the backseat and cried. The man said nothing to her as she paid him. Everyone had tragedies these days, and he didn't want to ask. Some griefs were not meant to be shared.

She waited three hours for the train to Lausanne. More than enough time to change her mind. But she knew she couldn't do that. She knew with her entire being that her future was with Antoine. He had given up just as much for her. There was no way to know what the future held for them, but she had known that he was her destiny since the day they met. She hadn't seen him since September, but he was part of her now. He was her life, just as her parents belonged to each other. Brigitte belonged to the man she had married. They all had their destinies to follow. And with luck, she would see them again one day. For now, this was her path. It was inconceivable to her that her father would stick to this unreasonable position forever. Sooner or later, he would have to give up.

Beata was quiet as she got on the train that afternoon. Tears rolled down her cheeks most of the way to Lausanne, until she finally slept, and the old woman in the compartment with her woke her up. She knew that Beata was getting off in Lausanne. Beata thanked her politely, got off the train, and looked around the station. She felt like an orphan. She had sent Antoine a telegram from the station in Cologne. And then in the distance, she saw him, hurrying across the platform toward her. His arm was in a bandage held by a sling, but as he reached her, he grabbed her with one arm and held her so powerfully she could hardly breathe.

"I didn't know if you would come. I was afraid you wouldn't . . . it's so much to ask of you . . ." There were tears rolling down their cheeks as he told her how much he loved her, and she looked up at him in awe. He was her family now, her husband, her present and her future, the father of the children they would have. He was everything to her, as she was to him. She didn't care what hardships they would have to endure, as long as they were together. As painful as it had been leaving her family, she knew she had done the right thing.

They just stood there together for a long time on the platform, savoring the moment, clinging to each other. He picked up one of her bags in his good hand, and she picked up the other, and they went outside to where his cousin and his wife were waiting for them. Antoine was beaming when they emerged from the station, and Beata was smiling up at him. His cousin put her valises in the trunk of the car, and Antoine pulled her close to him. He hadn't dared to believe she would come. But she had. She had given up everything for him. They got into the backseat of the car, as he put his one good arm around her and kissed her again. There were no words to tell her what she meant to him. And as they drove slowly through Lausanne and into the countryside beyond, she sat quietly next to him. She couldn't allow herself to look back now, only forward. And as he had said he would, her father wrote her name in their family's book of the dead that morning. They had sat shiva for her the night before. She was dead to them.

4

THE FARM OWNED BY ANTOINE'S COUSINS WAS small and simple. The land was beautiful, the house was warm and without pretension. They had two small bedrooms side by side, one of which their three children had grown up in. They were long gone to cities. None had stayed to work the farm. There was a big comfortable kitchen, and a sitting room for Sundays, which no one ever used. It was a far cry from the house where Beata had lived in Cologne. They were related to Antoine on his mother's side, and somewhat distant cousins, he explained, but they were more than happy to help the young people out and grateful to have help on the farm. Two young boys lived in a tiny cottage to help with the plowing, the harvest, and the cows. And here, in the mountains above Lausanne, it was hard to imagine that there was trouble anywhere in the world. The farm was as far removed from the war as one could get.

Antoine's cousins, Maria and Walther Zuber, were warm, easygoing, pleasant people. They were well educated, had little money, and had chosen a life that suited them. The rest of their family lived in Geneva and Lausanne, although their children had emigrated to Italy and France. They were roughly the age of Beata's parents, although in talking to them she realized that they were older than that. Their rigorous, hard-working, healthy life had served them well. And the haven they had offered Antoine when he told them his plight was perfect for the young couple in their hour of need. Antoine was going to do what he could for them, in exchange for the lodging they provided, but with his injured arm, he was limited.

Beata was shocked to see how bad the damage was, when she helped him dress his wound and massaged the arm for him that afternoon. Shrapnel had all but destroyed both muscles and nerves of his left arm. And it still looked like a painful wound. They had told him he would be able to use it again eventually, but no one knew yet to what degree. And clearly, it would never be the same as it had once been. It changed none of Beata's feelings for him, and fortunately for him he was right-handed.

Antoine had offered to help Walther with the horses, as he was particularly skilled with them, and with only one good arm, he would do whatever else he could. Beata and the two young boys who worked there would do the rest.

As they ate lunch of soup and sausages in the cozy kitchen, Beata offered to do the cooking, and whatever else they felt she could do. Maria said she would teach her to milk the cows, as Beata looked at her with wide eyes. She had never been on a farm before, and knew she had much to learn. She had not only given up her family for Antoine, and the home where she'd been born, she had left the only city and life she had ever known and loved. She had given up everything for him, as he had for her. It was a fresh beginning for both of them, and without the Zubers they would have had nowhere to go, and no way to live. Beata thanked them profusely as they finished lunch, and afterward she helped Maria with the dishes. It was the first non-kosher meal she had ever eaten. And although it was unfamiliar to her, she knew she had no choice now on the farm. In the blink of an eye, her entire life had changed.

"When are you two getting married?" Maria asked, looking motherly and concerned. She had worried about Beata ever since Antoine had written to them and asked if the young couple could seek refuge with them. She and Walther had been hospitable and generous and quick to agree. Without their own children at hand, it was going to be helpful to them, too.

"I don't know," Beata answered quietly. She and Antoine hadn't had time to speak of it. It was all so new. They had so much to think about. She was still in shock after the last traumatic days in Cologne.

She and Antoine spoke of their plans late that night. He had made up a bed for himself on the couch in the living room, and gave Beata the small bedroom, which Maria had approved. Antoine had assured his cousins that he and Beata would be getting married soon. Maria didn't want the young people living in sin under her roof, and Walther agreed. There was no question of that. Beata and Antoine wanted to be married, too. He had looked into it as soon as he arrived and had discovered that as foreign nationals, they needed permission to marry in Switzerland. And in order to get the documents they needed, he borrowed Walther's truck and drove Beata into the neighboring town the next day. They needed their passports, a document that would allow them to marry in the registrar's office, and two Swiss citizens to vouch for them and act as witnesses. The fact that his maternal grandfather had been Swiss was of no use to them. His mother's nationality had been French, through her mother, as was his. The official who took the information from them said that they would have the papers they needed within two weeks.

"Will you be married civilly or by a priest?" the civil servant asked as a matter of routine, as Antoine looked blankly at her. Neither of them had thought about who would marry them, and Antoine had assumed they would just do it in a brief civil ceremony at the *mairie.* With no family at hand except the Zubers, and in their circumstances, it was simply an official act to obtain proper documents and legitimize their union so they could live together decently and in peace. There would be no ceremony, no fanfare, no reception, no party afterward, no celebration. Just a moment in time when they became husband and wife. How and where they would do it, and who would do it for them, hadn't even crossed either of their minds. After the clerk in the registrar's office asked the question, Antoine looked hesitantly at his wife-to-be. And as they walked back out into the summer sunshine, he hugged her with his right arm, and kissed her cautiously. Beata looked surprisingly calm as she smiled up at him.

"We'll be married in two weeks," she said softly. This wasn't the wedding she had anticipated in her girlhood, but in every other way, it was the fulfillment of a dream. They had met ten months before and fallen in love the moment they met, and all she wanted now was to spend the rest of her life with him. They didn't know yet where they would live after the war, or even how they would live, or if their families would welcome them back in their midst once again. Beata hoped they would, but all she knew and all she wanted now was to be with him.

"Who would you like to marry us?" Antoine asked gently. The registrar had asked a reasonable question. Antoine didn't know if she would want a rabbi to do it, although he had to admit, that idea made him somewhat uneasy. They could be married in the registrar's office, if they chose to, but Antoine realized as he thought about it that he would prefer to be married by a priest.

"I hadn't really thought about it. We can't be married by a rabbi. You'd have to convert, and do a lot of studying to do that. It could take years," Beata said sensibly. A mere two weeks seemed like an eternity to them. Neither of them was willing to wait years, particularly now that she was here, and they were living at the Zubers. Antoine had lain awake during most of the previous night, unable to sleep, knowing that she was in the bed they would soon share in the next room. After all they'd been through to be together, he was aching to claim her as his own.

"How do you feel about being married by

a priest?" Antoine asked her honestly. He wasn't going to force her, although it was clearly what he would prefer.

"I don't know. I never thought about it. Just being married by the registrar seems a little bleak. I'm not sure it matters whether we are married by a rabbi or a priest. I've always thought it was one God watching us and caring about us. I'm not sure it makes a difference what church or synagogue He belongs to." To Antoine, it seemed a novel idea. She was very liberal in her thinking, unlike her family.

On the way back to the farm they talked about it, and the possibility of her converting to Catholicism. She was surprisingly open-minded about it and said she would do it, if it meant a lot to him. She believed in her faith, but she loved Antoine, too. And if converting to Catholicism for him meant they could be married sooner, that was important to her. As they discussed it seriously, Antoine stopped the car at a little church. There was a small rectory behind it, and Antoine got out of the car, walked up the ancient stone steps, and rang the bell. A sign said that it was a tenth-century chapel, and the stone looked worn and weathered.

An elderly priest came out wearing his cassock, and smiled at the young man. They exchanged a few words as Beata waited in the car, and then Antoine gestured to her. She got out of the car, and approached cautiously. She had never spoken to a priest. She'd never seen one at close range, only walking past her on the street, but his face and eyes looked kind.

"Your fiancé tells me that you want to get married," he said as they stood in the morning sunshine and fresh mountain air. There was a field of yellow wildflowers just beyond, and a small crumbling cemetery behind the church, where people were still buried. There was a small chapel at the back of the church, and a well, which dated back to the fourth century.

"Yes, we do want to get married," Beata agreed, trying not to think of what her parents would say if they could see her talking to a priest. She half-expected to be struck by lightning, and another part of her felt surprisingly safe and at peace.

"You're not Catholic, I understand. You would need some private instruction, and I assume you want to convert." Beata gulped. It was strange hearing him say the word. She had never thought she would be any faith but Jewish. But she had also never thought she would be married to Antoine or someone like him. And her earlier religious studies had opened her mind to other faiths. She assumed that in time, for Antoine's sake, her heart would follow. She was willing to convert out of love for him. "We could put you in catechism classes with the local children, but the last group just made their first communion, and the classes won't start again until after the summer. I gather that you want to be married in two weeks." The priest glanced at Antoine's injured arm as he said it, and the innocence evident in Beata's face. Antoine had explained that he was French and Beata German, that he had been injured in the war, and they had no family to speak of, except two cousins with whom they lived. He made it clear that Beata had just arrived from Germany the day before, and they wanted their situation regularized, and did not want to live in sin. It was up to the priest to help them to meet their needs, and he agreed. He wanted to do all that he could. They looked like good people to him, and clearly their intentions were pure, or else they would not be stopping to see him. "Why don't you come inside for a moment, and we'll talk about it."

He invited them in, and Antoine and Beata followed him inside to a small dark room. There was an enormous crucifix on one wall, and the room was lit with candles. A shrine to the Blessed Mother stood in the corner, as the priest sat on a small battered desk and Antoine pulled up two chairs for them. The room seemed somehow depressing, and yet with the kind old priest smiling at them, Antoine and Beata both felt at ease.

"Could you come in to see me for an hour every afternoon, Beata?" She nodded cautiously in answer to his question. She wasn't sure yet what was expected of her on the farm, or if Antoine would have time to drive her to the church. If not, she would have to walk a long way, but she was willing to do that, too.

"Yes, I will," she said, feeling a little daunted. She wasn't sure what he wanted from her.

"If you do, I think we can cover all the catechism you'll need in order to convert. I prefer to do that over time, many months, so that you understand what you're learning, and are sure that you're ready for baptism. But in this case, I think we can move more quickly. You can study on your own, and I can teach you what you need to know. This is an important step in your life, even more important than marriage. It is a wonderful thing to embrace Christ."

"Yes," she whispered. "I know." As Antoine glanced at her, her eyes looked huge in her milk-white face. She had never looked as beautiful to him as she did now in the candlelit room.

"What if I don't feel ready? If I am not ready for . . . baptism . . ." She could barely say the word.

"Then of course you have to wait until you are. You can always wait to be married," he said kindly. "You cannot marry a Catholic unless you convert." He didn't even mention the option that Antoine could convert to Judaism, or they could be married civilly and not in church. In the eyes of the priest, there was only one valid marriage for a Catholic, one performed by a priest in a Catholic church. And Beata knew just from the little he had said that morning that Antoine felt that way, too. It was another huge step she was taking for him, another sacrifice that had to be made. And it wasn't practical for him to become Jewish, as they had agreed that morning. The studies to do so would have taken years. There was no rabbi nearby to teach him, if Antoine would even consider doing that. But for reasons practical and otherwise, it just didn't make sense. And it seemed too much to ask of him. Beata felt she had no choice but to convert, if she wanted to marry him and have their union sanctioned and blessed in the eyes of a religion, in this case his. And as she listened to the priest, she felt it was what she wanted to do. The Bible had always intrigued her. She loved the stories about Jesus, and had always been fascinated by the saints. Perhaps, she told herself, this was what was meant to be. And although it was the only religion she knew, Beata had never been so certain of her deep bond to Judaism. She was ready nonetheless to give it up for him, and embrace Catholicism. She felt it was part of what she owed him as his wife. Their love had required sacrifices of both of them from the beginning. And this was yet another one she was making for him.

They chatted with the priest for half an hour, and Beata promised to come back the following afternoon. He said he would have her ready for both conversion and marriage within two weeks. He followed them out and waved as the two young people drove away. Antoine was driving with his right hand, and seemed at ease doing so, as he rested the fingers of his damaged left hand on the wheel.

"So, what do you think?" Antoine asked, looking concerned. He felt as though he was asking so much of her, and if she truly objected to converting, he was willing to be satisfied with a civil ceremony. He didn't want her to do anything that violated her own beliefs. He had no idea how religious she was, or how strictly she adhered to Jewish traditions. He knew her family was Orthodox, which was why it was so un-thinkable to them that she should marry out of her faith. But he did not know how pro-foundly she herself believed, or how painful it might be to her to relinquish her faith for him.

"I think he's a nice man, and it will be very interesting to study with him," she said po-litely, but Antoine was relieved to see that she didn't look upset. She was oddly calm about what she was doing, as she had been about every step she took along the way.

"How do you feel about converting? You don't have to do it if you don't want to, Beata. We can just get married at the *mairie.* You've given up enough for me already." He was deeply respectful of her.

"And so have you," she said fairly. And then after a long moment, as she looked out the window as they drove along, "I think I would rather marry in church. Particularly if it means a lot to you." She turned back to him with a small smile that lit her eyes.

"That is incredibly generous of you," he said, wishing he could take a hand off the wheel to put an arm around her, but obviously he couldn't. "I love you," he said gently, and then after a few minutes, he thought of something else. "What about our children? Do you want them to be Catholic or Jewish?" They were all questions they would have asked in a normal courtship, but in the dire circumstances they'd been in, and with the distance between them, they had never had the time or opportunity to ask each other these things. Beata sat and thought about it before she answered him,

and then looked at him with a serious expression. She had taken everything they'd
said that morning very much to heart. These
were important, even life-altering, decisions.

"I think if I'm going to be Catholic, and you
are, and it is what we both believe, then our
children should be, too. Don't you?" If nothing else, it seemed practical to her. She had
never had her parents' deep sentiments
about religion. She went to temple to please
them, and because it was their tradition.
And she had always found the Bible fascinating and exciting. She was convinced
that, married to Antoine, she would develop
a bond to Catholicism in time, and hoped
she would.

Antoine nodded gratefully at her. This was
why of course her parents had been so violently opposed to their marriage. The idea
that they would have Catholic grandchildren
was their worst nightmare come true. But to
Beata now it seemed a sensible idea. "It
would be too confusing if we did different
things, and believed in such different ideas,
although from what I've read, I'm not entirely sure that what we each believe is so
different." Antoine did not disagree, and

there was a sense of peace and unity between them as they reached the farm, and
got out of the car. He put an arm around her
then, and they went inside for lunch with the
Zubers.

They told Walther and Maria about their
meeting with the priest, going to the registrar's office, and about Beata's catechism
lessons for the next two weeks. Beata apologized for having to leave them every afternoon, but Maria thought it was wonderful
news. She had wondered what they were
going to do, once Antoine had explained to
them that Beata was Jewish. She thought
that Beata converting for him was a loving
thing to do, and she said as much to Beata,
after the men left and the two women
cleaned up the kitchen.

"This must all seem very strange to you,"
Maria said sympathetically. She was a large
motherly woman, with no worldly experience or interests. She had come to the
farm when she married Walther at nineteen. He had bought it two years before,
and worked hard. And since she had been
there, she had borne their children, done
her work, loved her husband, gone to
church. Although she read a great deal and

was intelligent, it was the epitome of a simple life, and it was a million miles removed from the large, elegant house Beata had grown up in, or the clothes and jewels worn by her mother and Brigitte. In fact, imagining them here was unthinkable. And she couldn't help but smile at how different her sister's and her own married lives would be. She and Antoine were not planning to stay in Switzerland forever, eventually they wanted to return to France, or Germany, depending which of their two families relented, and where the best opportunities would be. If he did not go back to run his own properties in Dordogne, Antoine didn't know what he would do. But after the war, with all the inevitable changes that would result, there would be others in the same situation in which they were. Starting new lives in new places. It was a new beginning for them, and Beata was just grateful to be here.

"It's not strange," Beata said calmly in response to Maria, "it's just different. I'm not used to being so far from my family." She missed her mother terribly. And all her life, she had been inseparable from her sister, but now with Brigitte married and living in Berlin, everything would have changed any-

way. What pained her most were the agonizing circumstances in which she had left
her family. To Beata, that still felt like an
open wound, as Maria could easily imagine
it would, probably for many years. She
hoped that both Antoine's family and
Beata's would come to their senses eventually and forgive them for the choices they
had made. They were lovely young people,
and Maria knew it would be hard for them if
their families never accepted them, and
their marriage, in future years. In the meantime, Maria and Walther were more than
happy to act as surrogate parents to them.
Having the young couple there was a blessing for the Zubers, too.

"Will you and Antoine be wanting children
soon?" Maria asked with interest, as Beata
blushed and wasn't sure what to say. She
didn't know if one had much choice in the
matter. She always thought that babies
came if they were meant to. And if there was
something one could do to prevent that
happening, or alter the course of events,
she had no idea what it was. And she didn't
know Maria well enough to ask.

"I think so," Beata answered quietly, looking embarrassed, as she put the last of the

clean dishes back in the cupboard, "whatever is God's plan." She wondered, as she said it, if Brigitte would be having babies soon, too. She somehow couldn't imagine Brigitte with children, she was still so much a child herself, even at eighteen. At twenty-one, Beata barely felt ready for the responsibilities of motherhood and marriage. Three years earlier she would never have been here. But in spite of their painful beginning, she felt equal to the task. It was an exciting time for them.

"It will be lovely to have a baby here," Maria said happily as she poured them each a cup of tea.

She hardly ever saw her own grandchildren because they lived so far away, and it was almost impossible for her and Walther to leave the farm. It warmed her heart to think of Antoine and Beata, and perhaps one day a baby being near at hand, if they were still there when one came. Maria's eyes lit up at the idea. Beata couldn't even think about that as a reality, all she wanted now was to take her catechism classes at the little church nearby, and to marry Antoine in two weeks. Beyond that, she didn't know what to expect or think. All she knew for certain was how much she loved him. And she regretted nothing that she had done or given up for him. And Maria and Walther both respected her profoundly for her loyalty to him. She was an impressive and obviously very determined young woman. And so loving. Maria felt closer to her each day. They had always been fond of Antoine, although they had seen little of him in recent years, but it had been an easy decision for them when he had asked if they could come to stay. She was only sorry that because of their nationalities, they couldn't stay for good. Sooner or later, after the war was over, the Swiss government would expect them to leave. They could come to Switzerland for asylum, but when their own countries were open and at peace again, they would have to return to whence they came. But given what was happening in the world after two years of war, who knew when that would be. Tucked away in the mountains, they were safe and at peace in the meantime.

Beata found her classes with Father André absolutely fascinating. They reminded her somewhat of the Bible studies she had done on her own. What he taught her was more geared to Catholicism. He taught her about the stations of the cross, the various devotions, the Blessed Mother, the Holy Trinity, taught her prayers and how to say the rosary. He explained the sacraments to her, and the importance of communion. And through it all, Beata asked him questions that told him she had given it all a great deal of thought. She didn't seem to be uncomfortable or at odds with any of the Christian concepts and ideas. Often she explained to him where there were intriguing similarities in her own childhood religion. She was a young woman with a fine mind, a deep appreciation for religion and philosophy, and a kind and loving heart. And he grew immensely fond of her during the two weeks they spent together, covering a lot of ground in intense religious study. And each day she came, she brought him something from the farm, along with greetings from the Zubers. She even made him laugh when she told him what it had been like learning to milk a cow. She laughed even harder to herself each morning, as she thought of Brigitte trying to attempt a similar endeavor. She would have swooned. The only thing that still pained Beata deeply was whenever she thought of her mother. And in spite of his unyielding stance about her marriage to Antoine, she missed her father, too. She worried constantly about the safety of her brothers. Just because she was far from home now, and had left with her father's wrath upon her, did not mean that she no longer loved them. She wasn't even angry at them, she just missed them, and had spoken of it to Father André, who was impressed with her sense of compassion and forgiveness. She seemed not to hold against them the fact that they had in essence driven her away. The ultimate compliment from him, in fact, was that he told her one afternoon that if she had not been born into another faith and were preparing now for her marriage, she would have made a wonderful nun. Antoine was not nearly as touched as she was when Beata told him about it that night.

"Good lord, I hope he's not trying to recruit you! I have other things in mind for you." He suddenly looked fiercely possessive of her.

"So do I. But it was sweet of him to say." She was flattered, it was high praise from the kindly old priest, as Maria agreed.

"Never mind how sweet it is," Antoine said disapprovingly, still sounding nervous, "I don't want any nuns in my family. I've always thought that's a sad life. People are meant to be married and have children."

"Not everyone perhaps. Not everyone is suited to marriage and having babies," Beata said fairly.

"Well, I'm glad you are," Antoine said, leaning over to kiss her at the dinner table, which made Maria smile. He had been working hard on the farm with Walther, and Beata noticed when she dressed his wound at night that his arm was better. The wound was healing, although the arm was still stiff and not as useful as he hoped it would be again in the future. But he was managing extremely well, even with only one good arm. And to Beata, he was as beautiful as ever. She smiled shyly at him when he kissed her. It embarrassed her a little when he talked about having babies, and reminded her of the new discoveries that were coming.

The morning of Beata's baptism, on the way to church, Maria, Antoine, and Beata stopped at the *mairie*. A somber-looking clerk performed the brief civil ceremony that was the legal prelude to their church wedding the following day. For Beata, it was an awesome feeling knowing, as they drove to church afterward, that in the eyes of the law she was already Antoine's wife, just as she would become in the eyes of God the following day. Maria and Antoine were at the church with Beata for her baptism. Walther was unable to come as he had too much work to do at the farm. The ceremony was brief and simple, as she professed her beliefs and loyalty to the Catholic Church. Antoine and Maria acted as her godparents, and promised to renounce the devil on her behalf, and help her to adhere to her faith, and live it in future. After her baptism, she received communion for the first time, and cried as Father André gave it to her. It all meant far more to her than she had expected, and anything that she had experienced in Judaism until then. She had always found the time they spent in synagogue intensely boring. They sat there for hours, and it had always annoyed her that the men were segregated from the women. It bothered her too that there were no female rabbis, which she thought extremely unfair. Her father had gotten angry at her whenever she said it, and said sternly that that was the way it was. She was disappointed to learn that there were no female priests either. But at least there were nuns.

Brigitte too had thought being Orthodox too restrictive, and had said before her wedding that when she moved to Berlin with Heinrich, she was no longer going to follow Orthodox dietary laws, since her husband and his family didn't. But she had never dared to say that to her parents. She thought the strict rules of Orthodoxy were silly. Beata had never viewed it in quite that way, but there were things about Judaism she had always disagreed with. And much to her own surprise, she suddenly liked the idea of being Catholic. It was another way of being closer to and more in harmony with Antoine. She even found it remarkably easy to believe in the concept of miracles, like the one of the virgin birth and the subsequent birth of Jesus. She felt different and lighter, and renewed in a sense as she walked out of church as a Catholic. She looked radiant and was beaming at Antoine. Between the civil marriage ceremony and the baptism, it had been an extraordinary day.

"I'm still sorry you don't want to be a nun," Father André teased her gently. "I think with a little more study and some time to discover your vocation, you'd have made a good one." Antoine looked panicked at the prospect.

"I'm glad you only had two weeks then," Antoine said, and meant it. The idea of losing his bride to the convent, after he had fought so hard to win her, filled him with horror. But he knew the priest meant well.

As they left the church, they promised to return the next day, for their wedding. Their paperwork was in order. The civil marriage gave them the ability to be married in church as well. After a celebratory dinner that night, to acknowledge her becoming a Catholic, Beata retired to her room early. It was the last night she would spend alone in the bed she would share with him after their wedding. And she still had work to do that night, on a secret project. She had brought nothing with her from Germany that she could wear for her wedding. Everything she had brought with her was practical and suited for farm work. But Maria had given her two beautiful lace tablecloths that had been given to her by her grandmother, and had become worn in places over the years. Beata said that didn't matter. When she hadn't been studying for her baptism, milking cows, or helping Maria prepare meals, she had been in her room, frantically sewing. The wedding dress she had made from the two tablecloths was nearly finished. She had managed to cut and drape and place the lace over her chest and shoulders and down her arms, and had just enough left over to shape into a little cap with a veil. And as she was so small, the dress even had a small train. She had sewn tiny pleats over the bust and tacked them down. The dress fit perfectly at her narrow waist, and the skirt was a gentle bell, appliquéd with what was left of the once-damaged lace. She had cut out all the old worn spots and small tears. The dress was a work of art, and even Maria hadn't seen it completed, but could hardly wait. She expected it to be simple, and somewhat awkward in design. There was only so much you could do with two old tablecloths, or so she thought. She had no idea of the extent of Beata's talent, and delicate needlework.

Antoine had agreed to walk down to the church an hour before the wedding, so he wouldn't see Beata when she emerged. She wanted to surprise him when she walked down the aisle of the ancient stone church and met him at the altar. He had no idea what she had been doing when she retired early to her room at night, and thought she was simply exhausted by the rigors of her activities on the farm. Even Maria didn't know that she had stayed up more than one night till dawn, and had performed all her duties the next day without the benefit of sleep the night before so she could complete the dress in time for her wedding day. Her wedding gown was the most beautiful dress she had ever sewn, worthy of a Paris collection, and if it had been made in silk or satin instead of the fine linen and handmade lace she had had to work with, it would have been a truly spectacular gown worthy of any important wedding, which to her this one was. Even made of the delicate white linen, it was an exquisite dress, and in some ways better suited to the simple church in the mountains than a more elaborate gown would have been. Maria gasped when she saw her.

"Oh my God, child . . . where did you get that dress? Did Antoine take you into Lausanne?"

"Of course not." Beata laughed with excitement at the effect it had on her godmother. The older woman stared at her and burst into tears. "I made it from the tablecloths you gave me. I've been working on it every night for two weeks."

"You couldn't have. I couldn't have done anything like it in two years!" She had never seen anything to compare with the gown Beata had made. She looked like a fairy princess. Maria had never seen a more beautiful bride. "How did you ever learn to sew like that?"

"It's fun. I used to make things for my mother and sister, and I always preferred making my own dresses to buying them." That way she always got what she wanted, instead of someone else's design.

"But not a dress like that." She spun Beata around by one hand, admiring the veil and train. It was the most beautiful dress Maria had seen in her entire life. "Wait until Antoine sees you . . . he'll faint dead away at the church."

"I hope not," Beata said, but she was

thrilled with the effect. And even Walther was amazed when he saw her, and helped Maria carefully arrange the dress and train in the backseat of the car. He and Maria rode up front, as Beata felt slightly guilty for having made Antoine walk to the church. But she hadn't wanted him to see the dress before they arrived. She had hidden in her room until he left, so he wouldn't see her that morning, for good luck. It was still hard for her to believe this was her wedding day. She had cried while she dressed, she missed her mother so much. It had never occurred to her that one day she'd be marrying without her mother there to see her, or her father to give her away.

Walther and Maria had provided their rings as well. They were simple and well worn. Walther had given Antoine his father's wedding ring, which he had put away in a box, and it fit perfectly on Antoine's injured left hand. Walther had it in his pocket, along with Maria's great-grandmother's ring, which was a narrow gold band with tiny diamonds on it. It was so small that no woman in the family had ever been able to wear it. It fit Beata as though it had been made for her, and inside the ring were engraved the words *Mon coeur à toi,* my heart for you. The ring looked loved and well-worn with time.

And in a gesture of great generosity, Walther and Maria were staying nearby with friends that night, so the young newlyweds would have the house to themselves. Walther was cooling a bottle of champagne he had saved for years, from his own son's wedding. Maria had left a small wedding feast for them, of delicacies they had prepared. It was all she could do for them and she had done it with tenderness and love. She wanted everything to be as lovely as possible for them, since this wasn't the wedding either of them would have had if they had remained with their families in their own worlds. For all they had lost, they both knew they had nonetheless gained much, and had each other. To both Antoine and Beata, it was enough, although it was hard not to think of those they had left behind, especially on this day.

The locals were just leaving the church after mass, when Beata and the Zubers arrived. Antoine was waiting in the rectory, as Beata had asked him to. And as people came out of the church they stared and exclaimed over the breathtaking dress and lovely bride. She looked like a fairy tale princess, with her dark hair beneath the lace cap, her milky white skin, and huge blue eyes. They had never seen a bride like her in all their years in the parish. Even Father André was stunned, and had to admit she made a prettier bride than nun. He said she was the most beautiful bride he had ever seen. His eyes were dancing a few minutes later when he led Antoine into the church, and told him he had an astonishing treat in store. Antoine couldn't imagine what it was, until the organist was playing the music Beata and he had selected, and he saw her walk slowly through the door on Walther's arm. She moved with the grace of a young queen, and her feet barely touched the floor. She was wearing the only pair of evening shoes she had brought with her, which were suitably a pair of creamy satin slippers with rhinestone buckles. But nothing had prepared Antoine for her dress. He had wondered what she would wear, and now as he saw her, he wondered if she had brought the wedding gown with her from Cologne. It looked as though it had been made in Paris before the war. But as soon as he took in the dress, all he could focus on was Beata.

He looked deep into her eyes, as tears rolled down both their cheeks. The lace had been fine enough for her to wear it as a veil covering her face, and as Maria lifted it for her, she could see that Beata's face was awash with tears of tenderness and joy. She had never seen a more beautiful young woman in her life, nor had any of them in the church.

Beata cried again as they exchanged their vows, and her hands were shaking violently as Antoine slipped on her ring, and she put Antoine's ring on his finger carefully so as not to hurt him. She had never been happier in her life as he held her close to him and kissed her when the priest declared them man and wife. Antoine could hardly bring himself to let go of her so they could walk out of the church into the summer sunshine. Some of the people from neighboring farms had stayed after mass to wait for them outside the church, so they could see the beautiful bride again. No one who had seen her that day would ever forget how she looked, least of all Antoine.

The Zubers and the priest joined them for lunch afterward, and that afternoon, they drove the priest back to his church, on their way to stay with friends. Beata and Antoine stood in the doorway of the Zuber home, as the others drove away, and then they turned to look at each other, finally alone. It did not happen often, living so closely with Walther and Maria, but now at least they would be able to share the same room at night. And just for today, they had the whole house to themselves, which was a remarkable gift the older couple had bestowed on them. Their night alone in the small farmhouse in the Alps was the only honeymoon they'd have, but it was all they wanted. All they needed in life was to be together. And they both knew they would never forget the magic of this day. Antoine stood looking at her rapturously in the late afternoon sun. She was still wearing her wedding dress, and he wished she could wear it forever. She had put a huge amount of work into it in order to show it off for only a few hours, as was the case with any wedding. But few brides would have been able to create a dress like that themselves. And still admiring the way it fit her graceful figure perfectly, Antoine followed her into the house.

They sat and talked quietly for a while in the living room, and then Antoine went to pour them each a glass of champagne. It had been so long since Beata had any, except for the little she had consumed at her sister's wedding weeks before, that she felt giddy, as they each took a sip and toasted each other. It was hard to believe how much their lives had changed in only a matter of weeks. A month before she would never have believed that she would be living on a farm in Switzerland, and married to Antoine at that moment. It was a dream come true for both of them, even though she had had to pass through a nightmare to get there. But the agonies she had gone through already seemed to be fading. And all that remained and would remain was the life they would share.

She offered to serve the dinner Maria had left for them, as the sun began to go down. They had sat talking all afternoon and holding hands. Neither of them was in any hurry to consummate their marriage, and Antoine didn't want to frighten her. He knew it was a big step she would be taking, and he wanted it to be as easy as possible for her. There was no hurry. But neither of them was hungry for dinner. At sunset, they were sitting in the living room, kissing, as the champagne began to have an effect on them, and both Antoine and Beata were suddenly overcome with passion, and could not hold back any longer. They had waited eleven months for this moment. It was the first of July and they had met the previous August. It seemed a lifetime ago since they had met at the lake, and he had bumped into her. And now they were married. It was everything they had both dreamed of and wanted since that first moment.

In spite of his injured arm, which had grown stronger, he managed to scoop her up in his arms in her wedding gown, and carried her gently into their bedroom, next to Walther and Maria's. He laid her ever so carefully on the bed, and began slowly to undress her. He wasn't sure if she was too shy to let him see her, but she seemed to have no qualms or fears about what he was doing. And in a few moments, the dress lay carefully put aside on the room's only chair, and he slowly peeled away the delicate satin and lace underwear that she had made months before and brought with her. She took his breath away as he looked at her. She looked like a perfect porcelain doll as he gently began to kiss her. And as he did, with trembling fingers, she began to un-dress him. She had no idea what she was doing, nor what he expected of her. She had some vague notion about making love with him from things Brigitte had said to her, but she was far less sophisticated and knowl-edgeable than her younger sister, who had always been much more interested in what transpired, or was supposed to, between the sexes. Instead, Beata came to him with her innocence and her love for him, and as Antoine took her in his arms and began making love to her, she found passion and fulfillment that she had never even dreamed of. He was gentle and loving with her, and after he made love to her, he lay beside her on their bed and held her, tracing her exqui-site form with a gentle finger. They talked for hours that night, and made love once again, and it was even better this time.

Finally, at midnight, ravenously hungry, they shared the feast that Maria had left for them. Antoine said he had never been so hungry in his life, and wearing the dressing gown Maria had given her as a wedding present, Beata giggled. They were sitting naked beneath their dressing gowns in the Zubers' kitchen. As he kissed her hungrily,

Antoine dropped the dressing gown from her shoulders and admired her beauty. He couldn't believe his good fortune, nor could Beata. Nothing about their wedding night had been a disappointment. And as she gnawed happily on a chicken bone, she looked at him with a question.

"Do you suppose we made a baby tonight? I assume that's how it's done, unless there's something you haven't shown me." She felt suddenly very grown up, after all the mysteries she had discovered, and he smiled in answer.

"We might have. Is that what you want, Beata? It's not too soon?"

"And if it is?" she asked, curious.

"If you want to wait, there are things we can do after tonight to prevent that happening too quickly." He preferred it this way, but he didn't want to do anything to upset her. If she didn't want to get pregnant right away, he was willing to wait, if that was what she wanted. He wanted above all things to please her and make her happy for the rest of her life.

"I don't want to wait," she said gently, leaning over to kiss him, "All I want now is your baby."

"Then we'll see what we can do to make that happen." They had already made a handsome effort. They cleared away the dishes, washed them, and put them away. He poured each of them a last glass of champagne, they had nearly finished the bottle by then. And when they had, he took her back to bed and made love to her again. It was the perfect wedding night for both of them. As the sun came up over the Alps, she sighed like a child and fell asleep in his arms, loving him more than she had ever dreamed.

5

ANTOINE AND BEATA'S WEDDING DAY REMAINED A magical memory not only for them but for everyone who had seen them. Her wedding gown was talked about in the village for months. Maria helped her put it away carefully in a box filled with tissue. She pressed some of the flowers she had carried in her bouquet. And after thinking about it for several days, she decided to write to her mother and sister. She knew that Brigitte would be in Berlin by then, and she wanted to share with her how lovely her own wedding had been, and to tell her that she still loved her. She wanted to tell her mother that she was well, and was sorry that the day she left had been so dreadful, and how much she thought about her and missed her on her wedding day.

Two weeks after she'd written to them, her letters came back to her, unopened. The one to Brigitte had nothing personal written on it. It was simply sent back with a stamp on it that said "addressee unknown." It told Beata that even while in Berlin Brigitte was not willing to defy their father. And the letter to her mother was returned with her father's meticulous penmanship on it, saying to return the letter to sender. They wanted no contact with her. It took her two days of silent tears to admit to Antoine what had happened.

"It's still fresh," he said quietly. "Give it time. You can write to them again in a few months. By then, things will have calmed down," he said with confidence. He had not written to his own parents, he was still angry at the position they had taken. And he had no desire to communicate with his brother either. But he was older than Beata and far angrier than she.

"You don't know my father," Beata said miserably. "He will never forgive me. He said that he and Mama were going to sit shiva for me." She explained to Antoine what that meant, it was the vigil for the dead, which shocked him profoundly. "I just wanted to tell Mama and Brigitte about the wedding, and that I love them." She wouldn't have dared write to her father. But even writing to the women in the family had gotten her nowhere. They were all too respectful of him and too afraid of him to defy him. Only she had dared to do that. And she knew he would never forgive her for it. She hoped the others would.

Antoine did his best to comfort her, and they made love every night like proper newlyweds. They made every effort to be quiet so as not to disturb the Zubers, but they were undeniably living in close quarters, so much so that Maria heard Beata vomiting in the bathroom early one morning six weeks after the wedding.

"Are you all right?" Maria asked through the door, sounding worried. The men had left the house at dawn, and the two women were alone. Beata had been about to go out to milk the cows when a wave of nausea overwhelmed her. She was green when she walked into the kitchen ten minutes later and sat down.

"I'm sorry. It must have been something I ate. Antoine picked all those blackberries for me yesterday. I already felt sick last night," Beata said, sitting down in one of the kitchen chairs and obviously feeling awful. "I didn't want to hurt his feelings and tell him."

"Are you sure it's the blackberries?" Maria asked kindly. She was not at all surprised to see Beata looking so ill. And in fact, it made her hopeful.

"I think so." She asked Beata a few pertinent questions then, and laughed at the innocent young woman's answers.

"If memory serves, my dear, I think you're pregnant."

"Do you?" Beata looked astonished, which made Maria smile broadly.

"Yes, I do. Why don't you wait until you're sure to tell your husband." There was no point worrying him unduly or getting his hopes up. Men were odd about things like that, Maria knew. It was better to tell them once one was certain.

"And when will that be? When would I be sure enough to tell him?"

"In another week or two, if nothing happens, and you continue to feel poorly. You'll know soon enough." Beata was smiling to herself as she went to milk the cows, and that afternoon she was so exhausted she came back to the house after her chores and slept for two hours before dinner.

"Is Beata all right?" Antoine asked Maria with a look of concern when he got home. His bride was usually so lively, and all she seemed to do was sleep now. He wondered if it was because he kept her up late, making love to her at night, but lying next to her, he found it impossible to keep his hands off her.

"She's fine. She's been out in the sun all day. I had her picking fruit for me," Maria said discreetly. But in addition to covering for her recent nausea and sleepiness, Maria was finding her to be a hard worker, and the younger woman was truly helpful to her.

Beata was certain herself about her pregnancy within two weeks, when nothing had happened to convince her otherwise, and even at this early stage she could no longer button her waistband. And she was constantly nauseous. She was taking a walk with Antoine one Sunday afternoon, on the way home from church, when she smiled up at him mysteriously, and he beamed down at her, wondering what she was thinking.

Life in close proximity to her was a constant, delicious mystery for him.

"You look like a woman with a secret," he said, smiling down at her proudly. He loved being married to her, and thinking ahead to their future together.

"I'll share it with you," she said softly, tucking a hand into his arm. They had decided to walk to church instead of driving. The weather was still beautiful, it was the end of August, and as closely as she and Maria could figure it, she was two months pregnant. She was sure she had gotten pregnant on their wedding night, and Antoine suspected nothing. "We're having a baby," she said, looking up at him, her eyes full of wonder, as he stared at her and stopped walking.

"Are you serious? How did that happen?" he asked in amazement, and she laughed at him.

"Well, when we go home, I'll explain it to you, or maybe I should just show you how we did it, to remind you." She was teasing him, and he laughed with her, feeling foolish.

"That's not what I meant, although I'd be happy for the reminder anytime, Madame de Vallerand." He loved saying her name now, and so did she. It seemed to suit her. "I meant when, and how do you know, and are you sure, and when is it coming?" And then suddenly, he looked worried. "Should you be walking?"

"Would you like to carry me home?" she asked sweetly, and then giggled at him. "I'm fine, although I've felt a bit sick lately, but Maria says that's normal. I remember hearing about girls I know who were dreadfully ill for several months. They couldn't even leave their bedrooms." But in the healthy atmosphere they lived in, leading a quiet life, Beata was sure that the nausea would pass quickly. It was already a little better. The first weeks had been truly awful. But now she was so excited at the thought of what was happening to her that she didn't mind it. "I think it happened on our wedding night, which means that we should have a lovely baby at the beginning of April. Perhaps in time for Easter." Out of habit, she had almost said Passover, but instead said Easter. In the Catholic faith, it was a time for resurrection and rebirth, and seemed a perfect time to her, and it would be nice to be able to take the baby out in the summer. It seemed better than having to bundle it up and keep it inside in the winter. To her, the timing was perfect. And Antoine was beside himself with excitement. He made her slow down, and not walk with such determination. If she had let him, he would have carried her home on his shoulders. And she could see that he was a little worried. He wasn't sure if he should make love to her anymore, and didn't want to hurt her. She assured him that everything was fine, and they could go on as normal.

But for the next several months, Antoine kept a constant eye on her. He came back to the house as often as possible to check on her, and he did most of her chores for her, although she insisted that there was no need to.

"Antoine, you don't have to do that, I'm fine. It's good for me to have exercise and stay busy."

"Who said so?" He finally took her to a doctor in Lausanne, just to reassure himself that everything was normal. The doctor reassured them both that everything was proceeding just as it should. The only thing Beata regretted frequently was that she couldn't share the news with her mother.

She had tried one more letter, which had come back to her this time even more quickly. She was entirely sealed off from her family. The only family she had now was Antoine and the Zubers and, in a few months, their baby.

By Christmas, at nearly six months, Beata was enormous. She was so tiny ordinarily that the addition of a growing baby to her small frame made her look far more pregnant than she was. By the end of January, she looked as though she was having the baby any minute, and Antoine hardly let her leave the house now. He was afraid she would slip and fall on the ice and snow and miscarry. And at night, he loved lying beside her and feeling the baby kick him. He thought it was a boy, and Beata hoped it was, but Antoine insisted it didn't really matter to him. It just seemed like a boy to him because it was so gigantic. Beata was healthy and in good spirits, but she could hardly move now. She had made some clothes that accommodated her growing form, and as always Maria was astonished by her sewing talent. She made some tops and skirts and dresses from old scraps of fabric she had lying around, and even a very stylish coat from a red plaid horse blanket Walther gave her. She looked young and beautiful and healthy. And when she went to church on Sundays, Father André was delighted to see her.

More than anything, Antoine was worried about who would deliver the baby. He thought about taking her to Geneva or Lausanne to have it in a hospital there, but the reality was he couldn't afford it. There was a doctor thirty miles away, but he had no telephone, and neither did the Zubers, and when the time came, there would be no way to reach him. Driving there and back would probably take longer than delivering the baby. Beata insisted she wasn't worried about it. Maria had given birth to her own children at home, and had gone to France to be with one of her daughters when she delivered. She had sat with friends over the years, and even without any official training, she was an experienced midwife. Both women felt assured that they could handle whatever happened. Or at least that was what Beata said. She didn't want to worry Antoine, but she admitted to Maria several times that she was frightened as well. She knew virtually nothing about having a baby, and the bigger it got, the more she worried.

"It won't happen till you're ready," Maria said confidently. "Babies know just when to come. They don't come when you're tired or sick or upset. They wait until you're feeling ready to greet them." It sounded overly optimistic to Beata, but in the face of Maria's calm, sensible ways, she was willing to give her the benefit of the doubt and believe her.

And much to her own surprise, in the last days of March, Beata found she had renewed energy. She even went to milk the cows one day, and when he found out that night, Antoine scolded her soundly.

"How can you be so foolish? What if one of them kicked you, and hurt the baby? I want you to stay home every day, and take it easy." It worried him considerably that he could provide no comforts or safe facility for her. He could do nothing to make this easier for her, and even though she was always a good sport about it, Beata was no farm girl. She had been brought up in the lap of luxury and was a delicate city girl. From what he could gather, she had never caught a cold without seeing a doctor. And now he was expecting her to deliver a baby in a cottage in the Alps, without even the help of a nurse or a doctor.

He wrote to a friend in Geneva and asked him to send him a book on midwifery. He read it at night surreptitiously after Beata went to sleep, hoping that he could learn something that would help her. And as the final days of her pregnancy went by, he grew increasingly nervous. If nothing else, her tiny frame panicked him. What if the baby was too big to be born? There was a chapter in the book about cesarean sections, which could only be performed by a doctor. And even then both mother and infant's lives were in jeopardy, and the book admitted that often births of that nature ended in disaster. Antoine couldn't imagine anything more terrifying than losing Beata. And he didn't want to lose their baby either. It was impossible to believe that a baby of the size she was carrying could emerge successfully from such a tiny mother. Beata seemed to be growing smaller and the baby bigger by the hour.

He was sleeping fitfully the night of March 31, when he heard Beata get up and go to the bathroom. She had grown so huge that she was wearing Maria's enormous night-gowns, which were big enough to accommodate her and the baby. She came back to bed with a yawn after a few minutes.

"Are you all right?" he whispered, looking worried. He didn't want to wake the Zubers.

"I'm fine." She smiled sleepily at him, and settled back in bed on her side, with her back to him. She couldn't lie on her back anymore. The baby was so heavy that it made her feel as though she were suffocating. He put his arms around her, with a hand resting gently on her enormous belly and, as always, felt the baby kick him.

Antoine couldn't go back to sleep again, and this time Beata couldn't either. She turned awkwardly from one side to the other, and finally lay facing him, and he kissed her.

"I love you," he whispered again.

"I love you, too," she said happily, looking beautiful and contented, as her long dark hair lay spread out on her pillow. She turned her back to him then, confessed that it ached, and asked him to rub it, which he was happy to do for her, and as always he marveled at her tiny body. The only part of her that was huge was her distended belly.

And as he rubbed her back, he heard her groan, which was unlike her.

"Did I hurt you?" he asked softly.

"No . . . I'm fine . . . it's nothing." She didn't want to tell him she had been having pains since the night before. They seemed like nothing to her, and she thought it was indigestion, and now her back hurt. She was drifting back to sleep again, when he got up before dawn an hour later. He and Walther had a lot of work to do that day, and they had planned to get an early start. Beata was still dozing when he left the house with Walther, as Maria moved quietly around the kitchen.

Beata didn't emerge from their bedroom until two hours later, and when she did, she looked frightened, and came to find Maria in the kitchen. "I think something's happening," she whispered.

Maria smiled at her with a look of pleasure. "You're right on time. It's your nine-month anniversary today. Looks like we're going to have a baby."

"I feel awful," Beata confessed. Her back was killing her, and she felt violently nauseous, and she had a tremendous sense of downward pressure in her belly. She had the same nagging pains in her back and lower belly she'd had the night before, and it no longer felt like indigestion. "What's going to happen?" Beata looked panicked and like a child herself, as the older woman put a gentle arm around her and led her back to her bedroom.

"You're going to have a beautiful baby, Beata. That's all that will happen. I want you to lie down, and think about that. I'll be back in a minute." She had put towels and old sheets aside for the delivery, and several tubs and washbasins, and she went to fetch them once she settled Beata back in her bed, looking anxious and wild-eyed.

"Don't leave me."

"I'm just going out to the pantry. I'll be back in a minute."

"Where's Antoine?" Beata was starting to panic as the first serious pain ripped through her. It caught her entirely by surprise—no one had ever told her it would be like that. It was like a butcher knife reaching up from her groin right through her belly. Her stomach felt hard as rock, and she couldn't catch her breath, as Maria held her.

"That's fine, that's fine. I'll be back in one second." Maria ran to the kitchen, grabbed one of the tubs and began heating water, and with that she grabbed the towels and sheets she'd set aside and ran back to Beata. She was lying on her bed, looking dazed. The second pain hit her just as Maria came through the doorway, and this time Beata screamed in terror and reached out to the older woman. Maria gripped her hands, and told her not to push too soon. They had a long way to go before the baby was ready. If she pushed too early, she would exhaust herself too quickly. Beata allowed Maria to look then, but she could not see the baby. The pains she had had the night before had started things along, but the real work still lay ahead. Maria guessed that it would be many hours before Beata held her baby. She just hoped it would be easy for her. Sometimes when it was fast, it was worse, but then at least it was over. But as this was her first one, and the baby was large, Maria suspected it would be slow.

With the next pain, Beata's water broke, and flooded the towels Maria had put under her and around her. She carried them out to the kitchen and put more towels under her. But as Maria knew would happen, once her water had broken, the pains began with a vengeance. Within an hour, Beata was in agony as the pains rolled over her in waves, giving her only seconds to catch her breath between them. And when Antoine came in for lunch, before he even opened the door to the house, he heard her screaming, and came running.

"Is she all right?" he asked Maria with a look of terror.

"She's fine," Maria said quietly. She didn't think he should be in the room, but he had walked right in, and instantly put a gentle arm around Beata.

"My poor baby . . . what can I do to help you?" At the sight of him, she began crying. She was terrified, but Maria staunchly refused to appear worried. The one thing she did know was that it was a big baby, but the force of the pains she was experiencing would help them. She was already in as much pain as most women when they were about to deliver, and each time Maria looked, there was no sign of the baby.

"Antoine . . . I can't . . . I can't . . . oh God . . . it's so awful . . ." She was gasping for air between pains, and Antoine was beside himself as he watched her.

"Go and have some lunch with Walther,"

Maria said calmly, but Antoine wasn't moving.

"I'm not leaving," he said firmly. He had
done this to her, as far as he was concerned, and he was not going to leave her
to face it without him, which seemed like an
unusual approach to Maria. But it seemed
to calm Beata a little to have him near her.
She made every effort not to scream when
the next pains came, and he watched her
belly tighten. It was as hard as a rock when
he felt it. Maria left them for a moment then,
to see to Walther in the kitchen, and Antoine
asked her to tell him he was going to stay
with Beata until they had the baby safely
delivered. She came back with a cool cloth,
but it did nothing to help, as the pains continued to rip through her.

It went on that way for hours as Beata
screamed endlessly. It was nearly sundown
when Maria gave a victorious cry. She had
finally seen the baby's head. She saw it now
each time a pain came, and the patch of
scalp and hair grew with each contraction.
Maria and Antoine both encouraged her, but
Beata no longer cared. She felt as though
she was dying. She just continued to
scream, barely pausing for breath. There

was no relief now, as Maria told her to push as hard as she could. Beata's face contorted and turned purple as she pushed and nothing happened. Antoine couldn't believe what he was seeing, it was beyond awful, and he swore to himself and silently to her that they would never have another baby. He would never have put her through this if he had known what it would be like for her. She had been in labor all day and into the evening. And by seven o'clock, Antoine was desperate. Beata refused to push anymore, she just lay there and cried and said she couldn't.

"You have to," the usually mild-mannered Maria shouted at her. She was watching the head come and go with each contraction, and she knew that if it took too long now, they would lose the baby. "Push!" she shouted so firmly that Beata obeyed her. "That's it! Push! Again!" She told Antoine to hold up her shoulders, and told Beata to brace her feet against the footboard. The sounds in the room were horrifying as Beata sounded as though she was being murdered. But as Antoine held her, the baby's head finally came halfway through, as Maria shouted at her to push again, and when she did this time, they heard a wail in the room that stunned them all. Beata was still screaming, but she looked at Antoine in amazement as she heard their baby. Maria told her to push again, and this time the shoulders were free, and with two more pushes, the baby lay on the bed, covered in blood, and wailing loudly. It was a girl.

The sheets around Beata were drenched with blood, and Maria saw she had lost a lot of it, but not so much that she was panicked. The baby was as enormous as they had suspected. And as Antoine and Beata watched, Maria expertly tied the cord in two places and cut it. She cleaned the baby quickly, wrapped her in a sheet, and handed her to her mother, as Antoine hovered over them, with tears pouring down his cheeks. He had never seen anything more beautiful than his wife at that moment and their baby daughter.

"I'm so sorry," he said to her, sounding grief-stricken. "I'm so sorry it was so awful," he said, as she put the baby to her breast and smiled up at her husband.

"It was worth it," she said, smiling up at him, still looking exhausted and ravaged, but blissful. It was hard to believe that this was the same woman who had been screaming and in agony since early that morning. Beata looked worn out, but happy and peaceful. "She's so beautiful."

"So are you," he said as he touched her cheek ever so gently, and then touched the baby's. She was looking at both of them, and seemed interested to meet them. Beata kept her at her breast, and lay back against the pillows exhausted. No one had ever told her what to expect. She had been in no way prepared for the rigors of childbirth. She couldn't imagine why no one had ever told her. Women always seemed to speak of these things in hushed whispers, and now she knew why. Perhaps if the women had been honest with her, she wouldn't have had the courage to do it. Antoine still looked shaken.

They lay side by side in the bed, cooing and talking to their baby, and then Maria asked Antoine to leave the room and go and have some dinner and a brandy. He looked as though he could use it. It was after nine o'clock by then, and she wanted to clean up Beata, the baby, the bed, and the room. She invited him back an hour later, and he had never seen anything so peaceful. Beata was lying on clean sheets with combed hair, a clean face, and the baby sleeping in her arms. The scene of carnage and terror he'd witnessed all afternoon and evening had entirely vanished. And he smiled gratefully at Maria.

"You're amazing," he said as he hugged her.

"No, you were. Both of you. I'm very proud of you. Your daughter weighs almost five kilos," Maria said proudly, as though she had given birth to her herself, which she was relieved she hadn't. She had never seen anyone deliver such a big baby. And given Beata's size, it was even more impressive. There had been one or two frightening moments when she had been afraid she would lose them, but she had never let on to either of them that she was beginning to panic. Nearly five kilos was ten pounds. Even lying in her mother's arms she looked bigger than a newborn, and Maria had never seen prouder parents. "What are you going to call her?" she asked, as Walther peeked in from the doorway, and smiled at the handsome couple holding their new baby.

Beata and Antoine looked at each other. They had talked about names for months, and they had consistently been undecided about a girl's name. But as Beata saw her, she knew they had found the right one among their earliest suggestions.

"What do you think of Amadea?" she asked Antoine, and he considered it for a moment. He had originally thought of naming a girl Françoise after his own mother, but after how hateful she had been about his marrying Beata, he no longer felt right about using her name. They both knew Amadea meant "loved of God," and she certainly was, as well as loved by both her parents.

"I like it. It suits her. She's such a big beautiful baby girl, she should have a special name. Amadea de Vallerand," he said, trying it out, as Beata smiled. The baby stirred then and let out a small sound, halfway between a sigh and a gurgle, and all her admirers laughed. "She likes it, too."

"That's it then," Beata concluded. She looked like herself again, in such a short time after the birth. She looked as though she could have gotten up and waltzed around the room, although Antoine was grateful that she didn't. "Amadea," she said, as she beamed at her firstborn daughter, and looked ecstatically at her husband.

They looked like proud parents. And as
Antoine held Beata close to him that night,
he thought about all they'd been through
that day, in utter amazement. And as Beata
drifted off to sleep with the baby in a basket
beside her, Antoine whispered a silent
prayer of thanks for the miracle they had
shared. Amadea. She was loved of God in-
deed and he prayed she always would be.

6

AMADEA DE VALLERAND WAS NINETEEN MONTHS and ten days old when the war finally ended in 1918. She was blond and blue-eyed and tall for her age, and the delight of her parents and the Zubers. Maria knew that as soon as the war ended, the young family who had lived with them for two years would move on, and she would be sorry when they did. But they couldn't stay in Switzerland forever. Once their own countries were back on their feet, the Swiss would no longer offer them asylum.

By Christmas 1918 Antoine and Beata had had endless discussions as to whether to go back to Germany or France. His family was firmer than ever that they would not welcome his Jewish wife in Dordogne, and their half-Jewish daughter. They had been brutally unkind about it. It made no difference to them that Beata had converted and was now a Catholic. As far as they were concerned, she was a Jew, whether or not she had converted. Their doors remained closed to Antoine. And Beata had fared no better. Letters sent separately to both her parents were returned just as the earlier ones had been. And she got the same result when she wrote to Brigitte. She wondered if by now she too had had a baby. Beata was open to the idea of having another one, and they had done nothing to prevent it. She was surprised that so far nothing had happened, since Amadea had been conceived so quickly. But for the moment, they were happy with Amadea. She was running everywhere, and chattering a mile a minute in her own language. The Zubers were enjoying her as much as any grandchild, and already knew how much they would miss her when they left.

In the end, it was February when Antoine received a letter that made the decision for them as to where they would go. A friend of his from Saumur, the cavalry academy where he had trained in the military, wrote to him and said that he had bought a splendid *Schloss* in Germany for pennies, and it had remarkable albeit crumbling stables. The friend's name was Gérard Daubigny, and he wanted to rebuild them. He was going to restore the *Schloss* for himself and his family, and he wanted Antoine to take charge of the stables and do whatever he deemed necessary to rebuild them, fill them with the finest horses money could buy, hire trainers and grooms, and run them. He knew that Antoine was an incomparable horseman and an equally talented judge of horseflesh. He knew about the injury to his arm, and Antoine had assured him that it didn't hamper him. He was able to use it adequately, although it had never healed completely. As a result, he was even more adept with his right one, enough so to compensate for his crippled left arm.

Coincidentally, the *Schloss* Gérard had bought was near Cologne, and although Beata's family had shown no sign that they would welcome them, it was always possible that if they lived nearby, they might relent eventually. And perhaps in time, some rapprochement could be encouraged. But the proximity of the Wittgensteins did not influence Antoine's decision. The salary Daubigny offered him was irresistible, and it was a job he knew he would enjoy. There was supposedly a lovely house on the grounds, which Gérard offered him. It was big enough for all three of them and several more children. Antoine accepted the offer by the end of February, and agreed to arrive at the *Schloss* in early April. It gave Antoine time to wrap things up at the farm, and do all he could to help Walther. The home the Zubers had given them for more than two years had literally saved them. Without them, Antoine and Beata wouldn't have survived the war, or certainly not together, nor would they have been able to marry when they did, or provide a home for Amadea. Both of them had been left penniless when their families banished them. And now, the job Antoine had been offered in Germany would save them.

Beata spent many nights before they left the farm teaching Antoine German, although his employer was French. But the grooms and trainers he would have to hire and the builders he would use for the restoration would all be German. He needed

to know the language, and he was not
overly skilled at it. But by the time they left,
he was nearly fluent. And they had long
since agreed that Antoine would speak to
Amadea in French, and Beata in German.
They wanted their daughter to be completely bilingual. And in time, Beata was determined to add English. If they could afford
it once in Germany, Beata wanted to hire a
young English girl to help her, so Amadea
would also be fluent in English. She and
Antoine both agreed that languages were
always useful.

Their financial situation was far from secure, although the salary he'd been offered
was respectable. And the job he was going
to was something Antoine loved and did
well. The opportunity they'd been offered
was a great blessing. And Beata was thinking of doing some sewing for some of the
elegant women she had known, if they were
interested. And she hoped that, in an indi-
rect way, it might be a conduit back to her
mother.

Antoine also mentioned that Madame
Daubigny had a great deal of money. It was
undoubtedly her money that Gérard was using to do the restoration of the *Schloss,* as

he had very little himself. He was from an aristocratic family that had been impoverished even before the war. Véronique's family had a considerable fortune. And Gérard had promised Antoine he could buy all the horses he wanted. They were starting a new life.

The Daubignys and Beata had never met, and they had no idea who she'd been before she married Antoine. She and Antoine discussed it and decided it was simpler if they didn't know she'd been Jewish. It was a piece of her history, and theirs, that they decided to keep to themselves. They felt private about that, and their family difficulties before they married. Without the Wittgensteins in their lives, there was no need to explain that Beata had been born Jewish, and she certainly didn't look it. Nor did Amadea. She was as blond and blue-eyed as babies came, and she had perfect cameo features like her mother. Beata's family's rejection of her was still a source of great sorrow and shame to her, and she didn't want anyone to know.

All five of them cried the day the Vallerands left the Zubers. Even Amadea wailed miserably as she held her arms out to Maria. The Zubers drove them to Lausanne to the train, and Beata couldn't stop crying as she hugged them both. It reminded her of the day nearly three years before when she had left her parents. They arrived in Cologne on Amadea's second birthday. And when they arrived at the *Schloss,* although Antoine was pleased to see his old friend, he had to confess to Beata that night that he found the project daunting.

The *Schloss* itself was in terrible shape and had been allowed to go to rack and ruin. The noble family who had owned it for centuries had long since run out of money, and the place had been uninhabited and was crumbling and had been allowed to deteriorate to a shocking degree during the war, and even before that. And the stables were even worse. It was going to take months, or even years, to get the place clean, whole, and up and running. But Antoine had to admit after a month or two, he found what he was doing exciting. And he couldn't wait to start buying horses for them. Beata loved hearing his plans when they talked about it at night.

In the end, their progress went faster

than expected. By Christmas, there was an army of carpenters, painters, architects, builders, stonemasons, gardeners, glaziers, and master craftsmen hard at work on the place. Véronique and Gérard Daubigny were relentless. According to Antoine, Véronique was building a palace. And much to his delight, they spared nothing on the stables. They were heated, immaculate, modern, beautifully built, and could house up to sixty horses. By the following spring, Antoine was buying horses at fabulous prices all over Europe for them. He made several trips to England, Scotland, and Ireland, and took Beata with him. She loved it. He also took several trips to France, and bought three beautiful hunters in Dordogne, within ten miles of the château where he had grown up, and where his family contin- ued to refuse to see him. He was quiet as they drove past the house on the way to an auction in Périgord, and Beata could see how much it upset him. She saw him look at the gates in sorrow as they rode by. Their families were as good as dead to them.

She had had the same experience herself when they returned to Cologne. She couldn't resist taking a taxi past her old house one day, and cried as she stood on the street outside, knowing that all the people she had once loved were there, and they wouldn't see her. She had written to them all again, when they returned to Cologne, and once again her letters had come back to her unopened. Her father had not relented. It was something she and Antoine had learned to live with, but it was still painful, like a scar that throbbed at times, or a limb that was no longer there. She was grateful that she had Antoine and Amadea, and somewhat disappointed that there was no second baby. Amadea was three by then, and Beata still hadn't gotten pregnant, although they'd tried. Things were busier and more stressful than they had been in Switzerland. And sometimes she wondered if that was the problem. Whatever the reason, Beata had begun to believe that a second baby would never come. But she was happy with Antoine and Amadea, and their new home. Gérard was not only a reasonable employer for Antoine, but the Daubignys were great friends to both of them.

It took another year for Antoine to fill the stables. He had bought fifty-eight

Thoroughbreds for the Daubignys, including several Arabians, and when Amadea was five, he bought her a pony. She was an excellent rider. And often he and Beata went on long rides in the countryside and took Amadea with them. Antoine wanted her to be an exceptional horsewoman. They lavished all their love and attention on her. And by then, she was as accomplished in the languages she spoke as Beata had hoped she would be. The child spoke fluent French, German, and English. And the following year she went to the local school with the Daubigny children. Véronique and Beata didn't spend a great deal of time together, as they were both busy, but they were always friendly to each other. Beata made evening gowns for her and several of her friends, at reasonable prices. She and Antoine hadn't amassed a fortune, but they were comfortable, and thanks to the house the Daubignys had given them, as part of Antoine's job, they lived extremely well, in a house that was handsome and impressive. It was a pleasant life in beautiful surroundings, and Antoine loved what he was doing, which was important to Beata. She was happy and at peace with her husband and daughter.

And only now and then were there reminders of her lost world, which inevitably distressed her. She saw her sister on the street in Cologne one day, and wondered if she was living there. She was with her husband and two small children, one of whom was the same age as, and looked almost exactly like, Amadea. Beata was alone, and she stopped dead in her tracks when she saw her. She had gone into town on the train to buy some fabric, and the moment she saw her sister, without thinking or hesitating, Beata called her name and approached her. Brigitte paused only for an instant, looked Beata in the eye, and then turned away, while saying something to her husband. She climbed hurriedly into a waiting limousine, while he lifted the children in beside her. And a moment later, they sped away, never having acknowledged Beata. It was a devastating feeling, she didn't even go to the fabric shop after that, and rode home on the train crying. She told Antoine about it that night, and he felt sorry for her. Neither of their families had relented in the seven years since they'd been married. They were heartless.

There had been another incident after that when she had seen her brothers leaving a restaurant with two women she assumed were their wives. Ulm had looked directly at her, and she could see that he had recognized her. His eyes met hers, and he looked right through her and walked past her with a pained expression. Horst had turned and walked away as he and his family got into a cab. She had cried that night, too, but this time she was angry. What right did they have to do that to her? How dare they? But more than anger, she felt sorrow, and the same loss she had felt the day she left her father's house to marry Antoine. It was a wound that she knew would never heal completely.

But the worst of all was the day she saw her mother, two years before she saw Brigitte. It was two years after they had returned to Cologne, and she had Amadea with her. She had taken her with her to do an errand in town, and unable to stop herself, she went to stand outside their old house for a moment, while Amadea asked her what they were doing.

"Nothing, darling. I just want to see something."

"Do you know the people who live in that house?" It was cold and Amadea was hungry, but Beata looked sadly at the windows where her room had been, and then at her mother's, and she saw her at the window. Without even thinking of what she was doing, she raised a hand and waved, and her mother stopped and saw her. Beata waved frantically then, as her daughter watched her. Beata's mother paused only for a moment, bowed her head as though in pain, and quietly pulled the curtains without responding. It was a sign to Beata that there was no hope for her. She knew she would never see her again. Even the sight of Amadea standing next to her had not been enough to soften her mother's heart, nor give her the courage to defy her husband. Beata was truly dead to them now. It was a lonely empty feeling, and her heart ached as she took Amadea to lunch, and home on the train, as the child questioned her about it.

"Who was the lady you waved to?" She had seen the ravaged look on her mother's face and didn't know what it meant, but she could see that she wasn't happy. Beata had looked deeply distressed.

Beata wanted to answer that it was her mother, but she didn't. "An old friend. I don't think she recognized me. I haven't seen her in a long time."

"Maybe she didn't see you, Mama," Amadea said kindly, as her mother nodded sadly. It took her a long time to tell Antoine about it. He had had no better luck with his parents and brother, although by law he would inherit his father's title and land one day, and the bulk of his fortune. But even knowing that did not induce his family to see him. In essence, their past was over. All they had now was their present and future with each other. Their history had vanished.

But other than the painful loss of their families, their life was pleasant. Antoine and Gérard got on well. And the stables prospered. Antoine bought new horses for him from time to time, organized a hunt for him, trained five of their best horses for the races, and bred their best stallions. Within a short time, Gérard Daubigny's stables were famous all over Europe, in great part thanks to Antoine, who knew far more about horses than Gérard did.

Things were going particularly well when
Beata went to see Véronique one afternoon
to fit an evening gown she was making for
her, when for no reason Beata could think
of, halfway through the fitting, as they were
chatting amiably, Beata fainted. Véronique
was instantly worried about her and made
her lie down on a chaise longue in her
dressing room, and walked her home afterward. Antoine happened to glance up and
notice her as she walked past the stables.
Beata was still extremely pale, and looked
unsteady. He had been giving Amadea a
riding lesson, and asked one of the grooms
to watch her for a minute. And then he hurried out to see his wife, walking home with
Véronique looking anxious beside her.
Beata had sworn Véronique to secrecy. She
didn't want to worry Antoine when he came
to check on her. Beata said that she thought
she was coming down with influenza, or
perhaps a migraine, though she rarely had
them.

"Are you all right?" Antoine asked, looking
worried. "You don't look well." He looked at
Véronique with concern, and she said nothing, as Beata had begged her not to. But
she was worried, too.

"I think I'm coming down with something." She didn't tell him that she had just fainted in Véronique's boudoir during a fitting. She had even forgotten to bring the dress home with her. "How is Amadea doing with her lesson?" Beata said to distract him. "You should force her not to be so reckless." She was seven, and absolutely fearless around horses. She particularly loved to jump over streams and hedges, much to her mother's horror.

"I'm not sure I can force her to do anything," Antoine said with a rueful grin. "She seems to have her own ideas on a multitude of subjects." She had her mother's sharp mind and interests on a myriad of topics, but she also had a daredevil quality to her that concerned them both. There appeared to be almost nothing she thought she couldn't do or was afraid of. It was a good thing in some ways, and terrifying in others. Beata was constantly afraid that something dreadful would happen to her. And as an only child, all her parents' love and attention was focused on her. Beata often thought too much so. But after seven years, it was obvious that Amadea was not going to have brothers or sisters, which was a circumstance both of her parents regretted. "Do you want me to walk you home?" Antoine asked, still looking concerned, and not successfully distracted from it. Beata was extremely fair-skinned normally, but when she wasn't feeling well, she developed an almost icelike pallor. And she appeared to be turning green as he spoke to her, and Véronique watched as well. Beata looked like she was going to faint again!

"I'm fine. I'm just going to lie down for a few minutes. Go back to our little monster." They kissed briefly, and Beata walked the short distance to their home with Véronique, who helped her into bed a few minutes later, and left.

Antoine was relieved to see that she looked better when he got home that evening. And then worried again when she looked considerably worse the next morning. She was a pale shade of green as she got Amadea ready for school, and she had been almost unable to get out of bed before that, when he left for the stables. He came back at lunchtime to check on her.

"How do you feel?" he asked, frowning at her. He hated it when she was sick. His wife and daughter were all he had in the world, and all that really mattered to him. And there had been a lethal strain of influenza going around the previous winter.

"I feel better actually," she said, trying to sound cheerful. She wasn't being entirely truthful with him, and he knew it. He knew her far better than that.

"I want you to see the doctor," he said firmly.

"He's not going to do anything. I'll take a nap this afternoon before Amadea comes home from school. I'll be fine by this evening." She insisted on making lunch for him, and she set it down in front of him, and sat next to him to keep him company, but he noticed that she didn't eat anything. She couldn't wait to get back to bed the moment he left for the stables.

Antoine was still worried about her a week later. Although she insisted she was fine, he could see that she felt no better, and he was frankly panicked. "If you don't go, I will take you myself. Now for heaven's sake, Beata, will you call him? I don't know what you're afraid of." What she was afraid of in fact was disappointment. She had begun to suspect what was wrong with her, and she wanted to wait just a bit longer until she was certain, and before she told Antoine. But finally, she relented and agreed to see the doctor. He confirmed her suspicions, and she was smiling that night when Antoine got back from the stables, although she still felt dreadful.

"What did the doctor say?" Antoine asked her anxiously after Amadea went upstairs to put on her nightgown.

"He said I'm healthy as a horse . . . and I love you . . ." She was so happy, she could hardly contain her excitement.

"He said you love me?" Antoine laughed at her answer. "Well, that's nice of him, but I already knew that much. What did he think was wrong that you've been feeling so poorly?" But she certainly seemed in better spirits, and very playful. She was almost giddy.

"Nothing a little time won't cure," she said obliquely.

"Did he think it's a mild form of influenza? If so, my darling, you really have to be careful." They both knew a number of people who had died of it the previous winter. It was lethal, and nothing to fool around with.

"No, not in the least," she reassured him. "Actually, it's a very definite and quite pro-

nounced case of pregnancy." She beamed
at him. "We're having a baby." Finally. After
all her prayers. When the baby came, there
would be eight years between their two children.

"We are?" Like her, Antoine had long since
given up hope of a second baby. After the
first easy conception and pregnancy, it had
simply never happened since then. "How
wonderful, my darling! How very, very wonderful!" he said, looking as happy as she
did.

"What's wonderful?" Amadea asked, as
she reappeared in her nightgown. "What
happened?" she inquired. She always liked
to be part of the excitement. She was a
strong-willed, but thoughtful, highly intelligent child, who adored her parents, which
was entirely reciprocal. For a moment,
Antoine was afraid she'd be jealous. He
raised an eyebrow as he looked at Beata,
and she nodded. She had just given him the
green light to tell her.

"Your mother just gave me some very
good news," he said proudly. "You are going to have a brother or sister." He was
beaming.

"I am?" She stared at him blankly, and

then looked at her mother, as they both suddenly feared that she would be jealous. She had had their full attention for so long, she might not be enchanted with the idea of a new addition, although she had frequently said that that was what she wanted. "When?"

"Two weeks after your birthday next year. You'll be eight then," her mother answered.

"Why do we have to wait that long?" She looked disappointed. "Can't we get it sooner? Ask the doctor."

"I'm afraid you can't rush up things like that." Beata smiled at her. She obviously thought you ordered babies from the doctor. Beata didn't care how long it would take, she was just thrilled they were having a baby. She would be thirty herself when the baby came. And Antoine had turned forty-two that summer. But most importantly, Beata was relieved to see that Amadea looked as excited as they were.

"Did you ask for a boy or a girl?" Amadea asked intently.

"You can't order that either. We'll have to take whatever God sends. Although I do hope it's a boy for your papa," Beata said warmly.

"Why does Papa need a boy? Girls are much better. I want a sister."

"Well, we'll have to see what comes." Antoine and Beata exchanged a warm look over her head and then smiled at their daughter. Antoine didn't care if it was a boy or girl, as long as it was healthy.

"It'll be a girl," Amadea said definitely, "and she will be my baby. I'm going to do everything for her. May I?"

"It will be wonderful if you help your mama," Antoine said gently.

"What shall we call her?" Amadea was being very practical about it.

"We'll all have to think about it," Beata said, feeling tired but excited. She had dreamed of this for so long, and now it had finally happened when she had stopped even hoping for it. "We have to pick boy and girl names."

"No. Just girl names. And I think it's really stupid that we have to wait so long." Beata was nearly three months pregnant, and the baby was due in mid-April. It did seem a long time, particularly to a child of seven.

Beata's pregnancy was not quite as easy

as the last one, but as the doctor pointed out, she was eight years older. She felt ill a lot of the time, and several times in the last two months, she felt as though she was going into early labor. The doctor told her to take it very easy. Antoine took wonderful care of her, predictably, and when he wasn't working, he spent as much time as possible with Amadea to relieve her mother. Beata spent most of her time knitting, and Amadea helped her. They knitted hats and booties and sweaters and blankets, and Beata made little dresses and nightgowns that could be worn by either sex, although Amadea continued to insist that she wanted a sister. She was fascinated to discover that the baby was growing in her mother's stomach, which was something she had never quite understood previously, since no one in her immediate circle had ever been pregnant. She had seen women like that before, but she just thought they were fat. Conversely, she thought that every fat woman she saw on the street now was having a baby, and Beata reminded her frequently not to ask them if that was the case.

Beata spent the last month of her pregnancy at home, and she wished that once again she had Maria with her. This time a doctor and a midwife were going to attend her. Antoine was relieved, but Beata admitted to him that she was disappointed. The doctor had already told her that Antoine could not be present. He felt it would be too distracting, and it was not how he did things. She much preferred having had Maria and Antoine with her in the simple farmhouse.

"Listen, my love, I'd much prefer knowing that you're in good hands. I don't want you going through the torture you did last time." Beata had forgotten the worst of it, but Antoine hadn't. He still shuddered at the memory of her endless screaming. "Maybe he knows some tricks to make it happen a little faster."

But as it turned out, Mother Nature did that for her. The doctor had warned her that it might be a long labor, almost like a first one. In eight years, her body had forgotten the previous birth. In his experience, he claimed, women who had many years between childbirths often experienced the same slow labors, or even longer ones, than they did the first time. Beata did not find that cheering. And when she met her, Beata wasn't crazy about his midwife. She wished that she and Antoine could just hop on a train and go back to Maria. They had stayed in touch over the years, and she had written to Beata to tell her how pleased she was to hear about the new baby, after Beata wrote to tell her. They had meant to go back and visit, but Antoine never seemed to be able to leave the stables. There was always too much going on.

Beata came home from a walk with Amadea late one afternoon. She was feeling better than she had in weeks and had more energy than she'd had in a long time. She and Amadea baked some cookies, and after that Beata made an elaborate dinner. She thought it would be a nice surprise for Antoine. She was just on her way up to change for dinner, when she felt a familiar pain in her lower abdomen. She had had pains like it for weeks, although not quite as strong, and decided to think nothing of it. She changed for dinner, combed her hair, put on lipstick, and went back downstairs to make sure nothing had burned in the kitchen. She had left a small turkey roasting in the oven. When Antoine came home, he found her in exceptionally good spirits, although she seemed restless at dinner. She had had the same small pains all evening, but they weren't severe enough to call the doctor, and she didn't want to worry Antoine. Amadea complained at dinner that the baby was taking forever, and her parents laughed at her and told her to be patient. It was only after Beata tucked her in cozily and went back downstairs to find Antoine that the pains got sharper.

"Are you all right?" he asked, looking at her. He was treating himself to a rare brandy, and thanked her for the excellent dinner. "You've barely sat down all evening."

"All I do is sit around. I think I've been resting too much. I've had lots of energy since yesterday. I feel so much better."

"Good. Then enjoy it. Don't wear yourself out. The baby will be here before you know it."

"Poor Amadea is so tired of waiting." Her mother sympathized with her, and suddenly felt a sharp pain, but she hated to tell Antoine. He was having such a nice time, relaxing with his brandy, and things had been exceptionally busy lately at the sta-

bles. They had just bought four new stallions.

Antoine sat admiring her then, enjoying
his brandy. She looked beautiful to him,
even though she was immensely pregnant.
And as he finished the last of the brandy,
much to his amazement, Beata doubled
over. She couldn't even speak to him, the
pain was so ferocious, and then as fast as it
had hit her, it was over.

"My God, what happened? Are you all
right? We'd better call the doctor." But they
both knew from the last time that even once
they did, it would take forever. This was just
the beginning. Beata remembered now that
it had been that way for hours the first time.
She had started labor in earnest at dawn,
and Amadea had finally appeared fifteen
hours later. And the doctor had warned her
this time might be longer. She wanted to
spend some quiet time with Antoine before
the doctor and midwife arrived and took
over. She preferred to spend her early labor
with her husband, since they wouldn't let
him stay with her once the midwife came.
Beata wanted time with him now.

"I'll just lie down for a minute. Even if this
is for real, the baby probably won't come

until tomorrow." It was ten o'clock in the evening, as she made her way slowly upstairs and Antoine followed. He offered to carry her, and she laughed at him. But she stopped laughing the moment she walked into their bedroom. The next pain hit her like a bomb, and she felt instant pressure on her back and lower belly. Antoine eased her gently onto their bed as she gasped in pain, wondering how she could have forgotten. It was all coming back to her now. It was only when she felt the first pains that she actually remembered what it had been like. Until then, the memory of the agony had faded. It was hard to believe now that she could have forgotten, but she had.

She lay down on their bed as Antoine watched her, and she insisted that he wait a while, or a few minutes at least, before he called the doctor. "They won't let you stay with me," she said, sounding frightened.

"I won't be far away, just in the next room. I promise."

Just as Maria had done eight years before, Beata had set aside a mountain of old sheets and towels, and she was worried about Amadea hearing frightening sounds from the next room during labor. With luck,

she'd be at school when the baby came,
and would miss the worst of it. Beata knew
she was in for a long haul. She remembered
it only too well now, from last time. She had
two sharp pains again then, and a tremendous sense of pressure that seemed unfamiliar. She felt as though a truck were driving through her, and with the next pain, she
suddenly looked frightened as she glanced
wild-eyed at Antoine.

"Oh my God . . . the baby's coming . . ."

"I know it is," he said calmly. The brandy
was helping. He recognized all the signs
that she was seriously in labor, but this time
he knew what to expect and he wasn't worried. "I'll call the doctor. Where's the number?"

"No, you don't understand," she said,
gasping for air, and clutching at him. "I
can't . . . don't . . . the baby's coming . . ."
And with no warning, she let out a terrible
groan, and her face turned first white, then
purple. She was pushing. She couldn't stop
herself. The pressure forcing her to was
overwhelming.

"Stop pushing . . . you'll wear yourself
out." He remembered Maria warning her of
that the first time. She had hours ahead of

her, but he definitely wanted to call the doctor. She wouldn't let go of him though. She
was clutching his hand, and he could see
that the pains were ripping through her
without stopping.

"Antoine . . . help me . . . take my clothes
off . . ." She managed to somehow pull off
most of her clothes, as he struggled to help
her, and as she did, he realized what was
happening. She wasn't just in labor, she
was having the baby, literally, at that moment. This was not at all what he had expected. And he felt slightly drunk from the
brandy as he looked between her legs and
saw the baby crowning. From all he knew,
she had been in labor for about five minutes. But in fact, she had been in labor since
early that afternoon and refused to notice.

"Lie down," he said firmly, with absolutely
no idea of what to do. All he remembered,
or knew, was what he had seen Maria do
during the endless hours before Amadea.
". . . you can't do this to me . . . Beata . . .
can't you wait till we call the doctor?" He
didn't dare leave her to find the number, and
there was no one to help them. He thought
of calling Véronique, but he suspected that
she knew even less than he did about deliv-

ering a baby. He made a move away from her to try and reach her address book, but she wouldn't let him.

"I need you . . . don't . . . oh my God . . . Antoine . . . please . . . oh no . . . someone help me . . ."

"It's all right, darling, it's all right . . . I'm here . . . I won't leave you . . . should you push now?" He had no idea what to do for her except be there, which was all she wanted.

"Get towels," she cried. He ran to her bathroom, and brought back an armload and put them under and around her. He could see that she was wracked with pain and he held her shoulders as he had the first time. But this time, she didn't have to do the work, the baby did it for her. Beata gave one scream, and within seconds a small face emerged, open-mouthed and wailing. They both looked shocked as they heard it, and Antoine had never seen anything so amazing. He talked Beata through the next pains, as she delivered the rest of the baby's shoulders and then the body. The baby lay there perfect and crying loudly. It was another girl, and he picked her up and placed her gently in a towel, then handed her to her mother. He leaned down and kissed them both, as Beata laughed through her tears. The entire process had taken less than half an hour. Antoine was still in shock as he asked her for the number and called the doctor. He told him not to cut the cord, and he would be there in five minutes. He lived within minutes of the *Schloss,* and knew where their house was. Antoine went to sit next to her then, and gently kissed both mother and baby.

"I love you, Beata, but if you ever do that to me again, I'm going to kill you . . . I had no idea what to do to help you . . . why didn't you let me call the doctor?"

"I didn't think the baby would come for hours, and I wanted to be with you . . . I'm sorry . . . I didn't mean to scare you." She had been afraid, too. It had all happened so quickly, she had never expected the baby to be born with so little warning. And with the exception of a few rough pains, it had been remarkably easy.

The doctor arrived moments later, cut the cord, checked mother and daughter, and declared them both in excellent condition.

"You didn't need me for this one, my dear. The next one is likely to come even faster."

"I'm putting myself in a hospital for that one," Antoine said, still looking shaken, as he thanked the doctor.

The doctor called and asked the midwife to come then, to clean up mother and baby and settle them in. And by midnight, mother and daughter were tucked into bed, looking immaculate and peaceful. This baby looked entirely different from Amadea. She was much smaller than Amadea had been, which was why the labor had been so much easier, and her arrival so speedy. She was tiny, and seemed to have the delicate frame of her mother. Amadea had continued to be tall and lanky, like her father. This baby had Beata's dark hair, and it was too soon to tell what color her eyes were. She seemed remarkably calm and relaxed as Beata held her.

In the morning when Amadea came in to them, she gave a shout of glee. She had heard nothing the night before, and Beata was grateful that she was a heavy sleeper.

"She's here! She's here!" Amadea said, dancing around the room, and then came to peer at her intently. "What shall we call her? Can I hold her?" Beata and Antoine had talked about names until they fell asleep, but they wanted to wait until they consulted Amadea.

"What about Daphne?" Beata suggested, and Amadea looked at the baby seriously, weighed the possibility for a long moment, and then nodded.

"I like it." Beata looked relieved, Antoine did, too. They all did. "Daphne. It's perfect." She climbed into bed beside her mother then, and Beata gently put the baby in her big sister's arms, and tears came to her eyes as she watched. She hadn't had the son she had hoped to give Antoine, but her heart filled with joy as she looked at her two daughters, the one beautiful and blond, and the other so small and dark. She was the image of her mother. And when she looked up, Beata saw Antoine smiling as he watched them from the doorway. They exchanged a long slow smile. It was the moment they had both waited eight years for.

"I love you," she mouthed to Antoine, more in love with him than ever. He nodded, as tears filled his eyes. No matter what they had lost in the past, they both had all they had ever wanted now.

7

BY THE TIME DAPHNE WAS TWO, AMADEA WAS ten, and there was no doubt in anyone's mind that she was Amadea's baby, just as Amadea claimed. She constantly fussed over her, indulged her, took her everywhere. She was like a live doll that Amadea never ceased to play with. Amadea was an extremely efficient little mother. Beata had nothing to do whenever Amadea was around. The only time she left her baby sister was when she went to school, and when she went to visit her father at the stables. At ten Amadea was an extremely proficient rider. She had won several jumping competitions and knew a great deal about horses. Antoine was justifiably proud of her, and adored both his daughters, as he did Beata. He was an extraordinary father and husband. Beata knew without a doubt that she was a lucky woman.

It was June, just after the girls had turned ten and two, two months before, that Antoine received a telegram, followed by a letter. Without ever speaking to him again, or forgiving him for the unpardonable crime he felt Antoine had committed, his father had died suddenly. And no matter how angry his father was at him, as the oldest son, the lands and fortune, as well as the title, had been passed to Antoine. He walked into the house late one afternoon, holding the telegram, with a startled expression.

"Is something wrong?" They knew each other well, and Beata was instantly worried.

"You've just become a countess." It took a moment to register, and then she understood. She knew what it meant to him to have remained estranged from his father. And now nothing would ever change that. Antoine counted it as an immeasurable loss.

"I'm sorry," she said softly, and then came to hold him. He clung to her for a long time, and then sighed and sat down. The telegram said that the funeral had been the week before. They hadn't even had the grace to let him attend it. The telegram was from his father's lawyer.

"I want to see my brother," he said, looking distracted. "This has gone on for too long. We have to fix this. I have to go to Dordogne to see the lawyers." There were decisions to be made, properties to run. He could not remain an absentee landlord. He had inherited the château and everything that went with it. And from the last he knew of it, there was a respectable fortune, a small portion of which would pass to his brother Nicolas. In fact, just in the few moments since he'd heard the news, Antoine had decided that he wanted to share the fortune equally with him. The title was Antoine's, and the land. But contrary to tradition, he thought the money should be evenly split. He had more than enough now to be able to afford to be generous with him. "I'll have to speak to Gérard tomorrow. I want to go to France in the next few weeks. I have no idea how long I'll have to stay there." But they both knew that their days at the Daubignys' château were over. They had spent a wonderful eight years there, but as Comte de Vallerand, Antoine had his own responsibilities. After being banished for eleven years, it was time for the prodigal son to go home now. And overnight, Beata had become a countess. It was a lot to absorb, and Antoine knew he would have to explain it to Amadea.

Antoine spoke to Gérard first. They had a long talk over breakfast the next morning. Antoine agreed to stay for the next few weeks, and after he spoke to the lawyers in France, he promised to come back to Germany for at least a month, to find and train a replacement. He had several suggestions, which sounded reasonable to Gérard. But he was devastated to lose him. They had been friends for years, and Antoine had been a genius with his stables. He had the most important horse farm in Europe. Their champions were famous.

Two days later, knowing that their long alliance was about to end, Antoine suggested to Gérard that they go out to try two new stallions. Antoine had just bought them for him at auction. They were highly spirited and spectacularly beautiful. Amadea watched them as they left the barn, and complained that her father wouldn't allow

her to go with them. Instead, she went back
to the house to play with her baby sister.
She was playing with her in her bedroom
later that afternoon, when she heard the
doorbell ring, and her mother let someone
in. She didn't think about it as she played
dolls with Daphne, and after a while, she
went downstairs to get Daphne a cookie.
She saw Gérard and one of her father's
chief trainers sitting in the living room,
speaking to her mother, and Beata was
wearing a glazed expression. She looked
dazed, as she turned and saw Amadea.

"Go back upstairs," she said tersely,
which was unlike her. Amadea was so startled by her tone that she turned and did as
she was told, but as she sat in her room
with Daphne, she was frightened. She knew
even before they told her that something
terrible had happened.

It seemed like hours before her mother
came upstairs, and when she did, she was
crying. She could hardly speak as she held
Amadea in her arms, and told her that her
father had been thrown by the new stallion.

"Is he hurt?" Amadea asked, looking terrified. Even with only one good arm, he was
a faultless rider. And all Beata could do was

sob and shake her head. It was an eternity before she could bring herself to say the words. Neither of them could believe it.

"Papa's dead, Amadea . . . Papa . . ." She choked on the words, as Amadea sobbed in her mother's arms. Véronique came a little while later to sit with the girls, and Beata went to see him at the stables. He had broken his neck and had been killed instantly. He was dead, the man she would have given her life for. It was almost beyond bearing.

The funeral was an endless agony, and the church was filled to bursting. Everyone who had ever known and worked with him had loved him. Gérard spoke at his funeral eloquently, and Véronique sat beside Beata with an arm around her shoulders. Afterward there was a reception at the *Schloss,* and the main hall was filled with mourning horsemen. Beata looked like a ghost as she drifted through the room, in widow's weeds, clinging to her daughters.

And afterward, there was so much to think of. This man she had loved so much, had given up her family for, who had loved and never betrayed or disappointed her, was suddenly gone. She had no idea where to go, what to do, or who to turn to. Gérard helped her as much as he could, and Véronique never left her. There was endless red tape to cut through, and Gérard offered his own attorneys in France to help her. The fortune that had been left to him by his father only weeks before was hers now. He had already agreed to share it equally with his brother Nicolas. But the half of the inheritance that Antoine had kept would be more than enough for Beata and the girls to live on. She would not live in grand luxury, but her future was secure. She could buy a house and support herself and the girls for as long as she lived. She no longer had to worry about petty economies, nor could she indulge frivolous excesses. But in essence, from a financial standpoint at least, she had few worries. The worst of it was that he was gone, and at thirty-two she was a widow. Amadea knew she would never forget the day her father died. And as quickly as was reasonable, they had to leave the house she had grown up in. Their life was about to undergo radical changes. Only Daphne was far too young to understand them. Amadea and her mother understood them all too well. Beata felt and looked as though her own life had ended.

The title passed to Nicolas, and the lands that went with them. The château was his now. Comte Nicolas de Vallerand was a rich man, just as Antoine would have been finally, if he had lived long enough to enjoy it. He had survived his father by less than two weeks. None of this was what Beata had expected. She didn't mind losing what she'd never had, and cared nothing for. All she cared about was that she had lost Antoine.

In time, a man Antoine had known and liked took over his job at the stables. Gérard and Véronique helped Beata find a house in Cologne. Beata and the girls moved into it that summer. She received a polite letter from her brother-in-law, extending his condolences, but he said nothing about wanting to meet her, or seeing Antoine's children. The letter was stiff, polite, and formal. Beata hated him for hurting Antoine. Just as her own family had been, his had been cruel to them as well. Beata and Antoine had been outcasts for their entire marriage. Their only close friends had been the Daubignys and each other. It was too late for Beata to want to meet her brother-in-law and he didn't suggest it. He seemed content to let things lie, especially now that Antoine was gone. And she had the distinct impression that Antoine's brother still blamed her for their estrangement, although he had had the grace and good manners to address her as Madame la Comtesse, which she still was now. As far as she was concerned, a title was a poor substitute for a husband. She never answered her brother-in-law's letter, nor did she explain the reasons for her anger at him to Amadea. She saw no point.

Beata moved around her new home like a ghost for the next year, and she was grateful that Amadea took full charge of her younger sister. She bathed her, dressed her, played with her, spent every waking hour with her when she wasn't in school. She was the mother to Daphne that Beata no longer could be. It was as though when Antoine died, he had taken her with him. She no longer wanted to live without him, and it frightened Amadea sometimes to see that her mother had become deeply religious. She spent most of her time in church. Often when Amadea came home from school, she found her mother gone, and Daphne being watched by the housekeeper, who just shook her head whenever Amadea asked for her mother. She was only eleven, but overnight she had become the only responsible member of the family. Not knowing what else to do, she sometimes spent hours in church, sitting silently beside her mother, just to be with her. It was the only place where Beata felt at peace and wanted to be. And rather than developing a horror of it, Amadea embraced it. She loved being in church with her. Amadea's best friend was from a large Catholic family, and when Amadea was thirteen, the girl's older sister became a nun, which Amadea found somewhat mysterious and intriguing. They talked a lot about Amadea's friend's sister's vocation, and Amadea wondered how you got one. It sounded like a good thing.

But just at that time, her mother began to confuse her. Not only did her mother go to church every day, sometimes more than once, but she went to a synagogue occasionally, too. It was a large imposing one filled with what looked like substantial people. She took Amadea with her once on a day she referred to as Yom Kippur. Amadea

found it fascinating, but a little scary. Her
mother had sat looking riveted, as she
stared at an older woman. The woman appeared not to see her. And that night, in
their living room, Amadea found her mother
staring at a lap full of framed, faded old pic-
tures.

"Who are those people, Mama?" Amadea
asked softly. She loved her mother so
much, and for three years now, she felt as
though she had lost her. In a way, the
mother she had known and loved had vanished with her father. There had been no
laughter in the house since he died, except
when Amadea played with Daphne.

"They're my parents and sister and brothers," Beata said simply. Until that day,
Amadea had never heard a word about
them. Her father had once told her that he
and her mother were orphans when they
met each other. She loved hearing about the
day they met, and how they had fallen in
love, how beautiful her mother had looked
on the day they were married. She knew
they had met in Switzerland, and lived there
with cousins of his until she was two, and
then came to the house she knew and had
grown up in. She still went to ride at the sta-

bles sometimes, but it made her sad now
and miss her father. Her mother had long
since sold her pony. Gérard and Véronique
said she was always welcome, but she
knew her mother didn't like it when she
went there. She was afraid that something
would happen, as it had to her father.
Amadea stopped going so as not to upset
her mother, although she missed it.

"Did they all die?" Amadea asked, as she
saw her mother staring at the faded pic-
tures. And then Beata looked at her
strangely.

"No, I did." She said nothing more then,
and after a while Amadea went back to
Daphne. She was a happy child of five, who
thought the sun rose and set on her older
sister. Amadea was like a mother to her.

After that first time when she took Amadea
with her, Beata went back to the synagogue
every year on Yom Kippur. It was the day of
atonement, a time to contemplate past sins,
and to allow God to judge you. She brought
her children up as Catholics, and profoundly
believed in what she taught them. But she
still went to the synagogue once a year, and
each time she went she watched them. Her
whole family. They were always there, the

men seated separately from the women.
And each year, she took Amadea with her.
She never told her why. It was too complicated, she felt, after all this time. She and
Antoine had always told her their families
were dead. Beata didn't want to admit she'd
lied. And as part of all that, she never told either of her daughters she had been Jewish
years before.

"Why do you want to go there?" Amadea
asked her, intrigued by it.

"I think it's interesting, don't you?" Beata
never offered any further explanation, and
Amadea admitted to her best friend when
she was fifteen that she thought it was
creepy. But there was no question in
Amadea's mind, ever since her father's
death five years before, her mother hadn't
been normal. It was as though the shock
had been too much for her, and Amadea
sensed correctly that she wanted to be with
him. She was only thirty-eight, and still
beautiful, but she was waiting to die now,
and Amadea knew it.

When Amadea was sixteen, Daphne was
eight, and that year Amadea had promised
to take Daphne to her ballet class on the
one day of the year that her mother went to

the synagogue, on Yom Kippur. She was relieved to have an excuse not to go. She
didn't know why, but she always found it
depressing. She much preferred joining her
mother in church, and lately Amadea had
been praying to know if she had a vocation,
like her friend's sister. She hadn't said anything to anyone but she was beginning to
think so.

Beata took her place in the synagogue, as
she always did, heavily veiled. And as she
did each year, she saw them. She knew she
could have gone at other times, but this always seemed the right day, to beg for their
forgiveness and her own. She thought her
mother looked frail this time when she saw
her. And by some miracle, she found herself
sitting in a seat just behind her. If she had
dared to, she could have reached out to
touch her. And then, as though by a miracle,
sensing Beata's eyes glued to her, she
turned and glanced at the woman behind
her. All she could see was a hat and a veil,
but she sensed more than saw something
familiar about her. And before she could
turn away again, Beata lifted the veil, and
her mother saw her. Their eyes met and held
for an endless moment, and then her

mother nodded and turned away again, looking transfixed. She was sitting alone, among the women. And when they left the synagogue, Beata fell into step beside her. She had no sense this time that her mother wanted to avoid her. And what had struck Monika and took her breath away was the bottomless sadness in the eyes of her daughter. The two women left the syna-gogue side by side, and as they did, their hands brushed and met. Beata gently took her hand in her own and held it, and her mother let her. And then without a word, her mother went to join her father. He still looked tall and proud, Beata saw, although he was much older. She knew that he was sixty-eight, and her mother sixty-three. She watched them leave the synagogue, and then Beata took a taxi home to her daugh-ters.

"How was it?" Amadea asked her that night at dinner.

"How was what?" Beata asked blankly. She rarely spoke at dinner, and tonight she looked particularly distracted. She was still thinking of her mother. They hadn't spoken in seventeen years now, and so much had happened. Her daughters had been born,

her husband had died, everything in her life
had changed, and she had become a
countess, which meant nothing to her, although she suspected it might have impressed her sister.

"Isn't today the day you go to the synagogue every year? Why do you do that,
Mama?" She knew that her mother had
been deeply intellectual, and she had always had a profound fascination with religion. Perhaps it was religious curiosity that
drove her there, or a gesture of respect for
other people. She knew how devoutly
Catholic her mother was.

"I like it." She did not tell her oldest
daughter that she went there to see her
mother, and today she had touched her.
They had not spoken a single word to each
other, but just holding her hand for a moment had revived her. Since Antoine had
died, she knew to her very core that she
needed to see her mother. It was some
sense of continuity from the past into the future. Monika was the link for her, as Beata
was between her mother and her daughters.

"I think it's disgusting that Jews can't be
newspaper editors or own land anymore.

And that some of them are being sent to work camps," Amadea volunteered at dinner with a look of outrage. Hitler had been appointed chancellor in January, and ever since then there had been laws passed against the Jews. Beata had been aware of it, as most people were, and thought it disgraceful, but there was nothing anyone could do to stop it. And as most people did, she had her own problems and worries. But the current anti-Semitism was of great concern to her for a number of reasons.

"What do you know about that?" Beata looked startled.

"I know a lot about it actually. I went to some lectures by a woman called Edith Stein. She said that women should become involved in politics, their community, and the nation. She wrote to the pope, condemning anti-Semitism. And I read her book about *Life in a Jewish Family.* She was born Jewish, and became a nun recently. She became a Catholic eleven years ago, but the Nazis still think of her as Jewish. They forced her to stop lecturing and teaching. Now she's in a Carmelite convent in Cologne. She's actually very famous."

"I know. I've read about her. I find her interesting." It was the first bond Beata and her daughter had made, on an adult level, the first serious conversation they'd had in years. Amadea was encouraged by it, and decided to open her heart to her. She was impressed that her mother knew of Edith Stein, too.

"Sometimes I think I'd like to be a nun. I spoke to a priest about it once. He thought it would be good." Beata looked upset as she glanced at her daughter. For the first time, she realized how absent she had been, and how lonely Amadea was. Other than her friends at school, her only companion at home was a child half her age. It was a wake-up call to Beata to pay more attention to her. Antoine had been gone for six years, and Beata felt as though she had died with him.

"Your father wouldn't like it if you became a nun." She remembered what he had said when the priest who had married them said that she should have become a nun. Antoine had strongly disapproved, not only for her obviously, but he thought it was a wasted life for women. He thought women should be married and have children. "You should get married when you grow up, and have babies." She tried to echo Antoine's words, as though she could speak for him, and in fact had an obligation to do so, since he could no longer speak for himself.

"Maybe not everyone is meant to have children. Gretchen's sister became a nun three years ago. She loves it. She took her first vows last year." The more Beata listened to her, the more she realized how out of touch she had been. Amadea sounded as though she were heading for the nearest convent, and Beata realized she had a responsibility to pay closer attention and talk to her, not just about taking Daphne to ballet, or dropping her off at school, but about the things that mattered to her. She hoped it wasn't too late to make that connection with her again. Beata realized with sudden shock that she had been drifting aimlessly since Antoine's death, and had all but lost touch with her children. Her body was there, but her spirit wasn't.

"I don't want you going to lectures like the ones Edith Stein gave, Amadea, or rallies organized by radicals, if that's what you're doing these days. And you should be careful about speaking up against Hitler's policies, except here."

"Do you agree with him, Mama?" Amadea looked shocked.

"No, I don't." Beata felt as though her head were clearing, finally, and it was interesting talking to Amadea. She was an extremely bright young girl. It reminded her of her own questioning at that age, and her passion for philosophy and political discussions. She had spent hours arguing with her brothers and their friends. Amadea had no one to talk to about things like that except her. "But it's dangerous to be oppositional. There's a lot of anti-Semitism in Hitler's policies. Even at your age, you could bring attention to yourself by speaking out. That could be dangerous for you." Amadea could see that her mother was serious, and Amadea made a comment about how disgusting it was that they had burned books in May. Amadea didn't like the things she was seeing and hearing publicly, and when she paid attention to them, neither did her mother.

"Why did they burn books?" Daphne entered the conversation finally, and looked confused.

"Because they're trying to frighten people

and intimidate them," Amadea volunteered. "And they're sending people to work camps because they're Jewish. The Nazis told people not to go to Jewish shops on my birthday this year."

"Because of you?" Daphne looked startled by what Amadea had said to her, and her older sister smiled at her.

"No, it was just a coincidence, but it was still a mean thing to do."

"Do Jewish people look different than other people?" Daphne asked then with interest, and Amadea looked outraged.

"Of course they don't. How can you say a thing like that?"

"My teacher said that Jews have tails," Daphne said innocently as both her mother and sister looked horrified.

"That's not true," Beata said, wondering if she should tell them that she had been born Jewish, but she felt awkward telling them now. She had been a Catholic for so many years. And some people said they were only going after the poor Jews, the homeless and criminals, not the ones like her family. The Nazis wanted to clean up Germany and disperse the criminal element. They would never go after respectable Jews. She was sure of that. But still not sure enough to tell her children she'd been Jewish.

It was an interesting conversation at the dinner table that night, and they lingered longer than usual. Beata had never realized how politically interested Amadea was, how socially conscious and independent. Nor had she realized that she was struggling to decide if she had a religious vocation, which she found far more disturbing than her more radical inclinations. She couldn't help wondering just how influenced by Edith Stein's lectures and writings she had been. Or worse yet, by the fact that Stein had become a nun. Things like that were powerful influences on a young girl. Not to mention the older sister of her best friend. Altogether it painted a portrait of a life Beata didn't want for her. But she herself had offered little to put any weight on the other side of the scale in recent years. She had no social life, no friends, saw no one except the Daubignys, and them rarely. For eleven years while Antoine was alive, she had devoted all her time to him and her children. And since his death, she had become a recluse. She saw no way of changing that now, and had no desire to. But at least she could pay more attention to what was happening in the world. Amadea seemed far better informed than she. She worried about her opinions about the Nazis' anti-Semitism, though, and hoped she wasn't voicing them in school. She reminded her to be careful when she left for school the next day. Disagreeing with the Nazis was a dangerous thing to do, at any age.

The following week Beata went back to the synagogue. She didn't want to wait another year before she saw her mother again. This time she sat just behind her purposely, and there was no need to lift her veil. Her mother recognized her the moment she saw her, and as they left after the service, Beata slipped a piece of paper into her mother's gloved hand. It had her address and phone number on it, and as soon as she had given it to her, and saw her mother close her fingers over it, Beata disappeared into the crowd and left. She didn't wait to see her father this time. All she could do now was pray that her mother would be brave enough to call. Beata wanted desperately to see her and hold her and talk to her again. More than anything, she wanted her to meet the girls.

It was an agonizing two days. By sheer coincidence, Amadea answered the phone when it rang. They were just leaving the table after dinner, and Beata had just asked Daphne if she wanted to play a game. Amadea had noticed that her mother seemed much better these days, and was making more effort to engage them, or emerge from her long depression after Antoine's death.

"There's someone on the phone for you," Amadea told her.

"Who is it?" Beata asked, momentarily forgetting the call she was expecting, and assuming it was Véronique. She had been asking Beata for months to make a dress for her for their Christmas party. She thought it would be good therapy for her. But Beata had been avoiding her. She hadn't sewn now in years, not since Antoine's death, except once in a great while, something simple for the girls. She no longer had any interest in making evening gowns or serious dresses. And she no longer had the need financially.

"She didn't say who she was," Amadea

explained, as she took Daphne upstairs, and Beata walked to the phone.

"Hello?" Beata answered, and her breath caught when she heard the voice. It hadn't changed.

"Beata?" she whispered, afraid someone might overhear. Jacob was out, but everyone knew she wasn't allowed to speak to her daughter. She was dead.

"Oh my God. Thank you for calling. You looked so beautiful at the synagogue. You haven't changed." After seventeen years, they both knew that wasn't possible. But to Beata, she looked the same.

"You looked so sad. Are you all right? Are you ill?"

"Antoine died."

"I'm so sorry." She sounded genuine. Her daughter had looked destroyed. It was why she had called. She couldn't turn her back on her any longer, no matter what Jacob said. "When?"

"Six years ago. I have two beautiful little girls. Amadea and Daphne."

"Do they look like you?" Her mother smiled as she asked.

"The little one does. The older one looks

like her father. Mama, would you like to see them?"

There was an interminable silence, and then she answered finally, with a sigh. She sounded tired. Things were difficult these days. "Yes, I would."

"That would be so wonderful." Beata sounded like a girl again. "When would you like to come?"

"What about tomorrow afternoon, for tea? The girls would be home from school then, I assume."

"We'll be here." There were tears rolling down Beata's cheeks. This was what she had prayed for for years. Forgiveness. Absolution. Touching her mother again. Just once. Holding her. A moment in her mother's arms. Just once.

"What will you tell them?"

"I don't know. I'll figure it out tonight."

"They'll hate me, if you tell them the truth," Monika Wittgenstein said sadly. But just as Beata wanted to see her, Monika wanted to see her own child again. And these days bad things were happening. Jacob was afraid that one day it could happen to them, too, although Horst and Ulm said that could never happen. They were Germans, not just random Jews roaming the streets. They said the Nazis were after the criminal element, not respectable people like them. Jacob didn't agree. And they were all getting old. She needed to see her daughter again. Needed to. Viscerally. Like a part of her heart that had been taken from her and needed to be restored.

"They don't have to know the truth. We can blame it on Papa." She smiled. They both knew her father would never relent. There was not even the remotest possibility that Amadea and Daphne would meet him. But Monika felt he could no longer force this tragedy on her, too. She could no longer do it to Beata or herself. "Don't worry. I'll figure it out. They'll be excited to meet you. And Mama . . ."—she nearly choked on the words—"I can't wait to see you."

"Me too." Her mother sounded as excited as she did.

Beata thought about it all that night, and in the morning, at breakfast, she said that there was someone who wanted to meet them, and she was coming that afternoon.

"Who is it?" Amadea asked with only minor interest. She had a test at school that day. She had stayed up late to study the night before, and she was tired. She was an exceptional student.

Beata hesitated for a beat. "Your grand-mother," she said, as both girls' eyes grew wide.

"I thought she was dead," Amadea said suspiciously, no longer sure which story was the truth.

"I lied," Beata confessed. "When I married your father, France and Germany were at war with each other, and people felt strongly about it. Both our families did. Papa and I met in Switzerland, when we were on vaca-tion with our parents. And my father wanted me to marry someone else. Someone I didn't even know." It was hard explaining it all to them now, their lives were so different. But they were riveted by what she was say-ing. It was not easy finding the words, or explaining what had happened so long ago. "Neither of our families wanted us to marry, because Papa was French, and I was German. We knew we'd have to wait until after the war, and even then it wasn't likely they'd approve. We were crazy and young, and I told my father I wanted to marry Papa, and would no matter what. He said that if I did, he would never see me again. Papa was wounded and waiting for me in Switzerland, and his cousins said we could live with them and be married. So I left, which was a very headstrong thing to do, but I knew I was right. I knew what a good man your father was, and I never regretted for a minute what I did. But my father has never seen me again, and he wouldn't let any of my family see me. Not my mother or sister or brothers. All my letters to them came back unopened. He never let my mother see me or speak to me again. I saw her somewhere the other day." She did not tell them it was at the synagogue, because she didn't think they needed the added complication of knowing they were part Jewish. It would only confuse them. Or perhaps even put them in danger at some point, given Hitler's feelings about Jews. "When I saw her I gave my mother our phone number and address. She called last night, and she wants to see you. She's coming here today after school." It was simpler than she had feared. Both her daughters were staring at her in disbelief.

"How could he be so mean?" Amadea

asked, looking outraged. "Is that what Papa's family did, too?"

"Yes, it is. They hated the Germans, as much as my family hated the French."

"How stupid. And how mean." Amadea's heart went out to her. "Would you ever do that to us?" Amadea knew the answer before she said the words.

"No, I wouldn't. But that was a long time ago, and it was an ugly war."

"Then why didn't he see you afterward?" Daphne asked sensibly. Like her sister, she was a bright child.

"Because he's a stubborn old man," Amadea said with rancor. Beata had forgiven him years before, and accepted what happened, though it had tormented her for years before she did.

"What about your sister and brothers?" Amadea asked, still shocked by what she had heard. "They're not dead either?" Beata shook her head. "Why won't they see you?"

"They don't want to disobey my father," Beata said simply. She didn't tell them that her father had said she was dead.

"He must be horrible if everyone is so afraid of him," Amadea said sensibly. She couldn't conceive of treating people that

way. But her own father had been a very
gentle man. "And Papa's family, too."

"Your mama must be very brave if she
wants to see us now. Will your father beat
her when she goes home?" Daphne asked,
looking worried.

"Of course not." Beata smiled at her. "But
she won't tell him she came here. He'd be
too upset. And now he's old. So is she. I'm
so happy she's coming to see us," Beata
confessed with tears in her eyes, which
touched both her girls. "I've missed her so
much. Especially since Papa died." Amadea
suddenly wondered if her yearly visits to the
synagogue had anything to do with it, but
she didn't want to ask. Her mother had
been through enough. "I just wanted you to
know before she came today." It had been
an extraordinary insight into their mother,
and both girls were still stunned by it as
they walked to school. It was odd finding
out that they had a grandmother who had
been alive for all these years, and whom
they had never seen. Not only a grandmother, but a grandfather, an aunt, and two
uncles.

"I'm glad for Mama that she's coming,"

Amadea said quietly. "But I think it was a terrible thing to do. Imagine if she did that to us," Amadea said, filled with compassion and sorrow for her mother. What a huge, huge loss, to lose everyone she had loved for a man. Although if she hadn't done it, Amadea realized, she and Daphne would never have been born.

"I'd cry a lot," Daphne said, looking impressed.

"So would I." Amadea smiled, taking her hand to cross the street. "You'd better never do anything stupid like not talk to me, or I'll come and beat you up," Amadea warned her, and Daphne laughed.

"Okay. I promise. I won't." Thinking about their mother, and the grandmother they were about to meet, the two girls walked the rest of the way to school, hand in hand, lost in their own thoughts. Amadea had already forgotten the question in her own mind about whether her grandparents had been Jewish. It made no difference to her. She knew that her mother was Catholic, so she had to have been wrong about that. If her mother was Catholic, then obviously her parents were too.

8

WHEN THE DOORBELL RANG AT FOUR O'CLOCK, Beata stood very still for a minute, smoothed her dress, and patted her hair. She was wearing a plain black dress and a string of pearls Antoine had given her for their tenth anniversary. Her face was startlingly pale. She looked serious and almost breathless when she opened the door and saw her mother standing there, in an elegant black coat over a purple dress. As always, she was beautifully dressed, and she was wearing black suede shoes, and a matching purse. Her black suede gloves were custom made. And she was wearing enormous pearls. Her eyes bored into her daughter's, and without a sound, they flew into each other's arms. Beata felt suddenly like a child who had lost her mother and finally found her. She just wanted to nuzzle her, feel her face, and the silk of her hair. She still wore the same perfume she had worn when Beata was a little girl. And as though it had happened yesterday, she could remember the horror of the day she left. But it was all over now. They had found each other again. The years since melted away. She led her mother into the living room, and they sat down next to each other on the couch, as they both cried. Beata couldn't speak for a long time.

"Thank you for coming, Mama, I missed you so much." More than she had allowed herself to feel, or could ever say. It all came rushing back to her now. The moments she wished she had been there, when she got married, when Amadea was born . . . and Daphne . . . for holidays and birthdays and every important moment in her married life . . . and when Antoine died. And all the ordinary moments in between. And now she was here. She felt no rage over the years they'd lost, only grief. And now, finally, relief.

"You'll never know what agony this has been," Monika said as tears rolled relentlessly down her cheeks. "I promised him I wouldn't see you. I was afraid to disobey him. But I missed you so much, every single day." She had never gotten over it. In the end, it was like a death.

"All my letters came back," Beata said as she blew her nose.

"I never knew you'd written. Papa must have returned them without showing them to me."

"I knew that," Beata said sadly, remembering her father's handwriting returning them to her. "The ones I wrote to Brigitte came back too. I saw her on the street once, and she wouldn't talk to me. And Ulm and Horst."

"We sat shiva for you," her mother said sadly. It had been the worst day of her life. "He won't allow us to even speak of you. And I think Brigitte is afraid to upset me, so she doesn't say anything."

"Is she happy?"

Her mother shook her head. "She's divorced. She wants to marry someone else. Papa doesn't approve. Are your children Jewish?" her mother asked hopefully, and Beata shook her head.

"No, they're not." She didn't tell her

mother she had converted when she married Antoine. Maybe hearing that would be too much for her. This was enough. And then her mother surprised her with what she said next. She assumed correctly that Beata had converted. She had somehow thought she would, once she married Antoine.

"Maybe it's better that way, with the way things are these days. The Nazis are doing terrible things. Papa says they'll never do it to us. But you never know. Don't tell anyone you were Jewish. It would take them a long time to find the records. If you're a Christian now, stay that way, Beata. You'll be safer that way." It was a powerful thing for her mother to say. And then she looked at her daughter with worried eyes. "What did you tell the children about me?"

"That I love you, Papa didn't want me to marry Antoine because he was French, and we were at war. I said his family felt the same way about me. The girls were shocked, but I think they understood." As best one could. It was a big bite, and tough to swallow, but Beata thought they had.

"Did his family ever see you?" Beata shook her head. "How did he die?"

"A riding accident. His father had died two weeks before." And then she smiled. "I'm a countess now." Her mother smiled, too.

"I'm impressed," she teased, with a sparkle in her eye. And with that, the girls came home, and walked cautiously into the room. They looked at the woman they knew was their grandmother, and saw the smile that lit up their mother's face. She introduced Amadea to her first, and then Daphne, as her mother sat looking at them with tears rolling down her cheeks, and she held out both hands to them. "Please forgive me for how foolish I have been. I'm so happy to meet you both. I'm so proud of both of you. You're so beautiful," she said, dabbing at her eyes with a lace handkerchief, as the girls slowly approached. Daphne thought she looked nice. And Amadea wanted to ask her questions about why she had let her husband be so mean to their mother, but she didn't dare. She thought she looked like a good person. She cried a lot, and their mother did, too. And as they all drank tea together, and talked, they realized that she reminded them a lot of their mother. She even sounded like her.

They had a lovely time together, and finally Monika stood up, as Daphne looked at her with interest.

"What are we supposed to call you?" It was a sensible question for an eight-year-old. Amadea had wondered about it too.

"Would Oma be all right?" Monika asked hesitantly, glancing first at them and then Beata. She hadn't earned it, but it was an endearing term for grandmother. "I'd be honored if you'd call me that." Both girls nodded, she hugged them both before she left, and then held Beata in her arms. They couldn't get enough of each other.

"Will you come again?" Beata asked softly as she stood in the doorway.

"Of course," her mother answered. "Whenever you like. I'll call you in a few days," she promised, and Beata knew she would. She had always kept her promises, and Beata sensed that she still would.

"Thank you, Mama," Beata said, and hugged her one last time.

"I love you, Beata," her mother whispered, kissed her cheek, and finally left. It had been an extraordinary afternoon, for all of them.

After her grandmother left, Amadea came to find her mother. Beata was sitting alone in the living room, lost in thought.

"Mama?" Beata looked up with a smile.

"Yes, sweetheart. What did you think?"

"I think it's sad that she was gone for so long. You can see that she loves you a lot."

"I love her too. I'm just glad she came back, and that she got to meet you."

"I hate your father for what he did to you," Amadea said in an icy voice, and her mother nodded. She didn't disagree with her, but she didn't hate him. She never had, although her father had caused her untold grief, as he had her mother. His decision to banish her had taken a huge toll on them all, and probably him too, although he would never admit it. But he and Beata had always been close. It had been a huge blow to him when she left. It was the ultimate betrayal, in his eyes. Beata had never expected her banishment to last the rest of their lives. But even if she'd known it before, she would still have married Antoine.

"Don't hate anyone," Beata said quietly. "It's too much work. And it only poisons you. I learned that a long time ago." Amadea nodded, as she listened to her. She suspected what her mother had just said was true. But she still thought her mother was a remarkable person for not hating her father. Amadea was sure that in her shoes, she would.

Amadea sat down on the couch where her grandmother had been, and hugged her mother close, just as Beata had hugged her mother, and was so grateful to have been able to do so after all these years.

"I love you, Mama," Amadea whispered, just as Beata had. It was an endless chain of echoes and bonds that went on and on. And in the end, in spite of distance and time, and unspeakable differences, it was an unbreakable bond. Her mother had proven that to her that afternoon.

9

FOR THE NEXT TWO YEARS, BEATA'S MOTHER came to visit them once a week. It became a tradition and a ritual that Beata came to count on, and for each of them, a precious gift. Beata and Monika got to know each other in ways they never had when she was young. She was a grown woman and a mother now, with children of her own, and both of them had suffered inordinately and grown wiser with time. Monika had even approached Jacob once and tried to get him to relent about their daughter—she said she had seen her on the street with two young girls—and his eyes were instantly fierce as he looked at her.

"I don't know what you're talking about,

Monika. Our daughter died in 1916." The
subject was closed. He was made of stone.
She never dared to bring it up again but
contented herself with their visits, as did
Beata. She no longer hoped to see the others again. Having her mother back in her life
was enough. She was grateful for that.

Her mother brought her photographs.
Brigitte was still beautiful, and she was living at home again, with her children. Their
mother was worried about her, said she
went to too many parties, stayed in bed all
day and drank too much, and she wasn't interested in her children. All she wanted was
another husband, but most of the men she
went out with were married to someone
else. Horst and Ulm were both doing well,
although one of Ulm's children was frail and
often sick, and Monika worried about her.
She had a problem with her heart. And during the years of their visits, she developed a
deep attachment to Beata's girls. Amadea
thought her grandmother was interesting
and intelligent, but she never quite forgave
her for allowing Jacob to banish their
mother. She thought it was cruel, and hung
back from her grandmother as a result. But
Daphne was young enough to fall unre-

servedly in love with her. She loved having a grandmother as well as a mother and sister. She didn't remember her father, and hers was an entirely female world. As was Beata's. She had never looked at another man since Antoine died, although she was still beautiful. She said that the memories of the years she'd spent with him were enough to last her a lifetime, and she wanted no one else. In 1935, two years after the visits with her mother began, she turned forty and her mother sixty-five. They were a great comfort to each other. The world had become a frightening place, although it had not touched them. Yet.

Amadea often spoke with outrage over the growing anti-Semitism in Germany. Jews had been banned from the German Labor Front, and were no longer allowed to have health insurance. They could no longer obtain law degrees, and had been banned from the military. It was a sign of things to come. Beata feared it would get worse before it would get better. Even actors and performers had to join special unions, and were rarely given work. The signs of the times were increasingly frightening.

Monika spoke to Beata about it quietly

one afternoon when they were alone, before
the girls got home from school. She was
worried about Beata's papers, and even the
children's. Even though she knew that
Beata was now Catholic and had been for
nineteen years, she had nonetheless been
born Jewish and the girls were half Jewish.
She was afraid it could make trouble for
them if things got worse. Poorer Jews, and
those without power and connections, had
been shipped off to work camps for the past
two years. Although Jacob insisted it
could never happen to them. Those being sent away were "marginals," or so the
Nazis claimed. Convicts, criminals, loiter-
ers, Gypsies, unemployed, troublemakers,
Communists, radicals, and people who
couldn't support themselves. But now and
then people they knew remotely were
caught up in it. Monika had a cleaning
woman whose brother had been sent to the
camp at Dachau, and subsequently her entire family was sent away, but admittedly her
brother was a political activist, who had
printed leaflets against the Nazis, so he had
brought it on himself and his family. But still,
Monika was deeply concerned. Little by little, Jews were being squeezed out of pro-

ductive society, singled out, and hampered at every turn. If things got worse, she didn't want anything to happen to Beata and the girls. And Beata had thought of it herself. They had no one to protect them and, if trouble happened, nowhere to turn.

"I don't think they'll cause problems for people like us, Mama," Beata said quietly. Monika always worried about how thin she was too. She had always been slight, but in recent years she was wraithlike, and without makeup her face was startlingly pale. She had worn black and no other color since Antoine's death. And overnight, it had turned her into a seemingly much older woman. She had closed her doors to the world, and all she had in her life now was her children. And at last, her mother once again.

"What about the children's papers?" Monika asked with concern.

"They don't really have any. All they have are student cards with 'Vallerand' on them, they were born Catholic. I'm Catholic. Our parish knows us well. I don't think it ever occurs to anyone that I wasn't born Catholic. And since we came here from Switzerland, I think some people think we're

Swiss. Even my marriage certificate to Antoine shows that we were both Catholic when we married. My passport expired years ago, and the girls never had any. Amadea was a baby when we came back, and she came in on mine. No one's going to pay any attention to a widow with two daughters with a noble French name. I'm listed everywhere as the Comtesse de Vallerand. I think we're safe, as long as we don't draw attention to ourselves. I worry more about the rest of you."

Everyone in Cologne knew the Wittgensteins and that they were Jewish. The fact that they had banished Beata two decades before and listed her as dead would protect her in a way, and her mother was grateful for that now. The rest of the family was far more visible, which was both good and bad. They assumed that the Nazis were not going to single out a family as respectable as theirs to persecute. As many were, they were convinced that it was the little people, the loose ends of society that they were after, as Jacob said. But anti-Semitism had certainly become the order of the day, and both her sons admitted that they were concerned. Both Horst and Ulm worked at

the bank with Jacob, who was thinking of re-
tiring. He was seventy years old. In the photographs Beata now saw of him, he looked
distinguished but ancient. She worried that in
disappointing him, she had contributed to his
looking so old. Unlike her mother, he looked
older than his years. Amadea refused to even
look at the photographs of him. And Daphne
said he looked scary. Their Oma wasn't.

She always brought them little presents,
which delighted them. Over time, she had
given Beata a few small pieces of her jewelry. She couldn't give her anything important, for fear that Jacob would notice. She
told him she had lost the small things, and
he chided her for being careless. But he
was often forgetful now, too, so he didn't
scold her too much. They were both getting
old.

The only real concern Beata had about
their Jewish origins was Amadea's desire to
go to university. She was desperate to
study philosophy and psychology, and literature, as her mother had wanted to do before her, and wasn't allowed to by her father.
Now it was the Nazis keeping Amadea from
it. Beata knew that if Amadea tried to go to
university, they would discover she was half

Jewish. The risk was too great. She would have to show not only her birth certificate, which was benign and showed both her parents to be Catholic at the time of her birth in Switzerland, but she would have to show papers as to her parents' racial origins. Antoine was no problem, but that was the only instance in which Beata's birth as a Jew was likely to surface, and Beata couldn't let that happen. She never explained it to Amadea, but Beata was adamant that she didn't want her going to university. It was too dangerous for them all, and the only way in which Beata could imagine their being put at risk. Even as a half-Jew, Amadea would be in serious trouble, as Beata had discussed with her mother. So Beata was intransigent about it. She told Amadea that in troubled times, a university was not the place to be, particularly for a woman. It was full of radicals and Communists and all the people who were getting into trouble with the Nazis, and being sent to work camps. She could even be caught in a riot, and her mother refused to let that happen.

"That's ridiculous, Mama. We're not Communists. I just want to study. No one's going to send me to a work camp." She couldn't believe her mother was being so stupid. And to her own ears, Beata sounded like the echo of her father.

"Of course not," Beata said firmly, "but I don't want you tossed in with those kinds of people. You can wait a few years, if that's really what you want, until things settle down. Right now there is too much unrest all over Germany. I don't want you in danger, even indirectly." And there was no question, applying to college would put her in great danger, but not for any reason she suspected. Her mother didn't intend to tell her she had been born Jewish, and that Amadea and her sister were half Jewish. It was no one's business. Not even theirs. She was adamant that the girls didn't need to know. The fewer people who knew, the safer it kept them, as far as she was concerned. No one in their world knew that Beata had been born Jewish. Her complete isolation and banishment from her family for nineteen years had in effect kept it a secret, and certainly none of them looked it, least of all Amadea, with her tall blond blue-eyed Aryan looks. But even Beata and Daphne looked Christian, although their hair was dark, but their features were delicate and fine and their eyes blue, in just the ways people associated with Christians, given their stereotypical views of Jews.

Amadea had been arguing about the university issue for months, but her mother remained rigid, much to their grandmother's relief. It was bad enough worrying about her other children who were openly Jewish, without agonizing over Beata and her daughters, too. And as was all too evident, without Antoine, Beata and the girls had no one to protect them or take care of them. Beata and her children were alone in the world, in part due to Beata's grief over losing her husband, and their having lost both their families decades before, which in the end had made her reclusive. She had no ties to anyone, except the girls, and the Daubignys whom she saw rarely. It was a lonely life for her. And the strife between her and Amadea over not allowing her to attend university was considerable. It put Amadea and her mother into pitched battle and fierce opposition, but Beata was relentless. There was no way for Amadea to disobey her, since her mother held the purse strings. Beata had suggested that she study on her own, until things calmed down in the schools. She would be finishing her school in June, two months after she turned eighteen. At not quite ten, Daphne had years to go, and still seemed like a baby to her mother and sister. She hated it when Amadea and her mother argued, and complained about it to her Oma, whom she adored. Daphne thought she was pretty, and she loved her jewelry and elegant clothes. She always let Daphne go through her handbags and play with the treasures she found there, like powder and lipstick. She let her wear her jewelry while she was there, and try on her hats. Monika was as elegant as ever. Beata no longer cared, and Daphne hated the dreary dresses and constant black her mother wore. It looked so sad.

Amadea was about to turn eighteen, when her grandmother failed to come for her weekly visits for two weeks in a row. She managed to call the first time, and told Beata she wasn't well. The next time, she simply failed to show up. Beata was worried sick, and finally dared to call her. A female voice she didn't recognize answered the phone. It was one of the maids, who re-

turned and said that Mrs. Wittgenstein was
too ill to come to the phone. Beata spent
the next week in an agony of concern over
her, and was immensely relieved the following week when her mother showed up. But
she looked extremely unwell. She was
deathly pale, and her face had a grayish
cast to it, she was having difficulty walking,
and seemed frighteningly short of breath.
Beata lent her a strong arm as she led her
into the living room and helped her to sit
down. For a moment, Monika could hardly
breathe, and then seemed better after a cup
of tea.

"Mama, what is it? What does the doctor
say?" Beata asked, with a look of deep concern.

"It's nothing." She smiled valiantly, but
was unconvincing. "It happened a few years
ago, and it went away after a while. It's
something with my heart. Old age, I guess.
The machinery is wearing out." But sixty-
five did not seem so old, and Beata thought
she looked ghastly. If things had been different, she would have spoken to her father
about it. Monika said he was concerned
too. She was going back to the doctor the
following day for more tests. But she said

she wasn't worried. It was just annoying. But she looked a lot worse than annoyed. This time, when she left, Beata walked her all the way out to the street to make sure that she got there safely, and hailed a taxi for her. Her mother always came in a cab, so their driver could not tell Jacob where she'd been. She trusted no one with their secret, for fear that her husband would stop her if he found out. And he would have been livid with her. She had been forbidden to ever see Beata again, and he expected his wife and children to obey him.

"Mama, promise me you'll go back to the doctor tomorrow," Beata said anxiously before her mother got into the cab. "Don't do something silly like cancel the appointment." She knew her mother.

"Of course not." Monika smiled at her, and Beata was relieved to see that she seemed to be breathing easier than she had when she'd arrived. Daphne had given her an enormous kiss when she left, and Amadea a distracted hug. Monika looked at her daughter for a long moment before she got into the waiting taxi. "I love you, Beata. Be careful and take care of yourself. I worry about you all the time." There were tears in

her eyes as she said it. She hated the fact
that her daughter had been shunned for
nineteen years, like a criminal to be punished for unpardonable crimes. In Monika's
mind, between people who loved each
other, there were none. And Beata always
looked so sad. Once Antoine died, she had
simply lost too much.

"Don't worry about us, Mama. We're fine."
She knew they were both overly concerned
about her origins and the girls' papers. No
one had ever questioned them about it.
"Take care of yourself." Beata hugged her
again. "And remember how much I love
you. Thank you for coming." She was always grateful to her for visiting them, particularly now, when she didn't feel well.

"I love you," Monika whispered again, and
put something into Beata's hand. Beata
didn't know what it was, as her mother
slipped onto the seat of the taxi. Beata
closed the door, and waved to her as they
drove off. She stood watching the cab disappear into the traffic for a long time, and
then looked into her hand, at what her
mother had left there. It was a small diamond ring that she had worn all her life, and
had been a gift from her own mother, who

had received it from hers. It was traveling down the generations, and when she thought of her mother's hands, Beata always thought of that ring. It touched her deeply as she slipped it onto her finger next to her wedding ring, and then it made her shiver for a moment. Why had her mother given it to her now? Perhaps she was sicker than even Beata realized, or maybe her mother was just worried. She said she'd had the same problem before, and it had gone away. But Beata worried about her all that night.

When she got up the next day, on a whim, she decided to call her, just to make sure that she was all right and still planning to go to the doctor. She didn't trust her to keep the appointment. She knew how much her mother hated doctors, and how independent she was. It was always awkward calling her, and Beata had only done so a few times in the last two years. But she knew her father would be at the office. And after nineteen years, there were no servants left in the house who would recognize her voice.

She dialed the number nervously, and noticed that her hands were trembling. It was always upsetting calling there, and this time

a man's voice answered. Beata assumed it
was the butler, and asked for her mother in
a businesslike voice. There was a long silence in response, and then he asked who
was calling. Not knowing what else to do,
she gave Amadea's name, as she had before.

"I regret to inform you, madame, that Mrs.
Wittgenstein is in the hospital. She col-
lapsed last night."

"Oh my God, how awful . . . is she all
right? Where did they take her?" She
sounded distraught and not businesslike at
all. The butler gave her the name of the hospital, but only because she sounded so distressed about it, and he assumed, whoever
she was, that she wanted to send his employer flowers. "She can only have visits
from her family," he said to make sure she
didn't try to visit her, and Beata nodded.

"Of course." A moment later she hung up,
and stared into space as she sat next to the
phone in her hallway. She didn't know how,
but she knew she had to see her. What if
she died? Her father couldn't possibly refuse to let her see her mother in extremis.
He just couldn't. She didn't even stop to
dress properly. She just put a black coat

over the black dress she was wearing, jammed on a hat, and grabbed her handbag and ran out the door. Within minutes, she was in a taxi, heading toward the hospital, to see her mother. And as they drove there, without thinking, she touched the ring her mother had given her the day before. Thank God she had seen her, she thought to herself, praying that her mother would recover.

She made her way into the hospital, and a nurse at the front desk told her which floor and which room to go to. She was in the best hospital in Cologne, and there were nurses and doctors and well-dressed people everywhere. Beata realized that she looked less than elegant in the haphazard clothes she wore, but she didn't care. All she wanted was to see her mother and be there for her. And as soon as she got off the elevator and turned into the first corridor, she saw them. Both her brothers and her sister and her father, standing in the hallway. There were two women with them that she didn't recognize, who she assumed were her sisters-in-law. Feeling her heart pound, she approached the group. She was within a foot of them, before Brigitte turned and saw her, and looked at her with wide eyes. She said nothing as the others noticed her expression, and slowly they each turned to see Beata, as did, finally, her father. He looked straight at Beata and said nothing. Absolutely nothing, and made no move toward her.

"I came to see Mama," she said in the terrified voice of a child, wanting to reach forward and hug him, and even beg his forgiveness if she had to. But he appeared to be made of stone. The rest of her family stood in shocked silence, watching her.

"You are dead, Beata. And your mother is dying." There were tears in his eyes as he said it, for his wife, not his daughter. He looked icy toward Beata.

"I want to see her."

"Dead people do not visit the dying. We sat shiva for you."

"I'm sorry. I am truly sorry. You can't keep me from seeing her," she said in a choked voice.

"I can and I will. The shock of seeing you would kill her." She realized how pathetic she must look in her old dress and coat, and her hat slightly askew. All she had thought of was getting there quickly, not how she looked. She could see in the faces of her sister and brothers, and even the women with them, that they felt sorry for her. She looked like what she was and had become, a misfit and an outcast. Her father did not ask how she knew that her mother was in the hospital. He didn't want to know. All he knew was that the woman who had been his daughter was dead as far as he was concerned. The one standing before him was a stranger, and he did not want to know her.

"You can't do this, Papa. I have to see her." Beata was crying, and his face was immovable, just as it had been when she left them. If anything, he looked harder.

"You should have thought of that nineteen years ago. If you do not leave, I will have you removed by the hospital." She looked and felt like a madwoman as she stood there, and she could easily imagine her father having her thrown out. "We do not want you. Nor would your mother. You do not belong here."

"She's my mother," Beata said, convulsed with tears.

"She was your mother. You are nothing to her now." At least Beata knew that was not true. The past two years of weekly visits had proved it, and she was so grateful they had had that, and that her mother had come to know and love her children, and they her.

"It is so wrong of you to do this, Papa. She would never forgive you for it. Nor will I." This time she knew she wouldn't. What he was doing was too cruel.

"It was wrong of you to do what you did. I have never forgiven you," he said without remorse.

"I love you," Beata said softly, and then looked at the others. They had not moved or said a single word. She saw that Ulm had turned away, and Brigitte was crying softly, but held out no hand to her. And none of them tried to convince their father to let Beata see her mother. They were too afraid. "I love Mama. I have always loved you. All of you. I never stopped loving you. And Mama loves me, just as I love her," Beata said fiercely.

"Leave now!" Her father spat the words at her, looking as though he hated her for tugging at his heart. It was impossible to fathom what he felt. "Go!" he shouted at her, pointing down the corridor from where

she'd come. "You are dead to us, and always will be." She stood looking at him for
a long moment, shaking from head to foot,
defying him as she had once before. She
was the only one who would. She had done
it the first time for Antoine, and now for her
mother. But she knew there was no way he
would allow her into her mother's room. She
had no choice but to go, before they physi-
cally threw her out. She looked at him one
last time, and then wheeled around and
walked slowly down the hallway with her
head down. She turned to look at them one
last time before she strode around the corner, and when she did, they were all gone.
They had gone into her mother's room,
without her.

She was crying as she rode down in the
elevator, and sobbed all the way back to her
home. She called the hospital every hour
through the afternoon to inquire about her
mother's condition, and at four o'clock they
told her. Her mother was dead. Beata sat
staring into space as she set the phone
down. It was over. Her last tie with her family had been severed and the mother she
loved was gone. She could still hear the
echo of her mother's voice the day before.

"I love you, Beata." And then she had hugged her tight. "I love you too, Mama," Beata whispered. And she knew she always would.

10

BEATA ATTENDED HER MOTHER'S FUNERAL THE next day, and observed it from a distance. She wore a fur coat, a good black dress, and a beautiful black hat Antoine had bought her before he died. She knew her mother would have been proud of the way she looked. And on her finger, she wore her mother's ring. She would never take it off again. Ever.

Beata sat riveted as she listened to the prayers, and prayed with them. According to Jewish tradition, Monika had to be buried within a day, and was. Beata followed them to the cemetery, and stood far away from them. They didn't even know she was there. She was like a ghost, watching them, as they each poured a shovel of dirt onto her mother's coffin after they lowered it into the ground. After they left, she went and kneeled beside the grave, and put a small pebble beside it, as a gesture of respect, according to tradition. She didn't know what she was saying, until she heard herself saying the Our Father. She knew her mother wouldn't mind. She stayed for a long time, and then she went home, feeling dead inside. As dead as her father said she was.

Amadea looked at her sadly when she got home, and put her arms around her. "I'm sorry, Mama." She had told the girls the night before, and they had cried. In their own way, they each loved their grandmother, although they had always had conflicted feelings, particularly Amadea, about the way their grandparents had treated their mother for marrying their father. It seemed wrong to them, and Beata agreed that it was. But she loved her mother anyway. And even her father. They were her parents.

Beata went to her room early that night, and lay on her bed, thinking back to all that had happened, and her early days with Antoine. It was a lot to think about, and absorb, a lifetime that had been worthwhile, though hard. She had paid a high price for love. Losing her mother reminded her that she had no one left now but her daughters. Her father had made that clear. Her whole life was them. She had no life of her own.

It was a month later in June when Amadea took her breath away, yet again. She heard the news as one more death blow to her heart. In some ways, it was like losing her mother, except that at least Amadea would be alive.

"I am going into the convent, Mama," Amadea said quietly, on her last day of school. Nothing had prepared Beata for the announcement her elder daughter made. She looked at her as though she had been shot, but Amadea's eyes were steady and calm. She had been waiting to announce this decision for months, and had grown more certain every day. There had been nothing hasty or frivolous about the choice she'd made.

"You're not," Beata said, as though there was no question of it. None. To her own ears, she sounded like her father, but she was not going to let this happen. Even Antoine wouldn't have wanted that, and he was a devoted Catholic. "I won't let you do that."

"You can't stop me." Amadea sounded like an adult for the first time. Her voice was solid, like rock. She had agonized too much over the decision to feel any uncertainty at all now. She was absolutely certain she had a vocation, and no one could shake her faith, not even the mother she loved. This was not a pitched battle to go to university. This was a grown woman who knew what she wanted, and was going to do it. Beata was frightened at the tone of Amadea's voice, as much as by the look in her eyes.

"Your father wouldn't want that," she reasoned, hoping to sway Amadea, by evoking her father's name. It didn't work.

"You don't know that. You gave up everything to marry him, because you believed in what you were doing. I believe in this. I have a vocation." She said it as though speaking of the Holy Grail. In truth, she had found all she wanted and needed. After talking to her priest for months, she was sure beyond a doubt, and it was written all over her.

"Oh my God." Beata sat down heavily and stared at her daughter. "You're too young to know that. You're bored, and you think it sounds romantic." Beata also knew that

Edith Stein had become her role model, and she had been in a convent for two years.

"You don't know what you're saying," Amadea said calmly. "I'm going into the Carmelites. I've already talked to them. You can't stop me, Mama." She repeated what she had said in the beginning. She didn't sound like a petulant child, but a woman with a holy purpose.

"That's a cloistered order. You will live like a prisoner for the rest of your life, shut away from the world. You're a beautiful young girl, you should have a husband and babies."

"I want to be a nun," she said clearly. Beata shuddered. Fortunately, Daphne was at a friend's, so she didn't hear them.

"You're doing it because Edith Stein did. She was a forty-two-year-old woman when she went in. She'd had a life. She knew what she was doing. You don't. You're too young to make this decision."

"I'll have plenty of time to find out," Amadea said sensibly. "It takes eight years before you take final vows." She knew all about it. "Mama, it's the life I want." Her eyes never left her mother's, and were filled with quiet determination, which terrified Beata.

"Why? *Why?*" Beata wailed, with tears running down her face. "You're beautiful and young, you have your whole life ahead of you. Why would you do that?"

"I want to serve God, and this is the best way I know how. I think this is what He wants. I want to be the bride of Christ, just the way you loved Papa. This is who I want. You're religious, Mama. You go to church. How can you not understand?" Amadea looked hurt that her mother was so unhappy about it, and something in her eyes reminded Beata of her own mother, when she told her about Antoine. Her mother had felt betrayed. And now so did Beata. It made her feel like her father, rigid and unyielding, and she didn't want to be that. But she didn't want her daughter going into the convent either. To Beata, it seemed abnormal.

"I admire you for your devotion," Beata said quietly, "but it's a hard life. I want something better than that for you. A man to take care of you, children who love you." And then she thought of Daphne. "What will your sister and I do without you?" She was devastated at the prospect.

"I will pray for you. That's far better than

anything I could do here. I will be of much greater use praying for the world than watching the terrible things people do to destroy each other, man's terrible unkindness to their fellow man." Amadea was deeply upset by the current injustices to the Jews, and had been since they began. It went against everything she believed, and she had strong beliefs. Beata loved her for it. But not this. Not this terrible waste of her daughter becoming a nun, locked away in a convent like a prisoner. "Will you think about it, Mama? Please? It's all I want . . . You can't stop me, but I want you to give me your blessing." It was exactly what she had asked her parents for when she married Antoine. Now Amadea was asking her blessing to follow Christ. It was a terrible decision for Beata. "I love you," Amadea said softly and put her arms around her as Beata sighed through her tears.

"How did this happen? When did you make this decision?"

"I talked to Ella's sister about it before she did it. I always thought I had a vocation, but I wasn't sure. I talked to our priest about it for months. Now I know it's right for me, Mama. I'm sure." She looked beautiful as she said it, which tugged at Beata's heart more than ever.

"Why? How can you be sure?"

"I just am. I feel so certain about it." As her mother looked at her, she saw eyes full of peace. Like a young saint. But Beata could not bring herself to be happy about it. It seemed a terrible waste, and a tragedy to her. To Amadea, it was a gift. The only one she wanted, along with her mother's blessing.

"When do you want to do this?" Beata hoped there would be time to dissuade her. Like maybe a year.

"I'm going in next week. There's no reason for me to wait any longer. I finished school." She had been waiting for that to tell her mother, but now it was happening very quickly.

"Does Daphne know about this?" Beata asked, and Amadea shook her head. Daphne was only ten, but the girls were close.

"I wanted to tell you first. I was hoping you could be happy for me, after you got used to the idea." It was so exactly what she had gone through with her parents over Antoine. Even the words they were using were the

same, except that she was not threatening
her daughter. She was begging her to rethink it, which was what her own mother
had done too. They thought the road she
had chosen was too hard, which was precisely what Beata thought of her daughter. It
was the echo of the past again. History re-
peating itself. The unbroken chain of repeti-
tion.

Beata lay awake in her bed all that night,
hearing the echoes of her past, reliving all
the terrible arguments with her parents,
knowing she was right, the agonizing day
when she left the house, and going to him in
Switzerland finally, and how perfect it had
been. For her. That was the point. The only
correct argument. That each person had to
follow their own destiny, whatever that was.
For her, it had been Antoine. Perhaps for
Amadea, it was the Church. And why had
they named her that, as though by some
terrible intuition? Loved of God. Beata
wished that He didn't love her quite so
much that He had called her, but perhaps
He had. Who was she to know? Who was
she to judge? What right did she have to try
to change her daughter's destiny and make
decisions for her? She had no more right to

do that than her father. Perhaps love meant sacrificing what you wanted for them, in order to let them follow their dream. And as morning came, Beata knew that she had no right to stop Amadea if that was what she wanted. If it wasn't right, she would have to find that out for herself. At least she had eight years to do it. She could always change her mind, although Beata knew she wouldn't. Her parents had probably hoped that she would leave Antoine too. But they had been so happy. He was her destiny. Just as this was Amadea's. Beata had never expected to have a daughter who was a nun, nor had Antoine. But she had the feeling that he would have let her do it too. What right did they have not to?

She looked ravaged when she went to Amadea's room before breakfast. Amadea could see in her mother's face, even before Beata spoke, that she had won, and held her breath as she waited to hear it.

"I won't stop you. I want you to be happy," Beata said, looking heartbroken, but with eyes filled with love. "I won't do to you what my parents did to me. You have my blessing, because I love you and I want your happiness, whatever that is to you." It was the ultimate gift to her, and the ultimate sacrifice to herself, which was what she thought parenting should be about. That was the hard part. The important things were never easy. That was what made them important.

"Thank you, Mama . . . thank you . . . thank you!" Amadea's eyes were filled with light, as she hugged her mother. She looked truly euphoric, and they had never been closer. There was no question of how much or how deeply they loved each other.

It was harder telling Daphne, who cried horribly. She didn't want Amadea to leave them, nor did Beata.

"We'll never see you," Daphne wailed miserably. "Ella never sees her sister, they won't let her. And she can't touch her or hug her." Beata's heart sank at the prospect.

"Yes, you will. You can come twice a year, and I can touch you through a little window. Besides, we can hug a lot now and that will last us for a long time." Amadea looked sorry for her, but remained convinced. And Daphne was inconsolable for the next week. Amadea was sad to leave them, but she seemed happier every day, as her entrance into the convent drew closer.

Hoping to make it easier for Daphne,

Beata asked Amadea to wait a few more weeks, but she shook her head. "It'll only make it worse, Mama. She'll get used to it. She has you." But that was hardly the same thing. Amadea was the light and joy in Daphne's life, as she was in Beata's. Beata had been solemn and depressed and withdrawn much of the time since her husband died. "It will do you good, too. You can do things with her, like go to movies, or the park, or museums. You need to get out more." Amadea had done all those things with her sister for years. Beata did very little. She was too depressed, and spent most of her time in her room. She wasn't sure she was up to what she had to do now. But someone had to do it. Antoine was gone. Her mother was gone. And now Amadea would be gone too. Beata felt almost as though Amadea would be dead to them, if they could not see her every day, or hold her in their arms ever again. It was grim.

"Can you write to us?" Beata asked, feeling panicked.

"Of course. Although I'll be busy. But I'll write to you as often as I can." It was as though she were leaving on a trip, for the rest of her life. Like going to Heaven. Or the first way station to get there. Beata couldn't imagine it, or wanting to do it. She had become a devout Catholic, but she still couldn't imagine wanting to go into religious orders. It seemed like a terribly restrictive life, but Amadea could hardly wait.

Beata and Daphne drove her there on the day she left. She wore a simple navy blue dress, and the hat she wore to church. It was a brilliantly sunny day, and Beata had rarely felt as depressed. Daphne cried all the way to the convent, as Amadea held her hand. When they got out of the car, Beata stood and looked at her for a long time, as though drinking her in for the last time, and carving her memory on her heart. The next time she would see her, she would look different. And be someone else.

"Always know how much I love you. How much you mean to me, and how proud I am of you. You are my gift from God, Amadea. Be happy and safe. And if it isn't right for you, it's all right to change your mind. No one will think less of you for it." Beata hoped she would.

"Thank you, Mama," Amadea said quietly, but knew she wouldn't. She knew to her very soul how right this was, and didn't doubt it for a second. She took her mother in her arms then, and held her. She held her like a grown woman, who knew what she was doing, and had no regrets. Just as Beata had done the day she left her mother to join Antoine. "Go with God," Amadea whispered as she held her, and tears rolled down Beata's cheeks and she nodded. It was Amadea who seemed like the adult now and not the child.

"You too," Beata said in a whisper, as Amadea kissed her little sister and smiled down at her. Amadea looked sad to leave them, but beyond that there was an over- whelming sense of joy and peace.

She had brought no suitcase with her. She had brought nothing except the clothes she wore, which they would dispose of the mo- ment she took them off. They would give them to the poor. She could bring no pos- sessions, and would eventually take vows of poverty, chastity, and obedience, all of which suited her. She was not frightened of what she was doing. She had never been happier in her life, and it was written all over her face. It was the same look Beata had worn when she met Antoine at the train sta- tion in Lausanne, and their life had been beginning. The same look she had worn the night Amadea was born. This was the beginning for Amadea. Not the end, as her mother feared.

She hugged each of them one more time, and then turned to ring the bell. She was ready. They answered the door quickly, and a young nun opened a tiny peephole, and then the door, without showing herself. And in an instant, Amadea was gone, as she stepped through the door without looking back at them. When it was closed, Beata and Daphne stood on the street alone, looking at each other, and then they clung to each other. This was all that was left now, all they had. Each other. A widow and a little girl. Amadea had her whole life ahead of her, in a life that would be far, far from them.

11

WHEN AMADEA ENTERED THE CONVENT, SHE WAS taken directly to the robing room by the young nun who had let her in. She said not a word to Amadea, but her peaceful smile and her warm eyes greeted her. Amadea understood. There was something deeply soothing about not having to say anything to her. She felt instantly as though she had entered a safe place, and knew it was the right one for her.

The nun looked at her, assessed her tall thin frame, and nodded as she set out a plain black garment that would reach her ankles, and a short white cotton veil that would cover her hair. It was not the habit of the order, but Amadea knew that it would be six months before she would be allowed to wear it, and only then if they felt she had earned it. It could take a lot longer, as the Mother Superior had explained to her before she went in, and the older nuns would have to vote on it. What she would wear in the meantime would identify her as a postulant. She would not receive the black veil of the order, until she took her solemn vows after eight years.

The nun left her alone for a moment to change all her clothes, down to her underwear. She had left a pair of rough sandals for her, which were the only shoes she would wear from now on, with bare feet. The order was discalced, which meant that they did not wear proper shoes, as part of the discomforts which they embraced.

Amadea put on what they left her, with a feeling of excitement. She wouldn't have been happier if she had been putting on her wedding gown, and she had the same feeling her mother had the day she had worn the white linen dress she'd made of lace tablecloths for her wedding. This was the beginning of a new life for Amadea, in some ways it was like being engaged to Christ. The

wedding would take eight years to prepare.
Even now, she could hardly wait.

The nun came back in a few minutes and
everything Amadea had worn coming in disappeared into a basket for the poor, including her good shoes. Her mother was keeping everything else for her, she said, in case
she changed her mind. More than that, she
was keeping it as one did the clothes and
possessions of dead children, out of senti-
ment, and the inability to part with them.
They meant nothing to Amadea now. Her
life was here.

Once dressed, she was led into the chapel
for prayers, with the other nuns. Afterward,
there was a long silence, during which the
community examined their consciences, as
they did each day, remembering the sins
they had committed, the unkind things
they'd thought of, the petty jealousies, the
longings they had for food or people or
comforts they had once thought were important and had to learn to strip themselves
of. It was a good place for Amadea to start,
as she reproached herself for her attachment to her mother and sister, more even
than to Christ. No one explained to her what

the silence meant, she had heard of it be-
forehand and used the time well.

While the other nuns ate lunch, she was
taken to the Mother Superior's office. She
would not eat until dinnertime that night,
which was the first sacrifice she would
make. As did the Mother Superior, in order
to talk to her.

"All is well, my child?" she asked kindly after greeting her with the words "Peace of
Christ," which Amadea repeated before she
spoke.

"Yes, thank you, Mother."

"We are happy to have you here." The
community was large these days. There
was no lack of vocations. Edith Stein joining
them two years earlier had not done them
any harm either. There had been more talk
of it than she liked, but it had awakened
others to their vocations, even as it had this
young girl. Edith Stein had become Teresa
Benedicta a Cruce the year before, and
Amadea would eventually meet her, although personal fascinations and admiration were strictly forbidden. They were a
community of sisters, not a collection of in-
dividuals with separate personalities and
their own ideas. They were here to serve

Christ and pray for the world, nothing more than that, and nothing less, as the Mother Superior reminded Amadea, and she said she understood.

"You will share a cell with three other sisters. We are silent except at meals and recreation, when you may speak about matters of the community, and nothing else. You will not have personal friends here. We are all friends of Christ." Amadea nodded again, in awe of her.

The Mother Superior was a tall spare woman with powerful eyes and a kind face. It was impossible to tell her age, and it would have been impertinent to do so. She was the mother who would guide them and guard them, and whom they must obey, as they would the Father who led them there. Entering Carmel brought her into a new family. No other existed now for her. She had been on loan to Beata, her father, and Daphne for eighteen years. Her time with them was done, her ties to them slight, except through prayer and occasional letters, out of kindness to them. She was told that she could write home once a week, as she had promised her mother she would do. But her work and chores must come first.

She was assigned to the laundry, and in her spare time she would scrub the kitchen down. If there was time left over, she would work in the garden, which was considered a privilege and an honor. The Mother Superior reminded her of the words of Saint Teresa of Àvila, that God reveals Himself to the heart in solitude. She was to work alone as much as possible, and pray constantly. She was to speak only at meals. The center and hub of her day and life was the sacrifice of the mass. "Remember that Saint Teresa taught us that the essence of prayer is not to think a lot, but to love a lot. You are here to love your sisters, and the world. And in time, if you have been blessed with a vocation, you will become the bride of God." It was an awesome responsibility and an honor beyond any that Amadea could imagine. This was why she was here. She had already thought of her name. She wanted to become Sister Teresa of Carmel. Until then, in her lowly state as postulant, she would be Sister Amadea. She was told she would be shown her cell that night after dinner. She already knew that one of the rules of the order was to abstain from meat perpetually, except if she was sick and a doctor prescribed it as necessary for her health. But even then, it was a sacrifice she could make, and most did. They fasted from September 14 till Easter every year. But food had never been important to Amadea, and she didn't care.

Lunch and recreation were over by the time Mother Teresa Maria Mater Domini had finished speaking to her, and she joined the other sisters for the litany of the Blessed Virgin, and tried to concentrate on it and not on all that the Mother Superior had said to her. There had been a lot to take in. There was reading afterward, and then she was sent to scrub down the kitchen before dinner. She was on her hands and knees for most of the afternoon, praying as she did so. And then she helped with the preparations for dinner. The nuns were constantly busy and working, and praying while they worked, which was why silence was so important. She was exhausted by the time they went to vespers, but exhilarated as they prayed in silence. And finally, the angelus announced dinner. She hadn't eaten since breakfast, and she had been too excited to eat much then. They ate beans and potatoes and vegetables for dinner, and fruit from the garden, while the nuns chatted

quietly over their food. There were a number
of girls Amadea's age, many of them wearing the garb of postulants, and others already wearing the habit of novices. Many
had come in even younger than she, or they
looked it. The nuns who already wore the
black veil of the order looked like saints to
her, with angelic faces, peaceful expressions, and warm, loving eyes. Amadea had
never been happier than she was here.
Many of them spoke kindly to her over dinner. And she saw that several of the younger
nuns were taking care of the elderly nuns,
some of whom were brought to dinner in
wheelchairs and sat chatting like grand-
mothers, flanked by their young aides.

After dinner and a brief half-hour of recreation, where they compared needlework
they were doing and vestments they were
making for the church, they prayed together
then for half an hour, and then prayed in silence for two hours until they prayed together for a last time and went to bed. They
had to be up at five-thirty and at prayer
again by six o'clock. They would pray then
for two hours, before mass at eight, followed by breakfast, and work until the daily
examination of conscience, and then lunch.

It was a full day, full of prayer and hard work. There was nothing about it that dismayed Amadea. She had known what she was coming to, and this was what she wanted. Her days and life would be full forever, and her heart light, in the bosom of Carmel.

When she entered her cell at ten o'clock that night, she saw the nuns whom she would share it with, two of them novices and another who was a postulant like her. They nodded their heads at each other, smiled, and turned the lights out to put on their nightgowns which were made of rough wool that had been washed a thousand times, and still scratched. There was no heating in their cells, and the gowns itched miserably, but it was a sacrifice they willingly made. They were to become the spouses of a crucified Christ, who had died on the cross in anguish for them. This was the least they could do for Him. Amadea knew she would get used to it in time. For an instant, she thought of the delicate silk and cotton nightgowns her mother had always made for her, and then reminded herself just as quickly that she would have to offer that thought up the next day during her examination of conscience. She could bring no such memories with her here. And whenever they intruded on her, she would have to do penance for it, and correct her thought as soon as it came to mind. She had no time to waste on mourning comforts of a past life.

She lay in bed that night, thinking of her mother and Daphne, and praying for them. She prayed that God would take good care of them, and keep them healthy and happy. And just for a moment, she felt tears sting her eyes, and reminded herself that she would have to pray about that, too. She was the monitor of her own conscience, and the porter at the door to her thoughts. She could allow nothing but thoughts of Christ in, as the Mother Superior had told her that day. She remembered them in her prayers, as she drifted off to sleep, and said a prayer for her grandmother who had died two months before and was in Heaven now.

And as she lay in bed that night, with Daphne lying next to her, having cried herself to sleep, Beata was thinking of her mother, too, and the child she had just lost to God. She prayed, as Amadea had, to keep her happy and safe. And then for no particular reason, she said a prayer for all Jews.

12

THE DAYS PASSED QUICKLY FOR AMADEA, FILLED with prayer and work. She was assigned to the kitchen and the laundry most of the time, although she worked in the garden once with Edith Stein. They had worked side by side in silence, and Amadea was just happy to be near her, and smiled at her from time to time. The thought came to her later that morning, in her examination of conscience, that she should have no personal interest in her. She avoided her thereafter, in an effort to clear her mind of the thought and what she knew of her, and admired in her, from the past. Sister Teresa Benedicta a Cruce was nothing more than one of her sisters in Carmel now, and not to be thought of as anything other than that.

She had regular letters from her mother and Daphne, and some small sense of what was going on in the world. The Nuremberg Race Laws against the Jews had been decreed in September, which made things even more difficult for them now. It gave Amadea something more to pray for. Her mother sent the entire convent oranges at Christmastime, which was an enormous treat. And in January the sisters voted to allow Amadea to begin her novitiate and bestowed on her the Holy Habit of Carmel, which felt like the most important day in Amadea's life. She was allowed to see her mother and Daphne in a brief visit after that. She beamed at them through the small grille, and her mother cried when she saw her in her habit, as Daphne stared at her.

"You don't look like you," Daphne said solemnly. She was almost scared of her, but not quite. And Beata saw instantly how happy she was, which nearly broke her heart.

"I'm not 'me.' I'm a nun." Amadea smiled at them. She could hardly wait to take her new name sometime in the coming year. "You both look wonderful."

"So do you," Beata said, staring at her, embracing her with her eyes. The three of them stuck their fingers through the grille to touch each other, but it was frustrating more than satisfying. Beata ached to hold her daughter in her arms, and knew she never would again.

"Are you coming home?" Daphne asked her hopefully, with enormous eyes, as Amadea smiled.

"I am home, sweetheart. How is school?"

"All right," Daphne said forlornly. Life wasn't the same without her. And their house was deathly quiet, although Beata was making an effort to spend more time with her. But they were both sad all the time. The house without Amadea seemed lifeless now. The spirit that had kept them all going and filled their days with sunlight was now here.

The visit was over all too quickly. And they didn't see her again until late in the year. Daphne was eleven and a half by then. Beata had taken her to the Olympics that summer, which had been terrific. Daphne had particularly loved the swimming, and had written all about it to her sister. By the time they saw her for that second time, she had become Sister Teresa of Carmel. Amadea de Vallerand no longer existed.

The following summer Sister Teresa of Carmel asked to make her temporary profession, which would bind her to the order by vows of poverty, chastity, and obedience. She was accepted by vote of the chapter and allowed to do so. She was still six years away from final vows. But already after her temporary profession, she felt as though she had been a nun all her life, after only two years. It was 1937.

The news of the world was disturbing that year, as Jews had been banned from countless professions, like teaching and dentistry. They could no longer be accountants. It was as though little by little Hitler's regime wanted to squeeze them out. They were being methodically removed from every arena, one by one. It gave the sisters of Carmel something to pray for. They had a lot to pray about these days.

In March of the following year, 1938, Nazi troops entered Austria and annexed it to Germany. The SS was put in charge of

Jewish affairs, and a hundred thousand Jews in Vienna were told to emigrate.

The following month, in Germany, Jews were told to register their wealth and property. Beata couldn't help wondering how this would affect her father and brothers. As far as she knew, they still owned and ran the bank.

Things got markedly worse over the summer, not long after Amadea renewed her temporary profession. By then she was working almost full-time in the garden, and sewing vestments for the church at night, according to her letters to her mother. In July, any Jewish person over the age of fifteen was told to apply for an identity card from the police, to be shown on demand to any member of the police, at any time. Jewish doctors were forbidden to practice. With the same regulations against dentists the previous year, most of Germany no longer had a doctor or a dentist, and countless Jews in serious professions were out of work.

Beata looked worried when she and Daphne saw Amadea in the fall. Amadea was stunned by how much Daphne had grown up. She was thirteen, and grew more beautiful each year. She had the same elfin beauty as her mother, in contrast to her much taller older sister, who smiled proudly at her through the grille, and brushed her cheek with a kiss.

Amadea teased Daphne about liking boys, which made her blush. Her mother had told her as much in a letter. There was a boy she had a crush on at school, and who liked her. But it was easy to see why. She was a lovely looking child, and she had an innocence about her that touched Amadea's heart. With their letters, they still managed to keep her a part of their lives. It was hard to believe Amadea had been in the convent for three years. Beata felt as though she had been gone forever, and yet at other times, it felt like only months. They still missed her terribly, but with so much ugliness happening all around them, in some ways Beata was relieved that she was safe. She had still had no problem herself, and didn't anticipate having one. As far as the world knew, she and Daphne were Catholics. She was a harmless widow with a young child, who needed nothing official, brought no attention to herself, and had escaped all official notice. But the same was not true of the Wittgensteins, who

were fully visible as Jews. Beata scanned
the papers every day to see if there was
news of her family or the bank, if they had
been asked to give it up. But so far, she had
seen nothing.

In October 1938, seventeen thousand
Jews of Polish origin were arrested in
Germany and sent back to Poland. Then
came Kristallnacht on November 9 and 10.
And the whole world changed. Joseph
Goebbels organized a night of terror that no
one would soon forget, and got rapidly out of
hand. It was the culmination of the smolder-
ing anti-Semitism of the past five years,
which finally burst into flame and became a conflagration out of control. Across
Germany, a thousand synagogues were
burned, seventy-six destroyed. Seven thousand Jewish businesses and homes were
destroyed and looted, a hundred Jews were
killed, and thirty thousand Jews were arrested and sent to concentration camps. All
Jewish businesses were ordered turned
over into Aryan hands. And in a single day, all
Jewish pupils were expelled from public
schools. And to add insult to injury, the Jews
were told that they would collectively have to
pay for the repairs of the damage done on

Kristallnacht. The hatred in Germany had turned into a blaze. Listening to the news after the night of terror, Beata sat in her living room in shock.

It was a full two days before she dared to leave the house, with the unrest in the streets. She took a taxi and had him drive past her father's bank and house. There were police cordons around the bank, which showed marked damage to the exterior. And all the windows in her parents' house were broken. Both buildings looked deserted. She had no idea where her family had gone, and she didn't dare to ask the neighbors. Even appearing to be interested in the fate of Jews could have drawn attention to herself, and would have put her and Daphne at risk.

It was another week before she mentioned something casually at her own bank, which was entirely staffed by Aryans. She said she was very glad she had taken funds out of the Wittgenstein bank several years before, as she imagined they were in a mess now.

"They're closed," her bank officer said bluntly. She couldn't even imagine what had happened to the funds they held for their customers, and wondered if the money had been seized by the Nazis, as most of their clients had been Jewish.

"I'm not surprised," Beata said wanly. "What do you suppose happened to them?" Beata asked, trying to sound like nothing more than a curious housewife chatting with her banker in troubled times. The entire country was talking about Kristallnacht. As was the world.

Her bank officer lowered his voice to a near whisper when he answered, "My boss knew the family. They were deported last Thursday." The day after Kristallnacht.

"How sad," Beata said, feeling as though she were about to faint and determined not to show it.

"I suppose so. But they're Jews after all. They deserve it. Most of them are criminals anyway. They probably tried to steal everyone's money." Beata nodded dumbly.

"Did they take all of them?"

"I think so. They usually do. Or now anyway. They didn't used to. But I think they've finally figured out that the women are as dangerous as the men. You can smell them." Beata felt sick as she listened.

"They were quite a prominent family," she said, putting her money away. She had come to cash a check exclusively for this purpose, to see what she could find out. And she had. Her whole family had been deported.

"Just be glad you took your money out of the bank. They'd have robbed you blind." She smiled, thanked him, and left, feeling wooden, and wondering how she could discover where they'd been sent. There was no way to do so without exposing herself, anyone who inquired was at risk. And then in a last attempt, she asked the cab to drive past the house on her way home. It looked yawning and dark, and she could see that it had been looted. There were pieces of furniture on the street, the antiques her mother had loved so much. Clearly, the house had been destroyed on Kristallnacht, and its inhabitants were gone. She wondered if they were hiding somewhere, if they had the sense to flee. In desperation, she stopped at her church on her way home, and spoke to the priest. She explained that she had known a Jewish family years before, and feared that they had fared badly on Kristallnacht.

"More than likely, I'm afraid." The priest looked grim. Catholics weren't entirely safe

from Hitler either. He had no great fondness
or respect for the Catholic Church. "We
must pray for them."

"I was wondering . . . do you suppose
there's any way of learning what happened
to them? Someone said they were deported. But they can't all have gone, at least
not the women and children."

"You never know," the priest said quietly.
"These are frightening times."

"Well, I didn't want to cause you any trouble," Beata said apologetically. "I just felt so
badly when I heard now at the bank. If you
hear anything, let me know."

"What was their name?"

"Wittgenstein. Of the bank." He nodded.
Everyone in Cologne knew the name. It was
a big statement if they had deported
them. But anything was possible now.
Kristallnacht had opened the doors of hell,
and unleashed demons beyond anyone's
worst fears. The inhumanity of man in its
most shocking form and colors.

"I'll let you know. I know a priest in that
parish. He may have heard something, even
though they're Jewish. Eventually these
things get around. People see. Even if
they're afraid to talk." Everyone was afraid

now. Even Catholics. "Be careful," he ad-
monished her as she got ready to leave.
"Don't try to go there yourself." He knew
she was a kind-hearted widow with a young
child, and might try to do something foolish.
And she had a special place in his heart
because of Amadea. The mother of a
Carmelite could only be a good woman, and
he knew she was.

It was the last week of November when he
stopped her on her way out of church.
Daphne was distracted talking to a friend.
And Beata had written nothing to Amadea
about her concerns.

"You were right," the priest said quietly as
he fell into step beside her. "They're all
gone."

"Who?" she asked, looking distracted.
She remembered asking him, but he was
being so mysterious that she wasn't sure if
this was her answer, or if he was talking
about something else.

"The family you asked about. They took all
of them. The next day. The entire family.
Apparently the man who owned the bank
had a daughter and two sons, and another
daughter who died years ago. My friend
knew him well. He saw him walking in the

neighborhood quite often, and he would stop to talk. He said he was a nice man. A widower. They took them all. The widower, the children, even the grandchildren. He thinks they were sent to Dachau, but there's no way to know. In any case, they're gone. The house will be given to an officer of the Reich most likely. I'll say a prayer for them," he said, and then moved on. There were a lot of stories like that these days. Beata felt as though she was in shock, and said not a word to Daphne as they walked home.

"Are you all right, Mama?" she asked quietly. Her mother seemed very nervous these days, but everyone was. Several children had been taken out of her school, and everyone had cried. The teacher had scolded them for it and said they were only Jews, and didn't deserve to go to school, which Daphne thought was very rude, and sick. Everyone deserved to go to school. Or at least that was what her mother said. "Is something wrong?"

"No, I'm fine," she said tersely, suddenly grateful for what the priest had said, that Jacob Wittgenstein had had a daughter who died years ago. With any luck at all, the world would assume she was dead. So far, no one had bothered them at all. She was a Catholic widow, with one young daughter, and another who was a nun. Thank God for Antoine. "I just heard a sad story about a family I knew who got deported after Kristallnacht," she said softly. Her entire family was gone. Her father, brothers, sister, their children, her brothers' wives. Gone. It was beyond belief. God only knew where they were and if they would survive. One heard horror stories about the camps. They were supposed to be work camps, but many died. And her father was not young. He was seventy-three years old. Her mother would have been sixty-eight, and Beata was suddenly grateful that she had been spared that. At least she had died in peace, even if Beata wasn't there to comfort her at the end. Even now, she had no malice against her father. What had just happened was far worse than anything she could have done, and not what any of them had deserved. No one did. And she was frightened herself. But for now, they were safe. She was sure of that.

"How awful," Daphne said quietly, thinking of what her mother had said.

"Don't say that to anyone," Beata snapped at her. "If you're sympathetic to the Jews, they'll hurt you," she said as they walked into the privacy of their own home. It was warm and comfortable and safe. That was essential now. She couldn't get the vision of the destroyed facade of her old home out of her head, the broken windows, and the antiques strewn all over the street.

"But you feel sorry for the Jews, don't you, Mama?" Daphne looked at her with innocent eyes.

"Yes," Beata said honestly, "but it's dangerous to say that out loud these days. Look what just happened. People are angry and confused. They don't know what they're doing. It's better to keep quiet. I want you to remember that, Daphne." Her mother looked at her sternly, and she nodded sadly.

"I will. I promise." But it seemed so mean. It all did. So cruel. And so wrong. She couldn't help thinking how frightening it would be to be Jewish. To lose your home. To have people take you away, or maybe even lose your parents. It made her shudder to think about it. She was glad that she and her mother were safe. Even if she didn't have a father near at hand. But no one was going to bother them.

They were both quiet that night, lost in their own thoughts. And Daphne was startled when she walked into her mother's room and found her on her knees praying. She looked at her for a minute and then walked out of the room. She wondered if her mother was praying for the family she had talked about that afternoon, and suspected that she was. She was right. But Daphne had no idea what she was doing. She was doing what she had never done, and heard her father do. What they had done for her. What Orthodox women never did. She was saying Kaddish, the prayers for the dead. And praying that they were still alive. But if not, someone had to do it. She said all that she could remember, and then knelt there, by the side of her bed, with tears running down her cheeks. They had closed their doors to her years before, and their hearts, and had declared her dead. But she loved them anyway. And now they were gone, all of them. Brigitte, Ulm, Horst, Papa. The people she had grown up with and never ceased to love. She sat shiva for them that night, just as long before, they had done for her.

13

BEATA CALLED THE MOTHER SUPERIOR IN THE
first week of December and asked to visit
her daughter. She said it was important, and
the Mother Superior told her gently that she
would have to wait. They were very busy
these days. In fact, they had deep concerns, and a problem of their own. She gave
Beata a visiting time on December 15, hoping things would have calmed down by
then.

Beata was beside herself till then. She
didn't know why, but she felt compelled to
see Amadea and tell her what had happened. It didn't really affect them, but it
could. She had to know. She had that right.
She would have told Daphne, too, but she

was too young, and she might say something in school. She was not yet fourteen,
and too young to be burdened with deep
secrets. Particularly secrets that could cost
lives, even her own. But at least Amadea
was safe where she was, and her mother
valued her advice. She didn't want to make
these decisions alone. She had been thinking of going to Switzerland. But Antoine's
cousins were long dead. And there was
nowhere else to go. She would have had to
rent a house there and leave her own. She
hated to make decisions out of panic and
fear. There was no reason for her to be
afraid, but she was. Deeply afraid.

Amadea could see it the moment she
walked in. Something was wrong. Her
mother had come alone. Daphne was at
school. Beata hated to waste a visit without
her, and deprive her of the opportunity to
see her sister, but she felt she had no
choice. She knew she wasn't thinking
clearly. They were all Germans after all. She
was Catholic. No one knew who she was.
No one was bothering her. But still, you
could never be sure anymore. Her father
must have thought he was safe too. She
wasn't sure where to begin.

"Peace of Christ," Amadea said softly, smiling at her mother. It had been a sad week for them. Sister Teresa Benedicta a Cruce, Edith Stein, had left them three days before, to join a convent in Holland. A friend had driven her over the border and her sister Rosa had gone with her, and was going to be staying at the convent too. She had been afraid to jeopardize the other nuns. Born Jewish, she had asked the Mother Superior to send her away to keep the others safe. And it broke everyone's heart to see her go. It was not what they wanted, but what they knew had to happen, for her well-being as well as theirs. They had all cried when she left, and prayed for her daily. The convent didn't seem the same without her smiling face. "Mama, are you all right? Where's Daphne?"

"In school. I wanted to see you alone." She was speaking quickly, because she knew they didn't have much time, and she had a lot to say. "Amadea, my family's been deported."

"What family?" Amadea looked confused as she stared at her mother, and they held each other's fingers through the grille. They

were speaking in whispers. "You mean
Oma's family?" Beata nodded.

"All of them. My father, my sister, my two
brothers, their children, and my brothers'
wives." There were tears in her eyes as she
said it, and she wiped them away as they
spilled onto her cheeks.

"I'm so sorry," Amadea said softly, confused. "Why?"

Beata took a breath and plunged in.
"They're Jewish. Or they were." By now
they were probably dead. "I'm Jewish. I was
born Jewish. I converted to marry your father."

"I never knew," Amadea said, looking at
her with compassion. But she didn't seem
frightened, nor did she seem to understand
what it meant, or could mean to her, to all of
them.

"I never told you. We didn't think it was
important. And now it is. Very important.
Maybe I was afraid . . . or ashamed. I don't
know. No one has bothered us or said anything, and all my papers say I'm Catholic. I
really don't have any papers, except the
identity cards I've had since your father
died. There's no evidence of it anywhere,
and your birth certificate says that Papa and

I were both Catholic when you were born, and we were. Our marriage certificate even says I'm Catholic. But it's there, somewhere. My father told everyone I had died. He wrote my name in the book of the dead. The person I was then no longer exists. I was reborn when I married your father, as a Christian, a Catholic. But the truth is, you're half Jewish, and so is Daphne. And I'm fully Jewish, as far as the Nazis are concerned. If they ever find out, you will be in danger. You have to know. I want you to be aware of it so you can protect yourself." And the others, Amadea instantly thought to herself, remembering what Edith Stein had just done, to protect them all. But she was fully Jewish, and known to be. Amadea wasn't, and she was a nobody. Nobody knew or cared who she was. And her mother said there was no evidence of their heritage, or their Jewish relatives. Still, it was good to know.

"Thank you for telling me. I'm not worried," she said quietly, looking at her mother, and kissing her fingers. And then she thought of what Edith Stein, Sister Teresa Benedicta a Cruce, had said before she left about the potential risk to others by association. "What about Daphne, Mama?"

"She's safe with me. She's just a child." But so were the other children who were being deported and sent to camps. The difference was that they were fully Jewish. Daphne wasn't. But there was admittedly some small degree of risk. As long as no one bothered them, and didn't unearth anything from the distant past, all would be well. And how likely was it that they would? Even going to Switzerland seemed a little hysterical to her now. They had no reason to run away. It was just unsettling knowing what was happening to the others.

"Mama, Sister Teresa Benedicta told us about something before she left. It's a beautiful thing. It's a train run by the British to rescue Jewish children before they get sent away to work camps and deported. The first one left on December first, but there will be others. They are sending German children to England until this insanity stops. Only children, up to the age of seventeen. And the Germans are allowing it. It's legal. They don't want Jewish children here anyway. What about sending Daphne to be sure that she's safe? You can always bring her back later." But Beata instantly shook her head. She wasn't sending her daughter away. There was no need to. And going to stay with strangers in England could be dangerous too.

"She's not Jewish, Amadea. Only half. And no one even knows that. I'm not sending her unprotected to a foreign country with God knows who, like an animal on a freight train, to stay God knows where. It's too dangerous for her. She's just a child."

"So are the others. Good people will take them into their homes and take care of them," Amadea said gently. It seemed a wise opportunity to her, but not to Beata.

"You don't know that. She could be raped by a stranger. Anything could happen. What if these children fall into the wrong hands?"

"They're in the wrong hands here. You said it yourself." And then Amadea sighed. Maybe her mother was right. There was no real danger to them for the moment, and they could see how things went. There was always time to send her away later if something came up. Maybe she was right. Maybe it was better to just keep their heads down, keep quiet, and let the storm pass. Sooner or later it would.

"I don't know," Beata said, looking worried. It was hard to know what to do, what was right. There was blood in the air, but it wasn't theirs for now. All she had wanted was to warn Amadea, so she could be aware. She was safe in the convent. Edith Stein was a different story. She was fully Jewish, known to be, and had been something of a radical and an activist, not so long ago. She was exactly the sort of person the Nazis were looking for. Troublemakers. Amadea certainly wasn't that. And as the two women sat looking at each other, thinking, a nun knocked at the door, and signaled to Amadea that their time was up.

"Mama, I have to go." It would be months before they saw each other again.

"Don't write to Daphne that I was here. It will break her heart not to have seen you, but I wanted to see you alone."

"I understand," she said, kissing her mother's fingers. She was twenty-one, but she looked considerably older. She had grown up in her three and a half years in the convent, and her mother could see it now. "I love you, Mama. Be careful. Don't do anything foolish," she warned her, and her mother smiled. "I love you so much."

"So do I, my darling." And then she confessed with a sad smile, "I still wish you were at home with us."

"I'm happy here," Amadea reassured her, feeling a tug at her heart. She missed them both at times, but she was still certain of her vocation. In four and a half years, she would take her final vows. There was no question of that. She had never doubted it once since she'd been there. And then as her mother got up to leave, "Merry Christmas, Mama."

"Merry Christmas to you," her mother said softly and then left the little cell where they visited, divided by the wall with the narrow grille.

Amadea hurried back to work after that, and at the time set aside for examination of conscience, she thought of all her mother had said to her. She had a great deal to think about, but there was no doubt in her mind what she had to do next. She went to find the Mother Superior in her office directly after lunch, during the time normally set aside for recreation. She was relieved to find Mother Teresa Maria Mater Domini at work at her desk. She looked up as Amadea hesitated. She had been writing a letter to the Mother Superior of the Convent in Holland where Sister Teresa Benedicta had gone, thanking her for responding to their need.

"Yes, sister. What is it?"

"Peace of Christ, Mother. May I speak to you?"

She signaled to her to come in and sit down. "Did you have a nice visit with your mother, Sister?" The wise old eyes were taking her in. She could see that the young nun was worried about something, and looked disturbed.

"Yes, thank you, Mother, I did." Amadea had closed the door behind her when she entered the room. "I have something I have to tell you, which I didn't know when I came in." The Mother Superior waited. She could see that it was something serious. The young nun looked upset. "I never knew that my mother wasn't born Catholic. She told me today that she converted to Catholicism before she married my father. She was born Jewish. Her family was deported the day after Kristallnacht. I never knew them because they disowned my mother when she married my father, and never saw her again. My grandmother finally met us two years before I came in. But my grandfather never allowed my mother to see the rest of them again. They wrote her down as dead." She looked up at the Mother Superior, and took a breath. "She says that no one seems to have any record of her history. She never registered, she has no passport. My parents lived in Switzerland for three years before we moved back here. I was born there. She has her marriage certificate to my father, which says she's Catholic. My birth certificate says they both are. But I'm half Jewish, Mother. I never knew that before. And I'm afraid now that if I stay, I will put everyone at risk." It was exactly why Sister Teresa Benedicta had just left.

"We are not at risk, my child, and neither are you. From what you're telling me, no one knows your mother's circumstances. Is she planning to register as a Jew with the police?"

Amadea shook her head. "No, she's not. She leads a quiet life, and there is no reason for anyone to find out." It was not honest, admittedly, but it was practical, and there were lives at stake. Both Daphne's and hers, and Amadea's. Even those of the other nuns perhaps. The Mother Superior did not appear to disapprove. "Sister Teresa Benedicta's circumstances were entirely different from yours. She was born fully Jewish, and she was well known as a lecturer and an activist, before she came here. She's a convert. You're not. She brought a great deal of attention to herself before she became a nun. You are a young girl who grew up as a Catholic. And with any luck at all, no one will ever realize that your mother didn't grow up Catholic, too. If she stays quiet, hopefully no one will ever know. If something happens to change that, I'm sure she'll let us know. In that case, we can spirit you away somewhere. This is precisely what I didn't like about Sister Benedicta's circumstances—it panics everyone. There is no need for alarm in your case. You came here as an innocent young girl, not as a grown woman who was known, had converted, and drawn attention to herself. In her case, it was wisdom to leave. In yours, it is imperative to stay. That is, if you want to stay." She looked at her questioningly, and Amadea looked relieved.

"Yes, I do. But I was afraid you would want me to go. I will, if that is ever what you wish." If so, it would have been the ultimate sacrifice to Amadea, for the good of the others. And her "small way" of denying herself for them. Saint Teresa's "small way" was self-denial in God's name.

"It's not. And Sister,"—she looked at her sternly then, as a mother would to admonish a child—"it is very important that you not discuss this with anyone. No one. We will keep this information between us." And then she looked up with concern. "Do you know what happened to your mother's family? Has she heard anything?"

"She believes they were sent to Dachau." The Mother Superior said nothing and pursed her lips. She hated what was happening to the Jews, as they all did.

"Please tell her that I'm sorry when you write to her. But do it discreetly," she said, and Amadea nodded, looking grateful for her kindness.

"Mother, I don't want to leave. I want to take my solemn vows."

"If that is God's will, then you shall." But they both knew it was still four and a half years away. It seemed an eternity to the young nun. She was determined to get there and let nothing stand in her way. They had just overcome a great obstacle in the

last half-hour. "Do not confuse your circumstances with those of Sister Teresa
Benedicta. That is a very different case."
And it had been a severe one, with high
risk for all concerned. This was not, in her
opinion.

"Thank you, Mother." Amadea thanked
her again and left a moment later, as the
Mother Superior sat at her desk, looking
pensive for a long moment. She wondered
how many more of these circumstances existed behind the convent walls. It was possible there were others she wasn't aware of,
and perhaps the nuns themselves had no
idea, as Amadea hadn't. But it was better
not to know.

Amadea felt immensely relieved for the
rest of the day, although she was still concerned about her mother and sister. But
perhaps her mother was right, and the truth
of her origins would never come out. There
was no reason for them to. She prayed that
night for the relatives who had been deported and possibly even killed, whom she
had never known. She remembered then
the time her mother had taken her to the
synagogue, and Amadea couldn't understand why at the time. She had forgotten

about it afterward, but now, thinking back, she realized that she must have somehow been touching some piece of her past. She had never taken Amadea there again.

14

THE PERSECUTION OF THE JEWS CONTINUED, PRE-
dictably, into the following year. In January
1939, Hitler gave a speech, threatening
them, and making clear his enmity toward
them. They were no longer welcome citizens in their own country, as Hitler vowed to
make things tough for them, and already
had. The following month they were told to
hand over all gold and silver items. In April
they lost their rights as tenants and had to
relocate into entirely Jewish houses, and
could no longer live side by side with
Aryans.

As a result, Jews were trying to emigrate,
which was far from easy. In many cases, the
countries they wished to emigrate to would

not take them. They had to have relatives
and sponsors abroad and often didn't. They
had to have jobs to go to, and permission
from both the Germans and the countries
they wanted to go to, and were often denied
by either or both countries. And they had to
have money to pay for the entire process,
and most didn't. Few were able to pull all
the necessary elements together, in the time
allotted, with success. Many German Jews
still insisted and believed that things would
calm down again. What was happening was
hard to believe. This wasn't reasonable,
they were Germans. Nothing bad could
happen. But too many had already been deported and sent to work camps, and the re-
ports that filtered back were increasingly
alarming. People were dying of abuse, mal-
nutrition, overwork, and illness. Some simply disappeared in silence. Those who saw
the handwriting on the wall were already
panicked. But leaving Germany was nearly
impossible to do.

Throughout the year, the Kindertransport
that Amadea had told her mother about
was continuing to pick up children and
send them to England. It had been organized by the British, and the Quakers had

gotten involved with it. They were shipping
children out of Germany, Austria, and
Czechoslovakia. A few were Christian, but
almost all were Jewish. The British had
agreed to accept them without passports as
long as they were no older than seventeen,
so as not to jeopardize jobs for Britons. The
Nazis had agreed to let them go, provided
they took no valuables with them, and took
only a single small valise that they could
carry. Watching them leave from railway
stations, and the parents who took them
there, tore one's heart out. But it was the
only assurance their parents had now that
they would stay safe, and might escape the
fate the Nazis were condemning Jews to.
Parents told their children on railway plat-
forms that they would join them in England
soon. Parents and children alike hoped that
it would be true. Some begged the children
to find sponsors and jobs for them once in
England, which was an impossible burden
to put on children who had no way of helping them, but knew that their parents' lives
were at stake if they didn't. Miraculously, a
precious few achieved it.

   Britons on the other end took them into
their homes as foster children, sometimes in

groups. They were committed to keep them until things became less dangerous for the Jews again in their home countries, and no one had any idea when that would be. In some cases, even small babies were among what the British referred to on arrival as the "kinders." In an astounding burst of charity and humanity, one of the Rothschilds took in twenty-eight and set up a house especially for them. Others weren't able to be as generous, but the British outdid themselves in their efforts to house and care for them. And those who were unable to find foster parents were kept in camps and barracks and cared for there.

On the military front, the news continued to be distressing, some of which even filtered into the convent, mostly when they got deliveries from the outside world. In March the Nazis invaded Czechoslovakia, and by summer they appeared to be setting their sights on Poland. Amadea professed her temporary vows for the second time. Her mother and Daphne visited her shortly after. They had had no problems with anyone harassing them, or questioning their papers, and Amadea was relieved. Daphne was fourteen, and she still had no suspi-

cion of her mother's secret. Amadea was
pleased to see that her mother looked well,
and calm. But she said that the atmosphere
in the city was strained, with so many Jews
out of work, even those who had had respectable professions, and so many being
sent to work camps. The hemorrhaging of
Jews out of cities and into work camps
hadn't stopped. Many of them were being
held in marshaling camps outside the city,
waiting to be sent elsewhere, men as well
as women and children.

By then her mother had heard of the
Kindertransport herself, and the work they
were doing. But it was out of the question
for her to send Daphne. She insisted there
was no reason to. She and Amadea said
nothing about it in front of her, except to
praise what the British were doing. Two of
Daphne's previous friends from school had
already left for England, and she had heard
that several more were leaving soon. They
were still waiting for permission. She said it
seemed so sad for them to be leaving without their parents. But the alternatives were
far worse, they all agreed.

Beata was pleased too to see Amadea
looking so well. She was thriving as Sister

Teresa of Carmel, and it was obvious that
she loved it. Knowing that was the only
thing that made Beata resign herself to the
choice Amadea had made. And as always
the visit went too quickly. She said before
she left that she had seen the Daubignys
and they were well.

Two weeks after their visit, the Nazis invaded Poland, and on the same day, Jews
in Germany were given a nightly curfew.
They had to be indoors by nine o'clock at
night, which would be shortened to eight
o'clock in the winter. Two days later France
and England declared war on Germany.
On that morning, the last Kindertransport
pulled out of the station. It was to be the last
one of its kind. Having declared war, they
would no longer be able to get Jewish children out. They had operated for exactly nine
months and two days, and had rescued ten
thousand children. A miracle in itself. As the
last "kinders" left Europe for England, the
Poles put up a valiant fight for survival, to no
avail. They surrendered nearly four weeks
later. The stories of Warsaw brought tears to
Beata's eyes when she heard them.

A month later all Jews were ordered to be
evacuated from Vienna, and all Polish Jews

from fourteen to sixty were sent to forced labor. The horrors continued, and seemed endless.

Given what was happening, and the fact that Germany was at war, it was a bleak Christmas, even in the convent, where they had several cheerful letters from Sister Teresa Benedicta from Holland. Her sister Rosa was still with her at the convent, and they both felt safe there, although Sister Teresa Benedicta said she missed the Sisters in Cologne, and prayed for them daily, as they did for her.

Amadea turned twenty-three in April 1940. Her mother and sister came to visit her. Daphne was turning fifteen, which was hard for even Amadea to believe. She was truly beautiful, and looked almost exactly like photographs of their mother at the same age. But much to everyone's horror, eight days later the Nazis invaded Denmark and Norway. A month later, in May, they took Holland and the Lowlands, which no one had expected, and put Sister Teresa Benedicta at risk once again. Speaking of it in whispers over lunch, the sisters were panicked for her. It was impossible to know what was going to happen anymore. Hitler appeared to be taking over all of Europe. In June they took France. By then Amadea had renewed her temporary profession once again. She had three years left before taking her solemn vows, which would attach her permanently to the order. She felt solidly attached to it now. She could no longer remember or imagine any other life. She had already been there for five years.

The Nazis invaded Romania in October, shortly after Daphne went back to school. And in November the Cracow Ghetto was sealed off, containing seventy thousand Jews, and the Warsaw Ghetto, containing four hundred thousand. What was happening was unthinkable. But in spite of all that was occurring, and the relentless Nazi policies to eliminate Jews at every level of society, Beata insisted to Amadea when she saw her at Christmas that she had had no problems. No one had ever questioned her, or asked for documents that could expose her. It was as though they had forgotten she existed, or never knew. No one seemed to care. She was just a Catholic widow, living alone with a daughter, minding her own business. In essence, she had been overlooked. Amadea was always relieved to hear from them that all was well.

It was in the spring of 1941, just after Daphne's sixteenth birthday and Amadea's twenty-fourth, that Beata was at the bank and saw a woman who looked oddly familiar to her. She stared at her for a long time, while they both stood at separate windows, but no matter how often she glanced at her, she couldn't place the face. Beata was making a sizable withdrawal that day, which was something she rarely did, but it had occurred to her after a dream she'd had recently that it might be a good idea. She had spoken to Gérard Daubigny about it, and he was amenable. She wanted to leave some money with him, in case anything ever happened to her, so that he could hold it for the girls, in an emergency. He didn't see why she couldn't leave it all in the bank, but Beata had always seemed nervous to him since Antoine died, and if it made her feel better, he was willing to humor her and do it. He was happy to do what he could for the wife of his old friend. It had been obvious to him and Véronique for years that she had never recovered from his death. The years since had taken a heavy toll on her, and at forty-six, she looked ten years older than she was. She was planning to ride out to the *Schloss* that afternoon, to give him the money, in cash, that she wanted him to hold. It wasn't much, but it would tide the girls over if anything went wrong. She had even written to Amadea about it, and told her that Gérard Daubigny would be holding funds for them, in case anything happened to her. Amadea hated to hear her thinking that way, but she knew that her mother had worried for years about what would happen if she fell ill, or worse, particularly with Daphne still so young. Now, with such uncertainty around them everywhere, it was even easier to become anxious, and Amadea knew she was nervous about the Nazis and the steady progression of the war.

The woman Beata had been looking at in the bank finished her business at the same time, and the two women headed for the door almost side by side on the way out. Beata almost fainted when the woman called out, "Miss Wittgenstein!" Feeling her knees nearly buckle under her, she walked outside with a determined stride. All she wanted to do was get away from her as quickly as possible, and hail a cab. She showed no sign of recognition and raised her arm as a taxi sped by. But the woman had caught up to her and was looking her right in the face with a broad smile. It was only then that memory stirred for Beata, and suddenly she knew who she was, despite the ravages of time. She had been a young Czech girl who worked as a maid for her parents nearly thirty years before. She had been there in fact when Beata left home. "I knew it was you!" she said victoriously. "I thought I was seeing a ghost. Your father told us you died in Switzerland."

"I'm sorry . . . I have no idea . . . I . . ." As she looked at her, Beata tried to keep all sign of recognition from her face, pretending there was some mistake. But the woman clearly knew who Beata was and would not let it go. "I don't know who you mean," Beata said coldly, shaking with terror over the possibility that someone might have heard the woman call her by her maiden name. It was not a name Beata could afford to acknowledge. To do so might put her life at stake.

"Don't you remember me? Mina . . . I worked for your parents." In fact, Beata now

remembered that she had married her father's driver, some thirty years before. It all
came rushing back to her, on a wave of fear,
knowing what this chance meeting could do
to her.

"I'm sorry . . ." Beata smiled vaguely, trying to be polite and anxious to escape, as a
cab slid mercifully to a stop beside her.

"I know who you are," Mina said with a
dogged look, as Beata slid into the cab and
turned away. All she could hope now was
that Mina would believe she had made a
mistake. With luck, the unfortunate chance
meeting would come to naught, and the
woman would forget. She had no reason to
pursue Beata. She was just trying to be
friendly. She had been a sweet girl, and
desperately in love with the chauffeur. They
had gotten married not long before Beata
left, and Mina was pregnant at the time.
Beata knew Mina must have been surprised
to see her, since her father had said he
would tell the entire household she was
dead. In fact, she was very much alive.
Perhaps that was why Mina was so determined to acknowledge her. But in these
frightening times, Beata could not afford to

be identified as a Wittgenstein, even at the risk of being rude to their former maid.

Beata was surprised to find that she was shaking violently in the cab. It had been one of those unnerving chance encounters that meant nothing, but hearing her call Beata's maiden name across the bank was risky business. It was a name she could no longer afford to admit ever having had. Hopefully, Mina would simply let it go. There was nothing Beata could do about it. It had been a frightening moment, but it was over. And Beata had not admitted her identity to her. She had remained outwardly calm throughout, even if shaking inside. Hopefully it would be the last she'd see of her. On her way to Gérard and Véronique's *Schloss,* she put it out of her mind, determined not to let it panic her.

The Daubignys had been lucky to keep the property intact, despite the war. Fortunately, Gérard had had the foresight years before to take German citizenship, as had Véronique, although Beata knew from conversations with him that he deplored what Hitler was doing to the Jews. He said it made him sick. He didn't question her as to why she wanted to leave money with him.

He thought it was more anxious eccentricity than due to anything else. She was an unhappy, lonely woman on her own with a child. It was understandable that she was nervous. With a war on, and all of Europe up in arms over the fate of the Jews, these were frightening times for everyone, and the entire world seemed unstable. He suspected that what she was worried about was that the banks would fail. It was the only explanation for the amount she gave him that afternoon. She had given him an envelope with the equivalent of twenty thousand dollars in it, which she said would tide the girls over for a while, if anything happened to her, until they could get the rest. He assured her he would take good care of it, and put it in the safe. He sat down and had tea with her then, since Véronique was out.

The stables were still beautiful, she saw when she went in, although he said he had far fewer horses than he had when Antoine was alive. He had never found anyone to compare to him, to run the horse farm for him. Antoine had been gone by then for fourteen years. They reminisced for a time, and after a while, he called a cab for her to take her back to the city.

Daphne was already at home when she got back, and she was excited about a new boy she'd met in school. His father was in the army in Austria, and she said he was very handsome, with a twinkle in her eye, which made her mother laugh. The two of them had a quiet dinner that night. Daphne said she wanted to visit Amadea soon. They hadn't seen her in months. She was going to be taking her temporary vows again for the fourth time. She accepted Amadea being a Carmelite now as a matter of course. It was harder for Beata, who still hoped that one day she would change her mind. She had two more years before she took her final vows. It was the spring of 1941.

It was the following week that Beata went to the bank to take some money out for minor purchases. She wanted to buy some fabric for a few summer dresses for Daphne, and it was easier doing business in cash than writing checks, although there were fewer places to buy fabrics these days. All the stores she had patronized previously for those purposes had been run by Jews and were long since closed. She was thinking about what she needed when the bank teller handed her back her check, instead of cash.

"I'm sorry, madame," he said coldly, "this check cannot be cashed." There was obviously some mistake.

"I beg your pardon? Of course it can. I have more than adequate funds in that account to cover the check." She smiled at him, and asked him to look it up again.

He handed the check back to her without checking anything. He knew he had read the notation correctly the first time. There was no mistaking those. The manager had made the notation himself, and the teller had no intention of challenging it. "Your account has been closed."

"That's ridiculous. Of course it hasn't." She was annoyed by their mistake, and about to ask for the bank manager, when she saw something in the young man's eyes. "By whom?"

"The Third Reich," he said briskly, as she stared at him, opened her mouth, and closed it again. She put the check back in her handbag and turned around and walked out as quickly as she could. She knew exactly what that meant. Someone had re-

ported her. All she could think of was Mina,
her parents' former maid. She was the
only one who knew. Or perhaps they had
heard her call out "Miss Wittgenstein" and
checked it out. However it had happened,
they had closed her account, undoubtedly
because someone knew that she was
Jewish, and had been born a Jew. There
was no other reason to close her account.
Only Mina knew, although Beata had admitted nothing to her.

Beata walked quickly away from the bank,
hailed a taxi on the street, and five minutes
later she was home. She had no idea what
to do, if she should wait to see what happened, or if they should leave immediately.
And if they did, where would they go? She
thought of the Daubignys, but she didn't
want to endanger them either, no matter
how sympathetic he said he was to the
Jews. It was one thing to feel sorry for them,
and another matter entirely to hide them.
But maybe they could stay there for one
night and he could advise her what to do.
She had no passport, and she knew that
she and Daphne would never be able to
cross the borders. Besides which, she now
had no money, except for what she had left

with him previously, which she didn't want to use. The girls might need it later. Beata tried to fight waves of panic, as she took out two suitcases and began packing. She put her jewelry and some clothes for herself into one of them. And then she went into Daphne's room, and was throwing things into the suitcase when Daphne came home from school. The moment she saw her mother's face, she knew that something terrible had happened.

"Mama, what are you doing?" she asked, looking frightened. She had never seen her mother look like that. There was raw terror on her face. Beata had always feared this day would come, and now it had.

"We're leaving. Give me anything you want that will fit in this one case." Her hands were shaking while she packed.

"Why? What happened? Mama . . . please . . ." Without even knowing why, Daphne started to cry. Her mother turned to look at her then, and the compounded griefs of twenty-five years showed in her eyes.

"I was born Jewish. I converted to marry your father. No one knew. I've kept it a secret for all these years. I didn't mean to, but

once they started going after the Jews, I
had to. I saw a woman at the bank last week
who knew me when I was young. She called
out my maiden name across the bank lobby.
When I went back today, they had closed
my account. We have to leave now. I think
they're going to arrest us . . ."

"Oh, Mama . . . they can't . . ." Daphne's
eyes filled instantly with panic and shock.

"They will. Hurry. Pack. I want to leave this
afternoon." There was desperation in her
voice as Daphne tried to take it all in. It was
a lot to swallow at one gulp.

"Where will we go?" She wiped her eyes,
trying to be brave.

"I don't know. I haven't figured that out.
Maybe we can stay with the Daubignys for
one night, if they let us. After that we will
have to work it out." They could be on the
run for years. But better that than caught.

"What about the convent? Can we go
there?" Daphne's eyes were wide as she
started putting random items into her suitcase. None of it made any sense. It was too
much to absorb for a girl of sixteen, or anyone. They were about to leave their home,
possibly for good. It was the only home

Daphne had ever known. They had lived there since she was two.

"I don't want to risk Amadea or the nuns," Beata said tersely.

"Does she know? About you, I mean."

"I told her after Kristallnacht. They took my family then, and I thought she should know."

"Why didn't you tell me?"

"I thought you were too young. You were only thirteen." As she said the words, there was a knock on the door. The two women looked at each other in terror, and Beata looked her daughter in the eyes with unexpected strength. "I love you. Remember that. That's all that matters. Whatever happens, we have each other." She wanted to tell her to hide, but wasn't sure if that was the right thing. There was a frantic knocking on the door again, as Daphne stood there and cried. This was the worst day of her life.

Beata tried to regain her composure and walked to the front door. When she opened it, there were two soldiers and an SS officer standing there. It was all that she had feared. Now she wanted to tell Daphne to hide, but it was too late. She was standing in the bedroom doorway watching them.

"You're under arrest," he said in a terrifying voice. "Both of you," he said, glancing at
Daphne. "As Jews. Your bank reported you.
Come with us now." Beata was shaking
from head to foot, and Daphne screamed.

"Daphne, don't," Beata shouted to her.
"We'll be all right." She turned back to the
officer then. "May we bring anything with
us?"

"You may bring one suitcase each. You
are being deported."

Beata had already packed the bags. She
went to get hers, and told Daphne to bring
the bag they had just packed in her room.
Daphne looked completely panicked as her
mother took her in her arms and held her
tight.

"We have to do this. Be strong. Remember
what I told you. I love you. We have each
other."

"Mama, I'm so scared."

"Come now!" the officer shouted, and
sent the two men to get them. A moment
later, Daphne and Beata were escorted out
of the house, carrying their bags, their fate
and destination unknown.

15

THE PRIEST FROM BEATA'S PARISH CAME TO SEE the Mother Superior at the convent two days later. He had heard it from Beata's maid, who had come to him in tears. She had been out when it happened. The neighbors had told her what they'd seen. He thought Amadea should know. He wasn't sure why they had been taken, but he knew they had. Before coming to see her, he had done some quiet checking himself. According to his sources, Beata and her youngest daughter had been taken to the marshaling station outside Cologne. Normally they kept people there for weeks or even months. But there had been a train leaving for Ravensbrück, the women's camp, that afternoon, and they were put on it. They were already gone.

The Mother Superior listened in silence to what he said, and impressed on him the importance of his silence. But she knew that in a very short time, others would know. There were people in the parish who knew that Amadea had become a Carmelite six years before. There was no question in her mind that this was a very serious situation, and after thinking about it, once the priest had left, she opened a drawer, took out a letter, and made a single call. Beata had sent her a letter with a name and a phone number months before. It was for an event such as this. Without panicking unduly, or giving in to hysteria, Beata had tried to anticipate the worst. And now the worst had come. It was hard to believe they had been lucky for this long. Or so very unlucky in the end.

After she hung up, the Mother Superior bent her head in prayer, and then sent for Amadea. She had been working in the garden, and she looked happy when she walked in.

"Yes, Reverend Mother?" She couldn't imagine why she'd called her to her office.

She was still looking slightly disheveled from her work in the garden.

"Sister Teresa, please sit down." She took a breath, and hoped that God would help her find the right words. This was no easy task. "As you know, these are hard times. For everyone. And God makes choices for us that we don't understand. We simply have to follow His paths, without questioning His ways."

Amadea looked at her, suddenly worried. "Did I do something wrong?"

"Not at all," she said, reaching a hand across her desk and taking Amadea's hand in hers. "I have some very hard news for you. Someone denounced your mother. She and your sister were arrested two days ago. They were sent to Ravensbrück yesterday. That's all I know. They were all right when they were last seen." But they both knew that the two women were unlikely to stay that way. Ravensbrück was a women's camp where the women were worked to death, and dropped like flies. No one returned. Amadea could hardly breathe as she heard the news. Her mouth flew open, and no sound came out. "I'm so sorry, I'm so sorry. But now we must decide what to do with you. Whoever denounced her knows about you. And if not, someone does. I do not want you at risk here." Amadea nodded in silence, and then thought instantly of the others. But all she could think of now was her mother and sister, and how terrible it must have been for them, how frightened they must have been. Daphne was only sixteen. She had been Amadea's baby since she was born. Tears rolled silently down her cheeks as she clutched the Mother Superior's hands, and the older woman walked around her desk and took her in her arms, as Amadea was engulfed in sobs. She couldn't even imagine it, it was so awful. "They're in God's hands," she whispered. "All we can do is pray for them now."

"I'll never see them again. Oh, Mother . . . I can't bear it . . ." She couldn't stop crying as the Mother Superior held her.

"Many survive." But they both knew most didn't, and there was no way of knowing if Beata and Daphne would be among the lucky ones. And Daphne was so beautiful, God only knew what they would do to her. It didn't bear thinking.

The Mother Superior was thinking of

Amadea now. She was her responsibility. And she couldn't send her to Holland as they had Sister Teresa Benedicta. Holland was occupied, and her presence in the convent there was already putting the sisters there at great risk. They couldn't take yet another danger in. Besides which, they'd never get Amadea across the border. Sister Teresa Benedicta had gone to Holland before the war began. Everything was different now. There was no way of getting Amadea out, which was why she had made the call she had. She had no other choice. He had agreed to come within the hour.

"I am going to ask you to do something very difficult," the Mother Superior said sadly, "for your sake, as well as ours. I have no other choice." Amadea was still too overwrought over what she had heard about her mother and sister to absorb much more, but she nodded and turned sad eyes to the older nun. "I am going to ask you to leave us, just for now. If you stay here, it could put the whole convent at risk. When this is over, when life is normal again, you will come back. I know you will. I have never doubted your vocation for an instant. Because of that, I am asking you to do this.

You will still be one of us, even in the outside world, wherever you are. Nothing will
change." She had professed her temporary
vows four times so far. She was due to do
so again in two months. She was two years
away from final vows. And this was yet another blow. She had lost her mother and sister, perhaps forever, and now she was being
sent away. But even in her distraught state,
she knew it was the right thing. It was a sacrifice she could make for them. As the
Mother said, she had no other choice, nor
did they. Amadea nodded her head.

"Where will I go?" Amadea asked in a broken voice. She had not been outside the
convent walls in six years. She had no place
to stay, nowhere to go.

"Your mother sent me a letter several
months ago. With the name of a friend. I
called him a few minutes ago. He said he
would be here within the hour."

"So soon?" She knew without asking who
it was. He was her mother's only friend, and
she had told Amadea as well to contact
Gérard Daubigny if something went wrong.
She had even said he had money for her.
But she couldn't put them at risk either. She
was a danger to everyone. "Will I be able to

say good-bye to the others?" The Mother Superior hesitated and then nodded. It would have been too cruel to her and to them otherwise. She rang the bell after that, which warned the sisters that something important had happened, and they were to gather in the dining hall. They were all there when Amadea and the Mother Superior walked in. All the familiar faces, all the nuns she had worked with, lived with, and loved for so long. The young ones, and the older ones, even the ones in wheelchairs. It was agonizing for her thinking of leaving them. But the Mother Superior was right. She had no choice. Wherever she went, to whichever convent, or if they kept her here, she presented a danger for the others. She loved them too much to do that to them. She had to leave them. But as the Mother Superior had said, she knew she would come back one day. This was the life she wanted. This was her home. She knew with utter certainty that she had been born to be a Carmelite, and serve God, in whatever way He chose.

Mother Teresa Maria Mater Domini offered no explanation. She said nothing. Even knowing the circumstances of Amadea's departure could be dangerous for them. If the police came afterward, they knew nothing. And the fact that she had left exonerated them. If anyone paid a price, it would be the Mother Superior and no one else. Amadea simply moved along their ranks, hugging and kissing each one of them, and saying "God bless you, Sister" softly to each one. It was all she said, but watching her do it, they all knew she was going, just as they had known when Sister Teresa Benedicta had left them three years before.

It took her half an hour to say good-bye to them, and she did not return to her cell to pick up her things. She had nothing to take with her. She had brought nothing and would leave with nothing. And now she had to go back out into a world she no longer understood and hadn't seen in so long. A world in which her mother and her sister no longer lived, where she had no home, and no belongings, and no one. All she had was her father's friend, and as she waited in the Mother Superior's office for him, he arrived, with grave eyes. Gérard Daubigny walked into the office and took Amadea gently in his arms.

"I'm so sorry, Amadea," he whispered. It

was beyond thinking that Beata and Daphne were gone. And given what he had heard of the camps, he thought it unlikely they would survive. But he said nothing to her of that now.

"What will I do?" she said softly to him, as he looked at her. He had forgotten how beautiful she was, and she was more so now. Even in her sadness, there was a luminous look to her, a great depth to her eyes. She seemed to be lit from within, and he could see she was a deeply holy person. It seemed a tragedy for her to come out, and a great loss to her, along with the others she had just sustained. He had no idea how she would adapt to the world after so long. The Mother Superior was worried about that as well. Amadea looked shell-shocked as she looked at him.

"We'll talk about that tonight," he said quietly. They had much to talk about. They had opened the convent gates for him, and he had driven his car behind the convent walls. He wanted her to lie on the floor of his car, with a blanket over her, so no one would see her leave. No one would suspect that he was leaving the convent with one of the nuns. And if they came for her at some

point, the Mother Superior could simply say
she was gone. She owed them no more explanation than that, nor would she offer one.
By then she herself would have no idea
where Amadea was. Although they would
keep her constantly in their prayers until she
returned.

"You must dress now," the Mother Superior reminded her. Amadea disappeared into
the robing room a moment later. She felt as
though she were peeling her skin away as
she took her habit off. Each piece of it was
like a part of her, and she stood alone in the
room, looking at it carefully folded on the
table. They had left a coat and shoes and
dress for her, a small ugly hat, and some underwear.

None of the clothes fit when she put them
on, but it didn't matter to her. Nothing mattered. Her mother and Daphne were gone,
in God's hands now, wherever they were,
and she was leaving the place where she
had sought refuge six years before, where
she had lived and worked and grown. It was
like leaving the womb, as she buttoned the
dress that was too short for her, with the
shoes that were too tight. She had worn
sandals for six years, and it felt strange to

wear shoes again. She was surprised to find how thin she was, as she put on normal clothes again. She had had no sense of it in her habit, and her hair was shorn as it had been for six years. She felt like a monster in the ugly outfit, after the simple beauty of her habit. She longed to put it on again, and wondered how long it would be before she came back to them. She could only pray now it would be soon. She had no desire to go back into the world, in fact, she would have done anything possible to avoid it.

Gérard was waiting for her in the courtyard, standing anxiously beside his car. He wanted to get back to the *Schloss* as soon as possible. He had already spoken to Véronique about it, and she was in full agreement. It was something they could do for Beata and Antoine who had been good friends to them, although this went beyond the bounds of friendship. But this was about more than that. It was about what was right, and so much these days wasn't. In fact, nothing was.

He was standing talking quietly to the Mother Superior, and the others had gone back to work. No one saw them as Amadea got into the car and lay on the floor in the back, as he put a horse blanket over her, that smelled of the stables, but it was a happy memory for Amadea. Before he covered her, she looked at the Mother Superior for a last time, and the two women's eyes met and held.

"God bless you, my child. Don't worry. You will be home soon. We'll be waiting for you."

"God bless you, Mother . . . I love you . . ."

"I love you, too," she whispered, as Gérard gently covered her, thanked the somber-looking nun, who stood watching him, as he backed slowly out of the courtyard, and drove to the *Schloss* without stopping. He drove at normal speed, as though he were doing nothing special, and kept his eye on the rearview mirror. They had given him a large basket of fruit and vegetables, to explain why he had come there. But no one followed him. They were not going to go to great lengths to look for a young nun. And even if the police came to inquire about her, they would soon forget about her. She was no great danger to them, and they knew it. Nor were Beata and Daphne, but once they were denounced, the Gestapo had no choice but to do something about it. In Beata's case, there was money and a house to be taken. Amadea had nothing except the clothes she had on her back, and the rosary beads the Mother Superior had given her as she left the convent.

He drove into the courtyard of the *Schloss* and around to the back of the house. It was lunchtime, and no one was around. Everyone was either eating or busy, when he escorted Amadea to their bedroom. Véronique was waiting for her there, and as she took the young woman into her arms, they both sobbed for all that had been lost, all the horror that had happened. Gérard quietly locked the bedroom door. He had already told the maids that his wife had a sick headache and no one was to disturb her. They had a lot to talk about. A lot to figure out. But for now, Amadea had to recover from the multiple shocks she had sustained that morning. She had lost everything. Her mother. Her sister. And the convent. She had lost the only way of life she had known for the past six years, and all the familiar people and landmarks of her childhood. She cried as though her heart would break, and had, as Véronique Daubigny held her.

16

GÉRARD AND VÉRONIQUE TALKED TO AMADEA long into the night. They waited until the servants left in the evening and went to their own quarters, and then Véronique went down to the kitchen herself and cooked Amadea dinner. She could barely eat it. She hadn't touched meat in six years, and she felt completely at a loss, staring at the sausages and eggs Véronique had cooked her. More than that, she felt naked without her habit. She was still wearing the ill-fitting clothes they had given her at the convent. But that was the least of her problems. Gérard had been thinking about what to do with her all evening.

He and Véronique were in full agreement.

They couldn't keep her forever, but for now at least, for as long as they could, they wanted to hide her. There was a locked storeroom with a small window high up in one of the towers, and Gérard was convinced that no one would find her there. She could come down to their rooms at night, for air and space, and the rest of the time, in the daytime, she could stay there. There was even a tiny bathroom.

"But what will they do to you, if they find me?"

"They won't," Gérard said simply. For the moment, it was the best plan they could think of, and she was grateful to them.

She had a bath in Véronique's bathroom that night, and afterward she was startled when she saw herself in the mirror. She had not seen herself in six years, and she was surprised to see herself look so much older. In six years she had become a woman. Her pale blond hair was short. She cut it herself each month, without looking, and it looked it, not that it mattered to her. It didn't. It was a travesty for her to be out in the world. She knew with her entire being that she belonged in the convent. But this was her gift to them, to go out into the world so she did not risk them. It was a small price to pay for their safety, a sacrifice she was willingly making. Not to mention the sacrifice the Daubignys were making for her.

Véronique had gone through her closets to find something for her to wear. She had found a long blue skirt, a white blouse, and a sweater. They were almost exactly the same size, and she had put out underwear and a pair of red sandals. Amadea felt sinful wearing it. It all looked much too pretty. But she was fulfilling her vows, she told herself as she put the clothes on. She was being obedient to the Mother Superior. She had told her to go out in the world again until she could come back, without risking her sisters. But her heart felt heavy as Gérard walked her up to the tower. He had pulled a mattress out of another storeroom and laid it on the floor, with a pillow and a stack of blankets.

"See you tomorrow," he said gently, as he closed and locked the door, and she lay down on the mattress. They were being so kind to her. She lay there awake, praying for her mother and sister for the rest of the night. She spent the next day in prayer, as she would have in the convent. He came once during the day to bring her food and water. At night, he unlocked the door again and led her back down to their bedroom, where she bathed again, and Véronique once more cooked her dinner.

It became a daily ritual for them all through the summer. Her hair had grown down to her shoulders by September. She looked as she had when she went into the convent, only slightly older. There had been no news from her mother or sister. She knew that sometimes they were allowed to send a postcard to reassure their relatives and loved ones, but there had been none, neither from Beata nor Daphne. Gérard had checked with the convent. No card had come for Amadea. And mercifully, the authorities hadn't inquired about her either. Amadea had simply vanished, and been forgotten.

On the war front, the Nazis had invaded Russia that summer. There had been mass murders of Jews in occupied countries, and new concentration camps were under construction, and being opened. Gérard told her during one of their long conversations at night that all German Jews had been ordered to wear armbands with yellow stars on them, in September. They had begun a mass deportation of German Jews to all the concentration camps they'd established.

The Daubignys had hidden Amadea for five months by then, and so far no one seemed the wiser. Everything at the *Schloss* continued as normal. Gérard and Véronique saw no reason not to continue hiding her, although all three of them knew that if they were caught, they would be either shot or deported. But when she offered to leave them, they insisted that she stay with them. They had no children of their own. This was a risk they were choosing to take for her, and in memory of her parents.

Amadea knew there had to be Jews hiding in other places, and she said that if she had to, she'd find them. They both insisted that that was out of the question, and for lack of any other solution, she agreed to stay with them. She had nowhere else to go.

Things continued as they had for the next several months, and Amadea was shocked when Gérard opened her door one night to let her out, and told her about Pearl Harbor. The United States declared war on Japan and four days later on Hitler, after he had declared war on them. By then, Amadea had not been out of the building in eight months, and it was strange to realize that it was almost Christmas. She had nothing to celebrate that year, except the Daubignys' kindness in letting her stay there.

Two days before Christmas, Gérard looked deeply upset when he came to let her out of her cell, and she could tell that something had happened. She had heard noise outside all day, and the sounds of horses. He told her that the Gestapo had taken over the stables, and commandeered most of their horses. He was concerned that they would try to take over the *Schloss* as well. The *Kommandant* had said that he wanted a full tour of the premises shortly after Christmas. In the meantime, they were busy. But all three of them agreed that Amadea was no longer safe there. Before the Germans began to explore every nook and cranny, they had to find her another refuge. Gérard had been making discreet inquiries, and he had heard of a farmhouse nearby where they were concealing Jews in an underground tunnel. But getting her there wouldn't be easy. Up till now, they had been remarkably lucky. But with the German army camped on their doorstep, she was once again in grave danger.

"You've been so good to me," she said to

both of them, as they shared a Christmas goose on Christmas Eve in the kitchen. All she could think about, as she picked at it, was if her mother and sister were still alive then. There had been no message from them since they were taken to Ravensbrück in April. Sometimes when they arrived at the camps, deportees were allowed to send a single postcard, and Beata would have sent hers to the Daubignys so they could pass the word to Amadea. None had come.

It was the day after Christmas, before dawn, that Gérard opened her door, looking grim-faced. The *Kommandant* had told him the night before that he wanted a full inspection tour the next morning. So far, Gérard was sure he suspected nothing. But in the morning, he would be unlocking every door, from the wine cellar to the tower. They had already helped themselves to a dozen cases of wine, and two barrels of cognac.

Gérard had the information Amadea needed. He knew where the farmhouse was, with the tunnel, and told her that they'd be waiting for her. He handed her a small map and explained how to get there.

"How will I find it?" she asked, looking worried, and realizing again how lucky she had been to be there since April. Now she had to take her chances. The farm was fifteen miles away, over rough countryside. If she could get there, they were willing to hide her. First, she had to get past the soldiers in the stables. Gérard said it was too dangerous to drive her. It would draw attention to the farm if he drove there, and they had asked him not to.

"I put one of the horses in a shed for you," he said quietly. "Just head north and keep going. The landmarks are written on the map. They'll be watching for you. You can let the horse loose and send him back when you get there." He wanted her to leave before sunrise. They sat in the dark in their room, talking softly. They didn't want the soldiers to see the lights on. Half an hour later, Gérard walked her downstairs with Véronique. They hugged her for a last time. Véronique had bundled her up warmly and kissed her like a daughter.

"Thank you," Amadea whispered one last time, and clung to her for a last moment, and then Gérard hugged her.

"Get there as quickly as you can. The horse I left for you is sure-footed." It was also one of his fastest. They opened the

door then, and she went out into the darkness. She was startled by how cold it was.
She hadn't been outside in eight months,
and the cold air was a shock to her lungs,
as she walked quickly toward the shed,
opened the door, patted the horse he had
left for her, and adjusted his saddle in the
darkness. She had the map shoved into her
pocket.

She led the horse outside, and he blew
steam into the air. There were no sentries
posted, and Gérard had told her all the soldiers were sleeping. She had nothing to fear
as she left the *Schloss.* All she had to do
was cover the fifteen miles to the farmhouse
before sunrise. She mounted the horse easily. As she swung into the saddle, it reminded her of her years riding with her father. This was second nature to her, and as
she always had, she left the grounds at a
slow gallop. She steered a wide berth
around the *Schloss,* and heard the horses in
the stables. They were aware of her, but apparently none of the men heard her. She
made an easy getaway, and enjoyed covering the distance. It was her first taste of
freedom.

She pulled the map out of her pocket half

an hour later. She could read it easily in the moonlight, and saw the first of the land-marks. She was only a few miles away now. The sky was a pale gray, but she knew she still had time to get there before sunrise.

She was within a mile of it, when she sud-denly saw lights on her left, realized it was a car hidden in a clump of bushes, and heard a gunshot. For an instant, she wasn't sure whether to go backward or forward, and then without thinking, she kicked the horse and raced across the final distance as the car followed at full speed. She was almost there, and then realized what she was do-ing. She was leading the Gestapo right to the farmhouse. There was no way she could outrun them. And then suddenly a truck pulled up ahead of her, as the car that had been following her pulled up behind her. They had her cornered.

"Halt!" two men shouted as the horse danced in the cold night air, and blew steam from his nostrils. She had pushed him hard for the last half-hour. "Who goes there?" She sat in her saddle as the horse pranced nervously, and she didn't answer.

They shone a bright light on her, and were startled to see it was a woman. She had rid-

den like a man, driving the horse hard over
rough terrain. One of the men walked up to
her, as she considered making a run for it.
But they would shoot the horse for sure, or
her. She knew then that she would never
make it to the farmhouse, and in the morning Gérard would know that. Worse than
that, from the brand, they would know she
was riding one of his horses. No matter
what happened, she didn't want to impli-
cate him, as she thought quickly.

"Papers!" the soldier shouted at her, holding out a hand, as another pointed a gun at
her. "Papers!"

"I have none." They had had none to give
her at the convent. And she had had none
since then. She had been out of the world
for six years.

"Who are you?" She thought of inventing
a name, but there was no point in that either. She might as well tell them the truth.

"Amadea de Vallerand," she said clearly.

"Whose horse are you riding?" they
asked, keeping their guns pointed at her in
case she made a run for it. The horse was
powerful, nervous and bucking, and they
could see easily that she was a skilled rider.
Even after all these years, she had no trou-

ble controlling one of Gérard's best horses. Her father had taught her well.

"I took it," she said, sounding fearless. But her whole body was shaking. She had no idea what they would do to her. "My father used to work at the stables. I stole it." She knew she had to protect Gérard and Véronique at all costs. She could not let them think the Daubignys gave it to her.

"Where are you going?"

"To visit friends." It was obvious that they did not believe her story, and there was no reason they should have. She just prayed they didn't find the map to the farmhouse in her pocket. It was a small scrap of paper, and she made no move to reach for it.

"Dismount," they ordered, and she swung easily out of the saddle, and held the reins until one of the soldiers took them from her. He led the horse away, as the other soldier pointed his gun at her. As she stood there, she wondered if he was going to shoot her. She was surprised at how unafraid she was. She felt as though she had nothing to lose. Only her life, which belonged to God. And if He chose to reclaim her, He would.

They pushed her roughly into the back of the car, and as they drove away, she saw one of the soldiers mount Gérard's horse and ride him back in the direction of the stables.

"How many horses have you stolen?" the soldier driving the car asked her. Another soldier had appeared and was riding with him.

"Just that one" was all she answered. She didn't look like a horse thief, but all of the men had noticed that she was an exceptional rider, and a beautiful young woman.

They drove her to a house nearby and left her alone in a small room. While they did, she shredded the map into particles, and dusted them around in corners and under the rug. They came back two hours later. They had asked her once to spell her name, and when they returned, they had spoken to Cologne. They had her records, or more importantly her mother's. There were clear records of her now, ever since the incident at the bank.

"Your mother was a Jewess," they spat at her. Amadea didn't answer. "She and your sister were arrested in April." Amadea nodded. She had all the poise and grace of a woman who knew she was protected. She stood there, looking at them, telling herself

she was wearing her habit. There was
something almost otherworldly about her,
and they sensed it, as she looked quietly at
them.

They took her back to Cologne that afternoon, and drove her directly to the warehouse where Jews were being held for
deportation. She had never seen or imagined anything like it. There were hundreds
of people pressed together like animals.
People crying, screaming, talking, shoved
against the walls and each other. Some had
fainted, but there was no room for them to
go anywhere, they still stood there. They
shoved her roughly in among them, still
wearing Véronique's old riding boots and
the clothes she had worn that morning. She
wondered if this was what it had been like
when they took her mother and sister away,
when they had gone to the marshaling station and then been loaded onto the train to
Ravensbrück. Amadea just stood there and
prayed, and wondered where she was going. They had told her nothing, and once in
the warehouse with the others, she had become just another body. Just another Jew
to be sent away.

They kept her in the warehouse for two

days, in the freezing cold and stench from all the bodies. They smelled of vomit, urine, sweat, and defecation. All she could do was stand there and pray. And then finally, they loaded them onto a train, without telling them their destination. It no longer mattered. They were just bodies. She had been thrown in with all the Jews they had rounded up and were deporting. People were frantically asking questions as they loaded them onto the train, and Amadea said nothing. She was praying. She tried to help a woman holding a small baby. And a man who was so ill, he looked like he was dying. She knew, as she stood there with them, that she had been put here for a reason. Whatever God intended for her, she had been sent here to share this with them, and perhaps to help whoever she could, even if only to pray.

She remembered what the Mother Superior had said to her the first day, that when she took her final vows, she would be the spouse of the crucified Christ. She was here now to share his crucifixion and theirs. When the train finally left the station after two days, she was faint with hunger and exhaustion, but she could hear the echo of her mother's voice telling her she loved her, and that of the Mother Superior telling her the same thing.

The man next to her died on the third day, and the woman's baby was dead in her arms not long after. There were children on the train and old people, men, women, dead people among the live ones. And every now and then, they would stop, open the doors, and push more people in. Amadea didn't know where they were going, nor did she care, as they made their way slowly across Germany toward the east. No one had any idea what their destination was, and it no longer mattered. All sense of humanity had been stripped from them. Whoever they had once been no longer existed. They were on the train to hell.

17

THE TRAIN STOPPED THIRTY-SIX MILES NORTH OF Prague, in Czechoslovakia, five days after they had left Cologne. It was the third of January 1942. Amadea had no idea how many people were on the train with her, but as they were told to leave the boxcars, people literally fell through the doors. They could no longer walk. Amadea had finally managed to find a small space where some of the time she could crouch. And as she stepped stiffly off the train, she could hardly bend her knees. She only glanced once behind her, and saw the bodies of several old people and a number of children left on the train. One of the women next to her had been holding a dead baby in her arms for two days. Some of the elderly hung back, as the guards were shouting at them to move. She could see that the signs that had been posted nearby were in Czech, which was her only clue as to where they were. It had been an endless trip. A few people were still clutching their suitcases, as they formed long lines as the soldiers ordered. When they moved too slowly, they were roughly shoved with their guns. She could see now, as the lines seemed to stretch for miles behind them, that there had been several thousand people on the train.

Amadea was standing next to two women and a young man. They looked at each other and said nothing. And as they walked, Amadea prayed. All she could think of was that her mother and sister had done this. And if they could do it, so could she. She thought of the crucified Christ and her sisters in the convent, and didn't allow herself to think of what was going to happen to her and the people around her. They were still alive, and when they got to wherever they were going, they would have to deal with whatever fate waited for them there. She said silent prayers, as she had for days, that there had been no reprisal against Gérard and Véronique. There was no evidence that they had concealed her, so she hoped that all was well with them. They seemed a lifetime from here, and were.

"Give me that!" a young soldier said to a man just behind her, and yanked a gold watch off his arm that had been overlooked in Cologne. She and the man next to her exchanged a glance and then looked away.

Amadea was still wearing Véronique's riding boots and was grateful to have decent shoes as they walked for the next hour. Some of the women had lost their shoes on the train, and were forced to walk on bleeding, torn feet, on frozen ground. They cried out in pain.

"You're lucky!" one of the guards said to an old woman who could hardly walk ten minutes after they had started. "You're going to a model city," he said smugly. "It's more than you deserve." As she stumbled, Amadea saw the men on either side of the woman hold her up and support her as she thanked them, and for the next mile or two, Amadea prayed for her. She was praying for all of them, including herself.

It was nearly an hour later when they saw it. It was an ancient fortress that had been built by the Austrians two hundred years before. A fading sign said TEREZIN in Czech, and beneath it a new one in German read THERESIENSTADT. It was in effect a walled city, they were marched through the main gates, and told to line up for "processing," as they watched people milling around in the narrow cobbled streets. It was more of a ghetto than a prison, and people seemed to be roaming around free. There were endless lines of people standing, holding tin cups and eating utensils. And beyond them a building that said COFFEE HOUSE, which seemed singularly odd to her. There was construction everywhere, men hammering and sawing, and putting up structures. Amadea noticed quickly that people weren't wearing prison uniforms, but their own clothes. It was a model prison camp of sorts, where the Jews living there were left to survive and fend for themselves. There were two hundred two-storied houses, and fourteen huge stone barracks. It had been built to accommodate three thousand, and there were more than seventy thousand people living there. For the most part, they looked hungry, tired, and cold, and none of them seemed to be wearing warm clothes.

Half a mile away, there was another smaller fortress, which was used as a prison for those who created trouble here.

It took seven hours for Amadea to be "processed," and all they were given while they waited was a cup of thin gruel. She hadn't eaten in five days. There had been water and bread on the train, but she had given her bread to the children, and the water made everyone sick, so eventually she didn't touch that either. But she had dysentery anyway.

The people she saw walking through the streets of Theresienstadt were an odd mixture. There were large numbers of old people who, she learned later, had been told that Theresienstadt was a retirement village for Jews, and had even been shown brochures so they would volunteer to come there, and beyond that there were crews of haggard-looking younger people who were part of construction groups working on putting the place together. There were even a considerable number of children. It looked more like a ghetto than a work camp, and because of its construction as a fortress and a walled city, it had the feeling of a village. But the people living there, other than the soldiers and guards watching them, looked ragged. They had the dead eyes and worn faces of people who'd been battered severely both before and after they got there.

When Amadea finally made it through the endless line, she was sent to one of the barracks with a dozen other women. There were numbers over doorways, and men and women inside. She was assigned to an area that had originally been built for fifty soldiers, and was inhabited now by five hundred people. There was no privacy, no space, no heat, no food, and no warm clothing. The prisoners themselves had built beds stacked three high, and close enough so the people in them could reach out and touch each other. Couples shared single beds if they had been lucky enough to come together and not get separated before they got here. Children were in a separate building, monitored by both guards and other prisoners. And on the highest floor, with broken glass in most of the windows, there were sick people in the attic. One old woman told her in hushed whispers that they were dying daily from the cold and disease. Both old and sick alike had to stand on line with everyone else for as long as six hours to get dinner, which consisted of watery soup and rotten potatoes. And there was one toilet for every thousand people.

Amadea had fallen silent as someone showed her her bed. As she was young and strong, she was assigned to a top bunk. The weaker, older people got the bottom ones. She was wearing wooden clogs they had given her during her "processing," when they had taken her boots and given her camp identity papers. They had ordered her to take off Véronique's custom-made leather riding boots, which had instantly vanished. Another guard had taken her warm jacket, and said she didn't need it, in spite of the freezing weather. It was a welcome that consisted of terror, deprivation, and humiliation, and reminded Amadea once again that she was the bride of the crucified Christ, and surely He had brought her here for a reason. What she couldn't imagine was her mother or sister enduring an existence like this, and surviving. She forced herself not to think of it now, as she looked at the people around her. It was nighttime by then, and everyone had come back from their jobs, although many were still outside on line, waiting for dinner. The kitchens cooked for fifteen thousand at a time, and even then apparently there was never enough to feed them.

"Did you just come on the train from Cologne?" a thin woman with a raging cough asked her. Amadea saw that her arm had been tattooed with a number, and her hair and face were dirty. Her nails were broken and filthy. She was wearing nothing more than a thin cotton dress and clogs, and her skin was almost blue. The barracks were freezing too.

"Yes, I did," Amadea said quietly, trying to feel like what she was, a Carmelite, and not just a woman. Knowing that and holding fast to it was her only source of strength and protection here.

The woman asked her about several people who might have been on the train, but Amadea knew no one's names, and people were all but unrecognizable in those circumstances. She recognized none of the names or descriptions the woman offered. Someone else asked the woman as they came in if she had been to the doctor. Many of the doctors and dentists who had been forced out of practice earlier had wound up here, and were doing what they could to help their fellow inmates, without benefit of medicines or equipment. The camp had only been open for two months, and already it was rife with typhoid, as someone warned her. They told her to drink the soup, but not the water. And as was inevitable, given the numbers living there, there were almost no facilities for bathing. Even in the freezing cold, the stench in the room was over-whelming.

Amadea helped an old woman get onto her bed, and saw that there were three women in the beds next to her. The bar-racks she'd been sent to were a mixture of women and children under twelve. Boys over twelve lived with the men separately. Some of the very young children were housed somewhere else, particularly those whose mothers had been sent on to other camps, or been killed. There was no pri-vacy, no warmth, and no comfort. But in spite of that, there was the occasional burst of good humor, as someone said some-thing, or cracked a joke. And in the dis-tance, Amadea could hear music. The guards walked among them from time to time, kicking someone roughly with a boot, or shoving someone, with their guns in evidence at all times. They were always looking for contraband or stolen objects. Stealing a potato, someone had told her, was punishable by death. If anyone disobeyed what rules there were, they were severely beaten. It was essential not to anger the guards, in order to avoid the inevitable reprisal that would result.

"Did you eat today?" the woman with the cough asked her. Amadea nodded.

"Did you?" Amadea was suddenly grateful for the fasting that had been a way of life in the convent. But there, their fasts had included healthy food and vegetables and fruit from the garden. This was literally starvation rations. Amadea noticed too that a number of people did not have tattoos, and she didn't know what the difference was between those who did and those who didn't, and was hesitant to ask them. They were already suffering so much, she didn't want to intrude on them further.

"It took me four hours to get dinner." They started serving in the morning. "And when I got there, they had no more potatoes, just soup, if you can call it that. It doesn't matter, I have dysentery anyway. The food here will make you sick quickly," the woman warned, "if you aren't already." Amadea had already seen that the toilet facilities were alarming. "I'm Rosa. What's your name?"

"Teresa," Amadea answered without thinking. It was so much a part of her by now that even after her months of seclusion with Gérard and Véronique, Amadea was unfamiliar to her.

"You're very pretty," she said, staring at her. "How old are you?"

"Twenty-four." Amadea would be twenty-five in April.

"So am I," Rosa said, as Amadea tried not to stare at her. She looked forty. "They killed my husband on Kristallnacht. I was in another camp before this. This one is better." Amadea didn't dare ask her if she had children. For most it was a painful subject, particularly if they'd been separated, and sent to another camp, or worse, killed before or after they'd been taken. The Nazis only wanted the children who could work. The younger ones were useless. "Are you married?" she asked with interest, as she stretched out her thin legs as she lay on her mattress. She had an old scrap of clothing she was using as a blanket. Many had none.

"No, I'm not." Amadea shook her head and smiled at her. "I'm a Carmelite."

"You're a nun?" Rosa looked first impressed, then shocked, and outraged. "They took you from the convent?"

"I left the convent in April. I've been with friends since then."

"You're Jewish?" It was confusing.

"My mother was. She converted . . . I never knew . . ." Rosa nodded.

"Did they take her?" Rosa asked softly. Amadea nodded, and for a moment couldn't answer. She knew now what it meant, and what it must have been like for her mother and Daphne. She would have done anything to spare them if she could have, even if it meant taking on more suffering herself. She had no doubt that she had come here to help those she could. It meant nothing to Amadea if she died here. She just hoped that her mother and Daphne would survive it, and were still alive wherever they were. She hoped that they were together and that she would see them both again someday. Although Gérard had admitted to Amadea, before she left, that her mother and Daphne's complete silence since the previous April was not a hopeful sign. There had never been a postcard, no message, or any kind of word.

"I'm sorry about your mother," Rosa whispered. "Did they tell you where you will work?"

"I have to go back tomorrow for a job assignment." Amadea wondered then if, when she did, they would tattoo her, and finally she got up the courage to ask Rosa about it, as they lay side by side in their bunks, close enough to speak in low whispers and still hear each other. The noise in the stone-walled room was tremendous.

"I got my number at the marshaling station before I came. They're supposed to do it when you get here, but there are so many of us and the camp is so new, they keep telling people to come back when they have more people to do it. They'll probably give you one tomorrow when they assign your job." Amadea didn't like the idea of being tattooed, but she was sure Jesus hadn't liked the idea of being crucified either. It was just one more small sacrifice she would have to make for her Father, in her "small way."

They lay in silence on their beds after that. Most of the people were too weak and tired and sick to talk, although a lot of the younger ones were very lively, despite the heavy work they did all day, and almost no food.

Later that night, after most of the inmates had gone to bed, there was the sound of a single harmonica playing. The random musician played some Viennese tunes, and some old German songs. It brought tears to people's eyes as they listened. Amadea had already heard that there was an opera company in the camp, and several musicians who played in the café, as many of the inmates had been musicians, singers, and actors before they were sent away. Despite the hardships, they tried to keep one another's spirits up, but the real terror for all of them was being deported elsewhere. The other camps were said to be much worse, and more people died there. Theresienstadt was the model camp that the Nazis wanted to use as their showpiece, to demonstrate to the world that although they wanted the Jews removed from society and isolated, they could still treat them humanely. The open sores on people's legs, the chilblains and the dysentery, the wan faces, the random beatings, and the people dying from conditions there said something very different. A sign above the camp at the entrance said WORK MAKES FREE. Death was the final freedom here.

Amadea lay in bed and said her prayers as she listened to the sound of the harmonica, and much as in the convent, they woke the inmates at five the next morning. There were lines for hot water and thin gruel, but they took so long that most people went to work on empty stomachs. Amadea went back to the processing center where she had been the day before for her job assignment. And once again, she stood on line for hours. But they told her that if she left, she would be punished, and the guard who said it to her shoved his gun into her neck, which was a clear indication that he meant it. He stood there for a long moment, looking her over, and then moved on to the next one. She heard noises outside shortly after that, and saw three guards beating a young man with clubs, as an old man in line behind her whispered.

"Smoking," he said softly, shaking his head. It was a crime punishable by severe beatings, although to the inmates even finding a cigarette butt was considered a rare

treat. One they had to keep carefully concealed, like stolen food.

When Amadea finally reached the officer
who was dispensing job assignments, he
looked like he'd had a long day. He stopped
for a moment and looked up at Amadea,
nodded, and reached for a sheaf of papers.
There were several officers lined up at
desks next to him, and official stamps and
seals being put on everything. She had
been given camp identification papers the
day before, and she handed them to him,
trying to look calmer than she felt. No matter how much she was willing to sacrifice for
the God she served, standing in front of a
Nazi soldier in a work camp was a frightening ordeal.

"What can you do?" he asked tersely,
making it clear he didn't care. He was trying
to weed out doctors and nurses and dentists and people with construction and
carpentry skills, who would be of use to
them. They needed engineers, stonemasons, cooks and lab technicians, and thousands of people to serve as slaves.

"I can work in the garden, cook, and sew.
I can do a little nursing, although I'm not
trained," but she had helped frequently with

the elderly, sick nuns, at the convent in Cologne. "I'm probably best in the garden," she added, although her mother had taught her some of her needlework skills, but the nuns she had worked with said she could make almost anything grow.

"You'd make someone a good wife," he joked, glancing at her again. "If you weren't a Jew." She was better looking than most of the inmates he saw, and she looked healthy and strong. Although she was thin, she was a tall girl.

"I'm a nun," Amadea said quietly. As soon as she said it, he looked up again, and then glanced at her papers, which said that her mother had been a Jew. He saw too then that her name was French.

"What order are you?" he asked suspiciously, as she wondered if there were other nuns there, and from what orders.

"I'm a Carmelite." She smiled, and he saw the same inner light that others noticed about her. Rosa had seen it too the night before, even here.

"There's no time for that nonsense here." She could see that he looked unnerved as he wrote something on her papers. "Fine." He looked up at her with a scowl. "You can work in the garden. If you steal any of it, you'll be shot," he said bluntly. "Be there at four in the morning tomorrow. You work till seven." It was a fifteen-hour day, but she didn't care. There were others being sent to other rooms, other buildings, other barracks, and she wondered if some of them were getting tattoos, but he seemed to have forgotten hers. She had the distinct impression that her being a nun had unnerved him. Perhaps even Nazis had a conscience, though given what she had seen so far, it seemed unlikely in the extreme.

She stood on line for food that afternoon, and was given one black rotting potato and a crust of bread. The woman just in front of her had been given a carrot. The soup had run out hours before. But she was grateful for what she got. She ate around the rotten part of the potato, and quickly gnawed on the bread. She thought about it on the way back to her room, and reproached herself for gluttony and devouring it so fast, but she was starving. They all were.

When she got back to her barracks, Rosa was already there, lying on her mattress. Her cough was worse. It was freezing that day.

"How was it? Did you get a number?"

Amadea shook her head. "I think they for-got. I think I made him nervous when I told him I was a nun." She grinned mischie-vously and looked like a young girl again. They all looked so serious and so old. "You should see one of the doctors for that cough," Amadea said, looking worried. She tucked her feet under the mattress then, they were freezing in the wooden clogs, and she was bare-legged in her riding pants, which felt paper thin in the freezing air. She'd been wearing the same filthy trousers for over a week. She had meant to go to the laundry that afternoon and see if she could trade for some clean clothes, but there hadn't been time.

"The doctors can't do anything," Rosa said. "They have no medicine." She shrugged and then looked around. She had a conspirator-ial look as she glanced at Amadea. "Look," she whispered, and pulled something out of her pocket. Amadea realized it was a sliver of an apple that looked as though a thou-sand people had stepped on it and prob-ably had.

"Where did you get that?" Amadea whis-pered, loath to take it from her, but her mouth watered when she saw it. There were no more than two bites there, or one good one.

"A guard gave it to me," she said, breaking it in half, and slipping it to Amadea. She already knew that stealing food was punishable by death. Rosa quickly put her half in her mouth and closed her eyes. Like two children sharing a single piece of candy, Amadea did the same.

They said nothing for a few minutes, and then a number of the other residents came into the room. They looked exhausted. They glanced at the two women and said nothing.

None of the men she'd encountered outside working on the construction crews had bothered Amadea in the short time she'd been there, but standing on line all afternoon, she had heard stories from the other women, several of whom had been raped. The Nazis thought the Jews were the lowest of the low, and the scum of the human race, but it didn't stop them from raping them whenever they wanted. The other women had warned her to be careful. She was too noticeable and too beautiful, and she looked as blue-eyed and blond as they did.

They told her to stay dirty and smell as bad as she could, and stay away from them, it was their only protection, and even that didn't always work, if the guards got drunk enough, which they often did, particularly at night. They were young and wanted women, and there were a lot of them in the camp. Even the old guards couldn't be trusted.

Amadea tried to get to sleep early that night, so she would be ready for work the next day. But it was hard sleeping with so many people around her. It even distracted her at times when she tried to say silent prayers. She tried to stick to her routine of the convent, as much as possible, just as she had while she was hiding at the *Schloss.* It had been easier there. But at least it was quiet when she got up at three-thirty. She had slept in her clothes, and for once there were only about thirty people waiting for the toilet. She was able to go before she left for work.

She made her way to where they had told her the gardens would be. There were about a hundred people reporting for work when she got there, mostly girls and some young boys, and a few older women. The night air was freezing, and the ground icy. It was hard to imagine what they would do there, as the guards handed them shovels. They were supposed to be planting potatoes. Thousands of them. It was backbreaking work. They worked eight hours straight until noon, their hands frozen and blistered as they pawed at the ground with the shovels, and the guards walked among them poking them with their guns. They let them stop for half an hour for some bread and soup. And as always, the soup was thin and the bread stale, but the portions were a little more plentiful. After that, they went back to work for another seven hours. As they left the gardens that night, they were searched. Stealing from the gardens was punishable by either beatings or death, depending on the guard's mood and how resistant they were. They searched Amadea's clothes, patted her down, and had her open her mouth. And as the guard searching her patted her, he grabbed her breast, and Amadea said nothing. She looked straight ahead. She said nothing about it to Rosa when she got back. She was sure she had endured worse.

The following week Rosa was moved to

another barracks. A guard had seen them talking and laughing on several occasions, and reported them. He said they were troublemakers and needed to be separated. Amadea didn't see her after that for months, and when Amadea saw her again, Rosa had no teeth. She had been caught stealing a piece of bread, and a guard had broken all of them, and her nose. The life seemed to have gone out of her by then. She died of what someone said was pneumonia that spring.

Amadea worked hard in the garden, doing what she could, but it was hard to get results given what they had to work with. Even she couldn't make miracles with the frozen ground and broken implements, but she planted row after row of potatoes every day for her fellow inmates. And in the spring, she planted carrots and turnips. She longed to plant tomatoes and lettuce and other vegetables as she had in the convent, but they were too delicate for what they needed. Some days all she got to eat was a single turnip, and more than once she was longing to steal a potato, and turned her mind to prayer instead. But on the whole, her stay there had been uneventful, and the guards left her alone. She was always respectful of them and kept to herself, did her work, and was helpful to the other inmates. She had started visiting some of the sick and the elderly at night, and when it rained too hard to work in the garden, she went to help with the children, which always buoyed her spirits, although many of them were sick. Most of them were so sweet and so brave, and it made her feel useful working with them. But there were tragedies even there. A whole trainload of them was shipped off to Chelmno in February. Their mothers stood by the trucks that took them to the train, and those who clung to them for too long or tried to fight the guards had been shot. There were horror stories every day.

By the time Amadea turned twenty-five in April, the weather was better, and she was moved to a new barracks closer to the gardens. They were working longer hours in the lengthening daylight, and sometimes she didn't get back to her barracks till nine o'clock at night. Despite the meager rations and continuing dysentery, Amadea was rail thin, but strong from her work in the gardens. And remarkably, like a few of the others, she had never been tattooed. They had just simply forgotten. They asked for her papers constantly, but never asked to see her number, and she was careful to wear long-sleeve shirts. Her hair was long by then, bleached even paler by the sun, and she wore it down her back in a long braid. But all who knew her knew that she was a nun. Among the inmates, she was treated with kindness and respect, which wasn't always the case for others. People were sick and unhappy, they watched tragedies happen constantly, the guards terrorized them frequently, beat them randomly, and sometimes even provoked them to fight with each other over a carrot or a parsnip or a piece of stale bread. But for the most part, people showed remarkable compassion toward each other, and once in a while even the guards were decent to them.

There was a young soldier who came to work as a guard in the garden in May, who was mesmerized by Amadea. He was German, from Munich, and he confessed to her one afternoon when he stopped to talk to her that he hated being there. He thought it was filthy and depressing. He was hoping for a transfer to Berlin, and had been asking for it since he arrived.

"Why do you always look so happy while you work?" he asked, lighting a cigarette, as some of the women eyed him with envy. But he didn't offer them any, although he had offered Amadea a puff and she declined. His commanding officer had left early that afternoon to attend a meeting, and the young soldiers unbent a little after he left. The one with the cigarette had been waiting for an opportunity to talk to Amadea for weeks.

"Do I?" she asked pleasantly, as she continued her work. They were planting more carrots that day. The ones she had planted so far had done well.

"Yes, you do. You always look like you have a secret. Do you have a lover?" he asked her bluntly. Some of the younger inmates had become involved with each other. It was a small ray of sunlight and warmth in a dark place. A last remnant of hope.

"No, I don't," Amadea said, and turned away. She didn't want to encourage him, and remembered the warnings the other women had given her. He was a tall, good-looking young man, with sharp features, blue eyes, and dark hair. Much like her mother's coloring. He was considerably taller than Amadea, and he thought her beautiful with her big blue eyes and blond hair. He suspected correctly that cleaned up she'd be a spectacular-looking woman. Even here, it was easy to see, with their filthy ill-fitting clothes and often-dirty hair. But in spite of that, many of the women were still pretty, especially the young ones, and Amadea certainly was.

"Did you have a boyfriend at home?" he inquired, lighting another cigarette. His mother sent them to him from home, and he was the envy of his barracks. He often traded them for favors.

"No, I didn't," Amadea said, removing herself mentally. She didn't like the turn of the conversation, and didn't want to encourage him in that direction.

"Why not?"

She stood to look at him then, and gazed right into his eyes without fear. "I'm a nun," she said simply, as though that were a warning to him that she was not a woman, but exempt from his attentions. For most people in the world as she knew it, that was a sacred state, and the look in her eyes said that she expected him to respect that, even here.

"You're not." He looked amazed. He had never seen a nun as pretty as she was, not that he remembered. He had always thought them rather plain when he'd seen them.

"Yes. I am. Sister Teresa of Carmel," she said proudly, as he shook his head.

"What a shame. Did you ever regret it? . . . I mean before you came here?" He assumed correctly that someone in her family had been Jewish, or she would never have come here in the first place. She didn't look like a Gypsy or a Communist or a criminal. She had to be a Jewess, to some degree.

"No. It's a wonderful life. I will go back one day."

"You should find a husband and have children," he said firmly, as though she were his little sister and he was reproaching her for being foolish, and this time she laughed.

"I have a husband. My husband is God. And these are all my children, and His," she said with a sweeping gesture at the garden, and for a moment he wondered if she was

crazy, and then knew she wasn't. She
meant it. She was unshakable in her faith.

"It's a stupid life," he growled at her, and
went to check on the others. She saw him
again that night as she left, and hoped
he wouldn't be the one searching her. She
didn't like the way he looked at her.

The next day he was back again, and
without saying a word, he slipped a piece of
chocolate into her pocket as he walked past
her without even acknowledging her. It was
an incredible gift, but a bad sign, and a dangerous one. She had no idea what to do
with it. If she was found with it, she could be
shot, and it seemed desperately unfair for
her to be eating chocolate when others
were starving. She waited until he walked
by again and said that she appreciated it,
but he should give it to one of the children,
and discreetly handed it back to him while
no one was looking.

"Why did you do that?" He looked hurt.

"Because it's not right. I shouldn't have
anything better than the others. Someone
else needs that more than I do. A child, or
an old person, or someone sick."

"Then give it to them," he said tersely,
shoved it back into her hand, and walked

away. But he knew it would melt in her pocket, and so did she, and then she would get in trouble. She didn't know what else to do, so she ate it, and felt guilty for the rest of the afternoon. She begged God to forgive her for being greedy and dishonest. But it had been so delicious, the taste of it haunted her all day. It was all she could think of until she left. And when she did, he smiled at her. And in spite of herself, she smiled at him. He looked like a big mischievous boy, although he was about her age. He came to talk to her again the following afternoon. He said they were going to make her the leader of a group because she worked so well. But what he was doing was granting her favors and putting her in his debt, which was an extremely dangerous thing. She had no idea what he wanted from her, but it was easy to guess. She tried to avoid him at every opportunity for weeks after that. The weather was getting warmer when he stopped to talk to her again. She had just finished her soup and bread, and was on her way back to work.

"You're afraid to talk to me, aren't you?" he asked softly as he followed her to where she had left her shovel. She turned to look at him.

"I'm a prisoner and you're a guard. That's a difficult thing," she said honestly, choosing her words carefully so she wouldn't offend him.

"Perhaps not so difficult as you think. I could make life easier for you, if you let me. We could be friends."

"Not here," she said sadly, wanting to believe he was a good person, but it was hard to tell here. Another trainload of inmates had been deported the day before. She knew one of the people who made the lists. So far her name wasn't on it, but it could be at any time. Theresienstadt seemed to be the gateway to other camps, most of which were worse. Auschwitz and Bergen-Belsen and Chelmno. They were all names that struck fear in everyone's hearts, even hers.

"I want to be your friend," he insisted. He had given her chocolate on two other occasions, but the favors were dangerous, and she knew it, and so was this. She didn't want to be put in the position of rejecting him. That would be even more dangerous. And she had no experience with men. She had been in the convent, sequestered from the world, since she was a young girl. At twenty-five, she was more innocent than girls of fifteen. "I have a sister your age," he said quietly. "I think of her sometimes when I look at you. She is married and has three children. You could have children one day too."

"Nuns don't have children." She smiled gently at him. There was something sad in his eyes. She suspected he was homesick, as many of the others were too. They got blind drunk at night to forget it, and the horrors they saw on a daily basis. It had to bother some of them too, though not many. But in some ways, he seemed like a sweet man. "I'm going back to my order when this is over, to take my solemn vows."

"Ah!" he said, looking hopeful. "Then you're not a nun yet!"

"Yes, I am. I was in the convent for six years," it had been almost a year since she left. If all had gone well and she hadn't been forced to leave the convent, she would have been a year from final vows.

"You can rethink it now," he said happily, as though she had given him a gift, and then he looked thoughtful. "How Jewish are you?" She felt as though she were being interviewed as his bride. The thought of it made her feel sick.

"Half."

"You don't look it." She looked more Aryan than most of the women he knew, including his mother, who was dark. His father was tall, thin, and blond like Amadea, as was his sister. He had his mother's dark hair, and father's light eyes. But Amadea certainly didn't look Jewish to him. Nor would she to anyone else, when this was over. He had a mad moment of wanting to protect her, and keep her alive.

She went back to work then and stopped talking to him, but every day after that, he stopped to talk to her, and every day he slipped something into her pocket. A chocolate, a handkerchief, a tiny piece of dried meat, a piece of candy, something, anything, to assure her of his good intentions. He wanted her to trust him. He wasn't like the others. He wasn't going to just drag her down a dark alley or behind a bush and rape her. He wanted her to want him. Stranger things had happened, he told himself. She was beautiful, obviously intelligent, and completely pure since she'd been in a convent for her entire adult life. He wanted her more than he had ever wanted any woman. He was twenty-six years old, and if he could have, he would have spirited Amadea away then and there. But they both had to be careful. He could get in as much trouble as she could, for befriending her. They wouldn't frown on it if he raped her, he knew that most of the men would find it amusing, plenty of them had certainly done it themselves. But falling in love with her was something else. For that, he would be killed or deported himself. This was danger-ous business, and he knew it. And so did she. She had far more to lose than he did. She never forgot that as she walked past him every day, and he slipped his little gifts into her pockets. If anyone saw them, she'd be shot. They were extremely dangerous gifts.

"You must not do that," she chided him as she walked past him one afternoon. He had put several candies in her pocket that day, and much as she hated to admit it, they gave her energy. She didn't even dare give them to the children she visited, because she'd be punished for having them in the first place, and so would the children, who would be so excited to have them that they would tell somebody, and then they'd all be in trouble. So she ate them herself, and told no one. His name was Wilhelm.

"I wish I could give you other things. Like a warm jacket," he said seriously, "and good shoes . . . and a warm bed."

"I'm fine as I am," she said, and meant it.

She was growing used to the discomforts, just as she had those of the convent. These were simply sacrifices she made for the crucified Christ. They were easier to accept that way. The one thing she hated and never got used to was seeing people die. And there were so many, for different reasons, illness as much as violence. Theresienstadt was the least violent of the camps, from what everyone said. Auschwitz was the one they all feared. Theresienstadt was child's play compared to that, and supposedly fewer people died here. They were even talking about bringing officials here to show it off as a model camp, and to show others, to demonstrate how well they treated the Jews. They had a *Kaffeehaus* and an opera company, after all. What more did they need? Medicine and food. And Wilhelm knew that, just as she did.

"You shouldn't be here," he said sadly,

and she agreed. But neither should anyone else. There was nothing either of them could do about it. He no more than she. "Do you have relatives somewhere else? Christian ones?" She shook her head.

"My father died when I was ten. He was French. I never met his relatives," she said as though it mattered now, which it didn't. But it was something to say in answer to his question. And then he lowered his voice, and spoke in a barely audible whisper.

"There are Czech partisans in the hills. We hear about them all the time. They could help you escape." Amadea stared at him, wondering if this was a trap. Was he trying to get her to escape, and then she would be shot trying? Was it a test? Was he mad? How did he think she would escape?

"That's impossible," she whispered back, drawn in by what he said, but suspicious nonetheless.

"No, it's not. There are often no sentries on the back gate, late at night. They keep it locked. If you ever found the keys, you could just walk away."

"And be shot," she said seriously.

"Not necessarily. I could meet you there. I hate it here." She stared at him, not know-

ing what to answer, and not knowing what
she would do if she did escape. Where
would she go? She knew no one in
Czechoslovakia, and she couldn't go back
to Germany. All of Europe was occupied by
the Nazis. It was hopeless, and she knew it.
But it was an interesting idea. "I could go
with you."

"To where?" They would both be shot for
what they were saying if anyone overheard
them.

"I have to think about it," he said, as his
commanding officer appeared and called
him. Amadea was terrified he would get into
trouble for talking to her. But the commanding officer showed him some papers and
laughed uproariously, and Wilhelm grinned.
Obviously, all was well. But she couldn't get
his words out of her head. She had heard
stories of men escaping, but never women.
A group of them had walked out a while
ago, appearing to be a work gang going
somewhere, the sentries hadn't been paying attention, and assumed they were au-
thorized to work outside the camp. They
said they were going to the nearby fortress
to work in the prison, and then they escaped. They had just walked out of camp.

Most of them had been caught and shot. But some had escaped. Into the hills, as Wilhelm said. It was an extraordinary idea. And of course it entailed leaving with him, which was a whole other problem. She had no intention of becoming his mistress, or his wife, even if he helped her escape. And if he turned her in, she could be sent to Auschwitz or killed right here. She could trust no one, not even him, although he did seem like a decent person, and he was obviously crazy about her. She had never before had a sense that she could have power over men just by the way she looked.

It was more than that in his case. He thought that she was not only beautiful but intelligent and a good person. She was the kind of woman he had wanted to find for years, and couldn't. And he had found her here. A half Jewess at Theresienstadt concentration camp, and a nun on top of it. Nothing in life was easy.

Lying on her mattress that night, all Amadea could think about was escaping, but once beyond the gates, then what? There was no way for it to work. He had spoken of Czech partisans in the hills, and how were they supposed to find them? Just walk into the hills and start waving a white flag? It made no sense. But the thought of it kept her going for days. And each day Wilhelm was kinder and spent more time with her. What he was trying to start was an innocent romance, and this wasn't the time or place, nor was she the right woman. But she no longer said that to him. Perhaps they could leave together, as friends. It was an extraordinary idea. Yet she also knew that there was nowhere in the world where they could be safe. He would be a deserter and she a Jew. And together, they would be doubly at risk.

There were rumors in the camp about something happening at the end of May. At first, the inmates didn't know what it was, but there were whispers among the guards. Two Czech patriots, serving with the British forces, had been parachuted into the countryside near Prague. On May 27 they had attempted to assassinate Gruppenführer Reinhard Heydrich, the Reich Protector. All hell had broken loose in Prague as a result. Fatally wounded, he died on the fourth of June. Within the next few days 3,188 Czech citizens were arrested, of whom 1,357 were shot. Another 657 died during interrogation.

The repercussions were massive, and the reprisals by the Nazis severe. Everyone in the camps waited to hear what was happening day by day.

On the afternoon of June 9 Wilhelm came to her in the garden, walked by her slowly without looking at her, and said a single word. "Tonight." She turned and stared. He couldn't mean what he had just said. Maybe he was propositioning her. But as she was finishing work, he stopped as though inspecting what she'd done and explained in a rapid whisper. "They are taking over the town of Lidice tonight. It's twenty miles from here, and they need our men. They're going to deport all the women and kill all the men, and burn the town to the ground, as an example to others. Two-thirds of our men are going there. They leave at eight o'clock. Nine at the latest, with most of the trucks and cars. Meet me at the back gate at midnight. I'll find the key."

"If anyone sees me leaving, I'll be shot."

"There'll be no one left to shoot you. Stay close to the barracks, no one will see you, and if they stop you, tell them you are going to the sick." He looked at her meaningfully then, and nodded, as though approving her work, and then he left. She knew what he had said was insane. It was a crazy plan, but there was no question that if there was ever going to be an opportunity, this was the night. And then what would they do? What would she do? But she knew that whatever happened, she had to try it.

She was thinking of the people in the town of Lidice as she walked home. They were going to kill the men and deport the women and children, burn the town down. It was a horrifying thought. But so was staying at Theresienstadt until the end of the war, or getting deported to another camp. She had been there for five months, and she was lucky. She wasn't as sick as most. They had never tattooed her. There were too many new arrivals, too much construction to or-ganize, too much to do. She had slipped through the cracks. And now they were go-ing to slip right out the gate. If they were caught, she would be killed or sent to Auschwitz, and he might be killed as well. She had much to lose. But perhaps more to lose by staying here. She might be sent to Auschwitz anyway. She knew she had to try, even if they killed her. She could not stay here, and they would never get another chance like this. This was the perfect opportunity.

She heard the trucks and cars roar out that night. Others noticed it, too. And even the guards roaming around the barracks were sparse. There was hardly anyone there. But Theresienstadt was a peaceful place. They were "good" Jews. They did as they were told. They worked. They built what they were meant to. They worked in their jobs. They played music. They did as the guards said. It was a peaceful night. And at midnight, Amadea got off her mattress, still wearing her clothes. Almost everyone slept in their clothes. If you didn't, they disappeared. Or got lost. She told the guard she was going to the bathroom, and wanted to check on a friend on the upper floor, in the attic, where the sickest ones were kept. He smiled and moved on. She had never given him any trouble, and he knew she wouldn't now. He knew she was a nun, and was always ministering to someone, either old people or children, or the sick, of which there were thousands. They were all sick to some degree.

"Goodnight," the guard said politely, as he moved on to the next barracks. It was going to be a quiet night with the others gone. There was no sign of unrest here. Just peaceful Jews. The better weather put everyone in a good mood, inmates and guards alike. The winter had been brutal, but the summer was gentle and warm. Someone was playing a harmonica as Amadea left. She stopped at the bathroom, and then just walked out of the barracks. There was no one there, and it was a short distance from where she was staying to the back gate. It was remarkable. There was absolutely no one around. The main square was a ghost town tonight. And he was there. Waiting for her. He had the key in his hand and showed it to her with a smile. With a single brief gesture, he put the enormous metal key in the lock, the same one that had been used for nearly two hundred years. The gate squeaked open, just enough to let them both through, and he closed it again, reached back inside to lock it, and then tossed the key away. If they found it, they would think a sentry had dropped it inadvertently and be relieved that no one had found it and unlocked the gate. And then they ran. They ran like the wind, both of them. Amadea never knew she could run so fast. Every moment, every second, she waited to hear shots, to feel a knifelike pain in her back or heart or her arm or her leg. She felt nothing. She heard nothing except Wilhelm's breath and hers. Until they reached the trees. There was a forest near Theresienstadt, and they plunged into it like two lost children, gasping for breath. They had done it! They were safe! She was free!

"Oh my God!" she whispered in the moonlight. "Oh my God! Wilhelm, we did it!" It was impossible to believe. She was beaming at him, as he smiled at her. And she had never seen so much love in a man's eyes.

"My darling, I love you," he whispered, and pulled her into his arms, as she suddenly wondered if this was just a plot to rape her. But it couldn't be. He had taken as much risk as she. Although he could always say that she had escaped and he had followed her, and then he would bring her back, after he raped her. She trusted no one now and looked at him suspiciously. He kissed her hard on the mouth, and she pushed him away. "Wilhelm, don't . . . please . . ." She was still out of breath and so was he.

"Don't be stupid," he said, sounding annoyed. "I didn't risk my life for you, so you could play nun. I'm going to marry you when we get back to Germany. Or before that." This was no time to be arguing about his illusions or her vows. "I love you."

"I love you for helping me, but not the way you mean," she said honestly, as he fondled her breast and then grabbed her. He wanted to make love to her right there. "Wilhelm, don't." She stood up, to get away from him, and he stood up with her, and grabbed her with powerful hands. He was trying to force her to the ground, as she pushed him away from her as hard as she could, and he lost his footing on a tree root, and pitched backward with a sharp sound and a stunned look on his face. His head hit the ground with a thud and instantly cracked.

There was blood everywhere as Amadea knelt next to him in shock and horror. She hadn't meant to hurt him, only to push him off. She had been afraid he was going to rape her in his enthusiasm and fervor, and now his eyes were open in a dead stare. He had no pulse. Wilhelm was dead, as she bowed her head in grief over what she'd done. She had killed a man. The man who had helped her escape. His death was on her soul. She looked at him, closed his eyes, and made the sign of the cross. And then, gingerly, she took his gun, and held it in her hand. He had a small canteen of water, and she took that, too. She found money, although very little, some candies, and bullets that she had no idea what to do with. She assumed the gun was loaded, but she had no notion of how to use it, and then she stood up.

"Thank you," she said softly, and then she walked deeper into the forest, with no idea where she was going, or what she would find. All she could do was keep walking, stay in the forest, and pray the partisans would find her. But she knew they would be busy that night. Lidice was already burning as Amadea walked away, and left the dead soldier beneath the trees. She would never know what he had really planned to do, if he would have hurt her or not, if he loved her or not, if he was a good man or bad. All she knew was that she had killed a man, and for now at least, she was free.

18

AMADEA WAS ALONE IN THE FOREST FOR TWO DAYS. She walked by day, and slept for a few hours at night. The air was cool and fresh, although at one point she thought she smelled fire in the air. Lidice. But the forest was dark. Even in the daytime it was deeply shaded. She had no idea where she was going, or if she would find anyone before she died of hunger, exhaustion, and thirst. The water in Wilhelm's canteen ran out. And on the second day she found a stream. She didn't know if the water was good or not, but she drank it anyway. It couldn't be any worse than the water they had drunk in Theresienstadt, standing stagnant in barrels, full of diseases. This water at least tasted clean. The forest was cool. There were no sounds except birds in the trees high above her and the ones she made. She saw a rabbit once, and a squirrel. It felt like an enchanted forest, and the enchantment was that she was free. She had killed a man to get here. She knew she would never forgive herself for that. It had been an accident, but still she would have to answer for it. She wished she could tell the Mother Superior. Wished she were back in the convent with her sisters. She had buried her papers under a clump of dirt. She had no identification now. None. She was a random soul, a lost person wandering through the forest. And there was no number on her arm. She could tell them whatever she wanted if they found her, but they would know. She looked like all the others in the camps. Thin, malnourished, filthy. The shoes she wore had almost no soles. She lay down finally at the end of the second day, and thought about eating leaves. She wondered if they were poisonous. She had found some berries and eaten those, and they had given her terrible cramps, and more dysentery. She felt weak and exhausted and sick. And as the light faded in the forest, she lay down to sleep on the soft earth. If the Nazis found her, maybe they would just shoot her there. It was a good place to die. She had seen no one in two days. She didn't know if they were look-ing for her, or if they cared. She was just one more Jew. And wherever the partisans were, they were surely not here.

She was alone in the forest, and remem-bered to say her prayers as she fell asleep. She prayed for Wilhelm's soul, and thought of his mother and sister and how sad they would be. She thought of her mother and Daphne and wondered where they were and if they were still alive. Maybe they had es-caped, too. She smiled thinking of it, and then she fell asleep.

They found her there the next morning, as the light filtered dimly through the trees. They came on silent feet and signaled to each other. One of them held her down, and the other covered her mouth so she wouldn't scream. She woke with a huge start and a terrified look. There were men with guns, six of them, surrounding her. Wilhelm's gun lay on the ground beside her. She couldn't reach it and didn't know how to use it anyway. One of the men signaled to her not to scream, and she nodded slightly.

There was no way of knowing who they were. They watched her for a moment, and then let her go, as five of them pointed guns at her and one of them searched her pockets. There was nothing. They found nothing, except for the last candy she had left. It was a German bonbon, and they eyed her with suspicion. The men spoke to each other in hushed voices in Czech. She had picked up a little in the camp, from Czechoslovak prisoners. She wasn't sure if they were good men or bad, if they were the partisans she had hoped to find. And even if they were, she didn't know if they would rape her, or what to expect from them. They pulled her roughly to her feet and signaled to her to follow. They had her surrounded, and one of the men took the gun. She stumbled often, and they walked fast. She was tired and weak, and when she fell, they let her pick herself up in case it was a trick.

Not one of them spoke to each other, except rarely, as they walked for several hours, and then she saw a camp in the forest. There were about twenty men there, and they left her with two of the men under guard, and then pulled her roughly into a clump of trees where a group of armed men sat talking. They looked up at her as she walked in. And the men who had walked with her to get there left. There was a long silence as they looked at her, and then finally one of them spoke. He addressed her in Czech first, and she shook her head. And then he spoke to her in German.

"Where did you come from?" he asked in proficient although heavily accented German, as he looked her over. She was filthy and thin, she had cuts and scratches everywhere, and her shoes were in shreds on her feet. The soles of her feet were bleeding. She looked him straight in the eyes.

"Theresienstadt," she said softly. If they were partisans, she had to tell them the truth. They couldn't help her otherwise, and maybe wouldn't anyway.

"You were a prisoner there?" She nodded. "You escaped?"

"Yes."

"You have no number," he said suspiciously. She looked more like a German agent with her tall blond good looks. Even dirty and exhausted she was beautiful, and obviously frightened. But she was brave, too, he could see, and he admired that.

"They never tattooed me. They forgot," she said with a small smile. He didn't smile back. This was serious business. There was a lot at stake. For all of them. Not only her.

"You're a Jew?"

"Half. My mother was German Jewish. My father was a French Catholic. She was a convert."

"Where is she? At Theresienstadt, too?"

Amadea's eyes wavered, but only for a moment. "They sent her to Ravensbrück a year ago."

"How long were you in Terezin?" He used the Czech name for it, not the one she used.

"Since January." He nodded.

"Do you speak French?" This time she nodded. "How well?"

"Fluently."

"Do you have an accent? Can you pass for German or French equally?" She felt weak as she realized they were going to help her, or try to. The questions he asked were brisk and efficient. He looked like a farmer, but he was more than that. He was the leader of the partisans in the area. He would be the one to decide if they would help her or not.

"I can pass equally," she said. But he realized as she did that she looked German. In this case, it was an asset. She looked entirely Aryan. And then she looked at him and dared to ask a question. "What will you do with me? Where will I go?"

"I don't know." He shook his head. "You can't go back to Germany if you're a Jew, not to stay at least. We can get you through with false papers, but they'll find you eventually. And you can't stay here. All the German women went back. The officers' wives come to visit sometimes. We'll see." He said something to one of his men then, and a few minutes later, they brought her food. She was so hungry she felt sick, and could hardly eat. She hadn't seen real food in six months. "You'll have to stay here for a while. There's trouble all around."

"What happened in Lidice?" she asked softly.

His eyes blazed with hatred as he answered. "All the men and boys are dead. The women were deported. The town is gone."

"I'm sorry," she said softly, and he looked away. He didn't tell her that his brother and his family had lived there. The reprisal had been total.

"We can't move you for weeks, maybe months. And it takes time to get the papers."

"Thank you." She didn't care how long they kept her. It was better than where she had been. Ordinarily, they would have moved her to a safe house in Prague, but they couldn't now.

In the end, she was there, living in the forest, in his camp until the beginning of August. Things had calmed down somewhat by then. She spent most of her time praying, or walking in a small area around the camp. Other men came and went, and only once a woman. They never spoke to her. And whenever she was alone, she prayed. The forest was so peaceful that it was hard to believe sometimes that there was a war raging beyond their camp. It was late one night after she'd been there for a few weeks, and they realized that she came from Cologne that they told her Cologne had been bombed from one end to the other by a thousand British bombers. They had heard nothing about it in Theresienstadt. The partisans' description of it was amazing. It had been a major hit to the Nazis. She hoped that nothing had happened to the Daubignys, but they were far enough out of the city that hopefully they had escaped major damage.

Almost two months after Amadea had come to them, the local leader of the partisans sat down with her and explained what was going to happen. They had heard nothing about her successful escape from local authorities. Presumably she was so unimportant that they felt that one Jew more or less, dead or alive, was not worth their notice. There was no way of knowing if they had connected it to Wilhelm's disappearance on the same evening, or if they cared about it. Hopefully, they didn't. She wondered if they had ever found him. The partisans had not wanted to get that close to the camp to retrieve him and bury him elsewhere.

The freedom fighters had had papers made for her in Prague, and they were astonishingly authentic looking. They said her name was Frieda Oberhoff, and that she was a twenty-five-year-old housewife from Munich. Her husband was stationed in Prague, and she had come to visit him. He was the *Kommandant* of a small precinct. He was going back to Munich with her on leave and from there they would go directly to Paris for a short holiday, before she went back to Munich and he returned to Prague. Their traveling papers looked impeccable. And a young woman brought clothes and a suitcase to her. She helped Amadea dress, and they took a photograph of her for her passport. Everything was in order.

She was going to be traveling with a young German who had worked with them. He had gone in and out of Germany into Czechoslovakia and Poland. This would be the second time he traveled into France on a mission like this one. She was to meet him the following day at a safe house in Prague.

She didn't know how to thank the leader of the group when she left the camp. All she could do was look at him and tell him that she would pray for him. They had saved her life, and were giving her a new one. The plan was for her to join a cell of the Resistance outside Paris, but she still had to get through Germany first, as the *Kommandant*'s wife. In her bright blue summer dress and white hat the day she left, she certainly looked the part. She even had high heels and white gloves. She turned to look at them for a last time, and then got in

the car with the men who were driving her
into the city. They were both Czechoslovaks
who worked for the Germans and were beyond reproach. No one stopped them or
checked their papers as they drove into the
city, and less than an hour after she had left
the partisan camp, she was in the basement
of the safe house in Prague. At midnight,
the man who was going to travel with her
arrived. He was wearing an SS uniform, and
he was tall and handsome and blond. He
was actually a Czech who had grown up in
Germany. His German was flawless, and he
looked every inch an SS officer as they introduced him to Amadea late that night.

They were leaving on a train at nine in the
morning. They knew that the train would be
full, the soldiers in the station distracted.
They would be checking papers randomly,
but it would never occur to them to be suspicious of the handsome SS officer traveling
with his beautiful young wife. One of the
men dropped them off at the station, and
they strode onto the platform chatting amiably, as he told Amadea in an undertone to
smile and laugh. It felt odd to be wearing
fashionable women's clothes again. She
hadn't done that since she was a girl of

eighteen. And she felt very odd to be traveling with a man. She was terrified that someone would recognize that her papers were
false, but neither the agent nor the soldier
watching people board the train questioned
them. They didn't even give them a cursory
glance and just waved them on. Amadea
and her traveling companion looked like
Hitler's dream for the master race. Tall,
blond beautiful people with blue eyes. They
settled into a first-class compartment as
Amadea stared at him with wide eyes.

"We did it," she whispered, and he nodded and put a finger to his lips. You never
knew who might be listening. The essence
of the masquerade was to consistently play
the part. They spoke to each other comfort-
ably in German. He discussed vacation
plans with her and what she wanted to see
in Paris. He told her about the hotel where
they would stay, and chatted with her about
her mother in Munich. As the train pulled
out of the station, Amadea watched with
haunted eyes as Prague slowly drifted
away. All she could think of was the day she
had come here in the cattle car. The agonies
and the miseries they had endured, the slop
buckets and the people crying and eventu-

ally dying all around them. She had stood up for days. And now she was sitting in a first-class compartment wearing a hat and white gloves, traveling with a freedom fighter in an SS uniform. All she could conclude was that, for whatever reason, thus far at least, the God she loved so profoundly had wanted her to survive.

The trip to Munich was uneventful and took just over five hours. She slept part of the way, and woke with a start when she saw a German soldier walk by. Wolff, the man she was traveling with, or the name he was using anyway, laughed at her and smiled at the soldier, and through clenched teeth told her to smile as well. She went back to sleep after that, and eventually dozed with her head on his shoulder. He woke her when they pulled into Hauptbahnhof station in Munich.

They had two hours to spare between trains. He suggested dinner at a restaurant at the station, and said it was a shame they didn't have time to go into town. But they agreed that they were anxious to get to France. Paris was a major holiday destination for Germans these days. With the Germans occupying it, everyone wanted to go to Paris. In the restaurant, Wolff talked to her about the fun they would have. But even as they chatted, she noticed that he was ever vigilant. He seemed to keep an eye on everyone and everything, all the while seeming to chat effortlessly with her.

Amadea didn't relax till she got on the train to Paris. They had a first-class compartment again, and she had scarcely been able to eat dinner, she was so worried that something terrible would happen and they'd get arrested on the spot.

"You'll get used to this eventually," he said in a low voice as they boarded the train. But with luck she wouldn't have to. She had no idea what they were going to do to hide her outside Paris, but the idea of circulating among German officers, pretending to be the wife of an SS officer on vacation, nearly made her faint with terror. It was almost as frightening as the night she had fled Theresienstadt. That had taken courage, but this took rigorous composure. She sat rigidly in her seat once again until the train pulled out. And this time they would be traveling overnight.

The attendant opened the beds for them,

and after he left, Wolff told her to put on her nightgown, as Amadea looked shocked.

"I'm your husband." He laughed. "You could at least take off your gloves and hat." Even she laughed at that.

She turned her back to him and put her nightgown on, pulling her dress off underneath it, and when she turned, he was wearing pajamas. He was a strikingly good-looking man.

"I've never done this before," she said, looking embarrassed as he smiled at her, and she hoped he wouldn't take the charade too far. He didn't look like that sort of man.

"I take it you're not married?" he asked softly. The noise of the train covered their conversation, and he was no longer worried. No one was listening to them now.

Amadea smiled in answer. "No, I'm not. I'm a Carmelite." He looked shocked for a minute and rolled his eyes.

"Well, I've never spent the night with a nun before. I suppose there's always a first time." He helped her onto her bed, and sat looking up at her from the narrow bench across from it. She was a lovely looking girl, nun or not. "How did you get to Prague?"

She hesitated for a moment before she answered. There were no simple explanations anymore, for anything. Only hard ones. "Theresienstadt." It explained everything with a single word. "Are you married?" she asked, curious about him too now. He nodded, and then she saw something painful in his eyes.

"I was. My wife and two sons were killed in Holland during the reprisals. She was Jewish. They didn't even bother to deport them, just killed them on the spot. I came back to Prague after that." He had been back in Czechoslovakia for two years, doing what he could to put a stick in the Germans' wheels. "What are you going to do after you get to Paris?" he asked, as they rode through Germany. They would be in Paris by morning.

"I have no idea." She had never been there before. If she had the opportunity, she wanted to visit her father's part of the world in Dordogne, and maybe even get a glimpse of their château. But she knew she wouldn't be free to move around. The partisans in Prague had assured her that she would be hidden by the underground in France, wherever they felt it was safest for her, more than likely somewhere outside Paris. They both knew that she had to wait and see what they told her when she arrived.

"I hope we travel together again sometime," he said as he stood up and yawned. She thought he was remarkably calm, given the potential dangers of their situation. But he had been doing missions like this for two years.

"I don't think I'll be leaving France." She couldn't imagine risking going back into Germany again until after the war. France would be difficult enough, given her situation. Germany was impossible. She would rather die than be deported again, next time more than likely to someplace worse. Theresienstadt had been bad enough. She couldn't help thinking of all the people there, and what would happen to them. It had been nothing less than a miracle that she'd escaped and was on this train.

"Will you go back to the convent again after the war?" Wolff asked with interest, and she smiled. Her whole face lit up as she did.

"Of course."

"Did you never have doubts about the choice you made?"

"Never once. I knew it was right the day I went in."

"And now? After all you've seen? Can you really believe it's right to be shut away from the world? There's so much more you can do for people out here."

"Oh no," she said with a look of wonderment, "we pray for so many people. There is so much to do." He smiled, listening to her, he wasn't going to argue with her. But he couldn't help wondering if she'd really go back one day. She was a beautiful girl, and she had much to discover and learn. It was an odd feeling for him knowing that he was traveling with a nun. She certainly didn't look like one to him. She looked very human and desirable, although she seemed to be unaware of it, which he thought was part of her appeal. She was a very attractive woman in a distinguished sort of way.

He lay awake on his bunk that night, listening for problems on the train. They could be stopped and boarded at any time, and he wanted to be awake if that happened. He got up once or twice, and saw that Amadea was fast asleep.

He woke her the next morning in time to dress before they reached the station. He

dressed and stood outside the compartment while she washed her face and
brushed her teeth and changed. And a few
minutes later, he accompanied her to the
bathroom and waited for her. She looked
very composed when they went back to the
compartment and she put her hat and
gloves on again. She had her passport and
traveling papers in her purse.

She looked with fascination as they pulled
into the Gare de l'Est. Her eyes were wide at
the bustling activity on the platform. And he
whispered to her before they left the compartment.

"Don't look frightened. Look like a happy
tourist, excited to be here with your husband for a romantic vacation."

"I'm not sure what that looks like," she
whispered back with a grin.

"Pretend you're not a nun."

"I can't do that." She was still smiling, and
they looked like a happy young couple as
they left the train. They each carried their
suitcases, and she had a gloved hand
tucked into his arm. No one stopped them,
no one questioned them. They were two
splendid-looking Aryans on their way to en-

joy a holiday in Paris. And outside the station, Wolff hailed a cab.

They went to a café on the Left Bank, where they said they were meeting friends, and afterward would go to their hotel. The driver was sullen, and he didn't appear to understand German. Amadea had spoken to him in French, and he was surprised by how well she spoke it. He assumed she was German after listening to them talk in the backseat, but when she spoke to him, she sounded French. She looked German to him.

Wolff gave him a more than decent tip, and the driver thanked him politely and drove off. He knew better than to be rude to Germans, particularly officers of the SS. One of his friends had been shot by one six months before, just for mouthing off, and calling him a *"sale boche."*

They sat in the café, drinking coffee, or what passed for it these days, and the waiter brought them a basket of croissants. Ten minutes later they were joined by Wolff's friend, who was obviously thrilled to see him and clapped him on the shoulder. They were friends from student days, or so they said. In fact, they had never met, but they performed well, as Amadea observed them with a shy smile. Wolff introduced her as his wife. They sat together for a few minutes, and then Wolff's friend offered to drive them to their hotel. They got into his car with their bags. No one at the café appeared to be particularly interested. And once in the car, on the outskirts of Paris, Wolff changed his clothes into the ones their contact had brought. The SS uniform and all its accoutrements disappeared into a valise with a false bottom. He changed expertly as they drove along, while conversing with the driver. They paid no attention to Amadea, and appeared to be speaking in code. Wolff said he was going back tonight.

They stopped at a small house outside Paris, in the Val-de-Marne district. It looked like any other ordinary house. The kind of house where you would visit your grandmother or a widowed great-aunt. There was a pleasant old couple sitting in the kitchen having breakfast and reading the paper.

Their driver, whose name was Pierre, gave them a cursory glance. *"Bonjour,* Grandmaman, Grandpapa . . ." He walked right past them to a closet, opened a false door at the back of it, and then went down a dark stairway into the basement, as Wolff and Amadea followed. He walked them into the wine cellar, and stood there for a moment, without turning on a light, and then pushed a well-concealed door. Behind it lay a bevy of activity. Once the door was closed behind them, they saw a dozen men sitting around a makeshift table, two women, and another man on a shortwave radio. The room was cramped, and there were papers and boxes everywhere, a camera, several suitcases. They looked like they had been there for many days.

"Salut," the driver addressed one of the men, and the others nodded and acknowledged him.

"Salut, Pierre" echoed around the room, and one of them asked if he had brought the package. Pierre nodded toward Amadea. She was the package they had been waiting for. One of the women smiled at her and extended a hand.

"Welcome to Paris. Did you have a good trip?" She addressed Amadea in German, who in turn answered her in flawless French, much to their surprise. "We didn't know you spoke French." They didn't have many details on her yet, only that she was a camp survivor, and had been rescued by the partisans near Prague. They said she needed refuge in France. And word was she could be useful to them. No one had explained how. But it was obvious to them now. She looked German and spoke flawless German and French.

Wolff sat down with two of the men in a corner then, and filled them in on what was happening in Prague, and what the German movements and plans were there. They spoke in low voices, and Amadea couldn't hear what they said.

The man who appeared to be in charge was looking Amadea over carefully. He had never seen a more typical Aryan, and she seemed to be equally at ease in French and German. "We were going to put you on a farm in the South if we could get you there safely. You certainly look like a German, an Aryan for sure. You're Jewish?"

"My mother was."

He glanced at her arm—he knew she had come out of one of the camps. "You have a number?" She shook her head. She was perfect. He hated to send her away. They needed her in Paris. He was squinting thoughtfully as he looked at her. "Do you have good nerves?" he asked with a wry smile.

Wolff overheard them and vouched for her. "She was fine on the train." And then with an affectionate look at his traveling companion, he said, "She's a nun. A Carmelite."

"That's interesting," the head of the cell said, looking at her. "Isn't having good judgment one of the requirements for becoming a Carmelite? And a good nervous equilibrium, if I remember correctly."

Amadea laughed. "How do you know that? Yes, both, and good health."

"My sister entered an order in Touraine. They were crazy to take her. She has terrible judgment, and bad nerves. She stayed two years and came out and got married. I'm sure they were happy to see her go. She has six kids." He smiled at her, and Amadea felt a connection to him. They hadn't been introduced, but she had heard several people call him Serge. "I have a brother who's a priest." He was the head of a cell in Marseilles, which he didn't volunteer to Amadea. He had trained with Father Jacques in Avon, where he had been hiding Jewish boys in the school he ran. Serge's brother was doing much the same thing in

Marseilles, as were individual members of the clergy all over France, often on an independent basis. Serge knew a number of them. But he didn't want to make use of this young German woman as a nun. She could be far more useful in other ways. She could easily masquerade as a German, and pull it off flawlessly, if she had the guts. That's what he had to learn. "We'll keep you here for a few weeks. You can stay downstairs until we get your papers in order. After that you can stay with my grandparents. You're my cousin from Chartres. That should be religious enough for you." She realized then that Pierre and Serge were brothers. The darkened room had the atmosphere of a factory, there was so much going on. Someone was running a small printing press in a corner. They were printing bulletins to distribute to buoy French spirits and tell them what was really happening with the war.

One of the women took Amadea's photograph then, for her new French papers. And a little while later, the other woman went upstairs and brought back food for Amadea and Wolff. After what she had seen at Theresienstadt, food seemed so plentiful to her now everywhere. She was surprised to find she was ravenous, as Serge continued to interview her. And a few hours later, Wolff left. He was going back to Prague.

He stopped to say good-bye to her before he left. "Good luck, Sister," he said, smiling at her. "Perhaps we'll meet again."

"Thank you," she said, sad to see him leave. She felt as though they were friends. "God bless you and keep you safe."

"I'm sure He will," he said confidently. He stopped for a few minutes to talk to Serge again, and then he and Pierre left. He would change back into the SS uniform on the way back to the station. He seemed fearless to Amadea. They all did. They were a shining example of French courage. Although the country had surrendered to the Germans in three weeks, there were cells like this one all over France, fighting to free the French again, to keep Jews alive, and restore the country's honor. But more than anything, they were saving lives, and doing all they could to help the Allied war effort, working closely with the British.

Amadea slept on a narrow cot in the basement room that night, as the men talked until the wee hours. Her papers were ready the next day. They were even more remarkable than the German ones, which Serge said he would keep for her. He didn't want them on her, if she went out for him with the others. They had talked about her long into the night, and had made a decision. He was sending her to Melun. It was sixty miles southeast of Paris, and he thought she would be safer there. They needed her desperately. The British were parachuting supplies in to them there, and men. It was delicate work.

This time her papers said that she was an unmarried woman from a town near Melun. Her name was Amélie Dumas. They used her correct birthday, and said she had been born in Lyon. If asked, she had studied at the Sorbonne before the war. She had studied literature and art. He asked her if there was a code name she wanted, and without hesitating she said, "Teresa." She knew it would give her courage. She had no idea what they expected of her, but whatever it was, she would do it. Yet again, she owed these people her life.

She and the other two women drove to Melun that night, they were just three women who had come to Paris for a few days, and were going back to the farms where they lived. They were stopped once, their papers were checked, the German soldiers laughed and winked at them for a minute, tried to tease them with chocolate bars and cigarettes, and sent them on their way. They were harmless for once, and loved flirting with the French women. They had spoken to the three women in broken French.

It was after dark when they got to the farmhouse, and went in. The farmer and his wife seemed surprised to see Amadea. The other two women introduced them, and the farmer's wife showed her to a small room behind the kitchen. She was to help them on the farm and help with the chores. The farmer's wife had terrible arthritis and could no longer help her husband. Amadea was to do all they directed her to do, and at night she was to work for the local cell. One of the men would come to see her the next day. The farmer and his wife had been in the Resistance since the occupation of France. They looked like harmless old people, but were not. They were extraordinarily courageous, and knew all of the operatives in the area. The clothes the farmer's wife gave her made Amadea look like a farm girl. She looked like a strong girl, and although she was still very thin, she was healthy and young, and she looked the part of a farm girl in a worn faded dress and an apron.

She spent the night in yet another unfamiliar bed, but was grateful to have one. The two women from the cell in Paris went back in the morning, and wished Amadea well. As she did with everyone now, she wondered if she would ever see them again. Everything about life seemed to be transient and unpredictable. People disappeared out of each other's lives in an instant. And each time you said good-bye, it could be forever, and often was. They were doing dangerous work, and Amadea was anxious to help them. She felt as though she owed them a lot, and wanted to repay the debt.

She helped with the chores on the farm that morning, and milked the few cows they still had. She carried wood, worked in the garden, helped cook lunch, and did the washing. She worked as tirelessly and as seriously as she had in the convent, and the old woman was grateful. She hadn't had that much help in years. And after dinner that night, their nephew came to visit. His

name was Jean-Yves. He was a tall gangly
man with dark hair and dark eyes, and there
was something faintly sorrowful about him.
He was two years older than Amadea and
looked like he had the world on his shoulders. His uncle poured him a glass of the
wine he made himself, and offered a glass
to Amadea, which she declined. She had a
glass of milk instead, from the cow she had
milked that morning. It was cold and fresh,
and she sat quietly at the kitchen table as
the two men talked. Afterward Jean-Yves
asked her if she'd like to go for a walk, and
she understood that it was expected. He
was the cell member she was meant to
work with. They strolled outside in the warm
air, like two young people getting to know
each other, and he looked at her somewhat
suspiciously.

"I hear you had a long trip." She nodded.
It was still hard to believe she was here. She
had left Prague only days ago. And her
refuge in the forest only shortly before that.
Her head was still spinning from it all, and
the stress of crossing borders with a partisan dressed as an SS officer, and carrying
false papers. She was Amélie Dumas now.
Jean-Yves was a Breton, and had been a

fisherman, before he came to Melun, but he actually was related to her hosts. It was all confusing for her at this point. It was a lot of information to take in and absorb. False identities, real jobs, secret agents of the Resistance, and all of them trying to free France.

"I'm lucky to be here," she said simply, grateful to them all for what they were doing for her. She was hoping to help them in exchange. It was better than hiding in a tunnel somewhere, praying that the Nazis didn't find her. She liked this better, and it made more sense to her.

"We need you here. We're getting a drop tomorrow."

"From England?" she asked softly, but there was no one to hear them in the gentle night air. He nodded in response. "Where do they come in?"

"In the fields. They radio us first. We go out to meet them. We use torches. They can only stay on the ground for about four minutes when they land. Or sometimes they just parachute things in. It depends what they bring." It was dangerous work, but they were anxious to do it. He was one of the leaders of his cell. There was a man above him, but Jean-Yves was one of their best men, and the most fearless. He had been a daredevil in his youth. She couldn't help wondering why he looked so sad. As they walked through the orchards, he looked mournful. "Do you know how to use a short-wave radio?" he inquired, and she shook her head. "I'll teach you. It's fairly simple. Can you use a gun?" She shook her head again, and then he laughed. "What were you before this? A fashion model or an actress, or just a spoiled girl?" She was so good looking, he assumed it had been something like that, and this time she laughed at him.

"A Carmelite nun. But if that was supposed to be a compliment, thank you very much." She wasn't sure being called an actress was a compliment, her mother certainly wouldn't have thought so. He looked startled by her response.

"Did you leave the convent before the war?"

"No. Only after my mother and sister were deported. For the safety of the others. It was the right thing to do." She didn't know it yet, but Sister Teresa Benedicta a Cruce, Edith Stein, and her sister Rosa had been deported to Auschwitz from the convent in

Holland only days before. By the time she was walking in the orchards in Melun with Jean-Yves, Edith Stein had been gassed and was dead.

"And you'll go back to the convent after the war?"

"Yes," Amadea said with the ring of certainty in her voice. It was what kept her going.

"What a waste," he said, looking at her.

"Not in the least. It's a wonderful life."

"How can you say that?" he said argumentatively. "All locked away like that. Besides, you don't look like a nun."

"Yes, I do," she said calmly. "And it's a very busy life. We work very hard all day, and pray for all of you."

"Do you pray now?"

"Of course I do. There's a lot to pray for these days." Including and most especially the man whose death she had caused on her escape from Theresienstadt. She still remembered Wilhelm's face with blood everywhere from his cracked head. She knew she would feel responsible for it all her life, and had a lifetime of penance to do.

"Will you pray for my brothers?" he asked suddenly, and stopped to look at her. He looked younger than she felt, although he was older than she. She felt very old these days. They had all seen too much by now, some more than others.

"Yes, I will. Where are they?" she asked, touched that he would ask her to pray for them. She would pray for them that night.

"They were killed two weeks ago by the Nazis, in Lyon. They were with Moulin." She had learned who he was from Serge. He was the hero of the Resistance.

"I'm sorry. Do you have other brothers and sisters?" she asked gently, hoping that he did, but he only shook his head.

"My parents are dead. My father died in a fishing accident when I was a boy. My mother died last year. She had pneumonia, and we couldn't get medicine for her." His brothers' recent deaths explained his mournful look. His entire family was gone, except for his aunt and uncle in Melun. Hers was too.

"My family is gone too. Or they may be. My mother and sister were deported a year ago June." There had been no news of them since that she knew of. "My father died when I was ten. My mother's family was all deported after Kristallnacht. They were

Jewish. And my father's family disowned him when they married, because my mother was German and Jewish. He was a French Catholic. They were in the first war then. People do such stupid things. Neither of their families ever forgave them."

"Were they happy?" He seemed interested, and Amadea was touched. They were two young people making friends. In hard times. Very hard times.

"Very. They loved each other very much."

"Do you think they regretted what they did, defying their families, I mean?"

"No, I don't. But it was hard on my mother when he died. She was never the same again. My sister was only two. I always took care of her," Amadea said, as tears sprang to her eyes. She hadn't talked about Daphne in a long time, and suddenly it made Amadea miss her more, and her mother too. "I think there are a lot of people like us now, who have no families left."

"My brothers were twins," he said as though it mattered now. It mattered to him.

"I'll pray for them tonight. And for you."

"Thank you," he said politely as they walked slowly back to the farm. He liked her. She seemed very mature, but she had been through a lot too. It was still hard for him to believe she was a nun, or to understand why she wanted to be. But it seemed to give her something very deep and peaceful that he liked about her. She was comforting to be with. He felt safe with her, and knew he was. "I'll pick you up tomorrow night. Wear dark clothes. We black our faces when we get out there. I'll bring you some shoe polish."

"Thank you," she said with a smile.

"It was nice talking to you, Amélie. You're a good person."

"So are you, Jean-Yves." He walked her back to the farmhouse then, and as he drove back to the farm where he lived, he was glad to know that she'd be praying for him. There was something about her that made him feel she had God's ear.

19

JEAN-YVES PICKED HER UP AT TEN O'CLOCK THE next night. He was driving an old truck and the headlights were turned out, and he had another man with him, a sturdy-looking farm boy with red hair. Jean-Yves introduced Amélie to him, and said his name was Georges.

She had worked hard on the farm all day, and had been a big help to Jean-Yves's aunt. She was grateful for Amadea's assistance, and she and his uncle were already in bed when they left. They asked no questions. They knew the routine. There had been no mention or acknowledgment of what Amadea would be doing that night. They just said goodnight and went upstairs.

And a few minutes later, Amadea left in the truck with Jean-Yves. The old couple made no comment to each other when they heard them leave. Amadea had worn dark clothes, as Jean-Yves had told her to. They drove straight over the fields and bumped along, without saying a word.

When they got there, there were two other trucks, which they parked in a clump of trees. There were eight men in all, and Amadea. They said nothing to each other. Jean-Yves handed her a small jar of shoe polish, and she put some on her face. If they got caught, it would give them away, but it was better to black out their faces. And as they heard a drone in the sky, the men began to spread out and then run. Minutes later they took out their flashlights and signaled to the plane. It was only seconds before she saw a parachute come slowly down. There was no man attached to it, just a large bundle, drifting slowly to earth, as they turned out the flashlights and the plane flew on. That was it. When the parachute landed near the trees, they all ran toward it. They unclipped the parachute, and one of the men buried it in the field as quickly as he could. The others took the bundle apart. It was filled with ammunition and guns, and they loaded them into the trucks. Twenty minutes later they had all dispersed, and she and her two companions were heading back to the farmhouse. They had already wiped the shoe polish off their faces.

"That's how it's done" was all Jean-Yves said. He had handed her a rag to wipe her face, and it looked clean again. It had been a remarkably smooth operation, and she had been impressed. They made it look easy, and it went off with the precision of a ballet. But she knew it wasn't always that way. Sometimes accidents happened. And if the Germans caught them, they'd be shot, as an example to the town. It happened all over France, and had happened to his brothers, whom she had prayed for the night before, just as she had promised him she would.

"Do they usually land, or just drop things off?" Amadea asked quietly, wanting to know more about their work and what would be expected of her.

"It depends. Sometimes they parachute men in. If they land, they have to take off again in less than five minutes. It's a lot dicier then." She could well imagine it would be.

"What do you do with the men?"

"It depends. Sometimes we hide them. Most of the time they take off. They're on missions for the British. It's harder getting them out. Sometimes they get hurt." It was all he said on the ride back. And Georges said nothing. He was watching Amadea and Jean-Yves. He teased him about her after they left. They had been friends for a long time, and been through a lot together. They trusted each other completely.

"You like her, don't you?"Georges asked him with a grin.

"Don't be stupid. She's a nun," Jean-Yves growled back at him.

"She is?" Georges looked shocked. "She doesn't look like a nun."

"That's 'cause she's not wearing the dress. She probably looks like one when she does, and the hat. You know, all that stuff." Georges nodded, impressed.

"Is she going back?" He thought if she did, it would be too bad. And so did Jean-Yves.

"She says she is," Jean-Yves said as they drove back to the farm where they lived. They were farmhands on a neighboring farm.

"Maybe you can change her mind." Georges grinned as they got out, and Jean-Yves didn't comment. He had been wondering the same thing.

The object of their interest was on her knees at that moment, thanking God that their mission had gone well. She had a moment of wondering how proper it was to be thanking God for helping them to bring guns in, which were likely to kill people. But there seemed to be no other choice at the moment, and she hoped He'd understand. She stayed on her knees for a long time that night, examining her conscience, as she had in the convent, and then she went to bed.

She was up before six, and went out to milk the cows, as she had learned to do. She had breakfast ready when her hosts got up. They ate a simple breakfast of fruit and porridge, and fake coffee. But it was a feast compared to what she had eaten for the earlier part of the year. She still thanked God every morning and night for bringing her safely to France. She sat pensively that morning, thinking of the mission she had participated in the night before.

There were two more like it over the next

weeks. And three in September where they brought men in. In one case the plane landed. In the other two they parachuted in, and one of the men got hurt. He sprained his ankle badly, and they hid him on the farm. Amadea ministered to him until he was well enough to leave.

It was October before German soldiers came to visit them. They were just checking the farms, and their papers. They looked at Amadea's, and her heart nearly stopped. But they handed them back to her without comment, took some fruit away in baskets, and moved on. It was obvious that Jean-Yves's aunt was badly crippled with arthritis and they needed a girl to help. And her husband was old too. Nothing seemed out of order to them.

She told Jean-Yves about it that night. They were on their way to another mission. They picked up more weapons and ammunition, and some radios that night.

"I was scared to death," she admitted to him.

"So am I sometimes," he said honestly. "No one wants to get shot."

"I'd rather get shot than go back where I was, or worse," she confessed.

"You're a very brave girl," he said, looking at her in the moonlight.

He liked working with her, and talking to her. He came by at night sometimes just to talk. He got lonely now that his brothers were gone. She was easy to talk to, and she had a good heart. He liked the rest of her as well, but he never said that to her. He didn't want to offend her, or scare her off. She talked about the convent a lot. It was all she knew now, and she missed it a great deal. He loved her innocence, and her strength at the same time. She was an odd combination of things. She never shirked work or responsibility, and wasn't afraid to take risks. She was as brave as any of the men. The others had commented on it too long since. They respected her, as did he.

She worked on every mission with them through the fall and into the winter. He taught her to use the shortwave radio, and how to load a gun. He taught her to shoot in his uncle's field. She was a surprisingly good shot. She had good reflexes and quick wits. And steady hands. And above all, a kind heart.

Two days before Christmas, she helped him transport four Jewish boys to Lyon.

Father Jacques had promised to take them in, and then couldn't. He was afraid to jeopardize the others, so they took them to Jean Moulin, just the two of them, and came back alone. One of the boys had been sick, and she held him in her arms and took care of him.

"You're a wonderful woman, Amélie," Jean-Yves said as they drove back to Melun. They were stopped by soldiers on the way, and their papers were checked, as the soldier glanced in. "She's my girlfriend," he said casually, and the soldier nodded.

"Lucky guy." He smiled. "Merry Christmas." And waved them on.

"Sale boche," Jean-Yves said as he drove off, and then he looked at her. "I wish it were true." She wasn't paying attention, she was thinking of the sick boy and hoped he would recover. He had been hidden in a hand-dug tunnel for three months, and had a fierce case of bronchitis as a result. He was lucky to be alive.

"What?"

"I said I wish it were true that you're my girlfriend."

"No, you don't." She looked startled. "Don't be silly." She sounded like a mother as she spoke, and he grinned and looked like a kid, instead of a man who was risking his life for France constantly.

"Yes, I do. And it's not silly. What's silly is you locking yourself up in a convent for the rest of your life. Now that's silly."

"No, it's not. It's the life I want."

"Why? What are you afraid of? What are you hiding from? What's so terrible out here?" He was almost shouting at her, but he had been in love with her for months, and he was frustrated by the way things were. They sounded like two children arguing as they drove along on the way home.

"I'm not hiding from anything. I believe in what I'm doing. I love the convent, and being a nun." She was almost pouting as she crossed her arms, as though slipping them into her habit. She still missed it and felt naked without it.

"I watched you with those children tonight, especially the sick boy. You need to have babies. That's what women were made for. You can't deny yourself that."

"Yes, I can. I have other things."

"Like what? You have nothing in there except sacrifice and loneliness and prayers."

"I was never lonely in the convent, Jean-

Yves," she said quietly, and then sighed. "Sometimes I am much lonelier out here." It was true. She missed convent life and her sisters there. The Mother Superior. And her mother and Daphne. She missed a lot of things. But she was grateful to be here.

"I'm lonely too," he said sadly, as he looked at her. He saw then that there were tears on her cheeks. *"Ma pauvre petite,"* he said, and pulled over. "I'm sorry. I didn't mean to shout at you."

"It's all right." Suddenly she was crying, and he was holding her. She couldn't stop sobbing. It was worse somehow because of Christmas. It had been the year before too. "I miss them so much . . . I can't believe they're gone . . . my sister was so beautiful . . . and my poor mother wanted to do everything for us. She never thought of herself . . . I always think of what must have happened to them . . . I know I'll never see them again . . . oh Jean-Yves . . ." She sobbed in his arms for a long time as he held her. It was the first time she had allowed herself to let go. She never let herself think of what must have happened to them. She had heard horror stories of Ravensbrück. It was unthinkable that they were gone forever, but in her heart she knew they were.

"I know . . . I know . . . I think those things too . . . I miss my brothers . . . We've all lost people we love by now. There's no one left who hasn't lost someone." And then without thinking, he kissed her and she kissed him back. All those months of standing back and respecting the vows she had taken, the life she said she wanted, the convent she wanted to flee to. He didn't want her to. He wanted to spend the rest of his life with her, have babies with her, and take care of her. All they had left now was each other. Everyone else they had ever loved was gone. Both of them. They were like two survivors alone in a lifeboat adrift in a stormy sea, and suddenly they were clinging to each other.

Amadea had no idea what was happening to her, but she was overwhelmed by such waves of desperation and passion, beyond reason, that they couldn't stop kissing and holding on to each other. And before either of them could stop it or control it or even think about it, he was making love to her in the truck, and it was all she wanted. It was as though she had instantly become someone else, someone other than the woman she had been for all these years. Wars did strange things and transformed people. Just as it had her. All her vows were forgotten, her sisters there, the convent, even her love for God. All she wanted and needed at that exact moment was Jean-Yves, and he needed her just as badly. They had both been through too much, lost too much, had been brave too many times for too many people, survived too many terrors while putting on a brave face. All their walls had come tumbling down that night, and he held her afterward, sobbing into her long blond hair and holding her, and all she wanted to do was comfort him. He was the child she had never had and never would, the only man she had ever wanted or loved. She had reproached herself for it a hundred times as she prayed in her room, and now all she wanted was to be his. They looked at each other like two lost children afterward, and he looked at her, terrified.

"Do you hate me?" He hadn't taken her by force, she had wanted him, and welcomed him. They had wanted each other, and needed each other more than they ever knew. They had simply been through too

much, and whether or not they acknowledged it, the toll it had taken on both of
them was huge.

"No. I could never hate you. I love you,
Jean-Yves," she said quietly. In some part
of her, she understood what they'd been
through, and forgave them both.

"I love you too. Oh God, how I love you.
What are we going to do?" He knew how
strongly she felt about her vocation, but it
seemed wrong to him, it always had. She
was too beautiful and loving a woman to
hide in a convent for the rest of her life. But
it was the life she'd said she wanted since
they met.

"Do we have to decide that right now? I'm
not sure if I've committed a terrible sin, or if
this is what was meant to be. Maybe this is
what God has in mind for me. Let's just see
what happens, and pray about it for a
while," she said sensibly as he held her
close to him. She had no idea where God
would lead her, but she knew she had to explore this new path for now. It felt oddly
right to her.

"If anything ever happens to you, Amélie,
I'll die."

"No, you won't. I'll just wait for you in

Heaven, and we'll have a wonderful time when you arrive." There were tears in her eyes, but she was so happy with him. She had never been as happy in her life. It was different than her love for the convent, but there was a definite sense of joy to this new life that she loved. For the first time in her life, she felt frivolous and young. For once, life didn't seem quite so serious, the tragedies all around them not quite as acute. This was what they both needed to counter the realities of their lives, at least for now.

"God, how I love you," he said with a broad grin, as they sorted themselves out, suddenly giggling like schoolchildren, and he started the truck up again. He wanted to ask her to marry him, but he didn't want to ask for too much too soon. She had made a big step that night. And maybe she was right, if it was meant to be, the rest would come. All in good time. They didn't have to decide everything in one night. If he had anything to say about it, she was going to be his wife, and the mother of his children. He just hoped that God agreed, and that Amadea would be willing to give up her dreams of returning to the convent now. But it was way too soon. She was still stunned by what they'd done, and so was he.

They talked quietly on the way home, and he kissed her and held her before she got out. "I love you. Don't forget that. Tonight was just the beginning. It wasn't a mistake," he said earnestly, "or a sin. I'll start going to church again regularly," he promised, and she smiled. He hadn't been since his brothers died. He was still too upset at God.

"Maybe that's why He sent me to you, to get you back to church." Whatever the reason, she looked as happy as he did, in spite of the shock of what they'd just done. Much to her own amazement, she didn't feel wrong about it, she felt happy, and in love. She knew too that it would take a long time to sort this out. It was one of the aftershocks of war.

As she lay in her bed that night, thinking of him, much to her own amazement, she didn't have a crisis of conscience, or even regret it. Oddly enough, it seemed right to her. She wondered if this was what God had in mind for her after all. She was still thinking about it when she drifted off to sleep. And when she woke up the next morning, he had dropped flowers off to her on his way to work. He had come by his uncle's farm and left a tiny bouquet of winter flowers outside the barn with a note, "I love you. J-Y." She tucked the note in her pocket with a smile, and went in to milk the cows that were waiting for her. She felt like a woman for the first time in her life. It was an unfamiliar sensation to her in every way. She was suddenly experiencing all she had denied herself, and had planned to deny forever. Her life had turned around entirely, and it was impossible to know which path was right, the enticing one she had just embarked on with Jean-Yves, or the one that had meant so much to her for so many years before. All she knew, and could hope, was that in time the answers would come, and the mystery would unfold.

20

FOR THE REST OF THE WINTER, AMADEA CONTIN-
ued running missions with him. Supplies
and men were steadily being parachuted in
by the British. They waited for a British officer to parachute in one night, and after they
helped him bury his parachute and sent him
on his way in an SS uniform, Jean-Yves
asked Amadea if she had heard of him. His
name was Lord Rupert Montgomery, and he
was one of the men who had helped start
the Kindertransport that got ten thousand
children out of Europe before the war
started.

"I asked my mother to put my sister on it,"
Amadea said sadly as they drove home.
"She never thought we'd have a problem,

and she was afraid of what would happen to her if she went. She was thirteen then, and was deported when she was sixteen. He did a wonderful thing for many children."

"He's a good man. I met him once before last year," Jean-Yves commented, with a smile at her.

Their affair had continued unchecked by then since Christmas. He had broached the subject of marriage to her, but she wasn't sure. She still didn't know if God wanted her to go back to the convent. But the prospect of that seemed more difficult now, even to her. She had killed one man, even if accidentally, and now she was deeply in love with another. They were making love to each other every chance they got. He could hardly keep his hands off of her. There was no way he was letting her go back to the convent after the war, he vowed to himself. Surely, that couldn't be what God wanted. It was an unnatural life, as far as he was concerned, and he was very much in love with her.

Serge came down from Paris in the spring to see them. It was 1943. And he could see what had happened between Amadea and Jean-Yves, without their explaining it to him.

He told his brother Pierre when he went back to Paris that he thought the Carmelite order was going to be minus one very pretty young nun after the war. But more than that, he was profoundly impressed by the work Amadea had done with Jean-Yves. They had been bringing in successful missions since she'd arrived, and from what Jean-Yves said, she was fearless, although always cautious not to put any of the members of their cell unduly at risk.

Serge and Jean-Yves had talked about blowing up a nearby German munitions dump in the next few weeks. Jean-Yves had insisted that he didn't want Amadea on the mission with him. Serge thought it should be up to her, but he understood what motivated Jean-Yves's concern. He was in love with her. The fact was, they needed her help, and she was good, and quick, from what he heard. Serge trusted her almost more than anyone else in Melun, with the exception of Jean-Yves.

They were still debating the matter hotly when Serge left, and Amadea agreed with Serge. She wanted to go on the mission with Jean-Yves. The war was starting to turn around. The Germans had surrendered at Stalingrad in February, in the first defeat of Hitler's army. They had to do everything they could now in France to defeat him here, too. And there was no question, blowing up their arsenal of weapons would be a major blow to them.

They planned the mission carefully over the next several weeks, and Amadea finally convinced him. It went against all his protective instincts, but Jean-Yves agreed to let her come. The final decision was his, as the leader of the cell. The fact was that they were short of men. Two of his best men were sick.

Jean-Yves, Amadea, two women, Georges, and another man set out for the munitions dump late one night. They took two trucks and an arsenal of explosives hidden in the back. Amadea was in the same truck as Jean-Yves. Two of the men got out and cut the sentries' throats. This was the most dangerous mission they had ever done. They set the explosives carefully around the munitions dump, and then as they had planned, all but Jean-Yves and Georges ran back to the trucks. They knew they only had minutes to light the fuses and get out. The explosives they were using were crude, but they were the best they could get. And before they even got back to the trucks, Amadea heard a tremendous explosion, and what looked like the biggest fireworks display she had ever seen lit up the night sky. She and the others looked at each other, as they started the trucks, and there was no sign of Georges or Jean-Yves.

"Go! . . . Go!" the man in the truck with her said, but they couldn't leave Georges and Jean-Yves. All of the local military forces would be arriving any minute, and if they found the other two, they'd be shot. The other two women were waiting in the second truck for Georges. Amadea was at the wheel of hers.

"I'm not leaving," she said through her teeth, but as she looked behind her, she saw an enormous ball of fire, and the second truck shifted into gear and took off.

"We can't wait," the man next to her begged her. They were going to get caught, and Amadea knew it too.

"We have to," she said, as a series of explosions erupted behind her and the truck shook. The fire was spreading as sirens went off, and without hesitating, she stepped on the gas and took off too. They bounced over the fields in the two trucks, and she was shaking from head to foot as they pulled into the barn where the trucks were stored. It was a miracle they hadn't gotten caught, and she knew they had waited too long. She had nearly jeopardized all the others for the sake of the man she loved. They stood silently in the barn in the darkness, listening to the explosions and crying softly. All they could do now was pray that Jean-Yves and Georges had gotten out, but Amadea couldn't see how they could have. The explosives had gone off much faster than they'd expected, and it seemed more than likely now that the two men had either been badly wounded or killed on the spot.

"I'm sorry," she said to the others, with a shaking voice. "We should have left sooner." They all nodded, they knew it was true, but they hadn't wanted to abandon the two men either. She had very nearly cost all their lives by waiting too long. They had just managed to get out.

She walked back to her own farm that night, listening to the explosions and looking up at the brightly lit sky. And she lay in bed for hours praying for him. The news was everywhere the next morning. The army was all over the countryside looking for evidence. But there was none. People on the farms were quietly going about their work. The Germans had found two men dead, burned beyond recognition, even their papers had turned to ashes. And not knowing what else to do, they took four boys off a neighboring farm and shot them, as a warning to the rest. Amadea sat in her room all that day, sick with grief and shock. Not only had Jean-Yves died, but four young boys had been killed as the result of what they'd done. It was a high price to pay for freedom, and for destroying the weapons the Germans would have used to kill so many others. But the man she loved was dead, and she had been responsible for the deaths of eight people, Georges and Jean-Yves, four young farm boys, and even the two German sentries whose throats had been cut. It was a lot to have on her con-science, for a woman who had once wanted to be the bride of God. And for the first time, as she mourned the only man she had ever loved, she knew that when it was all over, she had to go back. It would take her the rest of her life as a Carmelite to atone for her sins.

21

SERGE WAITED FOR THREE WEEKS BEFORE HE came down from Paris to Melun. He had heard the news in Paris, and he was pleased at the result of the mission. The Germans had been severely hampered by the damage they'd done. But he was devastated by the news of Jean-Yves's death. He had been one of their best men. And he wanted to talk to Amadea as soon as he could.

He found her grief-stricken and silent in her room at the farmhouse. The British had still been parachuting men and supplies in, but she hadn't been on a single mission since.

He sat and talked to her about it, and told

her they were too short-handed now to bring the men and supplies in safely. She looked at him with agonized eyes, and shook her head. "I can't."

"Yes, you can. He would still be out there if it had been you. You have to do it for him. And for France."

"I don't care. I have too much blood on my hands."

"It's not on your hands, it's on theirs. And if you don't continue the work you've been doing, it will be our blood."

"They killed four young boys," she said, looking sick. She was as tortured over them as she was devastated over the death of Jean-Yves.

"They'll kill more if we don't stop them. And this is all we've got. We have no other way. The British are counting on us. There's another big mission coming up soon. We don't have time to train more men. And I need you for something else right now anyway."

"What?" she asked. As he looked at her, she looked gray. He was putting pressure on her because he knew she had to get back out there. She was too good at it to give up. And he was afraid she would fall

apart completely from losing Jean-Yves.
She was ravaged by grief.

"I need you to get a Jewish boy and his
sister to Dordogne. We have a safe house
for them there."

"How old are they?" she asked without
much interest.

"Four and six."

"What are they still doing here?" She
sounded surprised. Most of the Jewish children, if not all of them, had been deported
out of France in the past year. The rest were
being hidden.

"Their grandmother was hiding them. She
died last week. We have to get them out.
They'll be safe in Dordogne."

"And how am I supposed to get there?"
She felt hopeless and looked tired.

"We have papers for them. They look like
you. They're both blue-eyed blondes. Only
their mother was Jewish. They deported
her, and the father was killed." Like so many
others, they had no family left at all.

She started to tell him she couldn't do it,
and then as she looked at him, she remembered her vows, and thought of her mother
and Daphne, and Jean-Yves. And she suddenly felt she owed it to them, maybe in

reparation for the lives she had cost. She
felt like a nun again. Jean-Yves had taken
the woman she had been with him. She
knew she would never be that person again.
But Sister Teresa of Carmel would not have
refused to do the mission. Slowly, she nodded. She had no other choice. "I'll do it,"
she said, looking at Serge and he was
pleased. He had taken on this particular
mission as much for her as for them. He
didn't like the way she looked since Jean-
Yves's death, and Jean-Yves wouldn't have
either. In a way, Serge was doing this for
him, as much as for her, and the two Jewish
children were orphans, Serge explained.

"We'll bring them here tomorrow night,
with their papers and yours. You'll have to
hide your other papers in the lining of your
valise. Your papers will show that you're
their mother, and you're going down to visit
family in Besse." It was in the heart of the
Dordogne, where her father was from. She
had never been there, and had always
wanted to go. She wondered if she would
see his château on the way, although she
had more important things to do. "You'll
have to borrow the car from the farm." He
knew that would be no problem.

She spent the rest of the day in prayer in her room, after she did her chores. She had hardly eaten in the last few weeks, and it showed. The next day she sewed her papers as Amélie Dumas into her suitcase. She knew she'd have the others by that night.

After dinner, they arrived. One of the women from the Paris cell had driven them down. They were beautiful children, and they looked terrified. They had been hidden in a basement for two years, and the only relative they had in the world had died. Serge was right. They were adorable, and they looked like her. They made her wonder what their children would have looked like if she and Jean-Yves had had babies. But there was no point thinking of that now. She sat down and talked to the children for a little while. They fed them dinner, and she tucked them into her own bed that night, and slept on the floor next to them. The little boy held his sister's hand all night. And they both understood what they had to do. They had to pretend she was their mother, and call her "Maman." Even if scary soldiers questioned them. She promised them that she wouldn't let anything bad happen to them, and prayed she was right.

They left right after breakfast the next morning, in Jean-Yves's uncle's car. She knew she could make the trip in six or seven hours. She brought food with them so they didn't have to stop anywhere. They passed one checkpoint, and she handed the soldiers her papers. They looked at her, glanced at the children, handed the papers back, and waved them on. It was the easiest mission she'd been on so far, and the children slept in the car, which gave her time to think. She felt better than she had in a while, and she was glad she had agreed to do it. They were sweet children, and she felt sorry for them. She was taking them to meet a member of a cell in Dordogne, and he was going to deliver them to the safe house that had been provided. He had said Amadea could spend the night there before she went back. It was a long trip.

It was four o'clock in the afternoon when they arrived in the rolling countryside that seemed not to know there was a war on. It looked lush and green and luxuriant. She drove to the address she'd been given, and found it easily. There was a young man waiting for her, who was as blond and blue-eyed as she and the children. He looked as though he could have been their father as easily as she could have been their mother. He thanked her for bringing them down.

"Do you want to come with me, or stay here?" he asked. The children looked panicked at the thought of leaving her. She was the only person there they knew, although they hadn't known her for long. But she had been nice to them. She tried to reassure them, but they both started crying, and she looked at the man she knew only as Armand.

"I'll come." He got into her car with the three of them, and told her where to go. Five minutes later, they were driving past an imposing château, and he told her to turn into the courtyard. "Here?" She looked surprised. "This is your safe house?" It was a beautiful old house, with many outbuildings, stables, and an enormous courtyard. "Whose house is this?" she asked, suddenly curious. They were not far from her father's boyhood home, although she wasn't exactly sure where it was either.

"Mine," he said, and she stared at him, as he laughed. "One day. In the meantime, it's my father's." She smiled in open admiration as she looked around and they got out. The children were staring up at the château in wonder. After two years in a basement on the outskirts of Paris, this was like going to Heaven. She knew they had papers for them that attested to their aristocratic birth. They were allegedly distant relations of the châtelain.

An old housekeeper led them away to get them dinner, as an older gentleman came down the steps of the château. Amadea assumed he was Armand's father. The distinguished-looking man shook her hand and was very pleasant to her, as Armand introduced them. All he knew of her was the name on her most recent set of papers. Philippine de Villiers. Which was how he introduced her to his father, whom he then introduced to Amadea. "May I introduce my father," he said politely, "Comte Nicolas de Vallerand." Amadea stood staring at him, and as she did, she saw the resemblance, although he was older than her father had been the last time she saw him. Her father was forty-four when he died, and would have been sixty now. As she looked from Armand to his father, she looked shocked, but said nothing. Armand could see that something had disturbed her severely, as the count invited her inside. They had prepared a meal for her, and served it elegantly in the dining room, as the two men joined her. She was quiet as she looked around, and the count noticed her pained silence but didn't comment.

"It's a beautiful old house. It was originally built in the sixteenth century. And rebuilt about two hundred years later. I'm afraid it's badly in need of repair these days. There will be no one to do it until the war is over. The roof leaks like a sieve." He smiled. He was looking at her as though there was something familiar about her too. She knew what it was, she was the image of her father. She wondered what would happen if she told him the truth. But things must have changed, if he was hiding Jewish children. It seemed the ultimate irony now, since her father had been banished and never seen again by any of them because he had a Jewish wife.

They finished dinner, and the count invited her to walk in the gardens. He said they had been done by the same architect who had designed the gardens at Versailles. It was a

strange feeling walking through the same
halls and rooms and places where her father had lived as a boy, and as she walked
outside, the thought of it brought tears to
her eyes. These same rooms had been filled
with the sounds of his voice and laughter as
a child and as a young man. They were
the echoes of her past, which she shared
with these two men, although they didn't
know it.

"Are you all right?" Armand could see that
she was deeply moved by something. His
father was already waiting for them in the
garden. She nodded as they went outside,
and he showed them around.

"You're a very brave woman to bring those
children down on your own. If I had a
daughter, I'm not sure I would let her do
that. In fact, I'm sure I wouldn't." He looked
at Armand then, frowned, and lowered his
voice. "I worry about Armand as well. But
none of us has any other choice these days,
do we?" In fact they did. There were others
who made different choices. She liked the
one she was making, and theirs.

As they walked around through the once-
beautiful gardens, the count asked her
nothing about herself. They were all better

off not knowing too much. Everyone was careful these days. It was dangerous to say too much to anyone. But as she sat down on one of the ancient time-worn marble benches that had been rubbed smooth by the elements, she looked up at him with sad eyes.

"I don't know why," he said gently, "but I have the feeling I know you, that we've met somewhere." There was no one around but Armand. "Have I?" He was in his late fifties, she knew, and not old enough to be senile. But he looked confused, as though he heard voices from another time, and wasn't sure what he was hearing, or seeing. "Have we met?" he asked her again. He didn't think it likely, but he might have forgotten. And as she sat there, looking at him, she looked remarkably like Armand.

"You knew my father," she said in a gentle voice, never leaving his eyes with her own.

"Did I? What was his name?"

"Antoine de Vallerand," she said calmly. Nicolas was his brother, and her uncle, and Armand her first cousin. There was absolute silence between the three of them for an endless moment, and then without saying a word, tears began to roll down his cheeks, and he took her in his arms.

"Oh my dear . . . oh my dear . . ." He couldn't say anything else for long minutes. He was overwhelmed by the memories she had brought with her. "Did you know when you came here?" He wondered if that was why she had taken the mission. But she hadn't known.

She shook her head. "Not until we drove in here, and Armand said your name. It was a bit of a shock, as you can imagine." She laughed through her own tears. "I wanted to say something at dinner, but I was afraid you'd ask me to leave. I wanted to savor it for a little while. My father always talked to me about all this, the place where he grew up."

"I never forgave my father for what he did. I hated him for it, and myself, for not having the courage to defy him. We were barely civil to each other after that. And when he died, I wanted to ask your father to come home and forgive us. He died two weeks later. And my wife died the year after. I wanted to write to your mother about how I felt about what happened, but I never knew her, and I felt sure she hated all of us."

Instead, he had written a proper letter of condolence, and nothing more.

"She didn't hate you," Amadea reassured him. "Her family was even worse to her. They wrote her name in the family's book of the dead, and wouldn't let her see her mother when she died, or go to the funeral. My grandmother had come to us two years before, and we got to know her. I never met the others."

"Where are they now?" he asked, looking concerned, as Amadea took a breath before she answered. The rest was all bad news.

"The entire family was deported on Kristallnacht. Some people thought they were sent to Dachau, but I don't know for sure. My mother and sister were deported to Ravensbrück two years ago. I haven't heard from them since." He looked horrified by what she had said.

"And you came here?" He looked confused as Armand watched her intently. She was an amazing woman. Armand had no sisters, and wished he had one like her. He was an only child, with no relatives other than his father. They had made the decision to join the Resistance together, all they had in the world was each other, and this house, which was in a genteel state of disrepair as was the property all around them.

"I was in Theresienstadt for five months. Friends hid me before that, after my mother was deported. I was in a Carmelite convent for six years before that."

"You were a nun?" Armand looked shocked.

"I still am, I suppose," although that had been questionable for a while. But she was sure again now. Ever since Jean-Yves died. She had found her vocation again. She wasn't sure now that she had ever lost it. She had just taken a brief detour, in extraordinary circumstances. "Sister Teresa of Carmel. I'll go back after the war. I had to leave the convent so as not to endanger the others."

"What a remarkable girl you are," her uncle said, putting an arm around her shoulders. "Your father would be very proud of you, if he were alive. I am, and I hardly know you." And then he looked at her wistfully. "Could you stay longer?" They had a lifetime of catching up to do. And he wanted to hear all about the years he had lost with his brother. There were a thousand things he wanted to know.

"I don't think that would be wise," she

said sensibly, showing Carmelite good judgment, as Serge would have said. "I'd like to come back, if I may," she asked politely. He could see that she was beautifully brought up.

"I'd be heartbroken if you didn't." They walked back inside then, and spent the rest of the night talking. They never went to bed, and then finally she went to lie down for a few hours before she left.

She went to kiss the children good-bye, and they cried when she left them. And she, Armand, and Nicolas all cried as she drove away. She had promised to come back, and her uncle had begged her to be careful and take care of herself. She could still see them in the rearview mirror, standing in the courtyard, waving, as she turned and they disappeared out of sight. It had been one of the best nights of her life, and she wished that Jean-Yves and her father could have been there. But as she drove back to Melun, she felt them close to her, along with her mother and Daphne. They were all part of an unbreakable chain, linking the present, the future, and the past.

22

Amadea's drive back to Melun went smoothly. She was stopped by soldiers only once, and although they admired her and chatted for a few minutes, they let her drive on fairly quickly. They had scarcely glanced at her papers. One of them waved with a big boyish grin as she drove off.

She was back in Melun at the farmhouse by late afternoon. By the following week, she was back with the others, picking up supplies parachuted in, and following their familiar routine. The British had sent them two more shortwave radios, which were concealed at neighboring farms.

It was late September when Serge came to visit them again. He liked to see the men and women who worked for him face to face whenever he could. He wanted to have a sense of them, to make sure that they weren't putting others at risk, and that they were as loyal as he believed. He had a sixth sense about those things. And this time there was something he wanted to discuss with Amadea. He had heard from others that she had been depressed for a long time about Jean-Yves, and still blamed herself not only for his death, and Georges's, but for the assassination of the four young boys. Even worse, she was afraid that Jean-Yves had died as punishment for her sins. Serge had grown fond of her in the time she had been doing missions for him, and he had a profound respect for her good judgment, great courage, and cool head. He wanted to make sure she was all right, and there was a mission he wanted to talk to her about. As always, when something was delicate, he wanted to speak to her in person. He sent a message to her, and they met at a neighboring farm.

As soon as she walked in, he saw that she looked drawn and tired, and her spirits were still lagging. She seemed to feel haunted by the deaths she felt she had caused, and talked a lot again about how anxious she was to go back to the convent after the war. She ate dinner with him, and filled him in on the supplies they had brought in, some of the new people working with them, and after dinner, they took a walk.

"There's something I want to talk to you about," he said after a few minutes. "I need an operative in Paris for a special mission. I don't know if you feel up to it, but I think you would be perfect." He had been asked by the SOE in England to find someone with specific qualifications, and she had them all. They needed someone who spoke German faultlessly, and could pass as a cool, sophisticated, aristocratic German woman. Amadea not only looked the part, but was in fact precisely that. And she could pass equally as French or German. They wanted to pose her as the wife or girlfriend of a high-ranking SS officer who was coming to visit Paris. The officer in question was going to be impersonated by a member of the British Secret Service who himself was half German and was also fluent in French. He needed a perfect match for him, and Amadea was it. The big question was if she would do it, and as always she had the choice.

Serge explained the mission to her as they walked along in the dark, and she listened to him in silence. For a long time, she didn't answer, and he didn't press her.

"When do you need to know?" She wanted to pray about it. She was happy in the countryside, doing what she could for them. It was far more dangerous for her going to Paris, and flaunting herself in the face of the SS. She didn't mind being shot by the Germans stationed in Melun, in the course of a midnight mission. The one thing she didn't want, and feared more than anything, was being deported back to the camps. That was more crucifixion than even she felt ready to risk, or face again. She knew she wouldn't be as lucky again, as she had been in escaping Theresienstadt. So far, not a single soul had escaped from Auschwitz, or most of the other camps. It had been a sheer fluke, the night of the leveling of Lidice, that she had been able to escape the Nazis' "model camp." They were in fact at that moment preparing to show their "Town for Jews" to the International Red Cross. Deportation to any other camp, or even that one now, was almost certain death, after unthinkable torture. Serge's invitation to

Paris, masquerading as the wife of an SS officer, sounded risky to her. Too much so.

"We don't have much time. And you're our only real possibility," Serge said honestly. "The agent who is running the mission is coming in at the end of this week. I was going to tell you about it tonight anyway. He's coming in with three men." She already knew what those landings were like, and had assisted them often with Jean-Yves and the others. They landed a tiny Lysander for less than five minutes, while the men got out, the plane took off again, and the men dispersed quickly. They were the same planes that did their supply drops, and sometimes parachuted agents in. The landings were far harder. They came in without lights, and relied on the freedom fighters on the ground to guide them with flashlights and protect them. So far, in Amadea's time of working with them, they hadn't had a single mishap, nor lost a single man. Although on several occasions they had come close.

"He must be someone important," Amadea said thoughtfully, wondering who it was and if she'd heard of him. She knew many of the names now of the people they worked with in England. She heard their code names on the radio, when she manned it, which she did from time to time. She was proficient now with the shortwave. Jean-Yves had taught her well. And loved her well, for the brief time they shared.

"He's very important," Serge admitted, referring to the British agent. "He can do the mission alone if he has to, but it will provide a diversion if he has a 'wife.' " He looked at her honestly then. "You're the only one who can do it." None of their other operatives spoke German as fluently as she did, and could pass for German. Even if they spoke it well, which some did, it was obvious that they were French. Amadea looked completely Teutonic. Not only German, but Aryan to the nth degree. As did the officer she'd be working with. Like her, he was half German, although not Jewish. His mother was a Prussian princess, well known as a great beauty when she was young.

"Who is he?" She was curious about him now and, in spite of herself, intrigued by the mission.

"His code name is Apollo." She knew she had heard the name before, and thought she might have met him once. It rang a chord of memory, but she could not place the face that went with it. And then suddenly it hit her. He had landed there once before. She had met him with Jean-Yves. Rupert Montgomery. He was one of the men who had started the Kindertransport. "He's a British lord."

"I've met him." Serge nodded. He knew that she had.

"He remembers meeting you, too. He thought it would be a good match. You're the right look." And the right personality. Although she wasn't aware of it, in times of crisis, she had nerves of steel and exquisite judgment. Everyone who had worked with her said so. There was an endless silence as they walked back to the farmhouse. The air was getting cold. Winter was coming early. And as they reached the gate in the fence, Amadea looked at him with a sigh. It was what she owed them all, and perhaps the only reason why she had been spared so often. To serve the Lord, no matter how frightening. "I'll do it," she said softly. "When does he come?"

"I'll send you a message," he had said at the end of the week. As they stood there, it was Monday. She looked at Serge with troubled eyes. He knew it was a lot to ask of her.

Maybe too much. But she was willing to do it. Any price for victory and freedom, even if only to save one life.

"I'll be waiting," she responded and Serge nodded. She had made an impression on Colonel Montgomery, too. He had remembered her code name. Teresa. They used it for messages, and on the shortwave. She would be listening for it now.

"Thank you. He's careful. He knows what he's doing." She nodded. She had decided to do it because of what he had done for the Jewish children. She wanted to help him.

Serge hugged her then, and went into the barn where he was staying, as she walked home alone. She wasn't afraid of anything in the countryside of Melun. In spite of what they did there, she felt safe among the farms. And the Germans were pretty tame here, except in the case of reprisals.

"Go with God," she said before she left him, and he nodded.

She heard her code name on the short-wave radio two days later. It said only "Teresa. *Samedi.*" Saturday. Which meant Friday. Their missions were always a day earlier than stated. They would start watching and listening for the tiny plane around midnight. And as always, they would have to work fast.

The following Friday night she was in the field with seven of the others. There were two groups of four working together, holding flashlights. And then they heard it, the dull purring of the little Lysander. They spread out and switched on their torches. The plane came in fast, landed hard, and taxied for a short distance. Before it stopped, four men got out. They were wearing rough farm clothes and wool caps. The plane was in the air again in less than three minutes. The drop had been perfect. And within less than two minutes, the locals had disappeared and returned to their farms. The three men Colonel Montgomery had brought in went with them. They were on other missions, and would not see him again until they were back in England. They were dispersing to the south later that night. He was working alone, as he often did. With Amadea this time. She led him back to the farm where she lived, without saying a word. And took him to an old horse stall at the back of the barn. There was a trapdoor in the floor that she pointed to, in case he heard someone coming. There were blankets, and a jug of water under the trapdoor. They were to drive to the outskirts of Paris the next day to meet with Serge.

Amadea said nothing to the man known as Apollo, she simply looked at him and nodded as he watched her, and as she was about to leave, he whispered, "Thank you." He meant not only for that night and the warm blankets, but for her willingness to do the mission. He knew everything about her background and the risk she was taking. The only thing he did not know about was Jean-Yves, which was unimportant in relation to what they were doing. He was a member of the British Secret Service, and of extremely high rank. He also knew that in her past life she had been a nun, which he had found intriguing. He knew she had left the convent to save the others.

She nodded again, and left to go to her own room at the back of the kitchen. In the morning, she brought him breakfast. He was wearing the same rough clothes as the night before, He looked clean, rested, and neatly shaven. And even in the rough work clothes, he looked impressive. He was as tall as her father had been, and had once been as blond as she was. Now the fair hair was mixed with gray. He looked to be in his early forties, roughly the same age her father had been when he died, and there was a vague resemblance, although her father had been French not British. But she could see how this man could easily pass for German. He looked like the ideal specimen of the master race. It would have been hard for him to pass unnoticed anywhere except in a crowd of Germans. He looked anything but French. And when she brought him breakfast, he spoke to her in German. His was just as flawless as hers, and as natural to him as English, as French and German were to her. She spoke English, though not as well, and this time she answered him in German. She asked him if he had slept well.

"Yes, thank you," he said politely, looking deep into her eyes. He seemed to be searching for something, and she had no idea what it was. He needed to know her better, to sense her reaction to things, her timing. If they were going to pose as man and wife, he had to truly know her, and sense her, with more than just words.

"We leave at four this afternoon," she said quietly, avoiding the ever-searching eyes.

"Don't do that," he corrected her. "You

know me. You love me. You are not afraid of me. You look me right in the eyes. You are comfortable with me. We have been married for five years. We have had children to- gether." He wanted her to learn her role, and feel it, so that it was part of her.

"How many children?" she asked, looking at him again, as he directed. What he was saying was not unreasonable, and she un- derstood what he was trying to do. It had nothing to do with her. It was a role they had to play. Well enough to stay alive. Any slip either of them made could cost the other's life, or both, and she knew that. This was far more difficult and dangerous than meeting aircraft at midnight in a field.

"We have two. Two boys. Three and two. This is the first time you have left them since they were born. For our anniversary. I had business in Paris, for the Reich, and you decided to come along. We live in Berlin. Do you know it?" he asked with a look of con- cern. If not, he would have to teach her every- thing about it. Photographs, maps, restau- rants, shops, museums, streets, parks, people, movie houses. She would have to learn it better than the town where she was born.

"Well enough. My mother's sister moved there when she married. I didn't know her. But I visited it as a child." He nodded. That was a start. He knew she was from Cologne. He even knew her mother's maiden name. And the name of her sister. And the date they had been taken. He knew the school she had gone to before she entered the convent. There was very little he didn't know about Amadea. All she knew about him was his name and code name, and that he had been one of the organizers of the Kindertransport, but she didn't mention it. They were not making friends, but only learning a part.

They talked all the way to Paris, about the things she needed to know, as he drove a car someone had given him. His papers were impeccable, as was his French. According to his papers, he was from Arles, and was a teacher there. She was his girlfriend. The single soldier who stopped them waved them on. They looked like a very respectable couple. He left the car where he had been told to, half a mile from Serge's house, and they walked the rest of the way, still talking. She had three days to learn the part. And to look it. He wasn't worried about that. She had the makings of a beauty. The one thing she didn't look like to him was a nun. They were halfway to Serge's house from the drop where they left the car, when he asked her about that. "Why did you enter the convent? Were you disappointed in love?" She smiled at the question, people assumed such strange things about why one entered a religious order. It was far less dramatic than they suspected, particularly at the age she had been then. She was twenty-six now. And he was forty-two.

"Not at all. I did it because I love God. I had a vocation." He had no reason to ask, but he was growing curious about her. She was an interesting young woman.

"Are you married?" she asked as they walked along, her hand tucked into his arm, which was appropriate for the part, and a habit she would have to grow accustomed to with him. He was a little daunting, but as he had said, she had to become comfortable with him. It wasn't entirely easy. In spite of the rough clothes, there was an air of authority about him. And she knew who he really was. More or less.

"I was," he said as they strolled toward Serge's place. Their strides were an even match, which he found pleasant. She didn't take little geisha steps like very small women, which he had always found annoying. He did things quickly and well, and had a tendency to be impatient. The rest of the world didn't always move quickly enough for him. She did. "My wife was killed in a bombing raid. And my two sons. Early in the war." As he said it, Amadea felt him tense.

"I'm sorry," she said respectfully. They had all lost someone. Or many. She wondered if that was why he was so willing to risk his life now. Like her, he had nothing to lose. In his case, he did it for his country. In hers, she did it for whatever lives she could save, and for the crucified Christ, to whom she felt she was married, or would be one day, when she took her solemn vows. She would have taken her solemn vows that summer, if life were still normal. Instead, she had left the convent nearly two and a half years before. But at the appropriate time, she renewed her vows now each year on her own.

They reached the home of Serge's grandmother then, where Amadea had come when she first came from Prague, with Wolff, the partisan who had brought her there nearly fourteen months before. It seemed aeons ago. Now she was going to be putting herself at great risk again, with this man.

They stopped to greet Serge's grandparents, and within moments went down the stairs at the back of the closet. Within seconds they were in the bustling room where Amadea had first come. It looked welcoming and familiar to her. Some of the same faces were there, and there were many new ones. One of the men was manning a shortwave radio. A woman was printing leaflets. Others were talking around a table, and Serge looked up with pleasure as they walked in.

"Any problems?" They shook their heads in unison and then laughed. There hadn't been much humor between them, or small talk, except for his question about the convent, and hers about his wife. The rest of what they had said was all related to the information they needed to share for their mission.

Someone brought them both a meal after a little while, it was thick stew made of rabbit, there was a slice of bread for each, and a cup of the bitter coffee everyone drank. The meal was nourishing and warmed them both. There was a decided chill in the air.

The man known as Apollo was obviously hungry. Even Amadea ate well of the delicious stew.

They took photographs of both of them after that, for the miraculous artwork they did on passports and traveling papers. They seemed to be able to produce almost anything. Serge thought their German passports and military papers were their best work. Serge and Colonel Montgomery talked quietly in a corner for a long time, and one of the women took Amadea's measurements for the wardrobe she would need. She had no idea how, but they had ways of acquiring country dresses and suits, and elegant gowns, that were still hidden somewhere from before the war. People had relatives who had once been well dressed, and old trunks full of treasures. They even had a moderate amount of jewelry and some furs.

All of it appeared in a handsome leather suitcase two days later, along with their passports and papers, and all the necessary SS accoutrements for Apollo. He looked spectacular in the uniform and had worn it often before. They tried everything on, and it all fit perfectly. They made an impressive couple. Amadea was wearing an elegant gray wool dress that looked like one of her mother's, and a handsome string of pearls. The dress was by Mainbocher, and was in pristine condition, as was the fur coat she wore, and the stylish black hat. Remarkably, the shoes they had found for her were German. The bag was a black crocodile Hermès, and the gloves black suede and also a perfect fit. She looked like the beautifully dressed wife of a very prosperous man, which the officer he was impersonating was alleged to be. The actual officer whose name he had borrowed had been dead for two years. He had died in a boating accident on leave, and had been relatively obscure. What they needed was his name and identity. He had never been to Paris, and they were certain that no one knew him here. And even if they did, it was more than likely that the pair would get away with the charade they needed to for two days.

Colonel Montgomery needed to gather information at meetings of the Reich in Paris, and social events. Amadea was a decoy for him, and she would do her own information gathering while chatting with other women,

and dancing with the senior officers at parties. Colonel Montgomery had gotten a
room for them at the Crillon since it was
their anniversary, and had ordered champagne and roses for her. A lovely gold and
diamond Cartier watch was going to be
shown off as her anniversary gift. They had
thought of every detail.

"You're very generous," she said, admiring
the watch.

"Do you think so?" he asked, looking very
cool and British in the SS uniform. "I think
it's rather paltry myself. I frankly think you
deserve a large diamond brooch or a sapphire necklace after putting up with me for
five years. You're very easy to please."

"We don't see a lot of these in the convent." She smiled at him, still feeling like her
mother in the gray wool dress and fur. She
took the coat off and hung it up gingerly.
Her mother had never had furs until after
Amadea's father died. Before his inheritance, which had come only at the eleventh
hour, they couldn't afford them. After that,
she had always allowed herself one good
fur coat, but no more. And a jacket for the
girls when they were old enough to wear

them. Amadea hadn't been near furs in years.

"Perhaps I should have gotten you rosary beads as an anniversary gift," Colonel Montgomery continued to tease her, and this time she laughed openly.

"I'd like that very much." And then she thought of something that she really did want to do, if they had time. "Could we go to Notre Dame?" she asked him, sounding like a wife for the first time, and he looked pleased.

"I think that could be arranged." He wanted to take her shopping, too, or at least appear to. They were giving him quite a lot of German money to carry with him. It was going to be a lavish two days, suitable for a man of his position, and his pretty young wife. "Can you dance?" he asked her suddenly. He had forgotten about that completely. And since she had gone into the convent so young, he thought it was possible that she had never learned.

"I used to." She smiled shyly.

"We won't dance more than we have to then. My wife always assured me I was a dreadful dancer. I'll tread all over your toes, and elegant shoes," which of course had to be given back to whoever had lent them to her.

They shared as much information as they could in the next three days. Serge had long meetings with him. Montgomery was here to gather information on new bombs they were building, not so much technical details about the bombs themselves, although they were always welcome, as plans for the factory, the number of men manning it, storage facilities once the bombs were made, and who was in charge of the project. It was still in its early stages, but the British already knew it would have a huge impact on the war. All he needed to do in the next two days was make contact. It was a risky mission for him. If he was too well recognized, and ultimately remembered, it could jeopardize him for future missions, but he had been the only man they could send. What he was doing was essential to the war effort.

A cab was called, and they set off for the Crillon, with two handsome suitcases filled with everything they needed. Their papers were impeccable. Amadea's makeup and hair looked beautiful. She wore her long blond hair woven into a neat bun, and looked very stylish in her fashionable clothes. They looked breathtaking as they walked into the hotel. She stared when she saw their room a few minutes later, and then forced herself to clap her hands, exclaim with delight, and kiss her husband. But there were tears in her eyes when the bell-man left. She had seen nothing like it since she entered the convent eight and a half years before, and it reminded her of her mother.

"None of that," he said to her in German.

They went to Notre Dame, then Cartier, which was doing a remarkable business selling to German officers and their mistresses. He took her to lunch at Maxim's, and they went to a party at German headquarters that night. Amadea dazzled them in a white satin evening gown with a narrow diamond necklace, long white kid gloves, and rhinestone sandals. Her husband looked extremely proud of her as she was swept around the dance floor by nearly every young officer in the room, and he chatted amiably about the new munitions plans and what a challenge it would be to finish on time. He got all the information he wanted. The second night they attended a

smaller dinner party at the *Kommandant*'s
home, whose wife became very fond of
Amadea in a short time, got slightly drunk
and extremely indiscreet, and told her
everything her husband had been doing, or
all she knew, and made Amadea promise to
come back to Paris again soon. They were
the hit of the evening by the time they went
back to the Crillon for the second night,
and Amadea was tempted to suggest they
go back to Serge's then, but Colonel
Montgomery said they had to play it out until the end and wait until the next morning.

As they had the night before, they slept in
the same bed, she in a peach satin nightgown trimmed with cream-colored lace,
and he in silk pajamas that were short for
him, but Amadea was the only one who
would know. They lay side by side in bed,
whispering about the things that they had
heard that night, as he debriefed her. She
had picked up some important information
for him, and he was immensely pleased. As
they discussed the significance of it, they
might as well have been sitting in an office
wearing uniforms. The nightgown and pajamas meant nothing to either of them. They
were operating as agents of his govern-

ment, and this was work. Nothing more. They barely slept that night, and Amadea was anxious to leave the next day. She had been aware every moment of the risk they were taking, and as luxurious as their accommodations were, all she wanted was to be back in Melun on the farm.

"Not so quickly," he chided her, always in German while they were there. "This is our anniversary. We are spending it in Paris. You don't want to leave. You adore being here with me, away from the children. You're a wonderful mother, but an even better wife." And more than that, he realized, she was a still better agent. She had been invaluable to him for the entire two days, and he hoped to work with her again. She was brilliant at what she did, and better than she knew.

"You lied to me, by the way," he said over breakfast in their room. They were both dressed by then, and their bags were packed. He had roughed up the sheets considerably when they got up, as she looked at him, wondering what he was doing. "We had a fabulous night of passion," he explained with a grin. They had lain so still and so far apart that they had barely dented the sheets, and it looked like two corpses had been laid in the bed. When he was finished, it looked like quite a night, and she laughed.

"What did I lie to you about?" She looked puzzled. It was comfortable speaking German to him, although she hadn't spoken it in two years, but it felt like home again.

"You're a wonderful dancer. I saw you tripping around the room, flirting with everyone. I was extremely jealous." He was only teasing.

"Did I flirt?" She looked horrified. That had not been her intention. She just wanted to be charming and pleasant, and hoped she hadn't misbehaved.

"Not more than you should have, or I would have been forced to make a jealous scene, which fortunately I wasn't. I forgive you. Also for the lie." In fact, he had watched her dance once or twice, and seen how graceful and light she was on her feet. Particularly for a Carmelite.

They checked out of the hotel, called a cab, and went to the station. And from there they took another cab, went to Serge's house, and were back in the basement room within an hour of leaving the Crillon. As they walked in, Amadea took off her hat and sat down with a tremendous sigh. She was exhausted by the strain of the last two days. She had been terrified, although she hadn't looked it, every second of the day. Although some of the time, she had had fun with him. Particularly at Notre Dame.

Colonel Montgomery told Serge it was the most successful mission of its kind he'd ever done, and he considered it a huge success. He said that Amadea had been flawless in her performance as an SS officer's wife, and had culled a considerable amount of information herself. As the colonel was, Serge was pleased.

"When are we going back?" Amadea asked the colonel with a tired smile after she had changed her clothes back into her own. She felt a little like Cinderella at midnight. It had been fun wearing the beautiful clothes and staying at the Crillon, but her mind had been rarely off the risk of deportation. She was used to the everyday risk of her life in Melun. This had been far, far more extreme.

He had shed the SS uniform by then as well, and they had both returned their papers to Serge. The passports and papers could be used again with a little fine art-

work, and new photographs. Serge returned their old ones as Amélie Dumas, and
the schoolteacher from Arles. They both
knew they were playing a dangerous game,
but they were both adept at it.

"Are you hungry?" he asked Amadea in an
undertone, as she smiled at him. They had
come to sound like man and wife in the past
two days, and it was already a habit.

"I'm fine. I'll eat when we get back. When
do we go?"

"In two hours." He wanted to radio some
coded information back to England first.

They left Serge's house without ceremony, and drove back to Melun, just as they
had on the way up, in the borrowed car. But
this time they were entirely at ease with
each other. It really felt as though they
were man and wife. She had even slept
next to him for two nights, although they
had done so like sister and brother. He still
remembered her in the peach silk nightgown, and she him in the silly too-small pajamas. He was a tall man, and it was hard to
find even trousers long enough for his long
legs.

"You did a fine job," he said to her as they

drove back. "A very fine job. You did good work."

"Thank you, Colonel," she said, no longer feeling shy with him.

"You can call me Rupert." They had switched back to French again, just so they did not make the mistake of speaking German if they were stopped. "You know, you talk in your sleep in German," he said, smiling at her. "That's the sign of an impeccable agent. She talks in her sleep in the language of the mission she is on." Amadea found it a bit confusing now to be speaking to him in French again.

"I liked speaking German to you," she admitted. "It's awful to say in these times. But it reminds me of my childhood. I haven't spoken it in a long time." Not since she'd come to France.

"Your French is remarkable. So is your English," he said admiringly.

"So is yours." They both had German mothers, so it wasn't surprising that German was their native tongue. Although he had grown up in Britain with an English father. And she in Germany with a French one.

"I'd like to work with you again," he said simply.

"I'm not sure I've got the nerves for this kind of work," she said in French. "Not at the level you operate at. I kept waiting for the Gestapo to come to the door and deport me."

"That would have been disagreeable," he said dryly. "I'm glad that didn't happen."

"So am I," she said, looking sobered. It had been an interesting experience, working with him. "You know, I keep wanting to tell you how much I admire what you did with the Kindertransport. What an incredible thing to do."

"It was a wonderful thing. I'm glad we were able to get so many out. I have twelve of them at home myself." He said it as though admitting that he had a radio, or a lovely plant. As though there were nothing remarkable whatsoever about offering a home to twelve foster children, which was in effect what they were. They all had parents, or had when they left Germany. And those whose parents were still alive after the war would be going back one day. He had already made a decision to adopt the ones who didn't, and said as much to Amadea. He was an extraordinary man. She had seen that in the past two days. And even under extreme tension, which he had been under, too, he had been polite, considerate, respectful, and kind at all times. He had been in constant danger of exposure and arrest at all times, just as she had. More than likely he would have been shot if they were caught.

"It must be quite something to have twelve children at home."

"It's entertaining," he admitted with a smile. And it took the edge off his own grief of losing his wife and sons, although it wasn't the same. But it warmed the heart. "They're wonderful children. I speak German with them too. I have eight boys and four girls, from the ages of five to fifteen. The youngest was six months old when they put her on the train. She came with her sister. Two of the older boys are twins. Some families in England only wanted one or two from a family when there were actually more—we did the best we could to keep families together. Some of them have had to be re-placed, but most of the placements have been a success. They get terribly homesick sometimes, poor things. Not my little one, of course. She doesn't remember any other family but me and the other kinders. She's a little vixen. She has bright red hair and freckles." He smiled as he described her, and Amadea could see in his eyes the love he had for them. She suspected he must have been a good father, too, when his sons were alive.

They reached Melun just after nightfall, and Jean-Yves's aunt cooked them dinner. She did not ask where they'd been or what they'd done, and they said nothing about Paris. It was obvious to her that he was an agent from somewhere else, and one of some importance. They just ate dinner quietly, and talked about the farm and the weather. And afterward, Amadea and Rupert sat in the barn talking until it was time for him to leave.

"It sounds strange, but I had a nice time with you," he said pleasantly. "Do you miss the convent?" he asked, still curious about her. She was an interesting mix of many different things. Worldly, innocent, beautiful, humble, brave, shy, intelligent, and entirely without pretension. In an odd way, he could see why she would make a good nun, although he still thought it was a terrible waste. He still remembered how smashing she had looked in the white evening gown, and the peach nightgown. He never got involved with other agents. It would have been madness to do so, and would have complicated everything. This was work, not play. And people's lives were at stake.

"Yes, I do," Amadea admitted seriously, in reference to missing the convent. "All the time. I'll go back when it's over," she said, sounding certain, and he believed her. He had a feeling that she would.

"Save me a dance before you do," he teased. "You could teach me a thing or two."

They walked out to the field around eleven-thirty and met the others. The plane came for him right on time just after midnight. The men who had come into France with him were still on other missions. The plane was just landing as he turned to her and thanked her again.

"God bless you," she said over the purr of the plane. "Take care."

"You too," he said, touched her arm, saluted her, and then hopped into the Lysander the moment it landed. They took off again in less than three minutes, and she stood looking at it for a moment as the tiny plane flew away. She thought she saw him wave, and then she turned and walked back to the farm.

23

AMADEA DIDN'T HEAR FROM SERGE AGAIN UNTIL two weeks before Christmas, and then he came to see her again. She had been doing the same local missions as always. Twice she had rescued men who had parachuted in and were hurt. She had shimmied up a tree and cut one of them down when he got tangled up in the branches, and she had nursed him for several weeks. Her heroism and selflessness were no secret around Melun. The two men she had saved had been British, and the one she had cut down from the tree had sworn he would come back after the war to see her again. He thought she had been an angel of mercy. There was no question she had saved his life.

She was feeling sad before Christmas, thinking about Jean-Yves—the Christmas before, they had been together. But now she felt her religious vocation stronger than ever. She wondered if that had been why he had come into her life. She knew that in time all things were revealed.

When Serge came this time, even he hesitated to broach the mission to her. The request had come from Colonel Montgomery himself. It was of course optional for her.

The plans for the bomb factory in Germany had been advancing rapidly. Faster than the British had expected. And now he needed the technical details that he had not obtained in Paris. He needed Amadea to masquerade as his wife again, as a different officer and his wife this time. The greatest risk of the mission was that it was in Germany. They had to get safely in and out, which would be no small accomplishment. Either of them could easily be killed, and in Amadea's case, if not killed, she would surely be deported. This time Serge didn't even want to ask her, and discouraged her from going. He had to relay the message to her, but nothing more.

"To be honest with you, I don't think you

should." Listening to him, neither did she. He told her she had two days to decide.

She didn't want to go, but for the next two days she couldn't sleep. All she could think of were the faces she had known and seen in Theresienstadt. She wondered how many of them were still alive. Her mother and sister in Ravensbrück. Her mother's family in Dachau. If no one did these missions, they would be there forever, and all the Jews in Germany and the other occupied countries would eventually die. She remembered something that one of the inmates of Theresienstadt had said to her, an old man who had died the month before she left. He had said, "Whoever saves one life, saves a world entire." It was from the Talmud, and she had never forgotten it. How could she turn her back on them now, when she had a chance to make a difference, even if it meant being deported again? It was the last thing she wanted. But this was her chance to fight for them. What other choice did she have? She asked herself what choice Christ had had when faced with the cross.

Amadea radioed Serge that night. The message was only "Yes. Teresa." She knew he would understand, and pass the message on to the colonel. She got her instructions the next day. He was flying in to the east of her this time. And she had to travel to meet the cell there. They would give her papers, and whatever clothes she needed. It was winter, and they wouldn't be having an "anniversary weekend" in Paris at the Crillon. She didn't need anything as fancy, just substantial.

She left in the dark of night and reached Nancy by morning. Colonel Montgomery had landed in a field that night. This time he had been parachuted in. They were expected to be in Germany for five days. When he saw her, he broke into a broad smile.

"Well, Sister, how have you been?"

"Fine, thank you, Colonel. It's good to see you again." Their greeting was respectful and friendly. It was like meeting an old friend.

He was impressed that she had agreed to take on this mission, knowing full well how dangerous it was for her. He had felt guilty asking her, but the truth was, he needed her, and so did England. He was glad she was coming with him.

They got their papers, and he instructed her that night. They sat talking until daylight. It was complicated this time. He needed her help in culling information, and taking photographs for him. He gave her a tiny camera for that purpose, to conceal in a pocket of her handbag. He was wearing his SS uniform again, and they were taking the train into Germany that morning. As they had before, he spoke to her in German, so they would make no mistake while on their mission. German had to be their language of choice and habit with each other, just as it had been in Paris. And once again, she found she was happy speaking it to him. But they both knew that this mission would be even more delicate than the first one.

They both looked tired and pale when they boarded the train, as everyone did that winter. But they chatted good-humoredly as the train left the station, and after a while she fell asleep with her head on his shoulder. She was genuinely exhausted. He read while she slept, and when she awoke, she looked better. They were going to Salzal Thüringen, and staying at a hotel where officers and their wives were billeted. It was nothing to compare to the Crillon. And when they checked in, their room was pleasant. The desk clerk apologized that there were two narrow beds in the room instead of one big one. They were full up with wives visiting their husbands before Christmas. Rupert told them it was no problem, it wasn't their honeymoon, and all three of them laughed. He could see as they walked into the room that Amadea was relieved. And this time the agents in the cell that had outfitted them had provided her with a warm flannel nightgown. This trip was far less romantic, and infinitely more danger- ous. Rupert was impersonating an SS offi- cer who did not exist. His name and papers were entirely fictitious, as were hers. They had agreed that it was perfectly all right for her to say she was from Cologne. She was less likely to make mistakes then, and so many of the records had been destroyed in the bombing of '42, the year before. It made conversation much easier and less self- conscious for her whenever she chatted with other officers or their wives.

They went to two formal Gestapo dinners in the evening. But most of the time, Rupert was working. On one occasion, she came with him for a tour of the factory. The Nazis were very proud of what they were doing. Amadea remembered everything she saw and wrote it down in the evening.

The entire trip was a constant strain, and on the fourth day, Rupert said quietly when they went to bed that he had done it. They were leaving in the morning, and everything had gone smoothly. But Amadea was awake all night with an anxious feeling. She still had it when they boarded the train the next day. She was silent for most of the trip through Germany. It was as though she had a strange premonition, which she didn't dare communicate to Rupert. There was no point making him nervous too. What they had done had been stunningly bold and courageous, and they both knew it.

Their papers were checked frequently on their way across Germany, and in the last station, two young soldiers seemed to take forever. They were very near the border, and she was sure something would happen. But once again their passports were handed back to them, and the train moved on.

Rupert smiled at her as they pulled away. And by morning, they were back in France. They were going to Paris, and from there

back to Melun. According to Rupert's papers, he was stationed at SS headquarters
in Paris. They were going to Serge, where
Rupert could radio into England, and then
to Melun, from where he would leave. It was
the week before Christmas.

They were hurrying through the station in
Paris, when an SS officer grabbed Rupert's
arm and called out his name. But it was the
name of the SS officer he had impersonated
three months before, and not the one he
was now. The reality of what that could
mean had Amadea shaking in her shoes.
But the two men wished each other well
and a Merry Christmas, as Amadea and
Rupert walked calmly out of the station and
hailed a cab. They went to a small café,
from there they would walk to Serge's place.
As they sat down at the café, and ordered
the coffee that was available, Amadea's
face was gray.

"Everything is fine," he said calmly, looking into her eyes to steady her, and speaking to her in French once again. It was nothing less than a miracle that they had pulled
it off from beginning to end.

"I am definitely not made for this," she
said softly, looking apologetic. She had

been feeling as though she were going to throw up since that morning. And he looked tired himself. The trip had been a tremendous strain, but also a huge success.

"You're much better at it than you think. Almost too good." She was so convincing as the wife of an SS officer that he was beginning to fear she would do more of this work. And he didn't think she should. You could only risk your life so many times. He always said he had at least ten lives. But she was young, and it somehow seemed like too much risk. At forty-two, he felt as though he had already lived. With his wife and boys gone, no one would miss him if he were gone, except his *kinders.* What he did, he did to pay the Germans back for his wife and sons, and also to serve his king.

They walked to Serge's grandparents' house after that, reported in, changed papers. Rupert used the radio for several hours, changing frequencies every fifteen minutes, so the Germans couldn't use their tracking devices to pinpoint their position, and listened in to what was happening in France. They did everything they had to do before they left, and Amadea decided that her premonition of something going wrong had been silly. It couldn't have been smoother.

In the end, they drove down to Melun that evening, and got back to her farmhouse before too late. She sat in the barn with him as they had before, and walked out to the field with him after midnight. It was so cold that there was frost on the ground, and there was a light snow in the air. She held his arm so she wouldn't slip on the patches of ice, and he steadied her several times. They had a familiar ease with each other, as though they really were man and wife now, or at the very least somehow related. They were waiting in a clump of trees for the plane to come. It all seemed very routine. It was hard to believe they had been in Germany the night before, and nearly for an entire week. She no longer even cared that it was Christmas. They had survived. That was all that mattered.

The plane came just before one that night. It had been a long wait in the freezing cold. Her hands were numb as she shook Rupert's and wished him a Merry Christmas and a good trip. This time he bent and kissed her cheek.

"You were extraordinary, as usual . . . I hope it's a good Christmas for you."

"It will be. We're still alive, and I'm not in Auschwitz." She smiled at him. "Enjoy Christmas with your *kinders*," as the children of the transport were called by their English foster parents, and all who knew of them.

He patted her shoulder then, and she watched the others signal the plane in. They didn't need her for it tonight. She had just come to see him off, like any dutiful wife at an airport. She stood back among the trees, and watched him run across the field to the waiting Lysander, and as he did, a shot rang out. He bent low for a minute, and she saw him clutch his shoulder, and then keep running. There were more shots, and she saw two of the men with the torches fall, with the beams from their flashlights pointing upward. Amadea sank deeper into the bushes. There was nothing she could do for any of them. She wasn't even armed. But she had seen that Rupert was wounded. Within seconds, they pulled him into the plane and took off, closing the door as the aircraft lifted. The other members of the cell had run across the field

and disappeared, dragging the two injured men with them, but both were dead.
Within minutes there were soldiers everywhere, and she knew that they would be
visiting all the neighboring farms. There
might be reprisals, or perhaps not, since no
Germans had been killed or injured, only
Rupert.

The soldiers headed off after the men
who'd fled, and she ran home as fast as she
could. She ran into her room, tore off her
clothes, and got into bed in her nightgown,
rubbing her hands and face as hard as she
could to warm them. But her room was ice
cold anyway.

Much to her amazement, they never
came. She couldn't believe the luck they'd
had getting out of Germany, accomplishing
their mission, and surviving his departure.
She was reminded of the premonition she'd
had ever since the last night in Germany,
which gave her new respect for her own instincts.

The two young freedom fighters were
dead, they were both old friends of Jean-
Yves. And the next day, Serge received a
message from the British on his shortwave
radio. Apollo had landed, with a scratch on

his wing, but nothing major, and warm thanks to Teresa. Serge duly passed on the message. And much to everyone's relief, it was a peaceful Christmas.

24

THE SYSTEMATIC EXTERMINATION OF JEWS CONtinued all over Europe through the winter of 1943. Nearly five thousand people a day were being gassed at Auschwitz. And 850,000 had been killed at Treblinka by the previous August. By October, 250,000 had been killed at Sobibor. In November, 42,000 Polish Jews had been killed. Jews from Vienna were sent to Auschwitz in December. There were mass deportations now from Theresienstadt to Auschwitz. And ghettos all over Europe had been leveled.

By March 1944, the Nazis had set their sights on 725,000 Hungarian Jews. In April, the Nazis were raiding French homes, looking for Jewish children. The tragedy of the

year before was that Jean Moulin, one of
the famed leaders of the Resistance, had
been arrested in Lyon.

In the spring of '44, Serge and everyone
else in the Resistance knew that the Allies
were coming. The question was when, and
how soon. The Germans were after everyone, and the plan for the Resistance was to
cripple them in every way they could, so
they wouldn't be able to stop the Allies
when they came.

Amadea wondered if Rupert was part of it,
and was sure he must have been. She had
heard nothing of him for four months since
their mission into Germany in December.
But there was no reason why she should.
She thought of him from time to time, and
his *kinders,* and hoped that he and the children he had brought to England were safe
and well.

She went on more missions than usual in
March. The weather was better, and it was
easier moving around than in the winter.
She had been made the head of her group,
and many of the decisions of her cell rested
on her.

In an effort to cripple the Germans' movements, she had decided with several others

to blow up a train. They had done things like that before, often with dire results, and severe reprisals, but the word they were getting from Paris was to slow the trains down in any way they could. Blowing up the train and the tracks east of Orléans seemed like a good move, although it was dangerous for all of them.

Coincidentally, the plan was set for the night of Amadea's twenty-seventh birthday. No one knew, and it meant little to her. Birthdays and holidays seemed irrelevant at that point. They always made her sad anyway. She was happier doing something useful, particularly if it hindered the Germans.

There were twenty people involved in their movements that night. A dozen men and eight women. Some of them were local, and others had come from nearby cells. One of the men had worked for Jean Moulin and had left Lyon the year before, when Moulin got arrested. Not surprisingly, Amadea thought he was remarkably well trained. And she couldn't help thinking as she lay in the dirt that night, waiting for the sentries to pass, that it was hard even for her to believe now that she had once been a nun. She spent her time preparing weapons, putting together explosives, damaging property, and doing everything she could to disrupt and destroy the enemy that was occupying France. She still intended to go back to the convent, but she wondered sometimes if they, or the God she loved, could ever forgive her for all that she'd done. But she was more determined than ever to do what she was doing. Until the war was over, she felt she had no choice.

Amadea herself helped set the explosives near the track that night. She had done things like it before, and knew how much to use. As always when they did things like that, it reminded her of Jean-Yves. But she was careful, and when they lit the fuse, she was about to run, just as a German sentry strolled by. She knew that within seconds he would be blown to smithereens, but if she didn't move, so would she. Instead of moving toward where some of the others were hiding, she had no choice but to fall backward, which separated her farther from them. She had just started to run, when the first explosion detonated. The German sentry was killed instantly, and Amadea was thrown backward with such force that she flew into the air like a rag doll, and landed not far from the tracks flat on her back. Much to her own amazement, she was still conscious and knew what was happening, but she couldn't move after what she'd been through. She had landed with a breathtaking blow to her spine.

One of the men had seen what happened, and he darted past the fire to where she lay. He threw her roughly over his shoulder and ran back to the others, just as the second explosion went off. The second one was huge, and would have killed her, just as had happened to Jean-Yves.

All she knew afterward was that someone carried her for a long time, and she felt nothing. She remembered being put in a truck with explosions in the distance and fire everywhere. After that, she lost consciousness and woke up two days later in a strange barn, among people she didn't know. She had been taken to a neighboring town and concealed.

She drifted in and out of consciousness for the next week, and two of the men from her own cell came to see her. They looked worried about her, and said the Germans were looking for her everywhere. They had

gone to Jean-Yves's aunt and uncle's farmhouse where she lived, and found her missing. The old couple said they had no idea
where she was, and miraculously they had
been spared. But she couldn't go back
there. Serge had radioed them from Paris
and said they had to get her out. But in addition to the Germans looking for her, her
second greatest problem was that she
couldn't move her legs or even sit up. Her
back had been broken when she had fallen.
Her legs were numb, and there was no way
she could leave on her own. In the condition
she was in, she had become a serious
handicap, and was no longer of any use to
them.

"He wants us to get you out," one of the
men she knew and had worked with for a
year and a half told her gently. They didn't
want to say it to her, but she looked like
death. She had been incoherent and hallu-
cinating for the past two days. Her back had
not only been broken but badly burned. She
felt nothing as she lay there, not even pain.

"To where?" Amadea said, trying to focus
on the problem. But she was so tired she
could hardly stay awake. She kept drifting
into unconsciousness when she talked to

them. In one of her brief moments of lucidity, they explained what was going to happen. Everything had been arranged.

"There's a plane coming for you tonight."

"Don't send me back to the camp," she pleaded with him . . . "I'll be good, I promise. I'll get up in a minute." But they all knew she couldn't. A doctor had come and said she would be paralyzed for life. And even in her condition, if the Germans found her, she'd be killed. They wouldn't even bother sending her to a camp. She was worthless to them now, even as a slave.

To make matters worse, it was too dangerous for them to keep her now. A young boy had informed, and the Germans knew that she was either part of or in charge of a cell. They all knew Serge was right. She had no choice but to get out. If they could get her out alive, which seemed doubtful. One of the Lysanders was coming for her that night. If they could get her on it. And if she survived. She was unconscious that night when they carried her out of the barn. One of the women had wrapped her in a blanket. She looked like a dead body, and they had covered her face. She moaned as they car-

ried her, but she didn't regain consciousness again.

A young boy who had known her since
she came to France ran across the field with
her, as the others shone their lights. It felt
more like a funeral than a rescue mission.
One of the men had cried and said she
would be dead before they got her off the
plane. And the others suspected he was
right.

The door was open as soon as the small
plane landed. And they literally threw her
onto the floor of the plane, still wrapped in
the blanket. There were two men on the
plane. One of them pulled her in, and then
slammed the door shut as they took off. The
pilot just managed to clear the trees, and
then turned and headed toward England as
the other man gently pulled the blanket off
her face. They knew they had come for a
French Resistance fighter they had to get
out. They knew nothing more than that.
They didn't even know her name. Serge had
radioed what they needed to know to the
British. All the pilots needed to know was
where to go and that there was someone to
pick up. They had.

"I think we made a bum run on this one,"

the man sitting next to her on the floor said as he saw her face. She was barely breathing, and she had almost no pulse. "I don't think she's going to make it." The pilot said nothing, and flew home.

They were both surprised to find that she was still alive when they got to England. An ambulance was waiting on the tarmac and took her. They took her to a hospital, where a bed was waiting for her, and when they saw her, they realized that she needed a lot more than a bed. She had third-degree burns all over her back, and her spine was broken. It was unlikely, the surgeon wrote in the report, after they had done what they could for her, that she would ever walk again.

They put her in the ward under the name on the papers she was carrying. Her French identification papers said her name was Amélie Dumas. Shortly afterward, a clerk from the British Secret Service office had called and identified her under the code name of Teresa.

"Do you suppose she's a British agent?" one of the nurses asked another when she saw the notation on the chart. They knew she had been picked up in France, but not why, or by whom.

"Could be. She hasn't spoken a word since she got here. I don't know what language she speaks."

The head sister looked at the chart intently. It was hard to tell these days. She wasn't British Army in any case, and she was in desperate shape. "She could be one of ours."

"Whoever she is, she's been through some pretty rough times," the other nurse said.

Amadea didn't regain consciousness until three days later, and when she did, she only did so for a minute. She looked up at the nurse ministering to her and spoke in French with haunted, unseeing eyes. She spoke in French, not German or English, and said only, *"Je suis l'épouse du Christ Crucifié"* . . . I am the bride of the crucified Christ. And with that, she lost consciousness again.

25

ON JUNE 6, THE ALLIES HAD LANDED IN Normandy, and Amadea cried when she heard the news. More than anyone in the hospital, it was what she had prayed for and fought for. It was mid-June before Amadea could be rolled out into the hospital garden in a wheelchair.

The doctors had told her that it was unlikely she would ever walk again, although not entirely certain. But highly unlikely, as they put it. She thought her legs were a small sacrifice to have made for the war effort, and to keep the people she had fought for alive. There were countless others who would never even see life from a wheelchair. And as she sat in the sunshine, with a blan-

ket over her legs, she suddenly realized that
she would be one of those old nuns in
wheelchairs that the young nuns took care
of. She didn't care if she had to crawl into
the convent, as soon as they let her out of
the hospital, she was going back. There
was a Carmelite convent in Notting Hill in
London, and she was planning to visit them
when she was able to get out. But the doctor said she couldn't consider it yet. Her
burns were still healing, and she needed
therapy for her back and legs. And she
didn't want to be a burden on the other
nuns just yet.

She sat in the garden with her eyes closed
and her face to the sunshine, when beside
her she heard a familiar voice. She couldn't
place it, and she had heard it in another language. It was like an echo of the distant
past.

"Well, Sister, you've certainly done it this
time." She opened her eyes and saw Rupert
standing next to her. He was wearing the
uniform of a British officer. And it seemed
strange to her not to be seeing him in the
uniform of the SS. She realized that the unfamiliar sound of his voice was that he was
speaking English, and not German or

French. She smiled as she looked at him. "I understand you tried single-handedly to destroy the entire French railway system and half the German Army with it. I hear you did a hell of a job."

"Thank you, Colonel." Her eyes lit up as soon as she saw him. He was the only friend she'd seen since she'd been there. And she had been having terrible nightmares about Theresienstadt. Worse than she'd ever had since she left. "What have you been up to?" It had been six months since they last met, after their last mission into Germany together, when he'd been shot as he left France. "How's your shoulder, by the way?"

"It aches a bit in the bad weather, but nothing that time won't take care of." In fact, he'd taken a nasty hit, but the doctors had done a good job putting him back together. Better than they had done with her. Or at least that was what he heard. The surgeon he had spoken to before visiting her said there was virtually no hope of her ever walking again, but they didn't want to tell her that quite that bluntly. He had said that for the moment at least, she appeared to be resigned to it. According to him, it was a miracle that she was alive. But miracles were her stock in trade.

"I got your message when you got back here. Thank you. I was worried," she said sincerely, as he sat down on the bench facing her.

"Not nearly as worried as I've been about you," he said seriously. "Sounds like you took a devil of a hit."

"I've never been good with explosives," she said, sounding the way some women did when they said they couldn't manage apple pies or soufflés.

"You might consider giving them up in that case," he said practically, with a twinkle in his eye.

"Have you come to ask me to go back to Germany, pretending to be your wife?" she asked mischievously. As terrifying as it had been, in retrospect she had enjoyed working with him. Almost as much as he had enjoyed working with her. "Maybe you could say I'm your grandmother, now that I'm in a wheelchair," she said, looking faintly embarrassed, and he brushed the comment off.

"Nonsense. You'll be running around again in no time. They tell me you'll be getting out next month." He had kept close

track of her, and had promised Serge he
would. But he had waited until he thought
she'd be up to a visit. He knew she had
been in bad shape until then. She'd had a
very rough two months.

"I thought I'd go to the convent in Notting
Hill, when I get out. I don't want to be a burden to them, but there's still a lot I can do.
I'll have to brush up on my sewing," she
said demurely, looking only for an instant
like a nun. But he knew her better.

"I don't suppose they'll want you blowing
up their garden. It could actually upset them
quite a lot," he said, smiling at her, happy to
see her. In spite of the rough spot she'd
been through, she looked well and, as always, beautiful. Her long blond hair hung
down her back and shone in the sunlight.
"Actually, I had a proposition for you. Not as
exciting as a mission into Germany, I'll admit. But close. And at times, almost as challenging for the nerves." She looked surprised as she listened. She couldn't imagine
that in her current condition the British
Secret Service would want her to do a mission with him. Her days as a Resistance
fighter were over. But hopefully in a while,
the war would be, too. She had fought a

good fight for a long time. Longer than most. "Actually, to be honest, I need help with my *kinders.* They're getting older. They've been with me for five years now. The little ones are not so little, and getting into all kinds of mischief. The older ones are nearly grown up, and causing all kinds of ruckus at my place. I'm here in London most of the time, and frankly I need some-one to keep an eye on them until this whole mess is over. And when it is, I'm going to need help tracking down their parents for them, if they're still alive. It could be quite a job. It's not easy for a man alone with twelve children," he said plaintively, and she laughed. "I don't suppose you'd put off reenlisting with your order for a bit, to help out an old friend. We were married for a few days at one point, as much as a week I'd say, all in all. I mean, you owe me at least that. You can't just walk off and leave me with twelve children on my own." She was laughing as she listened, and she sus-pected he was just being charitable, but also kind, which was typical of him.

"You're not serious, are you?" she asked with a strange expression. She felt an old stirring of friendship for him. Although they didn't know each other well, after all they had risked together, it created a powerful bond. In a sense, during their two missions, they had protected each other's lives. And done some terrific work. She was proud of what they'd done.

"Actually, I am serious. I adore them. But to be honest with you, Amadea, they're driving my housekeeper insane. She's seventy-six years old. She was my nanny when I was a boy, and my children's. These *kinders* need someone a bit younger to entertain them and keep them in line." He was being truthful with her.

"I'm not sure how useful I'd be at either these days." She glanced down at the wheelchair, and then back at him. "They might push me off a cliff if they don't like what I said."

"They're really good kids," he said, sounding serious finally. She could see that he meant what he had said. It was also easy to see that he loved them, but he was right. He had no wife, and a seventy-six-year-old housekeeper was no match for twelve lively young children, with no parent at hand. Rupert was away much of the time, on missions, or at work in London. He only got down to East Sussex on the weekends. On the other hand, she was anxious to get back to the convent. She had been out in the world long enough, and done all she was meant to. It was time for her to go back, and she said as much to him, as gently as she could. "Don't you suppose they could manage without you for a few more months?" he asked hopefully. "It's part of the war effort, after all. These children are victims of the Nazis, as you are. And it's going to be hard on them after the war, when a lot of them find out what happened to their parents. It could be very rough." He tore at her heartstrings, and she hesitated as she looked at him. The fates constantly seemed to conspire to keep her from the convent. She wanted to ask God what he wanted of her. But as she looked at the expression in Rupert's eyes, she knew. She was meant to take care of these children. Maybe that was why God had sent Rupert to her. It was endless. But after three years out of the convent now, she supposed she could wait a while longer. She was beginning to think she'd be ninety when she took her final vows. But she knew that eventually she would. Of that she was sure.

"I hadn't actually written to the Mother Superior yet," Amadea said, looking at him ruefully. "I was going to sometime this week. Are you sure I would be useful to you? I'm pretty useless in this thing." At times, in spite of her best efforts, she felt a little sorry for herself. But if it was God's will, she could live with it. She had been blessed in so many ways, so many times.

"I'm very glad to hear you haven't reenlisted yet. I was afraid you would before I got to you. And of course, you're perfectly useful the way you are now. Don't be silly. All you have to do is shout at them, and I'll give you a big stick. You can prod them along if you need to." He was teasing, and she laughed at him.

"When do you want me?" As she asked him, she already looked hopeful and excited. She couldn't wait to meet them. Taking care of them would give her life new purpose, particularly with Rupert gone so much. As they talked about it, she nearly felt married to him again, as she had in Paris and on the trip to Germany in December. They had a very odd relationship. In some ways they were strangers, in others they felt like best friends. And she was happy about

helping him with his *kinders.* The convent
could wait for a little bit. The war would be
over before long. And once they found their
parents and left him . . . her mind was rac-
ing as she sat in the wheelchair talking to
him, and suddenly she sat up straighter.
She wanted him to write down all their
names on a piece of paper before he left
that afternoon, and he promised that he
would.

He knew he had done a good thing for her
morale, and he sat smiling at her as they
talked for hours that afternoon, about the
children, his estate, the two days they had
spent in Paris, the five in Germany. They
seemed to have a lot to talk about, and she
looked happy and young and was laughing
when he wheeled her back to her room.
They had agreed that she would come
straight to his estate in East Sussex as soon
as the doctors released her in four weeks.
But he told her he would see her several
times before then. He wanted to make sure
she was doing well, and besides he enjoyed
her company.

He kissed her on the cheek when he left.
And after he was gone, she said prayers for
his *kinders,* and for him.

26

THE TRIP DOWN TO EAST SUSSEX FROM THE HOS-
pital was uncomfortable for her. She still
had some sensation in her lower spine and
her legs, though very little. It was more of a
tingling sensation than anything, but it was
just enough to give her pain if she stayed in
one position for too long. She had no control over her lower limbs. She felt completely numb from the waist down when the
chauffeur gently sat her in her wheelchair
when she got out of the car. Rupert was
waiting for her when she arrived. He had
come down the day before, to speak to the
children. He wanted them to be nice to her,
and not give her a hard time. He told them
how brave she had been, and that she had

even been in a concentration camp for five months, two years before.

"Did she meet my mummy?" a little girl with freckles and no front teeth asked him with interest.

"I don't think so," he said kindly, as the twins threw bread balls at each other and he told them to stop. "You're going to have to do better than that when she's here," he told them, scowling and trying to look fierce. But they knew him better than that and paid no attention to him. When he was at the estate in Sussex, they crawled all over him like puppies. And Rebekka, the little redhead, always wanted to sit on his lap and have him read her stories. She spoke no German, only English since she'd been six months old when she arrived. She was now six. But several of the others, who had been older when they got to England, still spoke German. He had told Amadea he thought she should speak German to them at least some of the time. When their parents came back, if they did, some of them would be unable to speak to their own children. He thought that keeping up their German would be a good thing. He had tried it himself, but he always got distracted and wound up speaking to them in English, although his German was as good as Amadea's, for the same reason, their mothers. "She's a lovely young woman, and she's very beautiful. You're going to love her," he had told the children almost proudly.

"Are you going to marry her, Papa Rupert?" twelve-year-old Marta inquired. She was fair and long and gangly and looked like a young colt.

"No, I'm not," he said respectfully. "Actually, before the war, she was a nun. And she's planning to go back to the convent after the war." He knew he had only waylaid her temporarily to help with his *kinders*. And he really did need her help. But he couldn't think of anything more pleasant now than coming home to the children and her.

"She was a nun?" Ten-year-old Friedrich stared at him, looking worried. "Is she going to wear one of those big dresses and the funny hat?"

"No, she's not. She's not a nun right now, but she used to be. And she's going to be again." Rupert didn't like it, and thought it a waste, but he respected it, and expected them to do the same.

"Tell me how she broke her back again?" Rebekka asked with a worried frown. "I forgot."

"She blew up a train," he said as though it were something sensible people did every day, like throw out the trash or walk the dog.

"She must be very brave," Hermann, the oldest boy, said in a hushed tone. He had just turned sixteen and had begun to look like a man and not a boy.

"She is. She's been in the Resistance in France for the last two years." They nodded. They all knew what that meant.

"Will she bring a gun?" a studious-looking eight-year-old boy named Ernst asked with interest. He was fascinated by guns, and Rupert had taken him hunting. They all called him Papa Rupert.

"I hope not," Rupert said, laughing at the image. And a few minutes later Amadea arrived. Rupert went out to greet her, as she looked around the grounds in awe. The ancestral house and grounds looked very much like her father's family's château in Dordogne. It was less formal than she had feared it would be, but impressive nonetheless.

He rolled her into the living room after

greeting her with a kiss on the cheek and a warm welcome. The children were all waiting for her in their best clothes, and Mrs. Hascombs had set up a long table in the library with a proper tea. Amadea hadn't seen anything so lovely since before the war. And the children were beautiful as she looked at them. And a trifle scared. A few of them looked worried by the wheelchair as she smiled at them.

"Now let's see," she said, smiling at them, and feeling like a nun again. At times it was the best way she had of making herself feel comfortable. If she pretended she was still wearing her habit and veil, she didn't feel quite so vulnerable and exposed. And they were all staring at her, trying to take her measure. But so far, for the most part, they liked what they saw. Papa Rupert was right. She was beautiful. And not old. In fact, she looked quite young, even to them. They were sorry about the chair, and her legs.

Amadea was smiling as she returned their gaze. "You must be Rebekka . . . You're Marta . . . Friedrich . . . Ernst . . . Hermann . . . Josef . . . Gretchen . . . Berta . . . Johann . . . Hans . . . Maximilian . . . and Claus . . ." She had named them all correctly, and pointed to each one of them. The only mistake she had made, and an understandable one even to them, was that she had confused Johann and Josef, but as they were identical, everyone did, even Rupert. He was amazed and so were they. She apologized politely to Johann and Josef for the mistake.

"I can't tell them apart either sometimes," Rebekka volunteered, and without warning, she hopped into her lap. But Amadea felt little, although for a moment Rupert panicked. He didn't want the child to hurt her, but fortunately she hadn't. And Mrs. Hascombs came to greet her with an extended hand and a kind look.

"We're so happy to have you," she said warmly, and looked as though she meant it. In fact, she looked immensely relieved. She was in deep water with twelve lively young children, and knew it. As did the *kinders,* and they took full advantage of it. Amadea wasn't sure she could control them either, but she was certainly going to try. She thought they were adorable and fell in love with them at first sight.

"Tell us about the train you blew up," Rebekka said cheerfully, as they all ate tea and scones, and Rupert looked slightly aghast as Amadea smiled. He had apparently briefed them about her. And she was sure he had also told them she was a nun, which was fine, too.

"Well, it wasn't a nice thing to do," Amadea said seriously, "but they were Germans, so for now it was all right. But it won't be all right after the war. You can only do things like that when there's a war on." Rupert nodded approval.

"They bomb us all the time, so there's nothing wrong with killing them," Maximilian said fiercely. He was thirteen, and already knew his parents were dead. Relatives had told him. He wet the bed sometimes. And had nightmares. Rupert had told her that, too. He had wanted her to know everything about them. He believed in full disclosure and didn't want her to be shocked. There were times when they made him want to tear his hair out. Twelve children were a lot for anyone, no matter how wonderful or well behaved they were.

"Do your legs hurt?" Marta asked kindly. She seemed the gentlest of all. Gretchen was the prettiest. Berta the shyest. The boys seemed full of life, and were moving all the time, even while drinking tea and eating scones. They were itching to go outside and kick a ball around, but Rupert had told them they had to wait until they'd finished tea.

"No, they don't hurt," Amadea said honestly about her legs. "Sometimes I don't feel them at all. Sometimes I do, a little." Sometimes her back was excruciating, but she didn't say that. And the scars from her burns were ugly.

"Do you think you'll ever walk again?" Berta finally asked her.

"I don't know," Amadea said with a smile, she seemed matter of fact about it, which tore at Rupert's heart. He hoped she would, for her sake. "We'll see," she said, sounding hopeful. She was philosophical about her fate.

And then she suggested they all go outside and walk around the grounds before dark. The boys were thrilled, and were outside playing ball in less than a minute.

"You're wonderful with them," Rupert said admiringly. "I knew you would be. You're just what they need. They need a mother. None of them has had one in five years, and may not again. Mrs. Hascombs is more like a grandmother to them." In some cases, most in fact, Amadea was too young to be their mother, she was more like an older sister to them, but they needed that, too. It reminded her of when Daphne was young. She had loved being her older sister. This was good for her, too.

At dinner that night, they spoke of many things, not only about the war. They told Amadea about their friends, school, the things they liked to do. And Rebekka came up with the perfect name for her. She called her "Mamadea." They all liked it, and so did she. They were now officially Mamadea and Papa Rupert.

The days sped by after that. Rupert went back to London after the weekend, and came back every Friday afternoon and stayed till Monday morning. He was vastly impressed by how well Amadea handled them. And he was touched when he saw what she had done on the first Friday night he was back. She had read about how to do it, and had done a Shabbat for them, with the challah bread. She lit the candles, and read the prayer. It was a deeply touching moment, and the first Sabbath they had celebrated in five years. It brought tears to Rupert's eyes, and the children looked as though they were drifting back in memory to a beloved place as she did it.

"I never thought of that. How did you know what to do?"

"I got a book." She smiled at him. It had touched her, too. And somewhere in her history there were Sabbaths like that, too, even though she had never known them.

"I don't suppose they did that in the convent," he said, and she laughed. She enjoyed his company and they were comfortable together. She had had her first glimpse of that in Paris when she was there with him. They talked about it once, and he reminisced nostalgically about the peach nightgown. He loved to tease her. "If you had slept any further from me in the bed, you'd have been levitating like some Indian soukh."

"I thought it was funny when you messed up the bed the next day." She laughed, but under the circumstances of their pretense, it had been a wise thing to do so as not to arouse suspicion.

"I had to preserve my reputation," he said rather grandly.

The days of summer rolled by easily, and for once Amadea didn't even miss the convent. She was too busy. She sewed, she read, she played catch with them, she scolded them, and dried their tears. She spoke German to those who wanted to and remembered it, and taught it to the others. And French. She told them it was a good thing to know. They thrived under her protection. And Rupert loved coming home on weekends.

"It's a shame she's a nun," Marta said mournfully one Sunday at breakfast with Rupert, after Amadea had gone out with the boys. She was going to fish with them in the lake on his estate. They called it Lake Papa.

"I think so, too," he said honestly. But he knew how determined she was to go back. They seldom talked about it, but she was loyal to her vocation, and he knew it.

"I forget sometimes," Marta admitted.

"So do I."

"Do you suppose you could ever change her mind?" she asked cautiously. The children spoke of it often. They wanted her to stay as long as they would.

"I doubt it. That's a very serious thing. And she was a nun for a long time. Six years. It wouldn't be right of me to try and dissuade

her." Marta had the impression he was saying it more to himself than to her.

"I think you should try." He smiled, but
didn't answer. There were times he thought
so, too. But he didn't dare. He was afraid
she would get angry at him and leave. Some
things were taboo. And he respected her a
great deal, even if he didn't like the path she
had chosen. But he recognized her right to
do that, whether he liked it or not. He had
no idea how to even broach the subject with
her. He knew by now how stubborn she
could be, particularly if she believed in
something. She was a woman with a strong
mind, and once in a while, she reminded
him of his wife, although they were very different. She had been a woman of strong
opinions too.

Seeing Amadea with the children, and the
odd family they had formed, sometimes
made him miss having a wife. But this was
in some ways the next best thing. They had
had a wonderful summer with each other.
And before the children went back to
school, they went on a family excursion to
Brighton. He pushed Amadea along the
boardwalk in her wheelchair, while the children went wild, playing games, and going

on the rides. She looked longingly at the beach. He couldn't push her on the sand.

"I wish I could walk sometimes," she said wistfully, although she managed very well in the wheelchair, could get around at full speed, and had no trouble keeping up with the children. It tugged at his heart the way she said it.

"Maybe we should go back and see the doctor one of these days." She hadn't seen him in three months. When she left the hospital, he had said there was nothing more he could do. The feeling would return in her legs, or not. And so far it hadn't. There had been no change or improvement, although she rarely if ever talked about it. And this was the first time he had heard her complain.

"I don't think there's anything he can do. I don't think about it most of the time. The children don't give me time to." She turned to look at him then with a tender look in her eyes that always made him wish things were different when he saw it. "Thank you for bringing me here, Rupert, to take care of your *kinders.*" She had never been as happy in her life, except in her early years in the convent. There was an irrepressible joy to every day. She loved being Mamadea, almost as much as she had loved being Sister Teresa. But she knew this would come to an end too. Many of them would go home, which was better for them in the end. They needed their parents. She and Rupert were only surrogates, although good ones. She thought Rupert was wonderful with them, and it always reminded her of how much he must miss his sons. There were photographs of them all over the house. Ian and James. And his wife Gwyneth. She had been Scottish.

"I don't know what we'd do without you," Rupert said honestly as he sat down on a bench on the boardwalk, where they could see the children, and she rolled the wheelchair close to him. She looked relaxed and happy as her long blond hair flew in the breeze. She often wore it down like one of the children, and loved brushing the girls' hair, the way her mother had done for her and Daphne when they were little. It was odd how history repeated itself constantly, generation after generation. "I can't even remember what it was like before you came," Rupert said, and looked distracted. And then he took the wind out of her with what he said next. "I'm leaving on a mission next Thursday." He wasn't supposed to tell her, but he trusted her completely.

"You're not," she said, as though denying it could make it not happen. But she knew from the look in his eyes that it would anyway.

"I am." He didn't look enthused about it either. He loved being at home with her and the children on the weekends. But there was still a war to win.

"To Germany?" she asked in a whisper, as terror struck her heart. They both knew all too well how dangerous that was. And she couldn't imagine life without him now either.

"Something like that," he said in answer to her question. She knew he couldn't tell her where he was going. It was top secret, and classified information. He had the highest security clearance. She wondered if he was going to Germany, or back into France, or somewhere worse, like farther east. She realized now that during her time in France, she had led a charmed life. So many had been killed and she hadn't, although she had come close several times.

"I wish I could go with you," she said, forgetting the wheelchair. But there was no question of that now. She could no longer do missions. She would be a handicap and not an asset.

"I don't wish that," Rupert said bluntly. He no longer wanted her risking her life. She had done enough. And been lucky. Even if she was in a wheelchair, she was lucky to be alive.

"I'm going to worry about you," Amadea said, looking deeply concerned. "How long will you be gone?"

"Awhile" was all he said. He couldn't tell her that either, but she got the feeling he would be gone a long time, and she couldn't ask. She fell silent for a long moment and then looked at him. There was so much to say, and no way to say it. For either of them. And they knew it.

The children noticed that she was quiet on the way home that night, and Berta asked her if she felt sick.

"No, just tired, sweetheart. It was all that good sea air." But she and Rupert both knew what it was. It was his mission.

She lay in bed for a long time that night, thinking about it and about him. He was doing the same in his bedroom. Their bedrooms were at opposite ends of the same hallway. She had been overwhelmed by the luxuriousness of the house at first. She had the best guest bedroom. She had told him to put her in one of the maids' rooms, but he wouldn't hear of it. He told her she deserved the handsome room she was in, which she insisted she didn't. It was difficult to adhere to her vow of poverty here. The others she could manage, or had until then.

Rupert left to go back to London the next morning, as he always did. And the children knew nothing about his impending trip, or worse yet, the possibility that he might never come back. Amadea was fully aware of it. He had requested permission to come down to Sussex for the day and night on Wednesday, before he left the following night. And until he returned, Amadea was nervous and anxious and out of sorts. And most unlike her, she snapped at one of the boys when he broke a window with a cricket ball, and then apologized to him for her bad temper. He said it was fine, his real mother had been much worse, and shouted a lot louder, which made her laugh.

But she was still immensely relieved to see Rupert return on Wednesday, and was quick to give him a kiss on the cheek and a

warm hug. She knew there was nothing she
could ask him. All she could do was pray for
him while he was gone and trust that he'd
come back. And all he could do was reassure her that he'd be fine. They tried not to
talk about it, and had a lovely dinner with
the children in the main dining hall, which
they normally only did on special occasions.
The children sensed easily that something
was going on.

"Papa Rupert is going on a trip," Amadea
said cheerfully, but the older children
searched her eyes and knew that something
was wrong, or at best scary. Amadea
looked worried.

"To kill Germans?" Hermann asked, looking delighted.

"Of course not," Amadea answered.

"When will you be back?" Berta asked,
looking worried.

"I don't know. You'll have to take good
care of each other and Mamadea. I'll be
home soon," he promised. They all hugged
and kissed him before they went to bed. He
said he'd be gone in the morning before
they got up.

He and Amadea sat and talked late into
the night, about many things and nothing in

particular. It was just comforting being together. It was nearly dawn when he finally
carried her upstairs and set her back in her
wheelchair on the landing of their respective
bedrooms. When he wasn't there, the older
boys always helped her. It was a communal
effort.

"I'll be gone when you get up," he said,
trying not to sound somber, but he felt it. He
truly hated to leave her.

"No, you won't." She smiled at him. "I'll
get up to say good-bye."

"You don't have to do that."

"I know I don't. I want to."

He knew her better than to argue with her.
He kissed her on the cheek, and she rolled
off to her bedroom, without looking back.
And for the next two hours, he lay in bed,
wishing he had the courage or audacity to
walk into her bedroom and take her in his
arms. But he didn't. He was too afraid that if
he did, she'd be gone when he got back.
There were boundaries between them that
he knew he had no choice but to respect.

True to her word, she was waiting for him
in the hall when he came out of his bedroom
just after dawn. She was sitting in the
wheelchair in her nightgown, with a robe

around her. With her long hair and pink dressing gown, she looked like one of the children. He looked serious and official in his uniform, and she saluted him, which made him smile.

"Will you get me downstairs?" she asked him easily, and he hesitated.

"You won't be able to get back up. None of the children are awake to help you."

"I have things to do anyway." She wanted to be with him for as long as she could. He gently carried her downstairs, set her in a chair, and then brought the wheelchair down, and she got in it.

She made him tea and heated up a scone for him, and then finally there was nothing left to say. They both knew he had to leave. She followed him out the door and onto the front steps in the September air. It was chilly and the air was fresh, as he kissed her on both cheeks.

"Take care of yourself, Mamadea."

"I'll pray for you." Her eyes looked deep into his.

"Thank you." He was going to need it. They were parachuting him into Germany on a mission they thought could take as long as three weeks.

They shared a long look, and he walked down the steps with a resolute step, without looking back. He was just about to get in his car when she called out to him. He turned then, and she was looking anguished as she stretched a hand out to him as though to stop him. "Rupert! . . . I love you." She could no longer stop the words, or the feelings she had for him. He looked as though she had splashed cold water at him, as he stopped in his tracks, and then retraced his steps and stood next to her. "Are you serious?"

"I think I am . . . no . . . I know I am . . ." She looked at him as though the world had just come to an end. She knew what this meant for her, and so did he, as a slow smile spread over his face and lit his eyes.

"Well, don't look so unhappy about it. I love you, too. We'll discuss it when I get back . . . just don't change your mind." He kissed her on the mouth and looked at her for a long moment, and he had to go. He could hardly believe what had just happened, nor could she. It had been coming for a long, long time. And he was immensely pleased.

He waved as he drove off, and he was

smiling. So was she as she waved, and blew him a last kiss. And then he turned and drove out the gate, as she sat in her wheelchair in the morning sun, praying he would come back. The decision had made itself.

27

THE TIME THAT RUPERT WAS GONE SEEMED IN-terminable to Amadea. At first she had been anxious and worried. Then she had told herself he would be fine. And after two weeks . . . three . . . four . . . she began to panic. She had no idea how long the mission was meant to be for. By the end of October, she knew something was wrong. Unable to contain herself any longer, she called the office of the Secret Service. They took her information down and said they'd get back to her. An officer called her back a week later. By then it was November. They said very little to her, and didn't tell her where he was, but they did say they hadn't heard from him "in quite some time."

Without actually saying it, they conveyed to her that he was out of contact, and was missing in action. She nearly fainted when they told her, but she put a good face on it for the children. She had to. They had already lost one set of parents, she didn't want them to think they had lost Rupert, too. Not until they knew. Amadea had never prayed so hard in her life. She was doubly glad now that she had told him she loved him. At least he had known. And she knew that he loved her. What they did about it, if they would even have the opportunity to, remained to be seen. The Secret Service had told her they would call her back if they heard anything. They didn't.

To keep from losing her mind entirely, she came up with an idea to entertain the children. She told them she thought Papa Rupert would be delighted if they surprised him by forming their own orchestra. She got them all instruments, and she played the piano with them so they could all sing for him. They were a long way from professional, but they had a wonderful time with it. And she enjoyed it too. It gave them a project to work on. And after a month of practice, they sounded pretty good.

They were playing a song one night, as Rebekka sat on her lap in the wheelchair. She was tired and sucking her thumb. She had a cold and didn't want to sing. And as they listened, she turned to Amadea with a grumpy look. "Stop tapping your foot, Mama. You're bumping me." Amadea stared at her, and one by one they stopped playing. The ones in the front row had heard her, and the others wanted to know what had happened, and why Mamadea looked that way.

"Do it again, Mama," Berta said gently as they all stared at her feet while she tried. Ever so gently she could tap her feet, and even move her legs a little. She had been so busy with them, and so worried about Rupert, she hadn't noticed the improvement.

"Can you stand up?" one of the twins asked her.

"I don't know," she said, looking scared as they stood all around her, and Josef held his hands out to her.

"Try. If you can blow up a train, you can walk." He had a point. She stood up very slowly, by pushing herself up on the arms of the wheelchair, and took a single step toward him, and nearly fell. Johann caught her. But she had taken a step. Her eyes were wide, and they were all watching her with excited expressions. She took another step, and another. In all she took four, and then said she had to sit down. She was shaking all over, and felt weak and faint. But she had walked. There were tears running down her cheeks as they all laughed and smiled and clapped their hands with excitement.

"Mama can walk!" Marta shouted with sheer glee. And after that, every day, they made her practice. They played music. And she walked.

By the beginning of December she could walk slowly across the room with one of the bigger boys to hold on to. She was still unsteady on her feet at times, but she was making consistent progress. The bad news was that there was still no news from Rupert. None. They hadn't pronounced him dead. But they seemed to know nothing. And as Amadea wasn't his wife, she had no right to know. He had been gone for nearly two months, and she knew instinctively that the mission had never been intended to last that long. She wondered every night if he was wounded as she had been, and no one

knew where he was. Or in a camp somewhere. If he had been found in a German
uniform and discovered as an enemy agent,
he would have been shot. A million terrible
things could have happened, and she had
thought of them all.

Two weeks later, not knowing what else to
do to distract them and herself, she celebrated Chanukah with them. They had been
celebrating Christmas since they'd been in
England, but she said that this year they
would do both. They made dreidls out of
paper, and they taught her how to spin
them. And they taught her Chanukah songs.
She loved knowing that the Hebrew letters
on the dreidl said "A great miracle happened here." Their little band was doing
very well, and she was walking slowly but
surely.

The children were standing all around her
as they lit the candles on the second night
of Chanukah, as Rebekka looked up and
gave a gasp.

"Are we celebrating Christmas early this
year?" There was a festive air in the room,
although the children were quiet as she lit
the candles. It brought back bittersweet

memories for many of them. Amadea
looked up at the sound of his voice.

"No, Chanukah," she said calmly, and
then gasped too. It was Rupert. All the children screamed and ran to him, and Amadea
walked slowly toward him as he stared at
her.

"You're walking," he said with a look of
wonder and disbelief. His arm was in a
sling, but the rest of him looked fine though
deathly thin. He had made his way across
half of Germany on foot for the past two
months, and had managed finally to meet
up with the Resistance in Alsace. They had
airlifted him out of a little village near
Strasbourg. It had been a harrowing three
months, for her as well. He just stood there
and held her in his arms. "I never thought
you'd walk again," he said honestly.

"Neither did I," she said as she nestled in
his arms. She had been desperately afraid
she would never see him again. "I was so
worried about you." He knew she would be,
but there was nothing he could do. It had
been difficult and frightening, even for him,
but the mission was a success.

"I had to come back after what you said
when I left." He hadn't forgotten, nor had

she. They had much to say and decide now, especially Amadea.

"Papa! We have a band!" Rebekka was shouting at him, and the others told her not to spoil the surprise. After she let the cat out of the bag, they played two songs for him, and he loved it. They were up till nearly midnight, and told him about Amadea celebrating Chanukah for them.

"You seem to be going backward in history," he teased her after they went to bed, and they were sitting holding hands by the fire. It felt like a dream having him back.

"I just thought it was important for them to have a piece of their history left intact and restored to them." It seemed strange, but it meant something to her, too. She could imagine her mother doing the same things as a child. And so many had died for being Jewish, it was a way to honor them now, too. It was as though she could hear their voices, not just her own, as she read the prayers.

"I'm not going to lose you again, Amadea. I walked halfway across Germany to come home to you. You can't leave me now," he said seriously. Her eyes never left his.

"No. I can't. I know that now. I knew it before you left, that's why I told you that I love you . . ." She looked sad for a moment then as she held his hand. But she knew now that she belonged here, with him, and their *kinders,* whichever ones stayed in the end. "I always thought I'd go back to the convent," she said sadly. But too much had happened. Too many people, too many lives, too many people she had contributed to killing, even if she had done it to save others. And now she wanted to be here with him. But it no longer seemed wrong. It seemed very right. And the only choice she could make. She could never have left him, although the convent and all it had meant to her would remain forever in her heart. It had been a difficult decision, but she felt pleased and relieved with the end results. While he had been away, she knew more than ever how much she loved him.

"I was so afraid you'd go back, and I didn't want to interfere with what you wanted," Rupert said kindly.

"Thank you for respecting that." She looked at him with eyes full of love. She had been so sure that she would always be a nun, and now she was his, in all the ways she had never dared to dream.

"I would have let you go if it was really what you wanted, and it made you happy . . . but that seems like a long time ago. Now, I couldn't bear it," he said as he pulled her close to him and held her. So often in the past three months, he had been so desperately afraid that he would never come home to her, and she had been afraid of the same thing. Finally, after all they'd been through, they both knew this was right. They had both crossed lifetimes to get here, lost people they loved, stared death in the face too many times. They had earned all that they had found.

He carried her up the stairs that night after they put the lights out. She still couldn't walk stairs easily, but she would in time. They hesitated on the landing, and he kissed her, and then with a shy smile she said goodnight and he laughed. This was not Paris and the peach nightgown. This was real life. They both knew what had to happen, and that it would soon, in the right way, at the right time. They had the rest of their lives.

28

A PRIEST MARRIED THEM, AND A RABBI SAID A blessing, as the children stood all around them. They were the first children they had shared, and they both knew that many of them would stay with them. And with luck, they would have children of their own, although his lost sons would never be forgotten. Amadea had finally taken her final vows, the ones she had been meant to take, though not the ones she had expected. Life with its twists and turns, terrors and pains and blessings, had led them to each other, through tortuous paths, to a peaceful place at last. They had found each other, amidst the echoes of all those they had once loved and who had loved them.

also by the editors at america's test kitchen

for a full listing of all our books
CooksIllustrated.com

AmericasTestKitchen.com

sunday suppers

sunday suppers

the editors at
america's test kitchen

Copyright © 2017

by the Editors at
America's Test Kitchen

Library of Congress
Cataloging-in-Publication Data

Names:
  America's Test Kitchen (Firm), author.
Title: All time best Sunday
  suppers / by the editors at
  America's Test Kitchen.
Other titles: Sunday suppers
Description: Boston, MA : America's Test Kitchen, [2017] |
  Includes index.
Identifiers: LCCN 2017000741 |
  ISBN 9781940352978
Subjects: LCSH: Cooking. | Dinners
  and dining. | LCGFT: Cookbooks.
Classification: LCC TX714 .A4436 2017 | DDC 641.5--dc23
LC record available at
  https://lccn.loc.gov/2017000741

AMERICA'S TEST KITCHEN
21 Drydock, Suite 210E, Boston, MA 02210

Manufactured in China

10 9 8 7 6 5 4 3 2 1

Distributed by Penguin Random House Publisher Services
Tel: 800.733.3000

Chief Creative Officer: Jack Bishop
Editorial Director, Books: Elizabeth Carduff
Executive Editor: Julia Collin Davison
Executive Editor: Adam Kowit
Editorial Assistant: Alyssa Langer
Design Director: Carole Goodman
Deputy Art Directors: Allison Boales and Jen Kanavos Hoffman
Production Designer: Reinaldo Cruz
Graphic Designer: Katie Barranger
Photography Director: Julie Bozzo Cote
Photography Producer: Mary Ball
Senior Staff Photographer: Daniel J. van Ackere
Staff Photographer: Steve Klise
Feature Photography: Keller + Keller and Carl Tremblay
Food Styling: Catrine Kelty, Marie Piraino, Elle Simone Scott, and Sally Staub
Photoshoot Kitchen Team:
  Senior Editor: Chris O'Connor
  Lead Cook: Daniel Cellucci
  Assistant Test Cooks: Mady Nichas and Jessica Rudolph
Production Director: Guy Rochford
Senior Production Manager: Jessica Lindheimer Quirk
Production Manager: Christine Walsh
Imaging Manager: Lauren Robbins
Production and Imaging Specialists: Heather Dube, Sean MacDonald, Dennis Noble, and Jessica Voas
Copyeditor: Cheryl Redmond
Proofreader: Pat Jalbert-Levine
Indexer: Elizabeth Parson

Pictured on front cover: Simple Pot-au-Feu (page 36)
Pictured on back cover: Flank Steak Peperonata (page 47), French Chicken in a Pot with Red Potatoes, Carrots, and Shallots (page 94), Miso-Glazed Salmon (page 135), Eggplant Parmesan (page 152)
Pictured opposite title page: Chicken Bouillabaisse (page 119)

contents

welcome to america's test kitchen

THIS BOOK HAS BEEN TESTED, WRITTEN, AND EDITED BY THE folks at America's Test Kitchen. Located in Boston's Seaport District in the historic Innovation and Design Building, it features 15,000 square feet of kitchen space including multiple photography and video studios. It is the home of *Cook's Illustrated* magazine and *Cook's Country* magazine and is the Monday-through-Friday destination for more than 60 test cooks, editors, and cookware specialists. Our mission is to test recipes over and over again until we understand how and why they work and until we arrive at the "best" version.

We start the process of testing a recipe with a complete lack of preconceptions, which means that we accept no claim, no technique, and no recipe at face value. We simply assemble as many variations as possible, test a half-dozen of the most promising, and taste the results blind. We then construct our own recipe and continue to test it, varying ingredients, techniques, and cooking times until we reach a consensus. As we like to say in the test kitchen, "We make the mistakes so you don't have to." The result, we hope, is the best version of a particular recipe, but we realize that only you can be the final judge of our success (or failure). We use the same rigorous approach when we test equipment and taste ingredients.

All of this would not be possible without a belief that good cooking, much like good music, is based on a foundation of objective technique. Some people like spicy foods and others don't, but there is a right way to sauté, there is a best way to cook a pot roast, and there are measurable scientific principles involved in producing perfectly beaten, stable egg whites. Our ultimate goal is to investigate the fundamental principles of cooking to give you the techniques, tools, and ingredients you need to become a better cook. It is as simple as that.

To see what goes on behind the scenes at America's Test Kitchen, check out our social media channels for kitchen snapshots, exclusive content, video tips, and much more. You can watch us work (in our actual test kitchen) by tuning in to *America's Test Kitchen* or *Cook's Country from America's Test Kitchen* on public television or on our websites. Listen to test kitchen experts on public radio (SplendidTable.org) to hear insights that illuminate the truth about real home cooking. Want to hone your cooking skills or finally learn how to bake—with an America's Test Kitchen test cook? Enroll in one of our online cooking classes. If the big questions about the hows and whys of food science are your passion, join our *Cook's Science* experts for a deep dive. However you choose to visit us, we welcome you into our kitchen, where you can stand by our side as we test our way to the best recipes in America.

facebook.com/
AmericasTestKitchen

twitter.com/TestKitchen

youtube.com/
AmericasTestKitchen

instagram.com/TestKitchen

pinterest.com/TestKitchen

google.com/
+AmericasTestKitchen

AmericasTestKitchen.com

CooksIllustrated.com

CooksCountry.com

CooksScience.com

OnlineCookingSchool.com

introduction

THE TERM "SUNDAY SUPPER" IS VERY SUBJECTIVE, LIKELY conjuring up memories of family, friends, long-standing traditions, and rituals. Whether it's a game day custom to have a large pot of chili simmering on the stove while cheering for your favorite team on television, or take-out from your favorite neighborhood restaurant, or a roast chicken recipe passed down from generations before, one common thread holds true: Sunday supper is more than just a meal; it's a time that can bring friends and family together.

Here at America's Test Kitchen, we believe Sunday supper should be a highlight of your week, not a chore, which is why we put together this carefully curated collection of 75 recipes—all perfect in their own way as a capstone for your weekend. Whether you're craving a cozy old-world classic straight out of Grandma's kitchen, like Rigatoni with Warm Spiced Beef Ragu (page 40), or you want to create new traditions with modern favorites like Seared Scallops with Squash Puree and Sage Butter (page 79), or Chicken, Spinach, and Artichoke Pot Pie (page 57), the foolproof recipes in this book guarantee perfect results every time. For those Sundays when you want to minimize your time in the kitchen, we've got you covered with recipes for the lazy cook like Roasted Pork Chops and Vegetables with Parsley Vinaigrette (page 97) and Almost Hands-Free Risotto with Chicken and Herbs (page 91). Want to try some international favorites? Check out Sunday Around the World. In this chapter you will find recipes that bring exotic flavors from across the globe into your home kitchen, such as Za'atar-Rubbed Butterflied Chicken (page 126) and Miso-Glazed Salmon with Sesame Sushi Rice (page 135). There's also a collection of recipes for meatless dinners with hearty dishes like Mushroom Bolognese (page 149) and Quinoa and Vegetable Stew with Eggs (page 171).

We've also included recipe times, so you'll know in advance exactly how long each recipe takes; this will help you plan ahead and eliminates any surprises. Keep in mind that the total time includes both active and inactive cooking time, so while some recipes require several hours, the majority of that time is actually hands-off, leaving you free to leave the kitchen. Complete with mix-and-match side dishes, make-ahead information, and meal-planning tips, *All-Time Best Sunday Suppers* will be your go-to guide for weekend cooking.

crafting your
sunday supper

the sunday supper matrix

tips for success

get organized
Before you start cooking, it's a good idea to read your recipes through carefully so you understand the timing and can plan accordingly. There is nothing more aggravating than getting involved in a recipe and suddenly realizing you should have planned on marinating or chilling time. Prepping all your ingredients ahead (known as *mise en place*) is also a good practice and will help ensure everything goes smoothly.

keep it simple
Unless you're the type of cook that likes to pull out all the stops for Sunday dinner, we suggest you put most of your energy into the main course of your choosing and rely on simple sides or a salad to round things out. Regardless of your cooking experience or style, you'll find lots of options across this book, plus an array of starters and sides, to add to the mix.

welcome help
If friends or family want to pitch in, it's a bonus and frees you up to concentrate on the main course. And in the process, you'll have more time to enjoy your weekend. Make assignments if you can!

declutter your kitchen
No matter how many people you're cooking for, it's helpful to get your kitchen completely cleaned up and organized before you start. A messy kitchen just adds to your stress level, and you don't want your guests walking in on any chaos. Starting with a clean sink and an empty dishwasher is super helpful, too.

If you like to think about categories of recipes when planning your Sunday dinners, then this fun matrix may inspire your selection whether you are looking for a homey casserole, a one-dish meal, or something that requires almost no effort to pull off.

hands-off recipes for the harried cook
- slow-roasted pork shoulder with peach sauce (page 27)
- slow-roasted beef (page 34)
- french chicken in a pot with red potatoes, carrots, and shallots (page 94)
- chuck roast dinner in foil (page 100)

last-minute wonders
- southwestern salmon cakes (page 74)
- mussels marinara with spaghetti (page 76)
- seared scallops with squash puree and sage butter (page 79)
- salmon with asparagus and chive butter sauce (page 109)
- stir-fried eggplant with garlic-basil sauce (page 160)

just add bread and wine
- beef burgundy (page 31)
- simple pot-au-feu (page 36)
- cod in saffron broth with chorizo and potatoes (page 69)
- roasted pork chops and vegetables with parsley vinaigrette (page 97)
- rosemary steak tips with gorgonzola polenta (page 103)

crowd pleasers
- chicken stew (page 21)
- meatballs and marinara (page 28)
- best ground beef chili (page 39)
- ancho-orange pork burritos (page 113)
- hearty vegetable lasagna (page 155)

set a nice table
(it's sunday, after all)
There's no time for formality on busy weeknights, but come Sunday night, it's always nice to slow down and carve out time for family and friends. Candles, a tablecloth, and your favorite dishes definitely signal that it's a chance to slow down and unwind with a meal uniting everyone, even if for a short time.

have dinner on the early side
Weekends are precious, so the last thing you want to be doing late on a Sunday is scrubbing pots and washing wine glasses by hand. Plus, no one wants to be out late and face starting the work week with a sleep deficit. Do yourself a favor and eat early rather than fashionably late. You'll be glad you did.

serve it family style
Many of the recipes in this book are well suited to serving family style, whether you're putting a beautiful casserole right on the table or assembling the main course and sides on a single large platter to pass around. It's a nice way to connect around the table; plus, it eliminates fussy in-kitchen plating and minimizes dealing with individual serving dishes later.

stress-free appetizers to kick off the evening

For a casual supper, we think appetizers are optional, but if you want to put out something for everyone to nibble on, here are some simple options that will satisfy but not push you over the limit in terms of time or energy.

prosciutto-wrapped figs with gorgonzola
serves 8 to 10

2 ounces Gorgonzola cheese

16 fresh figs, stemmed and halved lengthwise

1 tablespoon honey

16 thin slices prosciutto (8 ounces), cut in half lengthwise

Mound 1 teaspoon Gorgonzola into center of each fig half. Microwave honey in bowl to loosen, about 10 seconds, then drizzle over cheese. Wrap prosciutto securely around figs, leaving fig ends uncovered. Secure prosciutto with toothpicks and serve.

chunky guacamole
serves 4 to 5

3 ripe avocados

¼ cup chopped fresh cilantro

1 jalapeño chile, stemmed, seeded, and minced

2 tablespoons finely chopped onion

2 tablespoons lime juice

2 garlic cloves, minced

Salt

½ teaspoon ground cumin

1. Halve 1 avocado, remove pit, and scoop flesh into medium bowl. Add cilantro, jalapeño, onion, lime juice, garlic, ¾ teaspoon salt, and cumin and mash with potato masher (or fork) until mostly smooth.

2. Halve and pit remaining 2 avocados. Carefully make ½-inch crosshatch incisions in flesh with butter knife, cutting down to but not through skin. Insert spoon between skin and flesh, gently scoop out avocado cubes, and add to mashed mixture. Gently mash until mixture is well combined but still coarse. Season with salt to taste. Serve.

spiced nuts
serves 8 to 10

1 large egg white

1 tablespoon water

1 teaspoon salt

1 pound pecans, cashews, walnuts, or whole unblanched almonds

⅔ cup superfine sugar

2 teaspoons ground cumin

1 teaspoon cayenne pepper

1 teaspoon paprika

1. Adjust oven racks to upper-middle and lower-middle positions and heat oven to 275 degrees. Line 2 rimmed baking sheets with parchment paper. Whisk egg white, water, and salt together in medium bowl. Add nuts and toss to coat. Let nuts drain in colander for 5 minutes.

2. Mix sugar, cumin, cayenne, and paprika together in clean medium bowl. Add drained nuts and toss to coat. Spread nuts evenly over prepared baking sheets. Bake until nuts are dry and crisp, about 50 minutes, stirring occasionally.

3. Let nuts cool completely on baking sheets, about 30 minutes. Break nuts apart and serve. (Nuts can be stored at room temperature for up to 1 week.)

variation
curry-spiced nuts
Reduce cumin to 1 teaspoon and substitute 1 teaspoon curry powder for cayenne.

warm marinated artichoke hearts and olives
serves 6 to 8

1 cup extra-virgin olive oil

2 cups jarred whole artichoke hearts packed in water, halved and patted dry

Salt and pepper

3 sprigs fresh thyme

2 (2-inch) strips lemon zest plus 1 tablespoon juice

2 garlic cloves, sliced thin

1 teaspoon fennel seeds

½ teaspoon red pepper flakes

½ cup pitted kalamata olives, halved

4 ounces feta cheese, cut into ½-inch pieces (1 cup)

1 tablespoon minced fresh parsley

1. Heat 10-inch cast-iron skillet over medium heat for 3 minutes. Add 1 tablespoon oil and heat until shimmering. Add artichoke hearts and ½ teaspoon salt and cook until spotty brown, 7 to 9 minutes. Stir in thyme sprigs, lemon zest, garlic, fennel seeds, and pepper flakes and cook until fragrant, about 30 seconds.

2. Stir in olives and remaining oil. Reduce heat to low and cook until flavors meld and mixture is heated through, about 20 minutes.

3. Discard thyme sprigs and lemon zest, if desired. Gently stir in feta and lemon juice and season with salt and pepper to taste. Sprinkle with parsley. Serve.

baked goat cheese with olive oil and herbs
serves 8

12 ounces goat cheese

⅓ cup olive oil

2 teaspoons honey

½ teaspoon orange or lemon zest, grated

½ teaspoon dried herbes de Provence

¼ teaspoon salt

⅛ teaspoon pepper

⅛ teaspoon red pepper flakes

Crackers or thinly sliced baguette

Heat oven to 400 degrees. Using dental floss, slice chilled 12-ounce log of goat cheese into ⅓-inch-thick rounds. Shingle cheese into small casserole dish or shallow ovensafe bowl. Combine olive oil, honey, orange zest, herbes de Provence, salt, pepper, and pepper flakes in small bowl, then pour mixture over cheese. Bake cheese until oil is bubbling and cheese begins to brown around edges, 10 to 15 minutes. Serve warm with crackers or thinly sliced baguette.

smoked salmon with herbed crème fraîche and potato chips
serves 8

4 ounces cream cheese

1 cup crème fraîche

3 tablespoons minced fresh dill

2 tablespoons minced fresh chives

2 teaspoons grated lemon zest plus 1 tablespoon juice

Salt and pepper

12 ounces thinly sliced smoked salmon, cut into 1½-inch pieces

1 bag kettle-cooked potato chips

Microwave cream cheese in bowl until very soft, 20 to 25 seconds. Whisk in crème fraîche, dill, chives, and lemon zest and juice. Season with salt and pepper to taste. Cover and refrigerate until flavors meld, at least 30 minutes or up to 2 days. Transfer dip to serving bowl with spoon or spreader and serve alongside salmon and potato chips.

the art of making a good salad

how to measure salad greens

For a side salad we usually call for 2 cups lightly packed greens per person. To lightly pack greens, simply drop them by the handful into a measuring cup, then gently pat down, using your fingertips rather than the palm of your hand. We like to measure greens for a salad using a very large glass measuring cup.

washing and drying salad greens

To make a great salad, the only thing that is more critical than using crisp, fresh greens is using clean, dry greens. Trying to dress a salad while the greens are still wet is a losing battle—the dressing slides off, and the water from the greens will dilute the dressing. We believe that the only foolproof method for drying them is to use a salad spinner.

to wash greens Fill a salad spinner bowl with cool water, add cut greens, and gently swish them around. Do not run water directly over the greens, as the force can bruise them. Using your hands, gently move the greens to loosen grit, which will fall to the bottom of the bowl. Use the sink if you need to clean large amounts of greens.

to dry greens Dry greens in a salad spinner, stopping several times to dump out excess moisture. Keep spinning greens until no more moisture accumulates. After spinning them, we like to blot greens dry with paper towels; even the best salad spinners don't dry greens completely.

We've all experienced limp, over-dressed salads or a carelessly assembled bowl of mixed greens with bottled dressings on the side. We think there is an art to making a beautiful salad, and it doesn't necessarily mean you need to make a complicated homemade salad dressing (the vinaigrette on the next page is a winner and easy to make). All you really need is fresh greens, garlic, extra-virgin olive oil, vinegar, and a large wooden salad bowl. Make this once and you'll have it mastered forever.

rub bowl with garlic For just a hint of garlic flavor, rub inside of salad bowl with half clove of peeled garlic before adding lettuce.

add washed greens Add washed and dried salad greens to bowl. We suggest 2 lightly packed cups per person for a side salad.

drizzle with oil Slowly drizzle greens with extra-virgin olive oil. Toss greens gently and repeat drizzling and tossing as needed until greens are lightly coated.

season with vinegar, salt, and pepper Finally, sprinkle greens with small amounts of vinegar, salt, and pepper to taste while tossing gently until salad tastes just right.

a winning salad dressing (and more)

Most homemade salad dressings will keep only for a day or two in the fridge, but we developed this make-ahead vinaigrette, which is handy for busy home cooks. In addition to oil and vinegar, we made this vinaigrette foolproof with a combination of mayonnaise and molasses, which helped stabilize the emulsion. We used a 2:1 ratio of extra-virgin olive oil to vegetable oil, which prevented the oil molecules from solidifying in the refrigerator while still allowing the distinct flavor of the olive oil to come through.

make-ahead vinaigrette
makes about 1 cup
Regular or light mayonnaise can be used in this recipe. Do not use blackstrap molasses. You can substitute toasted hazelnut or walnut oil for the extra-virgin olive oil.

1 tablespoon mayonnaise

1 tablespoon molasses

1 tablespoon Dijon mustard

½ teaspoon salt

¼ cup wine vinegar

½ cup extra-virgin olive oil

¼ cup vegetable oil

1. Combine mayonnaise, molasses, mustard, and salt in 2-cup jar with tight-fitting lid. Stir with fork until mixture is milky in appearance and no lumps of mayonnaise or molasses remain. Add vinegar, seal jar, and shake until smooth, about 10 seconds.

2. Add ¼ cup olive oil, seal jar, and shake vigorously until thoroughly combined, about 10 seconds. Repeat, adding remaining ¼ cup olive oil and vegetable oil in 2 additions, shaking vigorously until thoroughly combined after each addition. (After third addition, vinaigrette should be glossy and lightly thickened, with no pools of oil on its surface.) Refrigerate for up to 1 week. Shake briefly before using.

homemade croutons
makes 4 cups
Homemade croutons are easy to make and they taste far better than those you can buy. You can make good croutons using nearly any type of bread, from stale pieces of baguette to the end slices of a sandwich loaf.

3 tablespoons olive oil

2 garlic cloves, minced

¼ teaspoon salt

4 cups (½-inch) bread cubes

Adjust oven rack to middle position and heat oven to 350 degrees. Whisk oil, garlic, and salt together in large bowl, add bread, and toss to coat. Spread bread onto rimmed baking sheet and bake until golden, 20 to 25 minutes. Let croutons cool before serving. (Store at room temperature in airtight container for up to 1 week.)

variation
parmesan croutons
Increase oil to 6 tablespoons and stir 1 cup grated Parmesan cheese into oil with garlic and salt.

how to store salad greens
For crisp lettuce, such as iceberg and romaine, core the lettuce, wrap it in moist paper towels, and refrigerate in a partially open plastic produce bag or zipper-lock bag. For leafy greens, such as arugula, baby spinach, and mesclun, store in the original plastic container or bag if prewashed. If not prewashed, wash and dry thoroughly in a salad spinner and store directly in the spinner between layers of paper towels, or lightly roll in paper towels and store in a zipper-lock bag left slightly open.

For tender lettuce, such as Boston and Bibb, if the lettuce comes with the roots attached, leave the lettuce portion attached to the roots and store in the original plastic container, a plastic produce bag, or a zipper-lock bag left slightly open. If the lettuce is without roots, wrap it in moist paper towels and refrigerate in a plastic produce bag or a zipper-lock bag left slightly open.

simple sides to mix and match

Some of the recipes in this book cry out for mashed potatoes or creamy polenta. And it's always handy to have a simple and foolproof recipe for rice to accompany a stir-fry or round out a meal. So here are some tried and true favorites for starches, along with a couple of welcome green vegetables that work well with recipes from across the book.

broiled asparagus with lemon
serves 8
Do not use pencil-thin asparagus here. For quick asparagus trimming, cut off all of the tough ends at once while the bunch is still banded together.

3 pounds asparagus, trimmed

1 tablespoon extra-virgin olive oil

Salt and pepper

½ lemon

Adjust oven rack 3 inches from broiler element and heat broiler. Toss asparagus with oil and season with salt and pepper to taste. Lay asparagus, in same direction, on rimmed baking sheet. Broil, shuffling asparagus from top to bottom every few minutes, until spears are tender and tips begin to brown, 5 to 10 minutes. Squeeze lemon over spears and serve.

creamy parmesan polenta

serves 6 to 8

Avoid instant and quick-cooking products, as well as whole-grain, stone-ground, and regular corn-meal. Do not omit the baking soda—it reduces the cooking time and makes for a creamier polenta.

7½ cups water

Salt and pepper

Pinch baking soda

1½ cups coarse-ground cornmeal

4 ounces Parmesan cheese, grated (2 cups), plus extra for serving

2 tablespoons unsalted butter

1. Bring water to boil in large saucepan over medium-high heat. Stir in 1½ teaspoons salt and baking soda. Slowly pour cornmeal into water in steady stream while stirring back and forth with wooden spoon. Bring mixture to boil, stirring constantly, about 1 minute. Reduce heat to lowest setting and cover.

2. After 5 minutes, whisk polenta to smooth out any lumps that may have formed, about 15 seconds. (Make sure to scrape down sides and bottom of pan.) Cover and continue to cook, without stirring, until grains of polenta are tender but slightly al dente, about 25 minutes longer. (Polenta should be loose and should barely hold its shape but will continue to thicken as it cools.)

3. Off heat, stir in Parmesan and butter, and season with salt and pepper to taste. Let stand, covered, for 5 minutes. Serve with extra Parmesan.

broccolini with browned butter

serves 8

You will need at least a 6-quart Dutch oven for this recipe. Make sure to watch the butter closely as it browns in step 3; it can go from nutty brown to black and burnt in a matter of seconds.

2 tablespoons olive oil

3 pounds broccolini, trimmed

Salt and pepper

¾ cup water

6 tablespoons unsalted butter

4 garlic cloves, minced

1 teaspoon minced fresh thyme

¼ teaspoon red pepper flakes

1. Heat oil in Dutch oven over medium-high heat until just smoking. Add broccolini and ½ teaspoon salt and cook, stirring occasionally, until beginning to brown, about 5 minutes.

2. Reduce heat to medium, add water, and cover. Cook broccolini, tossing often, until bright green but still crisp, 6 to 8 minutes. Uncover and continue to cook, tossing often, until water has evaporated, and broccolini is tender, 5 to 7 minutes longer. Transfer to large bowl.

3. Add butter to now-empty pot and melt over medium-high heat, swirling occasionally, until butter is browned and has nutty aroma, 2 to 3 minutes. Off heat, stir in garlic, thyme, pepper flakes, ½ teaspoon salt, and ¼ teaspoon pepper until fragrant, about 30 seconds. Add broccolini, toss to coat evenly with browned butter, and serve.

classic couscous

serves 4 to 6

Do not substitute large-grain couscous (also known as pearl or Israeli couscous) here; it requires a much different cooking method. To make this dish vegetarian, substitute vegetable broth for the chicken broth. This recipe can be easily doubled.

2 tablespoons unsalted butter

2 cups couscous

1 cup water

1 cup chicken broth

Salt and pepper

Melt butter in medium saucepan over medium-high heat. Add couscous and cook, stirring frequently, until grains are just beginning to brown, about 5 minutes. Add water, broth, and ½ teaspoon salt and stir briefly to combine. Cover, remove pan from heat, and let stand until grains are tender, about 7 minutes. Uncover, fluff grains with fork, and season with salt and pepper to taste. Serve.

variation

couscous with curry and mint
Stir 1½ teaspoons curry powder and 2 minced garlic cloves into toasted couscous and cook until fragrant, about 15 seconds, before adding liquids and salt. Gently fold 2 tablespoons minced fresh mint into couscous before serving.

quinoa pilaf with herbs and lemon

serves 4 to 6

If you buy unwashed quinoa, rinse the grains in a fine-mesh strainer, drain them, and then spread them on a rimmed baking sheet lined with a dish towel and let them dry for 15 minutes before proceeding with the recipe. Any soft herbs, such as cilantro, parsley, chives, mint, and tarragon, can be used.

1½ cups prewashed quinoa

2 tablespoons unsalted butter, cut into 2 pieces

1 small onion, chopped fine

¾ teaspoon salt

1¾ cups water

3 tablespoons chopped fresh herbs

1 tablespoon lemon juice

1. Toast quinoa in medium saucepan over medium-high heat, stirring frequently, until quinoa is very fragrant and makes continuous popping sound, 5 to 7 minutes. Transfer quinoa to bowl and set aside.

2. Return now-empty pan to medium-low heat and melt butter. Add onion and salt; cook, stirring frequently, until onion is softened and light golden, 5 to 7 minutes.

3. Increase heat to medium-high, stir in water and quinoa, and bring to simmer. Cover, reduce heat to low, and simmer until grains are just tender and liquid is absorbed, 18 to 20 minutes, stirring once halfway through cooking. Remove pan from heat and let sit, covered, for 10 minutes. Fluff quinoa with fork, stir in herbs and lemon juice, and serve.

foolproof baked white rice

serves 6 to 8

For an accurate measurement of boiling water, bring a full kettle of water to a boil and then measure out the desired amount. Basmati, jasmine, or Texmati rice can be substituted for the long-grain rice.

4½ cups boiling water

2⅔ cups long-grain white rice, rinsed

1 tablespoon extra-virgin olive oil

Salt and pepper

Adjust oven rack to middle position and heat oven to 450 degrees. Combine boiling water, rice, oil, and ¾ teaspoon salt in 13 by 9-inch baking dish. Cover dish tightly with double layer of aluminum foil. Bake until liquid is absorbed and rice is tender, 20 to 25 minutes. Remove dish from oven, uncover, and fluff rice with fork, scraping up any rice that has stuck to bottom. Re-cover dish with foil and let rice sit for 10 minutes. Season with salt and pepper to taste. Serve.

green beans amandine

serves 8

Use a light-colored traditional skillet instead of a darker nonstick skillet for this recipe to easily monitor the butter's browning.

⅓ cup sliced almonds

3 tablespoons unsalted butter, cut into pieces

2 teaspoons lemon juice

2 pounds green beans, trimmed

½ cup water

Salt

1. Toast almonds in large skillet over medium-low heat, stirring often, until just golden, about 6 minutes. Add butter and cook, stirring constantly, until butter is golden brown and has nutty aroma, about 3 minutes. Transfer almond mixture to bowl and stir in lemon juice.

2. Add green beans, water, and ½ teaspoon salt to now-empty skillet. Cover and cook, stirring occasionally, until green beans are nearly tender, 8 to 10 minutes. Remove lid and cook over medium-high heat until liquid evaporates, 3 to 5 minutes. Off heat, add reserved almond mixture to skillet and toss to combine. Season with salt to taste. Serve.

garlic mashed potatoes

serves 8 to 10

Cutting the potatoes into ½-inch pieces ensures that maximum surface area is exposed to soak up garlicky flavor.

4 pounds russet potatoes, peeled, quartered, and cut into ½-inch pieces

12 tablespoons unsalted butter, cut into pieces

12 garlic cloves, minced

1 teaspoon sugar

1½ cups half-and-half

Salt and pepper

1. Place cut potatoes in colander. Rinse under cold running water until water runs clear. Drain thoroughly.

2. Melt 4 tablespoons butter in Dutch oven over medium heat. Add garlic and sugar and cook, stirring often, until sticky and straw-colored, 3 to 4 minutes. Add rinsed potatoes, 1¼ cups half-and-half, ½ cup water, and 1 teaspoon salt to pot and stir to combine. Bring to boil, then reduce heat to low, cover, and simmer, stirring occasionally, until potatoes are tender and most of liquid is absorbed, 25 to 30 minutes.

3. Off heat, add remaining 8 tablespoons butter to pot and mash with potato masher until smooth. Using rubber spatula, fold in remaining ¼ cup half-and-half until liquid is absorbed and potatoes are creamy. Season with salt and pepper to taste. Serve.

old-world classics

roast chicken with root vegetables

why this recipe works There is nothing more homey and satisfying than a golden-brown roast chicken and caramelized root vegetables. The secret to great results, however, is keeping them separate until serving. To get good browning, we placed the chicken in a preheated skillet in a hot oven, allowing the dark meat to be in contact with the pan and finish cooking at the same time as the more delicate breast meat. The vegetables cooked on a separate baking sheet below the chicken until tender. We found that a variety of vegetables worked well as long as we cut them so that they all cooked through at the same rate. Once the chicken was done, we cranked the oven up to 500 degrees and tossed the vegetables with the chicken drippings. This recipe requires brining the chicken for 1 hour. If using a kosher chicken, do not brine in step 1, but season with ½ teaspoon salt in step 3.

serves 4 to 6
total time: 1 hour 45 minutes
(plus 1 hour for brining)

1 (3½- to 4-pound) whole chicken, giblets discarded

Salt and pepper

½ cup sugar

1½ pounds Yukon Gold potatoes, peeled and cut into 2-inch pieces

12 ounces carrots, peeled, halved crosswise, thick halves halved lengthwise

12 ounces parsnips, peeled, halved crosswise, thick halves halved lengthwise

4 teaspoons extra-virgin olive oil

¼ cup water

1 teaspoon minced fresh thyme

1 tablespoon minced fresh parsley

1. With chicken breast side down, use tip of sharp knife to make four 1-inch incisions along back. Using your fingers, gently loosen skin covering breast and thighs. Use metal skewer to poke 15 to 20 holes in fat deposits on top of breast halves and thighs. Dissolve ½ cup salt and sugar in 2 quarts cold water in large container. Submerge chicken in brine, cover, and refrigerate for 1 hour.

2. Adjust oven racks to upper-middle and lower-middle positions and heat oven to 450 degrees. Place 12-inch ovensafe skillet on upper rack and heat for 15 minutes. Spray rimmed baking sheet with vegetable oil spray. Arrange potatoes, carrots, and parsnips with cut surfaces down in single layer on baking sheet and cover sheet tightly with aluminum foil.

3. Remove chicken from brine and pat dry with paper towels. Combine 1 tablespoon oil and ½ teaspoon pepper in small bowl. Rub entire surface of chicken with oil-pepper mixture. Tie legs together with twine and tuck wingtips behind back.

4. Carefully remove skillet from oven (handle will be hot). Add remaining 1 teaspoon oil to skillet and swirl to coat. Place chicken, breast side up, in skillet. Return skillet to upper rack and place sheet of vegetables on lower rack. Cook for 30 minutes.

5. Remove vegetables from oven, remove foil, and set aside. Rotate skillet and continue to cook chicken until breasts register 160 degrees and thighs register 175 degrees, 15 to 25 minutes longer.

6. Transfer chicken to carving board and let rest, uncovered, for 20 minutes. Increase oven temperature to 500 degrees. Add water to skillet. Using whisk, stir until brown bits have dissolved. Strain sauce through fine-mesh strainer into fat separator, pressing on solids to remove any remaining liquid. Let liquid settle for 5 minutes. Pour off liquid from fat separator and reserve. Reserve 3 tablespoons fat, discarding remaining fat.

7. Drizzle vegetables with reserved fat. Sprinkle vegetables with thyme, 1 teaspoon salt, and ½ teaspoon pepper and toss to coat. Place sheet on upper rack and roast for 5 minutes. Remove sheet from oven. Using thin, sharp metal spatula, turn vegetables. Continue to roast until browned at edges, 8 to 10 minutes longer.

8. Pour reserved liquid over vegetables. Continue to roast until liquid is thick and syrupy and vegetables are tender, 3 to 5 minutes. Toss vegetables to coat, then transfer to serving platter and sprinkle with parsley. Carve chicken and transfer to platter with vegetables. Serve.

chicken parmesan

why this recipe works Who doesn't love chicken Parmesan, with its shatteringly crisp crust, blanket of cheese, and dollop of bright tomato sauce? But it can be time-consuming to prepare, between pounding and breading the chicken, frying it, and making the sauce. This recipe streamlines the process a bit and uses the broiler, making this dish perfect for a casual Sunday dinner. Replacing more than half the starchy bread crumbs with grated Parmesan helped to retain a desirable, crunchy exterior. And to keep the cheese topping tender, we mixed the usual shredded mozzarella with creamy fontina and placed the mixture directly on the cutlet, forming a waterproof layer between the crust and the sauce. A few minutes under the broiler melted and slightly browned the cheese. A sprinkle of shredded basil provided a vibrant, fresh finish and complemented the tomato sauce and cheese. Serve with pasta and extra sauce.

serves 4
total time: 1 hour

chunky tomato sauce
makes 4 cups

1 tablespoon extra-virgin olive oil

1 onion, chopped fine

Salt and pepper

3 garlic cloves, minced

¼ teaspoon dried oregano

⅛ teaspoon red pepper flakes

1 (14.5-ounce) can crushed tomatoes

1 (28-ounce) can diced tomatoes

Cook oil, onion, and 1 teaspoon salt in large saucepan over medium heat until onion is softened, 5 to 7 minutes. Stir in garlic, oregano, and pepper flakes and cook until fragrant, about 30 seconds. Stir in crushed tomatoes and diced tomatoes with their juice and simmer until sauce is slightly thickened and measures 4 cups, about 15 minutes. Season with salt and pepper to taste.

2 (6- to 8-ounce) boneless, skinless chicken breasts, trimmed

Salt and pepper

1 large egg

1 tablespoon all-purpose flour

1½ ounces Parmesan cheese, grated (¾ cup)

½ cup panko bread crumbs

½ teaspoon garlic powder

¼ teaspoon dried oregano

⅓ cup vegetable oil

2 ounces whole-milk mozzarella cheese, shredded (½ cup)

2 ounces fontina cheese, shredded (½ cup)

1 cup Chunky Tomato Sauce, warmed

¼ cup shredded fresh basil

1. Cut chicken horizontally into 2 thin cutlets, then cover with plastic wrap and pound to even ½-inch thickness. Pat chicken dry with paper towels and season with salt and pepper.

2. Whisk egg and flour together in shallow dish until smooth. Combine Parmesan, panko, garlic powder, oregano, and ¼ teaspoon pepper in second shallow dish. Working with 1 cutlet at a time, dip in egg mixture, then coat with Parmesan mixture, pressing gently to adhere; transfer to large plate.

3. Adjust oven rack 4 inches from broiler element and heat broiler. Heat oil in 10-inch nonstick skillet over medium-high heat until shimmering. Brown 2 cutlets until very crisp and deep golden brown on both sides, 3 to 4 minutes. Transfer to paper towel–lined plate; repeat with remaining cutlets.

4. Place cutlets on rimmed baking sheet. Combine mozzarella and fontina in bowl and sprinkle evenly over cutlets, covering as much surface area as possible. Broil until cheese is melted and beginning to brown, 2 to 4 minutes. Transfer chicken to serving platter, top each cutlet with 2 tablespoons sauce, sprinkle with basil, and serve.

to make ahead
Tomato sauce can be refrigerated for up to 3 days or frozen for up to 1 month; if frozen, thaw completely in refrigerator. Breaded chicken, prepared through step 2, can be refrigerated for up to 24 hours. Alternatively, cooked chicken, prepared through step 3, can be frozen for up to 1 month; to reheat, place frozen cutlets on wire rack set in rimmed baking sheet, top with cheese, bake in 400-degree oven on middle rack until crisp and hot throughout, 20 to 30 minutes, and continue with step 4.

chicken marsala

why this recipe works Beloved for its boozy, savory sauce, chicken Marsala is a restaurant favorite that we wanted to make more approachable for the home cook. First, we cut each chicken breast in half crosswise. Then, we cut the thicker half in half horizontally to make three identically sized pieces that could easily be pounded into cutlets. We salted the cutlets briefly and then dredged them in flour, which helped accelerate browning and prevented the meat from overcooking. For the sauce, we used reduced dry Marsala and chicken broth, along with cremini and dried porcini mushrooms for rich flavor and gelatin for a silky texture. It is worth spending a little extra for a moderately priced dry Marsala ($10 to $12 per bottle).

serves 4 to 6
total time: 1 hour 30 minutes

2¼ cups dry Marsala

4 teaspoons unflavored gelatin

1 ounce dried porcini mushrooms, rinsed

4 (6- to 8-ounce) boneless, skinless chicken breasts, trimmed

Kosher salt and pepper

2 cups chicken broth

¾ cup all-purpose flour

¼ cup plus 1 teaspoon vegetable oil

3 ounces pancetta, cut into ½-inch pieces

1 pound cremini mushrooms, trimmed and sliced thin

1 shallot, minced

1 tablespoon tomato paste

1 garlic clove, minced

2 teaspoons lemon juice

1 teaspoon minced fresh oregano

3 tablespoons unsalted butter, cut into 6 pieces

2 teaspoons minced fresh parsley

1. Bring 2 cups Marsala, gelatin, and porcini mushrooms to boil in medium saucepan over high heat. Reduce heat to medium-high and cook at vigorous simmer until reduced by half, 6 to 8 minutes.

2. Meanwhile, cut each chicken breast in half crosswise, then cut thick half in half again horizontally, creating 3 cutlets of about same thickness. Place cutlets between sheets of plastic wrap and pound gently to even ½-inch thickness. Place cutlets in bowl and toss with 2 teaspoons salt and ½ teaspoon pepper. Set aside for 15 minutes.

3. Strain Marsala reduction through fine-mesh strainer, pressing on solids to extract as much liquid as possible; discard solids. Return Marsala reduction to saucepan, add broth, and return to boil over high heat. Lower heat to medium-high and simmer until reduced to 1½ cups, 10 to 12 minutes. Set aside.

4. Spread flour in shallow dish. Working with 1 cutlet at a time, dredge cutlets in flour, shaking gently to remove excess. Place on wire rack set in rimmed baking sheet. Heat 2 tablespoons oil in 12-inch skillet over medium-high heat until smoking. Place 6 cutlets in skillet and lower heat to medium. Cook until golden brown on 1 side,

2 to 3 minutes. Flip and cook until golden brown on second side, 2 to 3 minutes. Return cutlets to wire rack. Repeat with 2 tablespoons oil and remaining 6 cutlets.

5. Return now-empty skillet to medium-low heat and add pancetta. Cook, stirring occasionally, scraping pan bottom to loosen browned bits, until pancetta is brown and crisp, about 4 minutes. Add cremini mushrooms and increase heat to medium-high. Cook, stirring occasionally and scraping pan bottom, until liquid released by mushrooms evaporates and mushrooms begin to brown, about 8 minutes. Using slotted spoon, transfer cremini mushrooms and pancetta to bowl. Add remaining 1 teaspoon oil and shallot to pan and cook until softened, 1 minute. Add tomato paste and garlic and cook until fragrant, 30 seconds. Add lemon juice, oregano, reduced Marsala mixture, and remaining ¼ cup Marsala and bring to simmer.

6. Add cutlets to sauce and simmer for 3 minutes, flipping halfway through simmering. Transfer cutlets to platter. Off heat, whisk in butter. Stir in parsley and cremini mushroom mixture. Season with salt and pepper to taste. Spoon sauce over chicken and serve.

chicken stew

why this recipe works There is something comforting about a big pot of stew simmering in the oven on a lazy Sunday afternoon. This old-fashioned chicken stew delivers big flavor in spades and is hearty enough to feed a crowd. We used two different cuts of chicken—wings and thighs. When cooked in the stew, the collagen within the wings converted to gelatin and added meaty flavor to the gravy. We used chicken thighs for chunks of fattier, dark stew meat, which could withstand a longer cooking time. Incorporating bacon, crisped in the pot before browning the wings, lent porky depth and just a hint of smoke. And while they may sound like strange additions, soy sauce and anchovy paste, both rich in glutamates, acted as meaty and savory flavor enhancers. You'll want to use small red potatoes measuring 1½ inches in diameter.

serves 6 to 8
total time: 2 hours 30 minutes

2 pounds boneless, skinless chicken thighs, halved crosswise and trimmed

Kosher salt and pepper

3 slices bacon, chopped

1 pound chicken wings, halved at joint

1 onion, chopped fine

1 celery rib, minced

2 garlic cloves, minced

2 teaspoons anchovy paste

1 teaspoon minced fresh thyme

5 cups chicken broth

1 cup dry white wine, plus extra for seasoning

1 tablespoon soy sauce

3 tablespoons unsalted butter, cut into 3 pieces

⅓ cup all-purpose flour

1 pound small red potatoes, unpeeled, quartered

4 carrots, peeled and cut into ½-inch pieces

2 tablespoons minced fresh parsley

1. Adjust oven rack to lower-middle position and heat oven to 325 degrees. Arrange chicken thighs on baking sheet and lightly season both sides with salt and pepper; cover with plastic wrap and set aside.

2. Cook bacon in Dutch oven over medium-low heat, stirring occasionally, until fat renders and bacon browns, 6 to 8 minutes. Using slotted spoon, transfer bacon to medium bowl. Add chicken wings to pot, increase heat to medium, and cook until well browned on both sides, 10 to 12 minutes; transfer wings to bowl with bacon.

3. Add onion, celery, garlic, anchovy paste, and thyme to fat in pot; cook, stirring occasionally, until dark fond forms on pan bottom, 2 to 4 minutes. Increase heat to high; stir in 1 cup broth, wine, and soy sauce, scraping up any browned bits; and bring to boil. Cook, stirring occasionally, until liquid evaporates and vegetables begin to sizzle again, 12 to 15 minutes. Add butter and stir to melt; sprinkle flour over vegetables and stir to combine.

Gradually whisk in remaining 4 cups broth until smooth. Stir in potatoes, carrots, and wings and bacon; bring to simmer. Transfer to oven and cook, uncovered, for 30 minutes, stirring once halfway through cooking.

4. Remove pot from oven. Use wooden spoon to draw gravy up sides of pot and scrape browned fond into stew. Place over high heat, add thighs, and bring to simmer. Return pot to oven, uncovered, and continue to cook, stirring occasionally, until chicken offers no resistance when poked with fork and vegetables are tender, about 45 minutes longer. Discard wings.

5. Season stew with up to 2 tablespoons extra wine and salt and pepper to taste. Sprinkle with parsley and serve.

to make ahead
Stew, prepared through step 4, can be refrigerated for up to 3 days. To reheat, bring stew, covered, to gentle simmer, stirring often; adjust consistency with hot broth as needed and continue with step 5.

herb-stuffed pork chops

why this recipe works Pork chops are a Sunday dinner favorite, and stuffing them takes the dish to another level. But they are rarely well executed, as they are typically crammed full of a soggy bread stuffing. We were after a perfectly cooked pork chop—thick and juicy, seared crusty brown on the outside—enhanced by a flavorful stuffing. We developed a stuffing mixture that incorporated enough moisture, fat, and assertive flavors to enhance the lean, mild pork. Baking the chops on a preheated baking sheet in a hot oven was an easy way to achieve a seared exterior and an evenly cooked interior. We found that tenting the chops with foil for a few minutes after they were done cooking helped them retain heat while they rested. While we prefer fontina cheese, Monterey Jack or Gruyère cheese work equally well.

serves 4
total time: 45 minutes

¼ cup vegetable oil

3 garlic cloves, minced

1 slice hearty white sandwich bread, toasted and torn into pieces

½ cup chopped fresh parsley

1 tablespoon chopped fresh thyme

3 ounces fontina cheese, shredded (¾ cup)

Salt and pepper

4 (6- to 8-ounce) boneless pork chops, about 1 inch thick, trimmed

1. Adjust oven rack to upper-middle position, place rimmed baking sheet on rack, and heat oven to 475 degrees. Combine oil and garlic in bowl. Pulse 2 tablespoons oil mixture, bread, parsley, thyme, fontina, ¼ teaspoon salt, and ¼ teaspoon pepper in food processor until coarsely ground, 5 to 10 pulses.

2. Pat pork dry with paper towels and season with salt and pepper. Using paring knife, cut 1-inch opening into side of each chop to make pocket for stuffing. Spoon herb mixture into pocket and insert toothpick through pork about ½ inch from opening.

3. Coat chops with remaining oil mixture and transfer to preheated baking sheet. Bake until browned and meat registers 145 degrees, 12 to 15 minutes, flipping chops halfway through cooking. Transfer to platter, tent with aluminum foil, and let rest for 5 to 10 minutes. Serve.

pork schnitzel

why this recipe works An Old World favorite, a schnitzel is simply meat that is pounded thin, coated in a classic bound breading, and then fried. Hugely popular in Germany and Austria, it is often made with veal, but to make it more accessible, stateside versions often use pork. We preferred to use pork tenderloin; pounded thin and fried, cutlets from the tenderloin were remarkably tender with a mild flavor similar to veal. We crisped the crumbs before coating the cutlets by simply microwaving cubes of bread on high power, then medium, and transferring to a food processor to grind. Instead of cooking the cutlets in a skillet, we used a Dutch oven to better accommodate the 2 cups of oil. Shaking the pan as the cutlets cooked in the hot oil sent the oil back over the top of the cutlets, speeding up the setting process and enhancing the puffed, golden-brown appearance of perfect schnitzel. The 2 cups of oil called for in this recipe may seem like a lot, but this amount is necessary to achieve a wrinkled texture on the finished cutlets. When properly cooked, the cutlets absorb very little oil. Cutting the pork tenderloin at about a 20-degree angle will yield pounded cutlets that fit easily into the pan. Serve with buttered egg noodles.

serves 4
total time: 1 hour

7 slices hearty white sandwich bread, crusts removed, bread cut into ¾-inch cubes

½ cup all-purpose flour

2 large eggs, plus 1 large hard-cooked egg, yolk and white separated and passed separately through fine-mesh strainer (optional)

1 tablespoon plus 2 cups vegetable oil

1 (1¼-pound) pork tenderloin, trimmed and cut on angle into 4 equal pieces

Salt and pepper

Lemon wedges

2 tablespoons minced fresh parsley

2 tablespoons capers, rinsed

1. Place bread cubes on large plate. Microwave on high power for 4 minutes, stirring well halfway through microwaving. Microwave on medium power until bread is dry and a few pieces start to lightly brown, 3 to 5 minutes, stirring every minute. Process dry bread in food processor to very fine crumbs, about 45 seconds. Transfer bread crumbs to shallow dish (you should have about 1¼ cups crumbs). Spread flour in second shallow dish. Beat eggs with 1 tablespoon oil in third shallow dish.

2. Set wire rack in rimmed baking sheet and line plate with triple layer of paper towels. Working with 1 piece at a time, place pork with 1 cut side down, between 2 sheets of parchment paper or plastic wrap and pound to even thickness between ⅛ and ¼ inch. Pat cutlets dry with paper towels and season with salt and pepper.

3. Working with 1 cutlet at a time, dredge cutlets thoroughly in flour, shaking off excess; coat with egg mixture, allowing excess to drip back into dish to ensure very thin coating; and coat evenly with bread crumbs, pressing on crumbs to adhere. Place breaded cutlets in single layer on prepared wire rack; let coating dry for 5 minutes.

4. Heat remaining 2 cups oil in large Dutch oven over medium-high heat to 375 degrees. Lay 2 cutlets, without overlapping, in pot and cook, shaking pot continuously and gently, until cutlets are wrinkled and light golden brown on both sides, 1 to 2 minutes per side. Transfer cutlets to paper towel–lined plate and flip cutlets several times to blot excess oil. Repeat with remaining cutlets. Serve with lemon wedges, parsley, capers, and, if desired, hard-cooked egg.

slow-roasted pork shoulder
with peach sauce

why this recipe works Seasoned with kosher salt and brown sugar overnight and then roasted for the better part of a day, this spectacular pork roast, served with a bright fruit sauce, makes for a showstopping but easy Sunday dinner. It also showcases the glories of old-fashioned, more flavorful (read: less lean) pork. The shoulder roast may take longer to cook than other cuts of pork, but it's also inexpensive and loaded with flavorful intramuscular fat; plus, it boasts a thick fat cap that renders to a bronze, bacon-like crust thanks to the sugar rub, which dries out the exterior and boosts browning. Elevating the pork shoulder on a V-rack and pouring water in the roasting pan kept the pork's drippings from burning as the meat roasted, and it also created a significant jus. Finally, a fruity sauce with sweet and tart elements cut the pork shoulder's richness. Pork butt roast is often labeled Boston butt in the supermarket. Add more water to the roasting pan as necessary to prevent the fond from burning. Serve with Garlic Mashed Potatoes (page 11).

serves 8 to 12
total time: 6 hours 30 minutes
(plus 12 hours for salting)

pork roast
1 (6- to 8-pound) bone-in pork butt roast

⅓ cup kosher salt

⅓ cup packed light brown sugar

Pepper

peach sauce
10 ounces frozen sliced peaches, cut into 1-inch chunks, or 2 fresh peaches, peeled, pitted, and cut into ½-inch wedges

2 cups dry white wine

½ cup granulated sugar

¼ cup plus 1 tablespoon rice vinegar

2 sprigs fresh thyme

1 tablespoon whole-grain mustard

1. for the pork roast Using sharp knife, cut slits 1 inch apart in crosshatch pattern in fat cap of roast, being careful not to cut into meat. Combine salt and sugar in bowl. Rub salt mixture over entire pork shoulder and into slits. Wrap roast tightly in double layer of plastic wrap, place on rimmed baking sheet, and refrigerate for 12 to 24 hours.

2. Adjust oven rack to lowest position and heat oven to 325 degrees. Unwrap roast and brush any excess salt mixture from surface. Season roast with pepper. Spray V-rack with vegetable oil spray, set rack in large roasting pan, and place roast on rack. Add 1 quart water to roasting pan.

3. Roast pork, basting twice during cooking, until meat is extremely tender and meat near bone registers 190 degrees, 5 to 6 hours. Transfer roast to carving board, tent with aluminum foil, and let rest for 1 hour. Transfer liquid in roasting pan to fat separator and let sit for 5 minutes. Pour off ¼ cup jus and set aside for sauce; discard fat and remaining jus.

4. for the peach sauce Simmer peaches, wine, sugar, ¼ cup vinegar, ¼ cup defatted jus, and thyme sprigs in small saucepan, stirring occasionally, until reduced to 2 cups, about 30 minutes. Off heat, discard thyme sprigs and stir in remaining 1 tablespoon vinegar and mustard; cover to keep warm.

5. Using sharp paring knife, cut around inverted T-shaped bone until it can be pulled free from roast (use clean dish towel to grasp bone). Using knife, slice roast. Serve with sauce.

meatballs and marinara

why this recipe works It doesn't get much better than sitting down to a heaping pile of spaghetti topped with juicy, flavor-packed meatballs, all married together by a bright tomato sauce. Our foolproof spaghetti and meatballs recipe hits every mark and is relatively fuss-free. While most meatball recipes call for equal amounts of pork and beef, we opted to use more beef than pork. The resulting drier, leaner mixture was better able to maintain its shape through cooking. Instead of browning the meatballs on the stovetop as most meatball recipes instruct, we utilized the oven so they would be more hands-off. Finishing the meatballs in the tomato sauce flavored both components and tied the dish together before serving.

serves 8 to 10
total time: 1 hour 30 minutes

sauce
¼ cup extra-virgin olive oil

3 onions, chopped fine

8 garlic cloves, minced

1 tablespoon dried oregano

½ teaspoon red pepper flakes

1 (6-ounce) can tomato paste

1 cup dry red wine

1 cup water

4 (28-ounce) cans crushed tomatoes

½ cup grated Parmesan cheese

¼ cup chopped fresh basil

Salt and pepper

meatballs and pasta
4 slices hearty white sandwich bread, torn into pieces

¾ cup milk

½ pound sweet Italian sausage, casings removed

2 ounces Parmesan cheese, grated (1 cup)

½ cup minced fresh parsley

2 large eggs

2 garlic cloves, minced

1½ teaspoons salt

2½ pounds 80 percent lean ground chuck

2 pounds spaghetti

1. for the sauce Heat oil in Dutch oven over medium-high heat until shimmering. Add onions and cook until golden, 10 to 15 minutes. Stir in garlic, oregano, and pepper flakes and cook until fragrant, about 30 seconds. Transfer half of onion mixture to bowl; set aside for meatballs.

2. Stir tomato paste into onion mixture left in pot and cook over medium-high heat until fragrant, about 1 minute. Stir in wine and cook until slightly thickened, about 2 minutes. Stir in water and tomatoes and simmer over low heat until sauce is no longer watery, 45 minutes to 1 hour. Stir in Parmesan and basil and season with salt and pepper to taste.

3. for the meatballs and pasta While sauce simmers, line 2 rimmed baking sheets with aluminum foil and spray with vegetable oil spray. Adjust oven racks to lower-middle and upper-middle positions and heat oven to 475 degrees. Mash bread and milk in large bowl until smooth. Mix in reserved onion mixture, sausage, Parmesan, parsley, eggs, garlic, and salt. Add beef and knead with your hands until well combined.

4. Shape meat mixture into 30 meatballs (about ¼ cup each) and place on prepared sheets, spaced evenly apart. Roast meatballs until well browned, about 20 minutes. Transfer meatballs to pot with sauce and simmer for 15 minutes.

5. Meanwhile, bring 8 quarts water to boil in 12-quart pot. Add pasta and 2 tablespoons salt and cook, stirring often, until al dente. Reserve ½ cup cooking water, then drain pasta and return it to pot. Add several spoonfuls of sauce (without meatballs) and toss to combine. Add reserved cooking water as needed to adjust consistency. Serve pasta with remaining sauce and meatballs.

to make ahead
Cooked meatballs in sauce can be refrigerated for up to 3 days or frozen for up to 1 month. If frozen, thaw completely in refrigerator. To reheat, bring sauce and meatballs, covered, to gentle simmer and adjust consistency with warm pasta cooking water as needed.

beef burgundy

why this recipe works Beef Burgundy is the king of all beef stews, with its heady wine-infused gravy and tender chunks of meat. To make the dish relatively hands-off, we moved the entire operation to the oven. Serve with Creamy Parmesan Polenta (page 9).

serves 6 to 8
total time: 4 hours 15 minutes
(plus 30 minutes for salting)

1 (4-pound) boneless beef chuck-eye roast, trimmed and cut into 1½- to 2-inch pieces, scraps reserved

Salt and pepper

6 ounces salt pork, cut into ¼-inch pieces

3 tablespoons unsalted butter

1 pound cremini mushrooms, trimmed, halved if medium or quartered if large

1½ cups frozen pearl onions, thawed

1 tablespoon sugar

⅓ cup all-purpose flour

4 cups beef broth

1 (750-ml) bottle red Burgundy or Pinot Noir

5 teaspoons unflavored gelatin

1 tablespoon tomato paste

1 teaspoon anchovy paste

2 onions, chopped coarse

2 carrots, peeled and cut into 2-inch lengths

1 garlic head, cloves separated, unpeeled, and smashed

½ ounce dried porcini mushrooms, rinsed

10 sprigs fresh parsley, plus 3 tablespoons minced

6 sprigs fresh thyme

2 bay leaves

½ teaspoon black peppercorns

1. Toss beef and 1½ teaspoons salt together in bowl and let stand at room temperature for 30 minutes.

2. Adjust oven racks to lower-middle and lowest positions and heat oven to 500 degrees. Place salt pork, 2 tablespoons butter, and beef scraps in large roasting pan. Roast on upper rack until well browned and fat has rendered, 15 to 20 minutes.

3. While salt pork and beef scraps roast, toss cremini mushrooms, pearl onions, sugar, and remaining 1 tablespoon butter together on rimmed baking sheet. Roast on lower rack, stirring occasionally, until moisture released by mushrooms evaporates and vegetables are lightly glazed, 15 to 20 minutes. Transfer vegetables to large bowl, cover, and refrigerate.

4. Remove roasting pan from oven and reduce temperature to 325 degrees. Sprinkle flour over rendered fat and whisk until no dry flour remains. Whisk in broth, 2 cups wine, gelatin, tomato paste, and anchovy paste until combined. Add onions, carrots, garlic, porcini mushrooms, parsley sprigs, thyme sprigs, bay leaves, and peppercorns to pan. Arrange beef in single layer on top of vegetables. Add water as needed to come three-quarters up side of beef (beef should not be submerged). Return roasting pan to oven and cook until meat is tender,

3 to 3½ hours, stirring after 1½ hours and adding water to keep meat at least half-submerged.

5. Using slotted spoon, transfer beef to bowl with cremini mushrooms and pearl onions; cover and set aside. Strain braising liquid through fine-mesh strainer set over large bowl, pressing on solids to extract as much liquid as possible; discard solids. Stir in remaining wine and let cooking liquid settle, 10 minutes. Using wide, shallow spoon, skim fat from surface and discard.

6. Transfer liquid to Dutch oven and bring mixture to boil over medium-high heat. Simmer briskly, stirring occasionally, until sauce is thickened to consistency of heavy cream, 15 to 20 minutes. Reduce heat to medium-low, stir in beef and mushroom-onion mixture, cover, and cook until just heated through, 5 to 8 minutes. Season with salt and pepper to taste. Stir in minced parsley and serve.

to make ahead
Stew can be refrigerated for up to 3 days or frozen for up to 1 month. If frozen, thaw completely in refrigerator. To reheat, bring stew, covered, to gentle simmer, stirring often, and adjust consistency with hot water as needed.

classic pot roast

why this recipe works With its tender, pull-apart meat and rich, beefy gravy, our Classic Pot Roast will give you the cooked-all-day feel of grandma's. We started by selecting a well-marbled chuck-eye roast. Splitting the roast along its natural seams meant we could trim off excess fat. To beef up the gravy, we used a combination of beef broth and red wine for the braising liquid. We also added a bit of glutamate-rich tomato paste. We determined that an initial sear wasn't necessary—we found that the "dry" part of the meat that stayed above the braising liquid eventually browned, even without searing. Blending the cooked vegetables with the defatted cooking liquid and extra broth gave us a full-bodied gravy, which we finished with balsamic vinegar and a bit more wine for brightness. We found that chilling the whole cooked pot roast overnight improved its flavor and made it moister and easier to slice. Serve with buttered egg noodles.

serves 6 to 8
total time: 4 hours 30 minutes
(plus 1 hour for salting)

1 (3½- to 4-pound) boneless beef chuck-eye roast, pulled into 2 pieces at natural seam and trimmed of large knobs of fat

Kosher salt and pepper

2 tablespoons unsalted butter

2 onions, halved and sliced thin

1 large carrot, peeled and chopped

1 celery rib, chopped

2 garlic cloves, minced

2–3 cups beef broth

¾ cup dry red wine

1 tablespoon tomato paste

1 bay leaf

1 sprig fresh thyme, plus ¼ teaspoon minced

1 tablespoon balsamic vinegar

1. Rub roasts thoroughly with 1 tablespoon salt, place on wire rack set in rimmed baking sheet, and let sit at room temperature for 1 hour. Pat beef dry with paper towels, season with pepper, and tie each with 3 pieces of kitchen twine.

2. Adjust oven rack to lower-middle position and heat oven to 300 degrees. Melt butter in Dutch oven over medium heat. Add onions and cook, stirring often, until softened and beginning to brown, 8 to 10 minutes. Stir in carrot and celery and cook until softened, about 5 minutes. Stir in garlic and cook until fragrant, about 30 seconds. Stir in 1 cup broth, ½ cup wine, tomato paste, bay leaf, and thyme sprig and bring to simmer.

3. Nestle meat on top of vegetables. Cover pot tightly with aluminum foil, then cover with lid and transfer to oven. Cook until beef is tender and fork slips easily in and out of meat, 3½ to 4 hours, turning meat halfway through cooking.

4. Transfer roasts to carving board and tent with foil. Strain liquid through fine-mesh strainer into 4-cup liquid measuring cup.

Reserve strained vegetables, discarding bay leaf and thyme sprig. Let liquid settle for 5 minutes, then skim fat and add broth as needed until liquid measures 3 cups.

5. Process liquid and strained vegetables in blender until smooth, about 2 minutes. Transfer gravy to medium saucepan and bring to simmer over medium heat.

6. Remove twine, slice meat against grain into ½-inch-thick pieces, and transfer to serving platter. Stir minced thyme, vinegar, and remaining ¼ cup wine into gravy and season with salt and pepper to taste. Spoon half of gravy over meat and serve with remaining gravy.

to make ahead
Before separating out meat, broth, and vegetables in step 4, contents can be cooled and refrigerated together for up to 2 days. To reheat, slice meat into ½-inch-thick slices, arrange in large baking dish, and cover with foil. Reheat in 325-degree oven for 45 minutes and continue with step 5.

slow-roasted beef

why this recipe works Sometimes you just want a simple beef roast to cap off your weekend, along with the leftovers for a head start on Monday. We wanted an inexpensive cut we could transform into a tender, juicy roast that could stand on its own at the Sunday dinner table. We chose an eye-round roast due to its exceptional flavor, relative tenderness, and uniform shape that guarantees even cooking. Searing the meat before roasting, as well as salting it as much as 24 hours before roasting, vastly improved its flavor. But the big surprise was the method that produced remarkably tender and juicy beef—roasting the meat at a very low 225 degrees and then turning off the oven toward the end of cooking. This approach allowed the meat's enzymes to act as natural tenderizers, breaking down the roast's tough connective tissue. Open the oven door as little as possible, and remove the roast from the oven while taking its temperature. If the roast has not reached the desired temperature in the time specified in step 4, reheat the oven to 225 degrees for 5 minutes, then shut it off and continue to cook the roast to the desired temperature. We don't recommend cooking this roast past medium. For a smaller (2½- to 3½-pound) roast, reduce the amount of kosher salt to 1 tablespoon and pepper to 1½ teaspoons. For a larger (4½- to 6-pound) roast, cut the meat in half crosswise before cooking to create two smaller roasts. Serve with Garlic Mashed Potatoes (page 11) and Horseradish Sauce.

serves 6 to 8
total time: 2 hours 30 minutes
(plus 18 hours for salting)

1 (3½- to 4½-pound) boneless eye-round roast, trimmed

4 teaspoons kosher salt

2 teaspoons plus 1 tablespoon vegetable oil

2 teaspoons pepper

1. Rub roast thoroughly with salt, wrap in plastic wrap, and refrigerate for 18 to 24 hours.

2. Adjust oven rack to middle position and heat oven to 225 degrees. Pat roast dry with paper towels, rub with 2 teaspoons oil, and sprinkle with pepper.

3. Heat remaining 1 tablespoon oil in 12-inch skillet over medium-high heat until just smoking. Brown roast well on all sides, 12 to 16 minutes; reduce heat if pan begins to scorch. Transfer roast to wire rack set in rimmed baking sheet and roast until meat registers 115 degrees (for medium-rare), 1¼ to 1¾ hours, or 125 degrees (for medium), 1¾ to 2¼ hours.

4. Turn oven off and leave roast in oven, without opening door, until meat registers 130 degrees (for medium-rare) or 140 degrees (for medium), 30 to 50 minutes.

5. Transfer roast to carving board and let rest for 15 minutes. Slice meat crosswise as thin as possible and serve.

horseradish sauce
makes about 1¼ cups

1 cup sour cream

3 tablespoons prepared horseradish

1 tablespoon mayonnaise

1 tablespoon lemon juice

1 garlic clove, minced

¼ teaspoon sugar

Salt and pepper

Combine all ingredients in bowl and season with salt and pepper to taste. Let sit at room temperature until flavors have blended, about 10 minutes.

to make ahead
Horseradish sauce can be refrigerated for up to 3 days. To serve, bring to room temperature and stir to recombine.

simple pot-au-feu

why this recipe works Although a French boiled dinner may feel out of date on today's dinner table, there is much to admire about this vintage recipe with tender meat and vegetables, a rich broth, and a robust sauce. By many accounts, pot-au-feu—which translates literally to "pot on the fire"—has been one of France's most celebrated meals since the French Revolution. A combination of beef and bones gave our broth a beguiling mix of beefiness and butteriness. Marrow bones (also called soup bones) can be found in the freezer section or the meat counter at most supermarkets. Use small red potatoes measuring 1 to 2 inches in diameter.

serves 6 to 8
total time: 4 hours 15 minutes

meat
1 (3½- to 4-pound) boneless beef chuck-eye roast, pulled into 2 pieces at natural seam and trimmed

Kosher salt

1½ pounds marrow bones

1 onion, quartered

1 celery rib, sliced thin

3 bay leaves

1 teaspoon black peppercorns

parsley sauce
⅔ cup minced fresh parsley

¼ cup Dijon mustard

¼ cup minced fresh chives

3 tablespoons white wine vinegar

10 cornichons, minced

1½ teaspoons pepper

vegetables
1 pound small red potatoes, halved

6 carrots, halved crosswise, thick halves quartered lengthwise, thin halves halved lengthwise

1 pound asparagus, trimmed

Kosher salt and pepper

Flake sea salt

1. for the meat Adjust oven rack to lower-middle position and heat oven to 300 degrees. Season beef with 1 tablespoon salt. Using 3 pieces of kitchen twine per piece, tie each piece into loaf shape for even cooking. Place beef, bones, onion, celery, bay leaves, and peppercorns in Dutch oven. Add 4 cups water (water should come halfway up roasts). Bring to simmer over high heat. Partially cover pot and transfer to oven. Cook until beef is fully tender and sharp knife easily slips in and out of meat (meat will not be shreddable), 3¼ to 3¾ hours, flipping beef over halfway through cooking.

2. for the parsley sauce While beef cooks, combine all ingredients in bowl. Cover and set aside.

3. Remove pot from oven and turn off oven. Transfer beef to large platter, cover tightly with aluminum foil, and return to oven to keep warm. Transfer bones to cutting board and use end of spoon to extract marrow. Mince marrow into paste and add 2 tablespoons to parsley sauce (reserve any remaining marrow for other applications). Using ladle or large spoon, skim fat from surface of broth and discard fat. Strain broth through fine-mesh strainer into large liquid measuring cup; add water to make 6 cups. Return broth to pot. (Meat can be returned to broth, cooled, and refrigerated for up to 2 days. Skim fat from cold broth, then gently reheat and proceed with recipe.)

4. for the vegetables Add potatoes to broth and bring to simmer over high heat. Reduce heat to medium and simmer for 6 minutes. Add carrots and cook 10 minutes longer. Add asparagus and continue to cook until all vegetables are tender, 3 to 5 minutes longer.

5. Using slotted spoon, transfer vegetables to large bowl. Toss with 3 tablespoons parsley sauce and season with salt and pepper to taste. Season broth with salt to taste.

6. Transfer beef to cutting board, remove twine, and slice against grain ½ inch thick. Arrange servings of beef and vegetables in large, shallow bowls. Dollop beef with parsley sauce, drizzle with ⅓ cup broth, and sprinkle with flake sea salt. Serve, passing remaining parsley sauce and flake sea salt separately.

best ground beef chili

why this recipe works Whether it's football season or not, chili seems a natural choice for any Sunday supper. To keep the meat tender, we treated it with salt and baking soda; this also helped the meat hold on to moisture and allowed us to brown 2 pounds of beef in just one batch. For intense flavor, we made our own chili powder, combining toasted dried ancho chiles, chipotle chiles in adobo, and paprika, along with a blend of herbs and spices to round it out. We made sure to stir in any fat that collected on the top of the chili before serving, since it contained much of the flavor from the fat-soluble spices in the chile powder. Serve with your favorite chili toppings.

serves 8 to 10
total time: 3 hours

2 pounds 85 percent lean ground beef

2 tablespoons plus 2 cups water

Salt and pepper

¾ teaspoon baking soda

6 dried ancho chiles, stemmed, seeded, and torn into 1-inch pieces

1 ounce tortilla chips, crushed (¼ cup)

2 tablespoons ground cumin

1 tablespoon paprika

1 tablespoon garlic powder

1 tablespoon ground coriander

2 teaspoons dried oregano

½ teaspoon dried thyme

1 (14.5-ounce) can whole peeled tomatoes

1 tablespoon vegetable oil

1 onion, chopped fine

3 garlic cloves, minced

1–2 teaspoons minced canned chipotle chiles in adobo sauce

1 (15-ounce) can pinto beans

2 teaspoons sugar

2 tablespoons cider vinegar

Lime wedges

Coarsely chopped fresh cilantro

Chopped red onion

1. Adjust oven rack to lower-middle position and heat oven to 275 degrees. Toss beef with 2 tablespoons water, 1½ teaspoons salt, and baking soda in bowl until thoroughly combined. Set aside for 20 minutes.

2. Meanwhile, place anchos in Dutch oven set over medium-high heat; toast, stirring frequently, until fragrant, 4 to 6 minutes, reducing heat if anchos begin to smoke. Transfer to food processor and let cool.

3. Add tortilla chips, cumin, paprika, garlic powder, coriander, oregano, thyme, and 2 teaspoons pepper to food processor with anchos and process until finely ground, about 2 minutes. Transfer mixture to bowl. Process tomatoes and their juice in now-empty workbowl until smooth, about 30 seconds.

4. Heat oil in now-empty pot over medium-high heat until shimmering. Add onion and cook, stirring occasionally, until softened, 4 to 6 minutes. Add garlic and cook until fragrant, about 1 minute. Add beef and cook, stirring with wooden spoon to break meat up into ¼-inch pieces, until beef is browned and fond begins to form on pot bottom, 12 to 14 minutes. Add ancho mixture and chipotle; cook, stirring frequently, until fragrant, 1 to 2 minutes.

5. Add beans and their liquid, sugar, tomato puree, and remaining 2 cups water. Bring to boil, scraping bottom of pot to loosen any browned bits. Cover, transfer to oven, and cook until meat is tender and chili is slightly thickened, 1½ to 2 hours, stirring occasionally to prevent sticking.

6. Remove chili from oven and let stand, uncovered, for 10 minutes. Stir in any fat that has risen to top of chili, then add vinegar and season with salt to taste. Serve, passing lime wedges, cilantro, and chopped onion separately.

to make ahead
Chili can be refrigerated for up to 3 days. To reheat, bring chili, covered, to gentle simmer, stirring often, and adjust consistency with hot water as needed.

rigatoni with warm-spiced beef ragu

why this recipe works Nothing says Sunday comfort food like a steaming bowl of pasta coated in a silky, savory meat sauce. Rustic Italian-style ragu is all about low-and-slow simmering—it relies on lots of time but minimal heat to turn the meat, cooked with tomatoes and red wine, fall-apart tender. For this recipe, we liked beef short ribs, which turned delicate and moist during braising; they gave the sauce a deep, savory flavor. Tomato sauce and crushed tomatoes made a sauce that was too smooth; although canned diced tomatoes created a chunkier sauce, we preferred the rustic texture and appearance of chopped whole canned tomatoes. Cinnamon and cloves, while unexpected, offered a subtle warmth. We also created a Greek-style version using lamb, oregano, and mint in place of beef, thyme, and parsley, increasing the amount of herbs and spices to balance the robust lamb flavor. This recipe will also work with flanken-style short ribs.

serves 6
total time: 3 hours

1½ pounds bone-in English-style short ribs, trimmed

Salt and pepper

1 tablespoon extra-virgin olive oil

1 onion, chopped fine

3 garlic cloves, minced

1 teaspoon minced fresh thyme or ¼ teaspoon dried

½ teaspoon ground cinnamon

Pinch ground cloves

½ cup dry red wine

1 (28-ounce) can whole peeled tomatoes, drained with juice reserved, chopped fine

1 pound rigatoni

2 tablespoons minced fresh parsley

Grated Parmesan cheese

1. Pat ribs dry with paper towels and season with salt and pepper. Heat oil in 12-inch skillet over medium-high heat until just smoking. Brown ribs on all sides, 8 to 10 minutes; transfer to plate.

2. Pour off all but 1 teaspoon fat from skillet, add onion, and cook over medium heat until softened, about 5 minutes. Stir in garlic, thyme, cinnamon, and cloves and cook until fragrant, about 30 seconds. Stir in wine, scraping up any browned bits, and simmer until nearly evaporated, about 2 minutes.

3. Stir in tomatoes and reserved juice. Nestle ribs into sauce along with any accumulated juices and bring to simmer. Reduce heat to low, cover, and simmer gently, turning ribs occasionally, until meat is very tender and falling off bones, about 2 hours.

4. Transfer ribs to cutting board, let cool slightly, then shred meat into bite-size pieces using 2 forks; discard excess fat and bones. Using a wide, shallow spoon, skim excess fat from surface of sauce. Stir shredded meat and any accumulated juices into sauce and bring to simmer over medium heat. Season with salt and pepper to taste.

5. Meanwhile, bring 4 quarts water to boil in large pot. Add pasta and 1 tablespoon salt and cook, stirring often, until al dente. Reserve ½ cup cooking water, then drain pasta and return it to pot. Add sauce and parsley and toss to combine. Season with salt and pepper to taste, and adjust consistency with reserved cooking water as needed. Serve with Parmesan.

variation

rigatoni with minted lamb ragu
Substitute 1½ pounds bone-in lamb shoulder chops, trimmed, for short ribs, 1 teaspoon minced fresh oregano for thyme, and 3 tablespoons minced fresh mint for parsley. Increase ground cinnamon to ¾ teaspoon and ground cloves to ⅛ teaspoon.

to make ahead
Ragu sauce, prepared through step 4, can be refrigerated for up to 3 days. To reheat, bring sauce, covered, to gentle simmer, stirring often, and adjust consistency with warm pasta cooking water as needed.

baked manicotti

why this recipe works In making this homey Italian American classic, we were determined to keep assembly as easy as possible. Manicotti pasta tubes were difficult to stuff, so to simplify the process, we used no-boil lasagna noodles. After a brief soak in hot water, they became pliable enough to roll up and were much easier to stuff with filling. Thoroughly covering the manicotti with sauce ensured that the noodles fully cooked. A sprinkle of Parmesan and just 5 minutes under the broiler provided a toasty crust of cheese—a must-have finishing touch. Some brands of no-boil noodles contain only 12 noodles per package so buy two. If your baking dish is not broiler-safe (and glass dishes are not), brown the manicotti at 500 degrees for 10 minutes. Serve with Broccolini with Browned Butter (page 9).

serves 6 to 8
total time: 1 hour 45 minutes

tomato sauce

2 (28-ounce) cans diced tomatoes

2 tablespoons extra-virgin olive oil

3 garlic cloves, minced

½ teaspoon red pepper flakes (optional)

Salt

2 tablespoons chopped fresh basil

cheese filling

1½ pounds (3 cups) part-skim ricotta cheese

8 ounces mozzarella cheese, shredded (2 cups)

4 ounces Parmesan cheese, grated (2 cups)

2 large eggs

2 tablespoons chopped fresh parsley

2 tablespoons chopped fresh basil

¾ teaspoon salt

½ teaspoon pepper

16 no-boil lasagna noodles

1. for the tomato sauce Pulse 1 can tomatoes with their juice in food processor until coarsely chopped, 3 or 4 pulses; transfer to bowl. Repeat with remaining can tomatoes.

2. Heat oil, garlic, and pepper flakes, if using, in large saucepan over medium heat. Cook, stirring often, until garlic turns golden but not brown, about 3 minutes. Stir in chopped tomatoes and ½ teaspoon salt, bring to simmer, and cook until thickened slightly, about 15 minutes. Stir in basil and season with salt to taste.

3. for the cheese filling Combine ricotta, mozzarella, 1 cup Parmesan, eggs, parsley, basil, salt, and pepper in bowl.

4. Adjust oven rack to middle position and heat oven to 375 degrees. Pour 2 inches boiling water into 13 by 9-inch broiler-safe baking dish. Slip noodles into water, one at a time, and soak until pliable, about 5 minutes, separating noodles with tip of sharp knife to prevent sticking. Remove noodles from water and place in single layer on clean dish towels; discard water and dry dish.

5. Spread 1½ cups sauce evenly over bottom of dish. Using spoon, spread ¼ cup cheese mixture evenly onto bottom three-quarters of each noodle (with short side facing you), leaving top quarter of noodle exposed. Roll into tube shape and arrange in dish seam side down. Top evenly with remaining sauce, making certain that pasta is completely covered.

6. Cover dish tightly with foil and bake until bubbling, about 40 minutes, rotating dish halfway through baking. Remove dish from oven and remove foil. Adjust oven rack 6 inches from broiler element and heat broiler. Sprinkle manicotti evenly with remaining 1 cup Parmesan. Broil until cheese is spotty brown, 4 to 6 minutes. Let manicotti cool for 15 minutes before serving.

to make ahead
Manicotti, prepared through step 5, can be covered with sheet of parchment paper, wrapped in aluminum foil, and refrigerated for up to 3 days or frozen for up to 1 month. If frozen, thaw completely in refrigerator. To reheat, remove parchment, replace foil, increase baking time to 1 to 1¼ hours, and continue with step 6.

modern family dinners

flank steak peperonata

why this recipe works Peperonata, an Italian mixture of sweet peppers, onion, tomato, and garlic, cooked in fruity olive oil until the peppers are soft and the flavors have melded together, is the perfect complement to tender, thinly sliced steak. We cut flank steak with the grain into three equal pieces, seasoned all sides with salt, pepper, and oregano, and wrapped the pieces in plastic for up to 24 hours to fully season the meat. Then we cooked the bell peppers, onion, and garlic in a hefty amount of extra-virgin olive oil until softened; added diced tomatoes, capers, and red pepper flakes; and cooked the mixture until the vegetables were softened. After wiping out the skillet, we seared the seasoned steak pieces on all sides to a perfect medium-rare. While the meat rested, we stirred fresh basil into the peperonata mixture. To serve, we sliced the meat into smaller pieces against the grain, seasoned the slices with salt and pepper and the accumulated meat juices, and arranged the meat with the peperonata. A final drizzle of extra-virgin olive oil balanced the tangy, meaty flavors. We prefer flank steak cooked to medium-rare.

serves 4 to 6
total time: 45 minutes
(plus 30 minutes for salting)

2 teaspoons dried oregano

Salt and pepper

1 (1½-pound) flank steak, trimmed

⅓ cup plus 1 tablespoon extra-virgin olive oil, plus extra for serving

4 red or yellow bell peppers, quartered, stemmed, seeded, and cut crosswise into ¼-inch-wide strips

1 onion, quartered through root end and sliced crosswise into ¼-inch-wide strips

6 garlic cloves, lightly crushed and peeled

1 (14.5-ounce) can diced tomatoes

2 tablespoons capers plus 4 teaspoons caper brine

⅛ teaspoon red pepper flakes

½ cup chopped fresh basil

1. Combine oregano and 1 teaspoon salt in bowl. Cut steak with grain into 3 equal pieces. Sprinkle steak with oregano mixture, wrap tightly in plastic wrap, and refrigerate for at least 30 minutes or up to 24 hours.

2. Heat ⅓ cup oil in 12-inch nonstick skillet over medium-high heat until just smoking. Add bell peppers, onion, garlic, and ½ teaspoon salt. Cover and cook, stirring occasionally, until vegetables are soft, about 10 minutes.

3. Stir in tomatoes and their juice, capers and brine, and pepper flakes and cook, uncovered, until slightly thickened, about 5 minutes. Season with salt and pepper to taste. Transfer peperonata to bowl, cover, and keep warm.

4. Wipe skillet clean with paper towels. Pat steaks dry with paper towels and season with pepper. Heat remaining 1 tablespoon oil in now-empty skillet over medium-high heat until just smoking. Cook steaks until well browned and meat registers 120 to 125 degrees (for medium-rare), 5 to 7 minutes per side. Transfer steaks to carving board, tent loosely with aluminum foil, and let rest for 10 minutes.

5. Stir basil into peperonata. Slice steaks thin against grain on bias. Season steak slices with salt and pepper to taste and drizzle with extra oil. Serve steak with peperonata.

pomegranate-braised beef short ribs
with prunes and sesame

why this recipe works Braised short ribs frequently appear on restaurant menus but can often be daunting to attempt at home. Our Mediterranean-inspired take on classic, red wine–braised ribs boasts meltingly tender beef and a deeply flavorful sweet but tart sauce made with pomegranate juice and prunes. Roasting the short ribs in the oven enabled us to render and discard a significant amount of fat. After braising, we defatted the cooking liquid, then blended it with the vegetables and part of the prunes to create a velvety sauce. Short ribs come in two styles: English-style ribs contain a single rib bone and a thick piece of meat. Flanken-style ribs are cut thinner and have several smaller bones. While either will work here, we prefer the less expensive and more readily available English-style ribs. If using flanken-style ribs, flip the ribs halfway through roasting in step 1. Ras el hanout is a complex Moroccan spice blend that traditionally features a host of warm spices; the flavor and spiciness of store-bought versions can vary greatly by brand. Serve with Creamy Parmesan Polenta (page 9).

serves 6 to 8
total time: 4 hours 30 minutes

4 pounds bone-in English-style short ribs, trimmed

Salt and pepper

4 cups unsweetened pomegranate juice

1 cup water

2 tablespoons extra-virgin olive oil

1 onion, chopped fine

1 carrot, peeled and chopped fine

2 tablespoons ras el hanout

4 garlic cloves, minced

¾ cup pitted prunes, halved

1 tablespoon red wine vinegar

2 tablespoons toasted sesame seeds

2 tablespoons chopped fresh cilantro

1. Adjust oven rack to lower-middle position and heat oven to 450 degrees. Pat short ribs dry with paper towels and season with salt and pepper. Arrange ribs bone side down in single layer in large roasting pan and roast until meat begins to brown, about 45 minutes.

2. Discard any accumulated fat and juices in pan and continue to roast until meat is well browned, 15 to 20 minutes. Transfer ribs to bowl and tent loosely with aluminum foil; set aside. Stir pomegranate juice and water into pan, scraping up any browned bits; set aside.

3. Reduce oven temperature to 300 degrees. Heat oil in Dutch oven over medium heat until shimmering. Add onion, carrot, and ¼ teaspoon salt and cook until softened, about 5 minutes. Stir in ras el hanout and garlic and cook until fragrant, about 30 seconds.

4. Stir in pomegranate mixture from roasting pan and half of prunes and bring to simmer. Nestle short ribs bone side up into pot and bring to simmer.

Cover, transfer pot to oven, and cook until ribs are tender and fork slips easily in and out of meat, about 2½ hours.

5. Transfer short ribs to bowl, discard any loose bones, and tent loosely with aluminum foil. Strain braising liquid through fine-mesh strainer into fat separator; transfer solids to blender. Let braising liquid settle for 5 minutes, then pour defatted liquid into blender with solids and process until smooth, about 1 minute.

6. Transfer sauce to now-empty pot and stir in vinegar and remaining prunes. Return short ribs and any accumulated juices to pot, bring to gentle simmer over medium heat, and cook, spooning sauce over ribs occasionally, until heated through, about 5 minutes. Season with salt and pepper to taste. Transfer short ribs to serving platter, spoon 1 cup sauce over top, and sprinkle with sesame seeds and cilantro. Serve, passing remaining sauce separately.

roast pork loin with sweet potatoes and cilantro sauce

why this recipe works This modern take on a roast pork dinner features a tender spice-rubbed pork loin, caramelized sweet potatoes, and a lively sauce. And, as an added bonus, it's a one-pan dinner—no piles of dishes to wash on a Sunday night. To ensure that the lean, boneless roast would emerge from the oven juicy and well seasoned, we brined the pork and cooked it at a moderate 375 degrees. A mixture of ground coriander, cumin, salt, and pepper gave the pork's exterior color and flavor and complemented a lively cilantro sauce. To complete the meal, we tossed sweet potato chunks with some oil and a pinch of cayenne pepper and roasted them along with the pork. By the time the pork was done, the vegetables were tender but a little pale, so we set the pork aside to rest, turned up the heat, and returned the roasting pan to the oven to give them some caramelization. A ¼-inch-thick layer of fat on top of the roast is ideal; if your roast has a thicker fat cap, trim it back accordingly. If the pork is enhanced (injected with a salt solution), do not brine in step 1 but season with salt in step 2. This sauce uses two entire bunches of cilantro, including the stems.

serves 6
total time: 1 hour 45 minutes
(plus 1 hour 30 minutes for brining)

pork and potatoes
½ cup sugar

Salt and pepper

1 (3-pound) boneless center-cut pork loin roast, trimmed

1 teaspoon ground coriander

1 teaspoon ground cumin

3 pounds sweet potatoes, peeled, quartered lengthwise, and cut into 2-inch pieces crosswise

3 tablespoons vegetable oil

⅛ teaspoon cayenne pepper

cilantro sauce
2½ cups fresh cilantro leaves and stems, trimmed (2 bunches)

½ cup extra-virgin olive oil

4 teaspoons lime juice

2 garlic cloves, minced

½ teaspoon sugar

Salt and pepper

1. for the pork and potatoes Dissolve sugar and ½ cup salt in 2 quarts cold water in large container. Submerge pork in brine, cover, and refrigerate for 1½ to 2 hours.

2. Adjust oven rack to lower-middle position and heat oven to 375 degrees. Remove pork from brine and pat dry with paper towels. Season pork with coriander, cumin, and ⅛ teaspoon pepper, and tie with kitchen twine at 1½-inch intervals.

3. Toss sweet potatoes in bowl with oil and cayenne, season with ¼ teaspoon salt and ⅛ teaspoon pepper, and spread evenly into 16 by 12-inch roasting pan. Lay pork, fat side up, on top of potatoes. Roast until pork registers 140 to 145 degrees, 50 minutes to 1 hour 10 minutes, turning pork over halfway through roasting.

4. for the cilantro sauce Meanwhile, pulse all ingredients in food processor until cilantro is finely chopped, 10 to 15 pulses, scraping down bowl as needed. Season with salt and pepper to taste.

5. Remove pan from oven. Transfer pork to carving board, tent loosely with aluminum foil, and let rest for 15 minutes. While pork rests, increase oven temperature to 450 degrees and continue to roast potatoes until nicely browned, about 10 minutes. Remove twine from pork, slice into ¼-inch-thick slices, and serve with potatoes and cilantro sauce.

italian sausage with grapes and vinegar

why this recipe works Originating as a quick meal for vineyard laborers in Umbria, Italian Sausage with Grapes and Vinegar has humble roots but complex, refined flavors perfect for the modern dinner table. The meatiness of sausage, a Sunday supper staple, perfectly balances the sweet tartness of grapes and vinegar. We found that using a combination of dry and moist heat was key to cooking the sausages. We cooked them over medium heat, turning once so that they browned on two sides. For savory-sweet backbone, we removed some of the fat and added halved red grapes and thinly sliced onion. We then immediately added water and covered the skillet to gently steam the links. Once the sausages were cooked through, we removed them from the pan but continued to cook the grapes, raising the heat to cook off excess moisture so that they would soften and caramelize but still retain their shape. To loosen the vinegar sauce's syrupy consistency and balance its sweetness, we deglazed the pan with wine and added fresh oregano during the last minute of cooking. Sprinkling chopped mint over the finished dish added a touch of color and freshness. Serve with Creamy Parmesan Polenta (page 9).

serves 4 to 6
total time: 45 minutes

1 tablespoon vegetable oil

1½ pounds sweet Italian sausage

1 pound seedless red grapes, halved lengthwise (3 cups)

1 onion, halved and sliced thin

¼ cup water

¼ teaspoon pepper

⅛ teaspoon salt

¼ cup dry white wine

1 tablespoon chopped fresh oregano

2 teaspoons balsamic vinegar

2 tablespoons chopped fresh mint

1. Heat oil in 12-inch skillet over medium heat until shimmering. Arrange sausages in pan and cook, turning once, until browned on 2 sides, about 5 minutes. Tilt skillet and carefully remove excess fat with paper towel. Distribute grapes and onion over and around sausages. Add water and immediately cover. Cook, turning sausages once, until they register between 160 and 165 degrees and onions and grapes have softened, about 10 minutes.

2. Transfer sausages to paper towel–lined plate and tent with aluminum foil. Return skillet to medium-high heat and stir pepper and salt into grape-onion mixture. Spread grape-onion mixture in even layer in skillet and cook without stirring until browned, 3 to 5 minutes. Stir and continue to cook, stirring frequently, until mixture is well browned and grapes are soft but still retain their shape, 3 to 5 minutes longer. Reduce heat to medium, stir in wine and oregano, and cook, scraping up any browned bits, until wine is reduced by half, 30 to 60 seconds. Remove pan from heat and stir in vinegar.

3. Arrange sausages on serving platter and spoon grape-onion mixture over top. Sprinkle with mint and serve.

mexican lasagna with pork, corn, and pinto beans

why this recipe works Combining the vibrant flavors of Mexico with the cozy casserole-feel of an Italian lasagna, this dish is easy to assemble and will leave your dinner guests very satisfied. We chose pork for its natural sweetness that paired well with earthy corn tortillas, and sautéed it with onions, spices, and canned chipotle chile. Pinto beans and frozen corn contributed contrasting sweet flavor to the spicy filling. Brushing the tortillas with oil and heating them briefly prevented them from becoming soggy during baking. And to make cutting and serving the casserole easier, we quartered the tortillas that made up the top layer. Ground turkey can be substituted for the ground pork. If Colby Jack cheese is unavailable, substitute Monterey Jack cheese. Serve with salsa, diced avocado, sour cream, and/or scallions.

serves 6 to 8
total time: 1 hour 30 minutes

3 tablespoons vegetable oil

1 onion, chopped fine

2 red bell peppers, stemmed, seeded, and cut into ½-inch pieces

Salt and pepper

3 garlic cloves, minced

1 tablespoon minced canned chipotle chile in adobo sauce

2 teaspoons chili powder

1½ pounds ground pork

2 tablespoons all-purpose flour

2 cups chicken broth

1 (15-ounce) can pinto beans, rinsed

1 (14.5-ounce) can diced tomatoes, drained

2 cups frozen corn, thawed

6 tablespoons minced fresh cilantro

2 tablespoons lime juice

18 (6-inch) corn tortillas

12 ounces Colby Jack cheese, shredded (3 cups)

1. Heat 1 tablespoon oil in Dutch oven over medium heat until shimmering. Add onion, bell peppers, and ½ teaspoon salt and cook until softened, 8 to 10 minutes. Stir in garlic, chipotle, chili powder, and ¼ teaspoon pepper and cook until fragrant, about 30 seconds. Stir in pork and cook, breaking up meat with wooden spoon, until no longer pink, 5 to 8 minutes.

2. Stir in flour and cook for 1 minute. Gradually stir in broth and bring to simmer. Stir in beans, tomatoes, and corn and simmer until mixture is slightly thickened and flavors have blended, about 10 minutes. Off heat, stir in ¼ cup cilantro and lime juice. Season with salt and pepper to taste.

3. Meanwhile, adjust oven racks to upper-middle and lower-middle positions and heat oven to 450 degrees. Brush both sides of tortillas with remaining 2 tablespoons oil. Spread tortillas over 2 baking sheets (some overlapping is fine) and bake until soft and pliable, 2 to 4 minutes.

4. Spread one-third of pork mixture over bottom of 13 by 9-inch baking dish. Top with 6 warmed tortillas, overlapping as needed, and sprinkle with 1 cup Colby Jack. Repeat with half of remaining pork mixture, 6 tortillas, and 1 cup cheese. Top with remaining pork filling. Cut remaining 6 tortillas into quarters and scatter over top. Sprinkle with remaining 1 cup cheese.

5. Bake on upper rack until filling is bubbling and topping is golden brown, about 15 minutes. Let casserole cool for 10 minutes. Sprinkle with remaining 2 tablespoons cilantro and serve.

to make ahead
Assembled, unbaked casserole can be refrigerated for up to 24 hours. To reheat, cover dish tightly with greased aluminum foil and bake in 450-degree oven until hot throughout, about 30 minutes. Uncover and continue to bake until topping is golden brown, about 10 minutes. Sprinkle with cilantro before serving.

chicken, spinach, and artichoke pot pie

why this recipe works Few dishes exemplify Sunday supper as well as chicken pot pie, with its creamy filling and flaky, golden crust. Instead of the usual peas and carrots, we opted for a modern spin on this quintessential favorite, incorporating the classic combination of spinach and artichokes. Mixing thawed frozen spinach with jarred artichokes and Boursin cheese gave us a flavorful, creamy base. Shredded carrots and capers upped the ante, introducing contrasting texture and a briny zing. To create a lush sauce, we stirred in broth, cream, and, for instant thickening, Wondra flour. We then sliced our chicken thin, tossed it with lemon zest, and placed the slices atop the vegetables, a surefire way to keep the meat from drying out. A buttery sheet of puff pastry made the perfect top to our updated pot pie. We prefer jarred artichoke hearts, labeled "baby" or "cocktail," that are 1½ inches or shorter in length. Larger artichoke hearts tend to have fibrous leaves. If you are using larger hearts, trim the top ¼ to ½ inch from the leaves. Do not use marinated or oil-packed artichoke hearts. To thaw frozen puff pastry, let it sit either in the refrigerator for 24 hours or on the counter for 30 minutes to 1 hour. You can substitute an equal amount of all-purpose flour for the Wondra flour, if necessary; however, the sauce will have a pasty, slightly gritty texture.

serves 4
total time: 1 hour

1¼ pounds frozen spinach, thawed and squeezed dry

1 (5.2-ounce) package Boursin Garlic & Fine Herbs cheese

1 cup jarred whole artichoke hearts packed in water, halved

2 carrots, peeled and shredded

¾ cup chicken broth

½ cup heavy cream

¼ cup capers, rinsed

1 tablespoon Wondra flour

12 ounces boneless, skinless chicken breasts, trimmed and sliced thin

1 teaspoon grated lemon zest

Salt and pepper

1 (9½ by 9-inch) sheet puff pastry, thawed

1 large egg, lightly beaten with 2 tablespoons water

1. Adjust oven rack to middle position and heat oven to 425 degrees. Spray 8-inch square baking dish with vegetable oil spray. Stir spinach, Boursin, artichokes, carrots, broth, cream, capers, and Wondra together in bowl, then transfer to prepared dish.

2. Toss chicken with lemon zest in separate bowl, season with salt and pepper, and spread in even layer over spinach mixture. Cut puff pastry into 8-inch square and place over top of chicken. Cut four 2-inch slits in center of dough, then brush dough with egg mixture.

3. Bake until crust is golden brown and filling is bubbling, 30 to 35 minutes, rotating pan halfway through baking.

4. Remove pot pie from oven and let cool for 10 minutes before serving.

to make ahead
Assembled pot pie can be refrigerated for up to 24 hours; bake as directed.

pan-roasted chicken and potatoes

why this recipe works For Sunday dinner–worthy chicken and potatoes you can make almost at the last minute, this recipe fits the bill. Here we made the most of the handy pan-roasting technique beloved by restaurant chefs; we browned bone-in chicken breasts on the stovetop and then transferred the skillet to a very hot oven to let the chicken cook through in a flash. Since we wanted to add potatoes to the mix, we had to parcook them to ensure they'd be done at the same time as the chicken. Enter the microwave, which softened them just enough so we were able to add them to the skillet with the chicken after it was browned. To pull the dish together and make it feel special, we made a quick sauce to drizzle over the chicken and potatoes before serving.

serves 4
total time: 45 minutes

1½ pounds small red potatoes, unpeeled, quartered

¼ cup olive oil

Salt and pepper

4 (12-ounce) bone-in split chicken breasts, trimmed

2 tablespoons balsamic vinegar

1 garlic clove, minced

½ teaspoon minced fresh thyme

¼ teaspoon red pepper flakes

1. Adjust oven rack to lowest position and heat oven to 450 degrees. Combine potatoes, 1 tablespoon oil, ½ teaspoon salt, and ¼ teaspoon pepper in bowl. Microwave, covered, until potatoes begin to soften, 4 to 7 minutes.

2. Meanwhile, pat chicken dry with paper towels and season with salt and pepper. Heat 1 tablespoon oil in 12-inch ovensafe nonstick skillet over medium-high heat until just smoking. Cook chicken until well browned, about 5 minutes per side. Transfer chicken to plate. Add potatoes to skillet and cook until beginning to brown, about 3 minutes. Arrange chicken, skin side up, on top of potatoes. Transfer skillet to oven and roast until chicken registers 160 degrees and potatoes are tender, 12 to 15 minutes.

3. Whisk vinegar, garlic, thyme, pepper flakes, and remaining 2 tablespoons oil together in bowl. Season with salt and pepper to taste. Drizzle vinegar mixture over chicken and potatoes. Serve.

chicken marbella

why this recipe works More than 25 years ago, Chicken Marbella was the signature dish of the famous Silver Palate gourmet shop in Manhattan and the cookbook it later inspired. And it's no wonder this chicken dish caught fire—marinated in a pungent mix of capers, olives, and prunes, it boasted big and, for the era, unusual flavors. That said, we felt it was time for some modern improvements. Instead of a marinade, we made a paste. After browning the chicken, we caramelized a portion of the paste in the skillet to bloom its complex flavors. After deglazing the skillet with wine and pouring the sauce around the chicken, we transferred everything to the oven. Using a skillet with low, flared sides allowed more steam to escape, resulting in a concentrated sauce. Once the chicken was half-cooked and the skin well rendered and browned, we added the remainder of the paste to coat the chicken. Last-minute additions of butter, vinegar, and parsley pulled everything together. Serve with Classic Couscous (page 9).

serves 4 to 6
total time: 1 hour 15 minutes

paste
⅓ cup pitted green olives, rinsed

⅓ cup pitted prunes

3 tablespoons extra-virgin olive oil

4 garlic cloves, peeled

2 tablespoons capers, rinsed

3 anchovy fillets, rinsed

½ teaspoon dried oregano

½ teaspoon pepper

¼ teaspoon kosher salt

Pinch red pepper flakes

chicken
2½–3 pounds bone-in, skin-on split chicken breasts and/or leg quarters, trimmed

Kosher salt and pepper

2 teaspoons olive oil

¾ cup chicken broth

⅓ cup white wine

⅓ cup pitted green olives, rinsed and halved

1 tablespoon capers, rinsed

2 bay leaves

⅓ cup pitted prunes, chopped coarse

1 tablespoon unsalted butter

1 teaspoon red wine vinegar

2 tablespoons minced fresh parsley

1. Adjust oven rack to middle position and heat oven to 400 degrees.

2. **for the paste** Pulse all ingredients in food processor until finely chopped, about 10 pulses. Scrape down bowl and continue to process until mostly smooth, 1 to 2 minutes. Transfer to bowl. (Paste can be refrigerated for up to 24 hours.)

3. **for the chicken** Pat chicken dry with paper towels. Sprinkle chicken pieces with 1½ teaspoons salt and season with pepper.

4. Heat oil in 12-inch skillet over medium-high heat until just smoking. Add chicken, skin side down, and cook without moving it until well browned, 5 to 8 minutes. Transfer chicken to large plate. Drain off all but 1 teaspoon fat from skillet and return to medium-low heat.

5. Add ⅓ cup paste to skillet and cook, stirring constantly, until fragrant and fond forms on pan bottom, 1 to 2 minutes. Stir in broth, wine, olives, capers, and bay leaves, scraping up any browned bits. Return chicken to pan, skin side up (skin should be above surface of liquid), and roast, uncovered, for 15 minutes.

6. Remove skillet from oven and use back of spoon to spread remaining paste over chicken pieces; sprinkle prunes around chicken. Continue to roast until paste begins to brown, breasts register 160 degrees, and leg quarters register 175 degrees, 7 to 12 minutes longer.

7. Transfer chicken to serving platter and tent with aluminum foil. Remove bay leaves from sauce and whisk in butter, vinegar, and 1 tablespoon parsley; season with salt and pepper to taste. Pour sauce around chicken, sprinkle with remaining 1 tablespoon parsley, and serve.

white chicken chili

why this recipe works A big pot of white chicken chili with all the fixings is a great casual way to bring people together around the dinner table. To make things easier, we put our food processor to work: First, we used it to chop the chiles. Later, we also used it to thicken the base of the chili, pureeing sautéed aromatics, a portion of beans, and broth. To ensure the chicken breasts stayed moist after we browned them, we poached the breasts in the chili itself. For a spicier chili, add the minced jalapeño ribs and seeds in step 6. If you can't find Anaheim chiles, add an additional jalapeño and poblano. Anaheim chiles are sometimes sold as New Mexican chiles. Serve with sour cream, tortilla chips, and lime wedges.

serves 6 to 8
total time: 1 hour 45 minutes

3 pounds bone-in split chicken breasts, trimmed

Salt and pepper

1 tablespoon vegetable oil, plus extra as needed

3 jalapeño chiles, stemmed

3 poblano chiles, stemmed, seeded, and cut into large pieces

3 Anaheim chiles, stemmed, seeded, and cut into large pieces

2 onions, cut into large pieces

6 garlic cloves, minced

1 tablespoon ground cumin

1½ teaspoons ground coriander

2 (15.5-ounce) cans cannellini beans, rinsed

3 cups chicken broth

¼ cup minced fresh cilantro

4 scallions, sliced thin

3 tablespoons lime juice (2 limes)

1. Season breasts with 1 teaspoon salt and ¼ teaspoon pepper. Heat oil in Dutch oven over medium-high heat until just smoking. Add breasts, skin side down, and cook until golden brown, about 4 minutes.

Using tongs, flip breasts and lightly brown second side, about 2 minutes; transfer to plate. When cool enough to handle, remove skin.

2. Discard ribs and seeds from 2 jalapeños, then mince and set aside. Pulse half of poblanos, half of Anaheims, and half of onions in food processor until consistency of chunky salsa, 10 to 12 pulses, scraping down sides of bowl as needed. Transfer mixture to medium bowl. Repeat with remaining poblanos, Anaheims, and onions. Add mixture to bowl with first batch (do not clean processor bowl).

3. Pour off all but 1 tablespoon fat from pot (add extra oil as needed) and set heat to medium. Add garlic, cumin, coriander, minced jalapeños, chile mixture, and ¼ teaspoon salt. Cover and cook, stirring occasionally, until vegetables have softened, about 10 minutes. Remove pot from heat.

4. Transfer 1 cup cooked vegetable mixture to now-empty processor. Add 1 cup beans and 1 cup broth and process until smooth, about 20 seconds. Add vegetable-bean mixture, remaining 2 cups broth, and breasts to pot and bring to boil

over medium-high heat. Reduce heat to medium-low and simmer, covered, stirring occasionally, until chicken registers 160 degrees, 15 to 20 minutes.

5. Transfer breasts to large plate. Stir in remaining beans and continue to simmer, uncovered, until beans are heated through and chili has thickened slightly, about 10 minutes.

6. Mince remaining 1 jalapeño, mincing and reserving ribs and seeds if desired, anΔd set aside. When cool enough to handle, use 2 forks to shred breasts into bite-size pieces, discarding bones. Stir cilantro, scallions, lime juice, chicken, and remaining minced jalapeño and, if using, ribs and seeds into chili and return to simmer. Season with salt and pepper to taste, and serve.

to make ahead
Chili, prepared through step 5, can be refrigerated for up to 3 days. To reheat, bring chili, covered, to gentle simmer, stirring often, and adjust consistency with hot water as needed; continue with step 6.

baked ziti with broccoli rabe and sausage

why this recipe works Broccoli rabe with sausage and pasta is a popular combination in Italy, and we wanted to transform these classic flavors into an approachable, easy-to-make Sunday pasta bake. Although orecchiette is the traditional pasta choice for these flavors, we turned to ziti, which stood up to baking better and provided plenty of surface area to which sauce could cling. A quick blanch and shock helped quell the bitterness of the broccoli rabe and prevented it from turning a dark, unappealing color. Wine, heavy cream, gooey fontina, and Parmesan made for a rich, creamy sauce. Broccoli cut into 1½-inch pieces can be substituted for the broccoli rabe.

serves 8
total time: 1 hour 45 minutes

1 pound broccoli rabe, trimmed and cut into 1½-inch pieces

Salt and pepper

1 pound ziti

2 tablespoons extra-virgin olive oil

1 pound sweet or hot Italian sausage, casings removed

1 onion, chopped fine

8 garlic cloves, sliced thin

2 anchovy fillets, rinsed and minced

2 teaspoons lemon zest plus 2 tablespoons juice

1 teaspoon red pepper flakes

⅓ cup all-purpose flour

2 cups chicken broth

1½ cups heavy cream

½ cup dry white wine

8 ounces fontina cheese, shredded (2 cups)

2 ounces Parmesan cheese, grated (1 cup)

1. Bring 4 quarts water to boil in large pot. Fill large bowl with ice water. Add broccoli rabe and 1 tablespoon salt to boiling water and cook until crisp-tender, about 1 minute. Using slotted spoon, transfer broccoli rabe to ice water and let cool, about 2 minutes; drain and pat dry.

2. Return pot of water to boil, add pasta, and cook, stirring often, until nearly al dente. Drain pasta in colander and toss with 1 tablespoon oil; leave in colander and set aside.

3. Adjust oven rack to middle position and heat oven to 400 degrees. Dry now-empty pot and heat remaining 1 tablespoon oil over medium heat until shimmering. Add sausage and cook, breaking up meat with wooden spoon, until no longer pink, about 3 minutes. Using slotted spoon, transfer sausage to paper towel-lined plate.

4. Pour off all but 1 tablespoon fat from pot, add onion and ½ teaspoon salt, and cook until softened and lightly browned, 5 to 7 minutes. Stir in garlic, anchovies, lemon zest, and pepper flakes and cook until fragrant, about 30 seconds. Add flour and cook, stirring constantly, until golden, about 1 minute. Slowly whisk in broth, cream, and wine, scraping up any browned bits and smoothing out any lumps. Bring to simmer and cook until thickened slightly, about 2 minutes.

5. Off heat, gradually whisk 1 cup fontina and ½ cup Parmesan into sauce until cheese is melted and sauce is smooth. Stir in lemon juice, broccoli rabe, pasta, and sausage, breaking up any clumps. Season with salt and pepper to taste. Transfer pasta mixture to 13 by 9-inch baking dish and sprinkle with remaining 1 cup fontina and remaining ½ cup Parmesan.

6. Place baking dish on aluminum foil-lined rimmed baking sheet and bake until golden and bubbling around edges, 25 to 35 minutes. Let casserole cool 20 minutes before serving.

to make ahead
Casserole, prepared through step 5, can be refrigerated for up to 24 hours. To bake, cover with greased aluminum foil and bake on foil-lined sheet in 400-degree oven until hot throughout, about 35 minutes; remove foil and continue to bake until cheese is golden, 25 to 35 minutes.

mediterranean-style shrimp and orzo casserole

why this recipe works This unusual casserole, which pairs succulent shrimp with saffron, garlic, and lemon-infused orzo, is a test kitchen favorite. Its vibrant colors and flavors and tangy topping of feta cheese make it especially appealing. Plus, there isn't a lot of last-minute work, which is unusual for a dish that features shrimp. We embedded the raw shrimp in the pilaf to shield them from the oven's direct heat, preventing them from drying out and toughening. A relatively hot oven, 400 degrees, cooked the shrimp evenly in about 20 minutes—just enough time for the flavors of the pilaf and the shrimp to marry. Though we normally shy away from combining cheese and fish, the salty, briny bite of feta cheese perfectly complemented the sweetness of the shrimp and fruitiness of the tomatoes and bell pepper. We found the cheese tasted better if baked on top of the casserole, where it browned and intensified in flavor. Make sure that the orzo is al dente, or slightly firm to the bite; otherwise, it may overcook in the oven. If you don't have saffron, ¼ teaspoon ground turmeric can add a similar orange-ish color (but not the flavor). Be careful not to add too much turmeric because its flavor is bitter when used in excessive amounts.

serves 6 to 8
total time: 1 hour 15 minutes

1½ pounds large shrimp
(26 to 30 per pound), peeled
and deveined

Salt and pepper

3 tablespoons extra-virgin olive oil

1 red onion, chopped fine

1 large red bell pepper, stemmed,
seeded, and chopped fine

6 garlic cloves, minced

1 pound orzo

1 pinch saffron

1 tablespoon grated lemon zest
plus 2 tablespoons juice

4 cups chicken broth

1 cup water

1 (28-ounce) can diced
tomatoes, drained

4 teaspoons chopped
fresh oregano

12 ounces feta cheese,
crumbled (3 cups)

4 scallions, sliced thin

1. Adjust oven rack to middle position and heat oven to 400 degrees. Season shrimp with salt and pepper; set aside.

2. Heat oil in 12-inch skillet over medium heat until shimmering. Add onion, pepper, and ½ teaspoon salt; cook, stirring occasionally, until vegetables are softened and beginning to brown, about 6 minutes. Add garlic and cook until fragrant, 30 seconds. Add orzo, saffron, and lemon zest; cook, stirring frequently, until orzo is coated with oil and lightly browned, about 4 minutes. Stir in broth and water; cook, stirring occasionally, until grains of orzo are mostly tender yet still slightly firm at center, about 12 minutes. Stir in tomatoes, oregano, and seasoned shrimp.

3. Pour into 13 by 9-inch baking dish. Sprinkle feta over the top and bake until shrimp are cooked through and feta is lightly browned, about 20 minutes. Sprinkle with lemon juice and garnish with scallions. Serve.

cod in saffron broth with chorizo and potatoes

why this recipe works Rustic yet refined, this Spanish take on cod and potatoes will impress your dinner guests and transport the flavors and aromas
of Spain to your kitchen. Cod's versatile, mild flavor serves as the perfect
backdrop for bright, pungent saffron. We created a flavorful broth, infusing
saffron into aromatics, white wine, and clam juice, in which we braised the
fish, then ladled the broth over the fillets for serving. For additional flavor,
we added spicy Spanish-style chorizo to the pan with the onions and sautéed the sausage until browned, lending a subtle heat and smoky flavor to
the broth. Waxy red potatoes, sliced into coins to mirror the slices of chorizo,
brought in just the right creaminess to soak up the flavorful broth. A hit of
lemon added brightness to the broth at the end of cooking, and a sprinkle
of parsley and drizzle of olive oil on the flaky fish, swimming in the fragrant
saffron liquid, brought it all together. Haddock and hake are good substitutes for the cod. Use small red potatoes measuring 1 to 2 inches in diameter.
Serve with crusty bread to dip into the broth.

serves 4
total time: 1 hour

1 tablespoon extra-virgin olive oil,
plus extra for serving

1 onion, chopped fine

3 ounces Spanish-style chorizo
sausage, sliced ¼ inch thick

4 garlic cloves, minced

¼ teaspoon saffron threads,
crumbled

1 (8-ounce) bottle clam juice

¾ cup water

½ cup dry white wine

4 ounces small red potatoes,
unpeeled, sliced ¼ inch thick

1 bay leaf

4 (4- to 6-ounce) skinless cod
fillets, 1 to 1½ inches thick

Salt and pepper

1 teaspoon lemon juice

2 tablespoons minced
fresh parsley

1. Heat oil in 12-inch skillet over
medium heat until shimmering.
Add onion and chorizo and cook
until onion is softened and lightly
browned, 5 to 7 minutes. Stir in
garlic and saffron and cook until
fragrant, about 30 seconds. Stir in
clam juice, water, wine, potatoes,
and bay leaf and bring to simmer.
Reduce heat to medium-low, cover,
and cook until potatoes are almost
tender, about 10 minutes.

2. Pat cod dry with paper towels
and season with salt and pepper.
Nestle cod skinned side down
into skillet and spoon some broth
over top. Bring to simmer, cover,
and cook until potatoes are fully
tender and cod flakes apart when
gently prodded with paring knife
and registers 140 degrees, 10 to
12 minutes.

3. Carefully transfer cod to
individual shallow bowls. Using
slotted spoon, divide potatoes
and chorizo evenly among bowls.
Discard bay leaf. Stir lemon juice
into broth and season with salt
and pepper to taste. Spoon broth
over cod, sprinkle with parsley, and
drizzle with extra oil. Serve.

prosciutto-wrapped cod
with lemon-caper butter

why this recipe works For a simple yet elegant cod dish, we found prosciutto to be just the ticket, as it added a strong, meaty-salty flavor to the mild fish. We wrapped the cod fillets in two thin sheets of prosciutto before arranging them in a skillet. To get good coloring and crispness, we first cooked the wrapped cod on the stovetop before transferring the skillet to the oven to cook the fish through. The prosciutto infused the fish with its salty pork flavor and provided a layer of insulation to the fish during cooking, keeping it moist. A warm butter sauce, enlivened by capers, parsley, lemon zest and juice, and garlic, brought the dish together. Do not season the cod with salt before wrapping with the prosciutto; the briny capers and salty prosciutto add plenty of salt to the dish. Halibut and haddock are good substitutes for the cod. You will need a 12-inch ovensafe nonstick skillet for this recipe.

serves 4
total time: 30 minutes

4 (6- to 8-ounce) skinless cod fillets, 1 to 1½ inches thick

Pepper

8 thin slices prosciutto (3 ounces)

1 tablespoon vegetable oil

4 tablespoons unsalted butter, softened

2 tablespoons capers, rinsed and minced

2 tablespoons minced fresh parsley

1 teaspoon grated lemon zest plus 1 tablespoon juice

1 garlic clove, minced

1. Adjust oven rack to upper-middle position and heat oven to 450 degrees. Pat cod dry with paper towels and season with pepper. Wrap each fillet widthwise with 2 overlapping pieces of prosciutto.

2. Heat oil in 12-inch ovensafe nonstick skillet over medium-high heat until just smoking. Brown prosciutto-wrapped cod lightly on both sides, 2 to 4 minutes. Transfer skillet to oven and bake until cod flakes apart when gently prodded with paring knife and registers 140 degrees, about 8 minutes.

3. Using potholders (skillet handle will be hot), remove skillet from oven. Transfer fish to serving platter. Add butter, capers, parsley, lemon zest and juice, and garlic to now-empty skillet. Cook over medium heat, swirling pan, until butter has melted. Spoon butter sauce over fish and serve.

sesame-crusted salmon with lemon and ginger

why this recipe works This elegant take on pan-seared salmon delivers flavor in spades, between the hearty coating of toasted sesame seeds and a fragrant tahini-ginger paste beneath the coating on both sides. To keep the fish moist and well seasoned, we first briefly soaked the fillets in a brine. Then, to liven the sesame flavor, we also submerged the seeds in some of the brine, drained them, and then toasted them whole in a skillet. As an added bonus, because the starch in the seeds absorbed water from the brine and then gelatinized during toasting, the seeds were crispier. For even more of a sesame punch, we made a paste with tahini, lemon juice, scallion whites, lemon zest, fresh ginger, and cayenne and smeared the flavor-packed mixture onto the fillets before pressing on the sesame seeds. A quick sauté browned the sesame seed coating before the fillets finished cooking in the oven. For even cooking, purchase fillets that are about the same size and shape. If any of your fillets have a thin belly flap, fold it over to create a more even thickness.

serves 4
total time: 45 minutes

Salt

¾ cup sesame seeds

4 (6- to 8-ounce) skinless salmon fillets

2 scallions, white parts minced, green parts sliced thin

1 tablespoon grated lemon zest plus 2 teaspoons juice

4 teaspoons tahini

2 teaspoons grated fresh ginger

⅛ teaspoon cayenne pepper

1 teaspoon vegetable oil

1. Adjust oven rack to middle position and heat oven to 325 degrees. Dissolve 5 tablespoons salt in 2 quarts water. Transfer 1 cup brine to bowl, stir in sesame seeds, and let stand at room temperature for 5 minutes. Submerge fillets in remaining brine and let stand at room temperature for 15 minutes.

2. Drain seeds and place in 12-inch nonstick skillet. Cook seeds over medium heat, stirring constantly, until golden brown, 2 to 4 minutes. Transfer seeds to pie plate and wipe out skillet with paper towels. Remove fillets from brine and pat dry.

3. Place scallion whites and lemon zest on cutting board and chop until whites and zest are finely minced and well combined. Transfer scallion-zest mixture to bowl and stir in lemon juice, tahini, ginger, cayenne, and ⅛ teaspoon salt.

4. Evenly distribute half of paste over bottoms (skinned sides) of fillets. Press coated sides of fillets in seeds and transfer, seed side down, to plate. Evenly distribute remaining paste over tops of fillets and coat with remaining seeds.

5. Heat oil in now-empty skillet over medium heat until shimmering. Place fillets in skillet, skinned side up, and reduce heat to medium-low. Cook until seeds begin to brown, 1 to 2 minutes. Remove skillet from heat and, using 2 spatulas, carefully flip fillets over. Transfer skillet to oven. Bake until center of fish is translucent when checked with tip of paring knife and registers 125 degrees, 10 to 15 minutes. Transfer to serving platter and let rest for 5 minutes. Sprinkle with scallion greens and serve.

variations
sesame-crusted salmon with lime and coriander
Substitute 4 teaspoons lime zest for lemon zest, lime juice for lemon juice, and ¼ teaspoon ground coriander for cayenne.

sesame-crusted salmon with orange and chili powder
Substitute orange zest for lemon zest, orange juice for lemon juice, and ¼ teaspoon chili powder for cayenne.

southwestern salmon cakes

why this recipe works With their crisp, golden-brown crusts surrounding tender, flaky interiors, salmon cakes make for a great-tasting, elegant, and deceptively simple Sunday meal. We found it was key to start with fresh, not canned, salmon. Assertive Southwestern-inspired flavors—chopped fresh cilantro, lime zest and juice, and spicy canned green chiles—were bold enough to stand up to the salmon's distinctive taste. To save time, we whipped up a mayonnaise-based dipping sauce and used a portion of it to flavor the salmon cakes. Dredging the cakes in panko bread crumbs gave them a crunchy exterior once they were fried. For the best texture, it's important to take the time to cut the salmon into even ¼-inch pieces. Serve with a simple green salad (page 6) and Quinoa Pilaf with Herbs and Lemon (page 10).

serves 4
total time: 30 minutes

½ cup mayonnaise

¼ cup sour cream

3 tablespoons chopped fresh cilantro

1 teaspoon grated lime zest plus 4 teaspoons juice, plus lime wedges for serving

Salt and pepper

1½ cups panko bread crumbs

1 pound skinless salmon fillets, chopped into ¼-inch pieces

1 (4-ounce) can whole green chiles, drained and chopped fine

2 scallions, sliced thin

½ cup vegetable oil

1. Whisk mayonnaise, sour cream, cilantro, and lime zest and juice together in bowl. Season with salt and pepper to taste.

2. Spread ¾ cup panko in shallow dish. Combine salmon, chiles, scallions, 3 tablespoons mayonnaise mixture, ½ teaspoon salt, ¼ teaspoon pepper, and remaining ¾ cup panko in bowl. Shape salmon mixture into four 3½-inch cakes. Coat cakes with panko, pressing gently to adhere.

3. Heat oil in 12-inch nonstick skillet over medium-high heat until just smoking. Add cakes and cook until golden brown and cooked through, about 3 minutes per side. Serve with lime wedges and remaining mayonnaise mixture.

mussels marinara with spaghetti

why this recipe works There is something festive about sharing mussels marinara with friends or family. But nailing perfectly cooked mussels and al dente pasta simultaneously can be tricky. Our modern and simple solution was to cook everything together in the same pot and stagger the ingredients, which simplified the timing and ensured that all of the mussel flavor stayed in the pot. To start, we built a tomato sauce with just the right texture by chopping canned whole tomatoes, which we simmered with some basic aromatics. We also added an anchovy and some bottled clam juice to reinforce the salty ocean flavor of the mussels. We cooked the pasta right in the sauce, added the mussels, and continued to cook the dish until they opened. More olive oil and some parsley finished off this perfectly cooked one-dish meal. When adding the spaghetti in step 3, stir gently to avoid breaking the noodles until they soften enough to be stirred more easily. If necessary, add hot water, 1 tablespoon at a time, to adjust the consistency of the sauce before serving. If desired, drizzle with additional extra-virgin olive oil before serving. Serve with crusty bread and a simple green salad (page 6).

serves 4 to 6
total time: 45 minutes

2 (28-ounce) cans whole peeled tomatoes

3 tablespoons extra-virgin olive oil

1 onion, chopped fine

6 garlic cloves, minced

1 anchovy fillet, rinsed and minced

½ teaspoon red pepper flakes

2 cups water

1 (8-ounce) bottle clam juice

1 pound spaghetti

2 pounds mussels, scrubbed and debearded

¼ cup minced fresh parsley

Salt and pepper

1. Pulse tomatoes and their juice, 1 can at a time, in food processor until coarsely chopped and no large pieces remain, 6 to 8 pulses; transfer to bowl.

2. Heat 2 tablespoons oil in Dutch oven over medium-high heat until shimmering. Add onion and cook until softened, about 3 minutes. Stir in garlic, anchovy, and pepper flakes and cook until fragrant, about 30 seconds. Stir in processed tomatoes and simmer gently until tomatoes no longer taste raw, about 10 minutes.

3. Stir in water, clam juice, and pasta. Cover, increase heat to medium-high, and cook at vigorous simmer, stirring often, until pasta is nearly tender, about 12 minutes. Stir in mussels, cover, and continue to simmer vigorously until pasta is tender and mussels have opened, about 2 minutes.

4. Uncover, reduce heat to low, and stir in parsley and remaining 1 tablespoon oil. Cook, tossing pasta gently, until well coated with sauce, about 1 minute. Season with salt and pepper to taste, and serve.

seared scallops with squash puree and sage butter

why this recipe works Elegant yet casual, these restaurant-worthy caramelized scallops served alongside a comforting, homey squash puree will make your Sunday supper guests feel spoiled. To keep your time in the kitchen to a minimum, you can make the squash puree in advance and simply cook the scallops and make the sauce just before serving. To make the squash puree and ensure that it would be silky smooth, we simply microwaved the squash and pureed it in a food processor with a little half-and-half, butter, and seasoning. We pan-seared the scallops and then made a quick shallot-sage browned butter sauce in the same pan. We recommend buying "dry" scallops, which don't have chemical additives and taste better than "wet." Dry scallops will look ivory or pinkish; wet scallops are bright white.

serves 4
total time: 45 minutes

2 pounds butternut squash, peeled, seeded, and cut into 1-inch pieces (5 cups)

4 tablespoons unsalted butter

1 tablespoon half-and-half

Salt and pepper

⅛ teaspoon cayenne pepper

1½ pounds large sea scallops, tendons removed

2 tablespoons vegetable oil

1 shallot, minced

2 teaspoons minced fresh sage plus 8 leaves

1 tablespoon lemon juice

1. Place squash in bowl, cover, and microwave until tender, 8 to 12 minutes, stirring halfway through microwaving. Drain, then transfer to food processor. Add 1 tablespoon butter, half-and-half, ½ teaspoon salt, and cayenne and process until smooth, about 20 seconds. Return to bowl and cover to keep warm.

2. Pat scallops dry with paper towels and season with salt and pepper. Heat 1 tablespoon oil in 12-inch nonstick skillet over high heat until just smoking. Add half of scallops and cook, without moving, until well browned, 1½ to 2 minutes. Flip scallops and cook until sides are firm and centers are opaque, 30 to 90 seconds. Transfer to plate and tent with aluminum foil. Wipe out skillet with paper towels and repeat with remaining 1 tablespoon oil and remaining scallops. Transfer to plate with first batch.

3. Melt remaining 3 tablespoons butter in now-empty skillet over medium heat. Continue to cook, swirling skillet constantly, until butter is starting to brown and has nutty aroma, 1 to 2 minutes. Add shallot, minced sage, and sage leaves and cook until fragrant, about 1 minute. Off heat, stir in lemon juice and season with salt and pepper to taste. Pour sauce over scallops and serve with butternut squash.

the lazy sunday cook

ziti with fennel and italian sausage

why this recipe works There is something magical about this recipe, which coaxes the ultimate flavor out of just a few humble supermarket ingredients, turning them into a rich-tasting and well-balanced pasta dish that will have your family reaching for seconds. After browning the sausage, we sautéed a hefty amount of sliced onions, along with sliced fennel, which added texture and flavor to the dish. And while it may seem like a mistake to add an entire can of tomato paste and no other tomato product to make the sauce, the concentrated, bold flavor of the tomato paste intensified during cooking and added rich notes to the dish. To pull everything together, we added 2 cups of boiling water, simmering the mixture until thick. Sharp Pecorino cheese, added to the sausage-onion mixture, enriched the sauce by giving it a salty bite. Chopped fennel fronds added pleasant anise notes upon serving.

serves 4 to 6
total time: 30 minutes

1 pound sweet or hot Italian sausage, casings removed

2 onions, halved and sliced thin

1 fennel bulb, fronds chopped, stalks discarded, bulb halved, cored, and sliced into ½-inch pieces

1 (6-ounce) can tomato paste

1 pound ziti

Salt and pepper

1 ounce Pecorino Romano cheese, grated (½ cup), plus extra for serving

1. Bring 4 quarts water to boil in large pot for pasta. Cook sausage in Dutch oven over medium-high heat, breaking up meat with wooden spoon, until no longer pink, about 4 minutes. Stir in onions and fennel, cover, and cook until softened, about 5 minutes. Uncover, reduce heat to medium, and continue to cook until vegetables are golden, 10 to 12 minutes.

2. Add tomato paste and cook until darkened, about 3 minutes. Stir in 2 cups boiling pasta water and simmer until thickened, about 5 minutes.

3. Meanwhile, add pasta and 1 tablespoon salt to boiling water and cook, stirring often, until al dente. Reserve 1½ cups cooking water, then drain pasta and return it to pot. Add sausage mixture, Pecorino, and 1 cup reserved cooking water and toss to combine. Season with salt and pepper to taste and add remaining cooking water as needed to adjust consistency. Sprinkle individual portions with fennel fronds and extra Pecorino before serving.

unstuffed shells with butternut squash and leeks

why this recipe works When we want to spend as little time in the kitchen as possible on a Sunday evening, we look to innovative one-pot meals to keep work and dishes to a minimum. For our cheesy jumbo unstuffed shells, we kept everything in one skillet, making for an impressive presentation and easy cleanup. Instead of the expected tomato-based sauce often paired with stuffed shells, we opted for vibrant, creamy butternut squash and sweet leeks. Cooking them briefly before adding the pasta and liquid deepened their flavors and ensured that the pasta and squash would finish cooking at the same time. Instead of stuffing the shells, which we found fussy and time-consuming, we sprinkled a little Parmesan cheese and dolloped a rich lemon-ricotta mixture over everything before sliding the skillet in the oven to brown and melt the cheesy toppings. A sprinkle of basil added a fresh finishing touch and pop of color. You can substitute large or medium shells, ziti, farfalle, campanelle, or orecchiette for the jumbo shells. The skillet will be very full when you add the shells in step 3 (stir gently to start), but will become more manageable as the liquid evaporates and the shells become more malleable. You will need a 12-inch ovensafe nonstick skillet for this recipe.

serves 4 to 6
total time: 1 hour 15 minutes

8 ounces (1 cup) whole-milk ricotta cheese

2 ounces Parmesan cheese, grated (1 cup)

1 teaspoon grated lemon zest

Salt and pepper

1 tablespoon extra-virgin olive oil

1½ pounds butternut squash, peeled, seeded, and cut into ½-inch pieces (5 cups)

1 pound leeks, white and light green parts only, halved lengthwise, sliced thin, and washed thoroughly

2 garlic cloves, minced

Pinch cayenne pepper

¼ cup dry white wine

4 cups water

1 cup heavy cream

12 ounces jumbo pasta shells

2 tablespoons chopped fresh basil

1. Adjust oven rack to middle position and heat oven to 375 degrees. Combine ricotta, ½ cup Parmesan, lemon zest, ¼ teaspoon salt, and ¼ teaspoon pepper in bowl; cover and refrigerate until needed.

2. Heat oil in 12-inch ovensafe nonstick skillet over medium heat until shimmering. Add squash, leeks, and ½ teaspoon salt and cook until leeks are softened, about 5 minutes. Stir in garlic and cayenne and cook until fragrant, about 30 seconds. Add wine and cook until almost completely evaporated, about 1 minute.

3. Stir in water and cream, then add pasta. Increase heat to medium-high and cook at vigorous simmer, stirring gently and often, until pasta is tender and liquid has thickened, about 15 minutes.

4. Season with salt and pepper to taste. Sprinkle remaining ½ cup Parmesan over top, then dollop evenly with ricotta mixture. Transfer skillet to oven and bake until Parmesan is melted and spotty brown, about 5 minutes. Remove skillet from oven (skillet handle will be hot). Let cool for 10 minutes, then sprinkle with basil and serve.

skillet pasta puttanesca

why this recipe works Puttanesca, a classic Italian sauce made with tomatoes, garlic, anchovies, capers, and olives, offers bold flavor and comes together fairly quickly—perfect for a Sunday supper. Cooking the tomato sauce in a skillet and then cooking the pasta directly in the sauce made things even speedier. For a lightly thickened sauce, we used whole peeled tomatoes, pulsed in the food processor, which gave us more consistent results than canned crushed tomatoes. Sautéing the anchovies, garlic, and red pepper flakes at the outset provided a rich, savory foundation of flavor; finishing the dish with chopped kalamatas and capers preserved their briny notes and provided the big flavor we were after. A sprinkle of nutty Parmesan and drizzle of fruity olive oil pulled everything together before serving. Be sure to simmer the tomatoes gently in step 2 or the sauce will become too thick.

serves 4
total time: 45 minutes

3 (14.5-ounce) cans whole peeled tomatoes

3 tablespoons extra-virgin olive oil, plus extra for serving

6 anchovy fillets, rinsed and minced

6 garlic cloves, minced

½ teaspoon red pepper flakes

Salt and pepper

2 cups water

12 ounces thin spaghetti or spaghettini, broken in half

¼ cup pitted kalamata olives, chopped coarse

¼ cup minced fresh parsley

3 tablespoons capers, rinsed

Grated Parmesan cheese

1. Pulse tomatoes in food processor until coarsely ground and no large pieces remain, about 12 pulses.

2. Cook 2 tablespoons oil, anchovies, garlic, and pepper flakes together in 12-inch nonstick skillet over medium-low heat, stirring constantly, until garlic is fragrant, 1 to 2 minutes. Stir in processed tomatoes and ½ teaspoon salt. Simmer gently until tomatoes no longer taste raw, about 10 minutes.

3. Stir in water and pasta. Cover, increase heat to medium-high, and cook at vigorous simmer, stirring often, until pasta is tender, 12 to 15 minutes.

4. Stir in olives, parsley, capers, and remaining 1 tablespoon oil. Season with salt and pepper to taste. Serve with Parmesan and extra olive oil.

shrimp piccata pasta

why this recipe works Though piccata dishes often center around veal or chicken, for an easy Sunday supper, we liked how quickly shrimp cooked and how well they paired with the classic piccata flavors of lemon juice, capers, and garlic. We seared the shrimp over high heat until just barely cooked through, then set them aside until the sauce was prepared. To maximize the flavor of the red pepper flakes, we first cooked them briefly with the garlic, before adding wine, clam juice, and lemon juice. A few minutes of simmering reduced the sauce to a desirable, syrupy consistency. Using just one pan for both the shrimp and the sauce allowed the sauce to pick up the flavors left behind by the shrimp and made for an easy cleanup. For cooking pasta, we recommend 1 tablespoon of table salt for every gallon of water. Be sure to toss the shrimp and sauce with the pasta immediately after draining. The hot pasta will heat the shrimp and melt the butter.

serves 4 to 6
total time: 45 minutes

1 pound linguine

Salt and pepper

2 tablespoons extra-virgin olive oil

1 pound large shrimp (26 to 30 per pound), peeled, deveined, and halved lengthwise

4 garlic cloves, minced

⅛ teaspoon red pepper flakes

½ cup dry white wine

1 (8-ounce) bottle clam juice

3 tablespoons lemon juice

3 tablespoons capers, rinsed

⅓ cup chopped fresh parsley

4 tablespoons unsalted butter, softened

1. Bring 4 quarts water to boil in large pot for pasta. Add pasta and 1 tablespoon salt and cook, stirring often, until al dente. Reserve ½ cup cooking water, then drain pasta and return it to pot.

2. Meanwhile, heat 1 tablespoon oil in large skillet over high heat. Add shrimp and cook, stirring, until just opaque, about 1 minute. Transfer to large plate. Heat remaining 1 table- spoon oil in now-empty skillet over medium heat. Add garlic and pepper flakes and cook until fragrant but not browned, about 30 seconds. Add wine, increase heat to high, and simmer until liquid is reduced and syrupy, about 2 minutes. Add clam juice and lemon juice, bring to boil, and cook until mixture is reduced to ⅓ cup, about 8 minutes.

3. Add capers, parsley, butter, shrimp, and sauce to pasta and toss to combine until butter melts and shrimp are warmed through. Season with salt and pepper to taste, and add reserved cooking water as needed to adjust consistency. Serve.

almost hands-free risotto with chicken and herbs

why this recipe works Sunday comfort food doesn't get much better than a bowl of steaming, creamy risotto, but the dish is infamous for the constant attention and stirring it requires. We found a way to achieve the same desirable, silky consistency with much less time standing over the stove. Instead of a traditional saucepan, we opted for a thick, heavy-bottomed Dutch oven that trapped and distributed heat evenly and ensured our risotto cooked consistently. And to make sure the bottom of our risotto didn't cook more quickly than the top, we stirred the pot for just a few minutes before reducing the heat, covering, and simmering until the rice reached a perfect al dente texture. To make the risotto a hearty main course, we added chicken, which we seared and then poached in broth before shredding and adding it to the rice. A final, bright splash of lemon juice and sprinkle of fresh herbs balanced the richness of the butter and Parmesan. We recommend that you use a timer when simmering the rice to ensure that it does not wind up soft and overcooked. If you prefer a brothy risotto, add the extra broth in step 6. For best results, make sure to use genuine Italian Parmigiano-Reggiano, not domestically made Parmesan cheese. Serve with Broiled Asparagus with Lemon (page 8).

serves 6
total time: 1 hour 15 minutes

5 cups chicken broth

2 cups water

2 (12-ounce) bone-in split chicken breasts, trimmed and halved crosswise

1 tablespoon olive oil

4 tablespoons unsalted butter

1 large onion, chopped fine

Salt and pepper

1 large garlic clove, minced

2 cups Arborio rice

1 cup dry white wine

2 ounces Parmesan cheese, grated (1 cup)

2 tablespoons chopped fresh parsley

2 tablespoons chopped fresh chives

1 teaspoon lemon juice

1. Bring broth and water to boil in large saucepan over high heat. Reduce heat to medium-low to maintain gentle simmer.

2. Pat chicken dry with paper towels. Heat oil in Dutch oven over medium heat until just smoking. Add chicken, skin side down, and cook without moving until golden brown, 4 to 6 minutes. Flip chicken and cook on second side until lightly browned, about 2 minutes. Transfer chicken to saucepan of simmering broth and cook until thickest part registers 160 degrees, 10 to 15 minutes. Transfer to large plate.

3. Melt 2 tablespoons butter in now-empty pot over medium heat. Add onion and ¾ teaspoon salt; cook, stirring frequently, until onion is softened but not browned, 4 to 5 minutes. Add garlic and cook until fragrant, about 30 seconds. Add rice and cook, stirring frequently, until grains are translucent around edges, about 3 minutes.

4. Add wine and cook, stirring constantly, until fully absorbed, 2 to 3 minutes. Stir 5 cups warm broth mixture into rice; reduce heat to medium-low, cover, and simmer until almost all liquid has been absorbed and rice is just al dente, 16 to 18 minutes, stirring twice during cooking.

5. Add ¾ cup warm broth mixture to risotto and stir gently and constantly until risotto becomes creamy, about 3 minutes. Stir in Parmesan. Remove pot from heat, cover, and let stand for 5 minutes.

6. Meanwhile, discard skin and bones from chicken and shred meat into bite-size pieces. Gently stir shredded chicken, parsley, chives, lemon juice, and remaining 2 tablespoons butter into risotto. Season with salt and pepper to taste. If desired, add up to ½ cup additional broth mixture to loosen texture of risotto. Serve.

lemon-thyme roasted chicken
with ratatouille

why this recipe works Roasted chicken and ratatouille is simplicity on a plate, perfect for a satisfying Sunday supper. Yet despite its simple nature, the preparation can be onerous, requiring multiple pans and cooking stages for the ratatouille alone. Seeking an easier method, we turned to a sheet pan; its large surface area could accommodate both the chicken and the vegetables, and exposing the food to dry heat would prevent the vegetables from becoming soggy—a hallmark of underwhelming ratatouille. We selected bone-in chicken breasts, which gave us juicy, tender meat without being too fussy or producing too much grease. To get nicely golden skin, we preheated the baking sheet, oiled it to prevent sticking, and placed the chicken breasts, skin side down, on the pan to sear them. We chopped eggplant and zucchini into bite-size pieces, tossed them with canned tomatoes, garlic, and thyme, and scattered them opposite the chicken. Halfway through roasting, we flipped the chicken, stirred the vegetables, and added lemon wedges to roast for a flavor boost. Peeking in 5 minutes later, we stirred the vegetables again to ensure that every piece was cooked and all the excess liquid could evaporate. A final squeeze of the roasted lemon wedges tied everything together.

serves 4
total time: 45 minutes

1 (14.5-ounce) can diced tomatoes, drained

12 ounces eggplant, cut into ½-inch pieces

2 zucchini (6 ounces each), cut into ½-inch pieces

3 tablespoons extra-virgin olive oil

1 tablespoon minced fresh thyme or 1½ teaspoons dried

2 garlic cloves, minced

Salt and pepper

4 (10- to 12-ounce) bone-in split chicken breasts, trimmed

1 lemon, quartered

2 tablespoons minced fresh parsley

1. Adjust oven rack to upper-middle position, place rimmed baking sheet on rack, and heat oven to 450 degrees. Toss tomatoes, eggplant, zucchini, 2 tablespoons oil, 1 teaspoon thyme, garlic, ½ teaspoon salt, and ¼ teaspoon pepper together in bowl. Pat chicken dry with paper towels and season with salt, pepper, and remaining 2 teaspoons thyme.

2. Brush remaining 1 tablespoon oil evenly over hot sheet. Place chicken, skin side down, on 1 side of sheet and spread vegetables in single layer on other side. Roast until chicken releases from sheet and vegetables begin to wilt, about 10 minutes.

3. Flip chicken, skin side up, and stir vegetables. Place lemon quarters, cut side down, on sheet. Continue to roast, stirring vegetables occasionally, until chicken registers 160 degrees and vegetables are tender, 10 to 15 minutes.

4. Remove sheet from oven, tent with aluminum foil, and let rest for 5 minutes. Transfer chicken to platter. Toss vegetables with pan juices, season with salt and pepper to taste, and transfer to platter. Sprinkle parsley over vegetables and serve with roasted lemon wedges.

french chicken in a pot with red potatoes, carrots, and shallots

why this recipe works A classic French dish in which a whole chicken bakes in a covered pot, *poulet en cocotte* is known for yielding unbelievably tender meat and a savory sauce of the chicken's own concentrated juices. To make this a more complete one-pot meal ideal for a Sunday supper, we wanted vegetables to accompany the chicken. We started by browning our chicken, which gave the skin an appealing color and left behind fond. While the chicken rested, we browned the vegetables in the same pot, making sure to scrape up the flavorful brown bits. Adding fragrant garlic and thyme, as well as wine and chicken broth, made for a savory jus. We returned the chicken to the vegetables and jus and transferred it all to the oven. About an hour later, we were left with succulent meat, crisped skin, superflavorful vegetables, and a killer sauce.

serves 4
total time: 2 hours

1 (3½- to 4-pound) whole chicken, giblets discarded

Salt and pepper

1 tablespoon vegetable oil

1½ pounds red potatoes, unpeeled, cut into 1-inch pieces

1 pound carrots, peeled and cut into 1-inch pieces

4 shallots, peeled and halved

3 garlic cloves, minced

1 teaspoon minced fresh thyme or ¼ teaspoon dried

½ cup dry white wine

½ cup chicken broth, plus extra as needed

1 bay leaf

2 tablespoons unsalted butter

1 tablespoon lemon juice

1 tablespoon minced fresh parsley

1. Adjust oven rack to lower-middle position and heat oven to 350 degrees. Pat chicken dry with paper towels, tuck wingtips behind back, and season with salt and pepper. Heat oil in Dutch oven over medium-high heat until just smoking. Add chicken, breast side down, and brown lightly, about 5 minutes. Carefully flip chicken breast side up and cook until back is well browned, 6 to 8 minutes; transfer to large plate.

2. Pour off all but 1 tablespoon fat left in pot. Add potatoes, carrots, shallots, and ½ teaspoon salt and cook over medium heat until vegetables are just beginning to brown, 5 to 7 minutes. Stir in garlic and thyme and cook until fragrant, about 30 seconds. Stir in wine, broth, and bay leaf, scraping up any browned bits.

3. Off heat, return chicken, breast side up, and any accumulated juices to pot, on top of vegetables. Transfer pot to oven and cook, uncovered, until breast registers 160 degrees and thighs register 175 degrees, 55 minutes to 1 hour 5 minutes.

4. Remove pot from oven. Transfer chicken to carving board and let rest for 20 minutes. Using slotted spoon, transfer vegetables to platter and cover with aluminum foil to keep warm.

5. Discard bay leaf. Pour liquid left in pot into fat separator and let settle for 5 minutes. (You should have ¾ cup defatted liquid; add extra broth as needed to equal ¾ cup.) Return defatted liquid to now-empty pot and simmer until it measures ½ cup, 5 to 7 minutes. Off heat, whisk in butter and lemon juice and season with salt and pepper to taste. Sprinkle vegetables with parsley, carve chicken, and serve with sauce.

roasted pork chops and vegetables with parsley vinaigrette

why this recipe works Thick-cut bone-in pork chops deliver the succulence of a larger roast but cook in just 10 to 15 minutes, making them perfect for a quick Sunday supper. They stand up to high heat and bold flavors, so it was natural to pair them with roasted root vegetables and to season everything well for a flavor-packed one-pan meal. We partially roasted the vegetables—a rustic mix of potatoes, carrots, and fennel—to give them a head start. To add base notes of flavor, we tossed them with fresh rosemary and whole garlic cloves, which turned deliciously sweet when roasted. Once the vegetables had softened and taken on some color, we added the pork chops, which we'd seasoned with a bold rub of pepper, salt, paprika, and coriander for a deeply flavored crust. We whisked up a simple parsley vinaigrette to drizzle over the pork, ensuring that our meal would end on a high note. Note that this recipe calls for kosher salt, not table salt; if using table salt, cut all salt amounts by half. Be sure to use pork chops that measure between 1 and 1½ inches thick for this recipe.

serves 4
total time: 1 hour

1 pound Yukon Gold potatoes, unpeeled, halved lengthwise and cut crosswise into ½-inch-thick slices

1 pound carrots, peeled and cut into 3-inch lengths, thick ends quartered lengthwise

1 fennel bulb, stalks discarded, bulb halved, cored, and cut into ½-inch-thick wedges

10 garlic cloves, peeled

2 teaspoons minced fresh rosemary or ¾ teaspoon dried

⅓ cup extra-virgin olive oil

Kosher salt and pepper

1 teaspoon paprika

1 teaspoon ground coriander

4 (12-ounce) bone-in center-cut pork chops, 1 to 1½ inches thick, trimmed

4 teaspoons red wine vinegar

2 tablespoons minced fresh parsley

1 small shallot, minced

⅛ teaspoon sugar

1. Adjust oven rack to upper-middle position and heat oven to 450 degrees. Toss potatoes, carrots, fennel, garlic, rosemary, 1 tablespoon oil, 1½ teaspoons salt, and ¼ teaspoon pepper together in bowl. Spread vegetables in single layer on rimmed baking sheet. Roast until beginning to soften, about 25 minutes.

2. While vegetables roast, combine 2 teaspoons salt, 1 teaspoon pepper, paprika, and coriander in bowl. Pat pork dry with paper towels and cut 2 slits, about 2 inches apart, through fat on edges of each chop. Rub chops with 1 teaspoon oil, then season thoroughly with spice mixture.

3. Lay chops on top of vegetables and continue to roast until chops register 145 degrees and vegetables are tender, 10 to 15 minutes, rotating sheet halfway through roasting.

4. Remove sheet from oven, tent with aluminum foil, and let rest for 5 minutes. Whisk remaining ¼ cup oil, vinegar, parsley, shallot, sugar, ½ teaspoon salt, and ¼ teaspoon pepper together in bowl. Drizzle vinaigrette over pork before serving.

spice-rubbed pork tenderloin with fennel, tomatoes, artichokes, and olives

why this recipe works When done right, nothing can match the fine-grained, buttery-smooth texture of pork tenderloin. The meat's mild flavors lend themselves well to bold seasonings. We found that a dry rub allowed us to skip a browning step, adding both flavor and color to our tenderloins without having to spend extra time in the kitchen on Sunday evening. Herbes de Provence, an aromatic blend of dried herbs from southern France, provided a distinct flavor profile; a little of this spice goes a long way, so just 2 teaspoons were sufficient to flavor and coat two tenderloins without overwhelming the pork. For a vegetable that would complement both the rub and the pork, we chose sweet, mild fennel and supplemented it with artichokes, kalamata olives, and cherry tomatoes. After jump-starting the fennel in the microwave, we cooked the tenderloins on top of the vegetables in a roasting pan. In less than an hour, we were transported to Provence with a dinner that was low on fuss but high on flavor. We prefer to use our homemade herbes de Provence, but you can substitute store-bought herbes de Provence, though flavor can vary by brand. While we prefer the flavor and texture of jarred whole baby artichokes, you can substitute 12 ounces of frozen artichoke hearts, thawed and patted dry, for the jarred.

serves 6
total time: 1 hour

2 large fennel bulbs, stalks discarded, bulbs halved, cored, and sliced ½ inch thick

2 cups jarred whole baby artichokes packed in water, quartered, rinsed, and patted dry

½ cup pitted kalamata olives, halved

3 tablespoons extra-virgin olive oil

2 (12- to 16-ounce) pork tenderloins, trimmed

2 teaspoons herbes de Provence

Salt and pepper

1 pound cherry tomatoes, halved

1 tablespoon grated lemon zest

2 tablespoons minced fresh parsley

1. Adjust oven rack to lower-middle position and heat oven to 450 degrees. Combine fennel and 2 tablespoons water in bowl, cover, and microwave until softened, about 5 minutes. Drain fennel well, then toss with artichokes, olives, and oil.

2. Pat tenderloins dry with paper towels, sprinkle with herbes de Provence, and season with salt and pepper. Spread vegetables in large roasting pan, then place tenderloins on top. Roast tenderloins and vegetables until pork registers 145 degrees, 25 to 30 minutes, turning tenderloins over halfway through roasting.

3. Transfer tenderloins to carving board, tent with aluminum foil, and let rest for 10 minutes. Meanwhile, stir tomatoes and lemon zest into vegetables and continue to roast until fennel is tender and tomatoes have softened, about 10 minutes. Stir in parsley and season with salt and pepper to taste. Slice pork into ½-inch-thick slices and serve with vegetables.

herbes de provence
makes about ½ cup

2 tablespoons dried thyme

2 tablespoons dried marjoram

2 tablespoons dried rosemary

2 teaspoons fennel seeds, toasted

Combine all ingredients in bowl.

to make ahead
Herbes de Provence can be stored at room temperature in airtight container for up to 1 year.

chuck roast dinner in foil

why this recipe works For the ultimate walkaway dinner that's always a crowd-pleaser, we looked to pot roast. Traditionally, the lazy cook's pot roast involves rubbing a chuck roast with onion soup mix, wrapping it in aluminum foil, and cooking it in the oven until tender. While we liked the ease of this one-pan dish, we weren't fans of its artificial, salty taste. We ditched the traditional monosodium glutamate in favor of soy sauce. To develop our own "soup mix," we combined onion powder, salt, brown sugar, pepper, thyme, celery seeds, espresso powder, and cornstarch. Though cornstarch may seem unusual, it was the key to browning the meat in the moist foil-packet environment. Cutting the roast in half gave us more surface area to apply as much of our flavorful mix as possible, and a 300-degree oven guaranteed ultratender meat. Using relatively large chunks of carrots, potatoes, and onions ensured that they didn't overcook during the lengthy roasting time. And as an added bonus, they contributed a great depth of flavor and volume to the meat's jus—no other sauce ingredients necessary. You will need an 18-inch-wide roll of heavy-duty aluminum foil for this recipe.

serves 6
total time: 5 hours 30 minutes

---

3 tablespoons cornstarch

4 teaspoons onion powder

2 teaspoons packed light brown sugar

2 teaspoons salt

1 teaspoon pepper

1 teaspoon garlic powder

1 teaspoon instant espresso powder

1 teaspoon dried thyme

½ teaspoon celery seeds

1 (4-pound) boneless beef chuck-eye roast

2 onions, peeled and quartered

6 red potatoes, unpeeled, quartered

4 carrots, peeled and cut into 1½-inch pieces

2 bay leaves

2 tablespoons soy sauce

2 tablespoons minced fresh parsley

---

1. Adjust oven rack to lower-middle position and heat oven to 300 degrees. Combine cornstarch, onion powder, sugar, salt, pepper, garlic powder, espresso powder, thyme, and celery seeds in bowl.

2. Pat roast dry with paper towels. Separate roast into 2 pieces along natural seam and trim fat to ¼-inch thickness. Tie kitchen twine around each roast at 1-inch intervals and coat thoroughly with cornstarch mixture.

3. Crisscross two 30 by 18-inch sheets of heavy-duty aluminum foil inside 16 by 12-inch roasting pan. Place onions, potatoes, carrots, and bay leaves in center of foil and drizzle with soy sauce. Set roasts on top of vegetables. Fold opposite corners of foil toward each other and crimp edges tightly to seal. Transfer pan to oven and cook until meat is completely tender, about 4½ hours.

4. Remove pan from oven and open foil pouch. Transfer roasts to carving board, tent with more foil, and let rest for 15 minutes. Using slotted spoon, transfer carrots and potatoes to platter, discarding onions and bay leaves. Strain contents left in roasting pan through fine-mesh strainer into fat separator. Let liquid settle, then pour defatted pan juices into serving bowl.

5. Remove kitchen twine from roasts, slice thin against grain, and transfer to platter with vegetables. Pour ½ cup defatted pan juices over meat. Serve with remaining pan juices and sprinkle with parsley.

rosemary steak tips
with gorgonzola polenta

why this recipe works As far as cooking steak goes, it doesn't get much easier or speedier than steak tips. And while steak tips are often grilled, here we bring them indoors and elevate their status by serving them atop creamy polenta, along with tart sautéed cherry tomatoes and a sprinkling of Gorgonzola cheese. Just a quick pat of rosemary, salt, and pepper was all the steak tips needed before searing in a hot skillet until well browned. While the steak rested, we cooked the tomatoes in the same skillet to soften them slightly and bring out their sweetness. Instant polenta provided a savory, creamy base for the steak and tomatoes in just minutes. Sprinkling Gorgonzola over the warm steak and polenta added tang and richness. You can substitute another mild blue cheese for the Gorgonzola, if desired.

serves 4
total time: 30 minutes

4 cups water

1 cup instant polenta

4 tablespoons unsalted butter

Salt and pepper

1 tablespoon coarsely chopped fresh rosemary

1½ pounds sirloin steak tips, trimmed and cut into 2-inch chunks

1 tablespoon vegetable oil

10 ounces grape tomatoes, halved

4 ounces Gorgonzola cheese, crumbled (1 cup)

1. Bring water to boil in large saucepan over medium-high heat. Whisk in polenta, reduce heat to medium-low, and cook until thickened, about 3 minutes. Off heat, stir in 3 tablespoons butter, 1 teaspoon salt, and ½ teaspoon pepper. Cover and keep warm.

2. Combine rosemary, 1 teaspoon salt, and 1 teaspoon pepper in bowl. Pat steak tips dry with paper towels and sprinkle with rosemary mixture. Heat oil in 12-inch nonstick skillet over medium-high heat until just smoking. Add steak and cook until well browned on all sides and meat registers 125 degrees (for medium-rare), about 7 minutes. Transfer to plate and tent with foil.

3. Melt remaining 1 tablespoon butter in now-empty skillet over medium-high heat. Add tomatoes and ½ teaspoon salt and cook until just softened, about 1 minute. Transfer to plate with steak. Serve steak and tomatoes over polenta, sprinkled with Gorgonzola.

meatloaf florentine

why this recipe works This effortless meatloaf, which requires no chopping or prep, tastes just as great as it looks—and its short ingredient list makes shopping a breeze. We started with meatloaf mix (a blend of ground pork, beef, and veal) and combined it with panko bread crumbs for structure. Two convenient pantry items—store-bought tomato sauce and pesto—gave our meatloaf a decidedly Italian feel and robust flavor. Extra sauce kept the exterior of our loaf moist as it cooked in the oven. For a unique, impressive-looking filling, we liked the combination of thinly sliced provolone with baby spinach; the provolone melted into a nice, gooey layer and the fresh spinach balanced the richness of the meat and cheese. Serve with Garlic Mashed Potatoes (page 11).

serves 6
total time: 1 hour 15 minutes

1 (25-ounce) jar tomato sauce

¾ cup panko bread crumbs

⅓ cup prepared basil pesto

1½ pounds meatloaf mix

Salt and pepper

3 ounces (3 cups) baby spinach

5 thin slices (3 ounces) deli provolone cheese

1. Adjust oven rack to middle position and heat oven to 350 degrees. Mash ¾ cup tomato sauce, panko, and pesto together in medium bowl with fork. Gently mix in meatloaf mix, ¼ teaspoon salt, and ¼ teaspoon pepper with your hands until thoroughly combined.

2. Shape half of meat mixture into 10 by 6-inch rectangle in center of 13 by 9-inch baking dish. Lay half of spinach on top, leaving ½-inch border at edges. Shingle provolone over spinach; top with remaining spinach. Form remaining meat mixture into 9 by 5-inch rectangle; gently transfer to baking dish on top of meatloaf. Reshape top layer as needed and tuck in edges of filling, leaving ½ inch of bottom meat layer exposed. Fold bottom edge of meatloaf over top layer; pinch edges together to seal.

3. Spread ½ cup tomato sauce on top of meatloaf; bake until meatloaf registers 145 degrees, about 45 minutes. Remove from oven; spoon off fat. Add remaining tomato sauce to dish and continue to bake meatloaf until it registers 160 degrees, 10 to 15 minutes. Skim fat from surface of sauce using spoon. Slice meatloaf and serve with sauce.

clams with pearl couscous, chorizo, and leeks

why this recipe works Cooking clams may seem daunting, but their short cooking time actually makes them perfect for a quick, yet luxurious, Sunday supper. To infuse this simple clam dish with big flavor, we added Spanish chorizo, thyme, and dry vermouth for a potent broth in which to steam our shellfish. We chose larger-grain pearl couscous instead of traditional small-grain couscous, as it was the perfect vehicle for soaking up the broth's flavors and also added textural appeal. We like the punch that dry vermouth adds, but dry white wine will also work. Do not substitute regular couscous in this dish, as it requires a different cooking method and will not work.

serves 4 to 6
total time: 30 minutes

2 cups pearl couscous

Salt and pepper

2 tablespoons extra-virgin olive oil

1½ pounds leeks, white and light green parts only, halved lengthwise, sliced thin, and washed thoroughly

6 ounces Spanish-style chorizo sausage, halved lengthwise and sliced thin

3 garlic cloves, minced

1 tablespoon minced fresh thyme or 1 teaspoon dried

1 cup dry vermouth or dry white wine

3 tomatoes, cored, seeded, and chopped

4 pounds littleneck clams, scrubbed

½ cup minced fresh parsley

1. Bring 2 quarts water to boil in medium saucepan. Stir in couscous and 2 teaspoons salt and cook until al dente, about 8 minutes; drain.

2. Meanwhile, heat oil in Dutch oven over medium heat. Add leeks and chorizo and cook until leeks are tender, about 4 minutes. Stir in garlic and thyme and cook until fragrant, about 30 seconds. Stir in vermouth and cook until slightly reduced, about 1 minute. Stir in tomatoes and clams, cover, and cook until clams open, 8 to 12 minutes.

3. Use slotted spoon to transfer clams to large serving bowl, discarding any that refuse to open. Stir couscous and parsley into cooking liquid and season with salt and pepper to taste. Portion couscous mixture into individual bowls, top with clams, and serve.

salmon with asparagus and chive butter sauce

why this recipe works For a restaurant-worthy meal that can be made in a flash at home, look no further than this ingenious recipe that delivers tender poached salmon, perfectly cooked asparagus, and a rich white wine pan sauce using just one skillet. Instead of using a steaming rack or other kitchen equipment to steam the salmon, we opted to resourcefully layer the asparagus spears in the pan to serve as a bed to elevate the salmon fillets above the liquid. This allowed the asparagus and fish to cook together in the same pan, making cleanup quick and easy. To make the white wine sauce, we simply added wine to the flavorful poaching liquid left behind after cooking the salmon and asparagus, simmering it down to the right consistency and then swirling in butter and chopped chives. Thinner asparagus spears will overcook, so choose spears that are at least ½ inch thick at the base. Serve with Classic Couscous (page 9) and lemon wedges.

serves 4
total time: 30 minutes

1 pound thick asparagus, trimmed

1 cup water

Salt and pepper

4 (6- to 8-ounce) skinless salmon fillets, about 1 inch thick

½ cup dry white wine

3 tablespoons unsalted butter

2 tablespoons chopped fresh chives

1. Lay asparagus in single layer on bottom of 12-inch skillet. Add water and ¼ teaspoon salt to skillet. Season salmon with salt and pepper and lay across asparagus spears. Bring water to boil over high heat, cover, and cook over medium heat until asparagus is tender and salmon is still translucent when checked with tip of paring knife and registers 125 degrees (for medium-rare), about 8 minutes. Transfer asparagus and salmon to platter.

2. Add wine to skillet, increase heat to medium-high, and simmer mixture to reduce, 5 minutes. Off heat, whisk in butter and chives and season with salt and pepper to taste. Pour sauce over salmon and asparagus. Serve.

sunday around the world

ancho-orange pork burritos

why this recipe works Fun and casual, burritos are always a dinnertime crowd-pleaser and are a fun, interactive way to get everyone involved. Too often though, burritos contain bland meat and rely on their condiments for flavor. We wanted to make an ultraflavorful, unique pork filling that didn't necessitate toppings. We took inspiration from the mildly spiced, orange-infused pork known as *chilorio*, one of the most popular dishes in Sinaloa, Mexico. Traditionally, the pork is slow-simmered until fall-apart tender, pulled into bite-size pieces and fried, and then cooked again in a chile sauce. We cooked boneless pork butt slowly and gently in the oven in a sauce base of orange juice, vinegar, chipotle chile in adobo, and dried ancho chiles. After a couple of hours of braising, the pork was meltingly tender and shreddable. We defatted the flavorful liquid left behind in the pot, pureed it until smooth, and tossed it with the shredded pork. Since we wanted the pork to be the star, we used just rice, no cheese or beans, when assembling these rich and satisfying burritos. If you are short on braising liquid for the sauce in step 2, you can make up the difference with chicken broth or water.

serves 8
total time: 2 hours 45 minutes

¾ cup orange juice (2 oranges)

½ cup distilled white vinegar

4 dried ancho chiles, stemmed, seeded, and torn into ½-inch pieces (1 cup)

2 tablespoons tomato paste

2 tablespoons minced canned chipotle chile in adobo sauce

5 garlic cloves, lightly crushed and peeled

2 bay leaves

2 teaspoons ground cumin

2 teaspoons dried oregano

Salt and pepper

4 pounds boneless pork butt roast, trimmed and cut into 2 inch pieces

2 cups water

1½ cups long-grain white rice, rinsed

¼ cup minced fresh cilantro

2 scallions, sliced thin

8 (10-inch) flour tortillas

1. Adjust oven rack to lower-middle position and heat oven to 300 degrees. Whisk orange juice, vinegar, anchos, tomato paste, chipotle, garlic, bay leaves, cumin, oregano and 1 teaspoon salt together in Dutch oven. Season pork with salt and pepper, stir into pot, and arrange in single layer. Cover and cook in oven until pork is very tender, about 2 hours.

2. Transfer pork to large bowl using slotted spoon and let cool slightly. Using 2 forks, shred pork into bite-size pieces. Strain braising liquid into fat separator, reserving solids, and let settle for 5 minutes. Discard bay leaves and transfer solids to blender. Add 1½ cups defatted liquid to blender and process until smooth, about 1 minute. Combine sauce and pork in now-empty Dutch oven; before making burritos, reheat mixture over medium heat until hot.

3. Meanwhile, bring water, rice, and 1 teaspoon salt to boil in medium saucepan over medium-high heat. Cover, reduce heat to low, and cook until rice is tender and water is absorbed, about 20 minutes. Remove rice from heat and let sit, covered, for 10 minutes. Add cilantro and scallions and fluff with fork to incorporate; cover to keep warm.

4. Wrap tortillas in damp dish towel and microwave until warm and pliable, about 1 minute. Lay warm tortillas on counter. Mound warm rice and pork across center of tortillas, close to bottom edge. Working with 1 tortilla at a time, fold sides then bottom of tortilla over filling, pulling back on it firmly to tighten it around filling, then continue to roll tightly into burrito. Serve.

to make ahead
Pork, prepared through step 2, can be refrigerated for up to 3 days or frozen for up to 1 month.

chinese cilantro pork

why this recipe works Stir-fried pork is a Sunday night Chinese take-out favorite, but we wanted to achieve the same distinctive Asian flavors at home. We first cooked thin slices of pork tenderloin until lightly browned. Once the meat was set aside, we added a combination of garlic and ginger to the skillet, heating until fragrant, and then added the cooked pork back into the skillet to absorb these flavors. A simple sauce brought a balance of sweet and sour flavors to this lighter, fresher stir-fry. We used cilantro as a vegetable in this stir-fry, rather than as a garnish. In an effort to keep the cilantro's flavor distinct, we added a full bunch to the skillet—stems and all—near the end of cooking. To make the pork easier to slice, freeze it for 15 minutes. Be sure to dry the canned bamboo shoots thoroughly with paper towels after rinsing; otherwise, the packing liquid will dilute the flavor of the sauce.

serves 4
total time: 30 minutes

sauce
¾ cup chicken broth

4 teaspoons soy sauce

4 teaspoons rice vinegar

1 tablespoon sugar

2 teaspoons cornstarch

¼ teaspoon red pepper flakes

stir-fry
3 tablespoons vegetable oil

1 tablespoon cornstarch

1 tablespoon all-purpose flour

2 teaspoons soy sauce

1 (1-pound) pork tenderloin, trimmed and sliced thin

3 garlic cloves, minced

1 tablespoon grated fresh ginger

1 large bunch cilantro, stems trimmed, cut into 1-inch lengths

1 (8-ounce) can sliced bamboo shoots, rinsed and dried

1. for the sauce Whisk all ingredients together in bowl.

2. for the stir-fry Whisk 2 tablespoons oil, cornstarch, flour, and soy sauce in medium bowl until smooth, then stir in pork. In separate bowl, combine garlic, ginger, and 1 teaspoon oil.

3. Heat 1 teaspoon oil in 12-inch nonstick skillet over high heat until just smoking. Add half of pork, breaking up any clumps, and cook, without stirring, for 1 minute. Stir pork and continue to cook until lightly browned, about 1 minute; transfer to clean bowl. Repeat with remaining 1 teaspoon oil and remaining pork mixture; transfer to bowl.

4. Add garlic mixture to now-empty skillet and cook over medium heat, mashing mixture into skillet, until fragrant, about 30 seconds. Add cooked pork and any accumulated juices, cilantro, and bamboo shoots, and toss to combine.

5. Whisk sauce to recombine, then add to skillet. Cook, stirring constantly, until sauce is thickened and cilantro is slightly wilted, about 1 minute. Serve.

peruvian roast chicken with swiss chard and sweet potatoes

why this recipe works Roast chicken is a Sunday supper classic, but for a more exotic take, we looked to *pollo a la brasa*, which boasts a bronzed exterior seasoned with a robust paste of garlic, spices, lime juice, chile, and mint. Lacking the spit traditionally used to roast the bird whole, we instead figured, why not use leg quarters? They fit neatly in our roasting pan and yielded more bronzed skin coated in a tasty paste. We smeared the paste over and under the skin before letting the chicken rest for at least an hour to allow the flavors to meld. We used our roasting pan to brown a side of sweet potatoes before arranging the chicken on top and roasting both together, allowing the chicken drippings to baste the potatoes as they became tender. We then removed the chicken and potatoes to rest while we cooked chard in the delicious juices left behind. Some leg quarters are sold with backbone attached; removing it (with a heavy chef's knife) before cooking makes the chicken easier to serve.

serves 6
total time: 1 hour 45 minutes
(plus 1 hour for marinating)

¼ cup fresh mint leaves

10 garlic cloves (5 chopped, 5 sliced)

¼ cup extra-virgin olive oil

1 tablespoon ground cumin

1 tablespoon honey

2 teaspoons smoked paprika

2 teaspoons dried oregano

2 teaspoons grated lime zest plus ¼ cup juice (2 limes), plus lime wedges for serving

Salt and pepper

1 teaspoon minced habanero chile

6 (10-ounce) chicken leg quarters, trimmed

3 pounds sweet potatoes, peeled, ends squared off, and sliced into 1-inch-thick rounds

4 pounds Swiss chard, stemmed and cut into 1-inch pieces

2 tablespoons minced fresh cilantro

1. Process mint, chopped garlic, 1 tablespoon oil, cumin, honey, paprika, oregano, lime zest and juice, 2 teaspoons pepper, 1 teaspoon salt, and habanero in blender until smooth, 20 seconds.

2. Using your fingers, gently loosen skin covering thighs and drumsticks and spread half of paste directly on meat. Spread remaining half of paste over exterior of chicken. Place chicken in 1-gallon zipper-lock bag and refrigerate for at least 1 hour or up to 24 hours.

3. Adjust oven rack to middle position and heat oven to 425 degrees. Toss potatoes with 1 tablespoon oil and ½ teaspoon salt in bowl. Heat remaining 2 tablespoons oil in 16 by 12-inch roasting pan over medium-high heat (over 2 burners, if possible) until shimmering. Add potatoes, cut side down, and cook until well browned on bottom, 6 to 8 minutes.

4. Off heat, flip potatoes. Lay chicken, skin side up, on top. Roast until thighs and drumsticks register 175 degrees and potatoes are tender, 40 to 50 minutes, rotating pan halfway through roasting.

5. Remove pan from oven. Transfer potatoes and chicken to platter, tent with aluminum foil, and let rest for 10 minutes. Being careful of hot pan handles, pour off all but ¼ cup liquid left in pan. Add sliced garlic and cook over high heat (over 2 burners, if possible) until fragrant, about 30 seconds. Add chard and ¼ teaspoon salt and cook, stirring constantly, until chard is wilted and tender, about 8 minutes; transfer to serving bowl.

6. Sprinkle cilantro over chicken and potatoes and serve with chard and lime wedges.

chicken bouillabaisse

why this recipe works Swapping readily available bone-in chicken breasts and thighs for the numerous and expensive varieties of fish in traditional bouillabaisse makes this update of the classic Provençal recipe an equally delicious but far more practical dish. We switched from stovetop to oven cooking and rested the chicken on the potatoes so the skin stayed out of the liquid. Serve with Rouille and crusty bread.

serves 6
total time: 1 hour 45 minutes

3 pounds bone-in chicken pieces (split breasts cut in half, drumsticks, and/or thighs), trimmed

Salt and pepper

2 tablespoons extra-virgin olive oil

1 large leek, white and light green parts only, halved lengthwise, sliced thin, and washed thoroughly

1 small fennel bulb, stalks discarded, bulb halved, cored, and sliced thin

4 garlic cloves, minced

1 tablespoon tomato paste

1 tablespoon all-purpose flour

¼ teaspoon saffron threads, crumbled

¼ teaspoon cayenne pepper

3 cups chicken broth

1 (14.5-ounce) can diced tomatoes, drained

12 ounces Yukon Gold potatoes, unpeeled, cut into ¾-inch pieces

½ cup dry white wine

¼ cup pastis or Pernod

1 (3-inch) strip orange zest

1 tablespoon chopped fresh tarragon or parsley

1. Adjust oven rack to middle position and heat oven to 375 degrees. Pat chicken dry with paper towels and season with salt and pepper.

Heat oil in Dutch oven over medium-high heat until just smoking. Brown chicken well, 5 to 8 minutes per side; transfer to plate.

2. Add leek and fennel to fat left in pot and cook, stirring often, until beginning to soften, about 4 minutes. Stir in garlic, tomato paste, flour, saffron, and cayenne and cook until fragrant, about 30 seconds. Slowly whisk in broth, scraping up any browned bits and smoothing out any lumps. Stir in tomatoes, potatoes, wine, pastis, and orange zest. Bring to simmer and cook for 10 minutes.

3. Nestle chicken thighs and drumsticks into pot with skin above surface of liquid. Cook, uncovered, for 5 minutes. Nestle breast pieces into pot, adjusting pieces to ensure that skin stays above surface of liquid. Transfer pot to oven and cook, uncovered, until breasts register 145 degrees and thighs/drumsticks register 160 degrees, 10 to 20 minutes.

4. Remove pot from oven and heat broiler. Return pot to oven and broil until chicken skin is crisp and breasts register 160 degrees and thighs/drumsticks register 175 degrees, 5 to 10 minutes.

5. Discard orange zest. Skim excess fat from surface of stew, stir in tarragon, and season with salt and pepper to taste. Serve.

rouille
makes about 1 cup

3 tablespoons boiling water

¼ teaspoon saffron threads, crumbled

1 (3-inch) piece baguette, crusts removed, torn into 1-inch pieces (1 cup)

4 teaspoons lemon juice

1 large egg yolk

2 teaspoons Dijon mustard

2 garlic cloves, minced

¼ teaspoon cayenne pepper

½ cup vegetable oil

½ cup extra-virgin olive oil

Salt and pepper

Combine boiling water and saffron in medium bowl and let steep for 5 minutes. Stir bread pieces and lemon juice into saffron-infused water and let soak for 5 minutes. Using whisk, mash soaked bread mixture until uniform paste forms, 1 to 2 minutes. Whisk in egg yolk, mustard, garlic, and cayenne until smooth, about 15 seconds. Whisking constantly, slowly drizzle in vegetable oil until smooth mayonnaise-like consistency is reached, scraping down bowl as necessary. Slowly whisk in olive oil in steady stream until smooth. Season with salt and pepper to taste.

latino-style chicken and rice
(arroz con pollo)

why this recipe works Mexican *arroz con pollo*, literally meaning "rice with chicken" is a satisfying one-dish meal that will bring the vibrant flavors of Mexico into your kitchen. The traditional method calls for stewing marinated chicken slowly with aromatic herbs and vegetables, creating a rich broth in which the rice is cooked once the chicken is fall-off-the-bone tender. We set out to streamline the traditional method without sacrificing its deep, rich chicken flavor. We opted for flavorful dark-meat chicken thighs and removed any visible pockets of fat and some of the skin before cooking to prevent the dish from becoming greasy. Once the chicken was done, we removed the skin; although it protected the meat during cooking, it didn't crisp in the moist environment of the closed pot. Using spoons rather than forks to pull the meat apart ensured that we ended up with chunks, not shreds. Cooking the rice directly in the pot with the chicken and sauce allowed it to absorb all the bold flavors of the dish and really complement the meat.

serves 4 to 6
total time: 1 hour 45 minutes

6 garlic cloves, minced

5 teaspoons distilled white vinegar

Salt and pepper

½ teaspoon dried oregano

4 pounds bone-in chicken thighs, trimmed

2 tablespoons olive oil

1 onion, chopped fine

1 small green bell pepper, stemmed, seeded, and chopped fine

¼ teaspoon red pepper flakes

¼ cup minced fresh cilantro

1¾ cups chicken broth

1 (8-ounce) can tomato sauce

¼ cup water, plus extra as needed

3 cups medium-grain white rice

½ cup green Manzanilla olives, pitted and halved

1 tablespoon capers, rinsed

½ cup jarred whole pimentos, cut into 2 by ¼-inch strips

Lemon wedges

1. Adjust oven rack to middle position and heat oven to 350 degrees. Combine garlic, 1 tablespoon vinegar, 1 teaspoon salt, ½ teaspoon pepper, and oregano in large bowl. Add chicken, toss to coat, and marinate for 15 minutes.

2. Heat 1 tablespoon oil in Dutch oven over medium heat until shimmering. Add onion, bell pepper, and pepper flakes and cook until beginning to soften, about 5 minutes. Stir in 2 tablespoons cilantro.

3. Clear center of pot and increase heat to medium-high. Add chicken, skin side down, to center of pot and cook until outer layer of meat becomes opaque, 2 to 4 minutes per side, reducing heat if chicken begins to brown. Stir in broth, tomato sauce, and water. Bring to simmer, cover, reduce heat to medium-low, and simmer for 20 minutes.

4. Stir in rice, olives, capers, and ¾ teaspoon salt and bring to simmer. Cover pot, transfer to oven, and cook, stirring every 10 minutes, until chicken registers 175 degrees, about 30 minutes. (If, after 20 minutes of cooking, rice appears dry and bottom of pot begins to scorch, stir in additional ¼ cup water.)

5. Transfer chicken to cutting board; cover pot and set aside. Using 2 spoons, pull chicken into large chunks, discarding skin and bones. Place chicken in large bowl, toss with pimentos, remaining 2 teaspoons vinegar, remaining 1 tablespoon oil, and remaining 2 tablespoons cilantro and season with salt and pepper to taste. Place chicken on top of rice, cover, and let stand until warmed through, about 5 minutes. Serve with lemon wedges.

indian-spiced chicken with yogurt sauce (tandoori chicken)

why this recipe works Tandoori chicken traditionally achieves its hallmark charred, crispy skin and juicy, flavorful meat from a combination of a three-day marinade and a superheated tandoori oven. We wanted to develop a streamlined, home-kitchen-friendly chicken dish inspired by this Indian classic. For the marinade, we chose a variety of traditional Indian spices and added oil to bloom them, as well as a good amount of salt so that the marinade would have the effect of a brine, guaranteeing juicy meat. We took advantage of the oven's broiler setting to achieve crispy, well-browned skin. To reinforce the flavors of the marinade, we created a quick yogurt sauce by reserving a few tablespoons of marinade and brightened it with fresh cilantro and lime juice.

serves 4
total time: 1 hour
(plus 1 hour for marinating)

½ cup vegetable oil

¼ cup water

1 tablespoon grated fresh ginger

1 tablespoon ground coriander

1½ teaspoons ground cumin

1½ teaspoons salt

1 teaspoon ground turmeric

½ teaspoon ground cinnamon

¼ teaspoon cayenne pepper

¼ cup plain whole-milk yogurt

2 tablespoons minced fresh cilantro

2 teaspoons lime juice

4 (12-ounce) bone-in split chicken breasts, trimmed and halved crosswise

1. Process oil, water, ginger, coriander, cumin, salt, turmeric, cinnamon, and cayenne in food processor until smooth, about 20 seconds. In small bowl, combine yogurt, cilantro, lime juice, and 2 tablespoons oil-spice mixture; cover.

2. Place chicken and remaining oil-spice mixture in 1-gallon zipper-lock bag, press out air, and seal; toss to coat.

3. Refrigerate chicken and yogurt mixture separately for at least 1 hour or up to 24 hours, flipping bag occasionally to ensure chicken marinates evenly.

4. Remove yogurt mixture from refrigerator and bring to room temperature while preparing chicken. Pat chicken dry with paper towels.

5. Adjust 1 oven rack to lower-middle position and second rack 6 inches from broiler element; heat broiler. Set wire rack in aluminum foil–lined rimmed baking sheet and spray with vegetable oil spray. Arrange chicken skin side down on prepared wire rack. Broil on lower rack until chicken registers 150 degrees, 22 to 26 minutes, flipping chicken halfway through broiling. Transfer chicken to upper rack and broil until skin is spotty brown and crisp and chicken registers 160 degrees, about 3 minutes.

6. Transfer chicken to serving platter. Stir yogurt-marinade mixture to recombine, then drizzle over chicken. Tent with aluminum foil and let rest for 5 to 10 minutes. Serve.

filipino chicken adobo

why this recipe works Most braised chicken recipes rely on many ingredients and a lot of prep—mincing garlic, chopping onions, and slicing myriad vegetables. With chicken adobo, the national dish of the Philippines, the approach is quite different. The ingredient list is very short and nothing—other than the chicken—requires prep time, making the dish ideal for a Sunday supper. This formula works because the key ingredients that go into this braise—soy sauce, vinegar, garlic, bay leaves, and black pepper—are each so potent. The end result is a pantry-ready braise with bold, tangy flavors. We chose bone-in chicken thighs because they contain more fat and collagen than chicken breasts, making them particularly well-suited to braising. Keeping the skin on allowed us to crisp it into a craggy crust—giving the sauce something to grab onto. A brief marinade in soy sauce helped tenderize and flavor the meat. We also added a can of coconut milk; the thick, rich milk mellowed the sharp saltiness of the traditional vinegar and soy sauce braising liquid—and it added welcome body to the sauce. To render the gummy fat layer in the chicken skin and crisp its surface, we started the meat in a room-temperature nonstick skillet and then turned up the heat, allowing the fat to melt before the exterior burned. We started the browned chicken pieces skin side down in the braising liquid and then, to preserve as much crispness as possible in the finished dish, we turned the chicken pieces skin side up, giving the skin a chance to dry out a little before serving. Serve with rice.

serves 4
total time: 1 hour
(plus 30 minutes for marinating)

8 (5- to 7-ounce) bone-in chicken thighs, trimmed

⅓ cup soy sauce

1 (13.5-ounce) can coconut milk

¾ cup cider vinegar

8 garlic cloves, peeled

4 bay leaves

2 teaspoons pepper

1 scallion, sliced thin

1. Toss chicken with soy sauce in large bowl. Refrigerate for at least 30 minutes or up to 1 hour.

2. Remove chicken from soy sauce, allowing excess to drip back into bowl. Transfer chicken, skin side down, to 12-inch nonstick skillet; set aside soy sauce.

3. Place skillet over medium-high heat and cook until chicken skin is browned, 7 to 10 minutes. While chicken is browning, whisk coconut milk, vinegar, garlic, bay leaves, and pepper into soy sauce.

4. Transfer chicken to plate and discard fat in skillet. Return chicken to skillet skin side down, add coconut milk mixture, and bring to boil. Reduce heat to medium-low and simmer, uncovered, for 20 minutes. Flip chicken skin side up and continue to cook, uncovered, until chicken registers 175 degrees, about 15 minutes. Transfer chicken to platter and tent with aluminum foil.

5. Remove bay leaves and skim any fat off surface of sauce. Return skillet to medium-high heat and cook until sauce is thickened, 5 to 7 minutes. Pour sauce over chicken, sprinkle with scallion, and serve.

za'atar-rubbed butterflied chicken

why this recipe works For an easy but impressive Sunday dinner, we turned to a simple dish of chicken rubbed with *za'atar*. Za'atar is the Arabic name for wild thyme but now commonly denotes an addictive spice mixture of thyme, sumac, and sesame seeds. So the fat would render quickly and allow the skin to crisp, we borrowed an Italian technique of cooking under a brick (or a pot in this case). A thick za'atar paste contributed a strong, complementary flavor to the chicken as it cooked through. To finish, we created a zesty vinaigrette that brightened up the chicken. We prefer to use our homemade za'atar, but you can substitute store-bought if you wish, though flavor can vary by brand.

serves 4
total time: 1 hour 15 minutes

5 tablespoons plus 1 teaspoon extra-virgin olive oil

2 tablespoons za'atar

1 (3½- to 4-pound) whole chicken, giblets discarded

Salt and pepper

1 tablespoon minced fresh mint

¼ preserved lemon, pulp and white pith removed, rind rinsed and minced (1 tablespoon)

2 teaspoons white wine vinegar

½ teaspoon Dijon mustard

1. Adjust oven rack to lowest position and heat oven to 450 degrees. Combine 2 tablespoons oil and za'atar in small bowl. With chicken breast side down, use kitchen shears to cut through bones on either side of backbone. Discard backbone and trim away excess fat and skin around neck. Flip chicken and tuck wingtips behind back.

2. Press firmly on breastbone to flatten, cover with plastic wrap, then pound breast to be same thickness as legs and thighs. Pat chicken dry with paper towels and season with salt and pepper.

3. Heat 1 teaspoon oil in 12-inch ovensafe skillet over medium-high heat until just smoking. Place chicken skin side down in skillet, reduce heat to medium, and place heavy pot on chicken to press it flat. Cook chicken until skin is crisp and browned, about 25 minutes. (If chicken is not crisp after 20 minutes, increase heat to medium-high.)

4. Off heat, remove pot and carefully flip chicken. Brush skin with za'atar mixture, transfer skillet to oven, and roast until breast registers 160 degrees and thighs register 175 degrees, 10 to 20 minutes.

5. Transfer chicken to carving board and let rest for 10 minutes. Meanwhile, whisk mint, preserved lemon, vinegar, mustard, ⅛ teaspoon salt, and ⅛ teaspoon pepper together in bowl until combined. Whisking constantly, slowly drizzle in remaining 3 tablespoons oil until emulsified. Carve chicken and serve with dressing.

za'atar
makes about ½ cup

½ cup dried thyme, ground

2 tablespoons sesame seeds, toasted

1½ tablespoons ground sumac

Combine all ingredients in bowl.

to make ahead
Za'atar can be stored at room temperature in airtight container for up to 1 year.

quick preserved lemons
It takes at least six weeks to make your own preserved lemons; however, if necessary, you can make a quick substitute: Combine four 2-inch strips lemon zest, minced, 1 teaspoon lemon juice, ½ teaspoon water, ¼ teaspoon sugar, and ¼ teaspoon salt. Microwave mixture at 50 percent power until liquid evaporates, about 1½ minutes, stirring and mashing lemon with back of spoon every 30 seconds. Makes about 1 tablespoon.

enchiladas verdes

why this recipe works Beloved for their vibrant green sauce, tender chicken, and gooey cheese topping, enchiladas verdes feature everyone's favorite Mexican flavors and textures. To mimic traditional recipes that dry-roast whole tomatillos and poblanos on the stovetop, we broiled the vegetables. We sprayed tortillas with vegetable oil spray and gently baked them for a few minutes, making filling and rolling easy. To increase spiciness, reserve some of the chiles' ribs and seeds and add them to the food processor in step 4. To avoid soggy enchiladas, be sure to cool the chicken filling before filling the tortillas.

serves 4 to 6
total time: 1 hour 45 minutes

4 teaspoons vegetable oil

1 onion, chopped

½ teaspoon ground cumin

3 garlic cloves, minced

1½ cups chicken broth

1 pound boneless, skinless chicken breasts, trimmed

1½ pounds tomatillos (16 to 20 medium), husks and stems removed, rinsed well and dried

3 poblano chiles, stemmed, halved, and seeded

1–2½ teaspoons sugar

Salt and pepper

8 ounces pepper Jack or Monterey Jack cheese, shredded (2 cups)

½ cup chopped fresh cilantro

12 (6-inch) corn tortillas

Vegetable oil spray

2 scallions, sliced thin

Thinly sliced radishes

Sour cream

1. Adjust 1 oven rack to middle position and second rack 6 inches from broiler element; heat broiler. Heat 2 teaspoons oil in medium saucepan over medium heat until shimmering. Add onion and cook, stirring often, until softened and lightly browned, 5 to 7 minutes. Stir in cumin and two-thirds of garlic and cook, stirring often, until fragrant, about 30 seconds. Decrease heat to low and stir in broth. Add chicken, cover, and simmer until it registers 160 degrees, 15 to 20 minutes, flipping chicken halfway through cooking. Transfer chicken to large bowl; place in refrigerator to cool, about 20 minutes. Measure out ¼ cup liquid and set aside; discard remaining liquid.

2. Meanwhile, toss tomatillos and poblanos with remaining 2 teaspoons oil. Arrange tomatillos cut side down and poblanos skin side up on aluminum foil–lined rimmed baking sheet. Broil on upper rack until vegetables blacken and start to soften, 5 to 10 minutes, rotating sheet halfway through broiling.

3. Remove tomatillos and poblanos from oven, let cool slightly, then remove skins from poblanos (leave tomatillo skins intact). Decrease oven temperature to 350 degrees. Discard foil from sheet and set sheet aside for warming tortillas.

4. Transfer vegetables, along with any accumulated juices, to food processor. Add 1 teaspoon sugar, 1 teaspoon salt, remaining garlic, and reserved cooking liquid to food processor and pulse until sauce is somewhat chunky, about 8 pulses. Season with salt and pepper to taste, and adjust tartness by stirring in remaining sugar, ½ teaspoon at a time; set aside.

5. When chicken is cool, use 2 forks to shred into bite-size pieces. Combine chicken with 1½ cups pepper Jack and cilantro; season with salt to taste.

6. Spread ¾ cup tomatillo sauce evenly over bottom of 13 by 9-inch baking dish. Place tortillas in single layer on 2 baking sheets. Spray both sides of tortillas lightly with vegetable oil spray. Bake until tortillas are soft and pliable, 2 to 4 minutes. Increase oven temperature to 450 degrees. Place warm tortillas on counter and spread ⅓ cup chicken filling down center of each tortilla. Roll each tortilla tightly and place in baking dish, seam side down. Pour remaining tomatillo sauce over top of enchiladas and spread into even layer so that it coats top of each tortilla. Sprinkle with remaining ½ cup pepper Jack and cover tightly with foil.

7. Bake enchiladas on lower rack until heated through and cheese is melted, 15 to 20 minutes. Uncover, sprinkle with scallions, and serve immediately, passing radishes and sour cream separately.

shrimp pad thai

why this recipe works With its sweet-and-sour, salty-spicy sauce, plump, sweet shrimp, and tender rice noodles, pad thai is Thailand's most well-known noodle dish. But making it at home can be a chore, thanks to lengthy ingredient lists with hard-to-find items. We found we could achieve just the right balance of flavors in the sauce using a simple combination of fish sauce, lime juice, rice vinegar, and brown sugar. With such a flavorful base at the ready, we didn't even need to season the shrimp—we merely sautéed them in the pan until barely pink at the edges, then stirred them in later to finish cooking. To get the texture of the rice noodles just right, we first soaked them in hot water so they'd start to soften, then stir-fried them in the pan. Scrambled eggs, chopped peanuts, bean sprouts, and thinly sliced scallions completed our easy and authentic-tasting pad thai. Do not substitute other types of noodles for the rice noodles here.

serves 4
total time: 30 minutes

8 ounces (¼-inch-wide) rice noodles

⅓ cup water

¼ cup lime juice (2 limes)

3 tablespoons fish sauce

3 tablespoons packed brown sugar

1 tablespoon rice vinegar

¼ cup vegetable oil

12 ounces medium shrimp (41 to 50 per pound), peeled, deveined, and tails removed

3 garlic cloves, minced

2 large eggs, lightly beaten

¼ teaspoon salt

6 tablespoons unsalted dry-roasted peanuts, chopped

6 ounces (3 cups) bean sprouts

5 scallions, sliced thin on bias

Lime wedges

Fresh cilantro leaves

Sriracha sauce

1. Cover noodles with very hot tap water in large bowl and stir to separate. Let noodles soak until softened, pliable, and limp but not fully tender, about 20 minutes; drain. In separate bowl, whisk water, lime juice, fish sauce, sugar, vinegar, and 2 tablespoons oil together.

2. Pat shrimp dry with paper towels. Heat 1 tablespoon oil in 12-inch nonstick skillet over high heat until just smoking. Add shrimp in single layer and cook, without stirring, until beginning to brown, about 1 minute. Stir shrimp and continue to cook until spotty brown and just pink around edges, about 30 seconds; transfer to bowl.

3. Add remaining 1 tablespoon oil and garlic to now-empty skillet and cook over medium heat until fragrant, about 30 seconds. Stir in eggs and salt and cook, stirring vigorously, until eggs are scrambled, about 20 seconds.

4. Add drained noodles and fish sauce mixture. Increase heat to high and cook, tossing gently, until noodles are evenly coated. Add cooked shrimp, ¼ cup peanuts, bean sprouts, and three-quarters of scallions. Cook, tossing constantly, until noodles are tender, about 2 minutes. (If necessary, add 2 tablespoons water to skillet and continue to cook until noodles are tender.)

5. Transfer noodles to serving platter and sprinkle with remaining peanuts and remaining scallions. Serve with lime wedges, cilantro leaves, and Sriracha.

thai curry rice with cod

why this recipe works Cod's mild flavor makes it the perfect fish to infuse with the zesty, aromatic flavors of Thai curry. Accompanied by a rice-and-vegetable side, we had an exotic-tasting, satisfying Sunday supper that conveniently cooked all in one skillet. Though this dish could easily have involved lots of prep and multiple pans, we layered the components all in one skillet and timed everything just right for a minimalist but boldly flavored meal. To start, we enhanced our rice with meaty mushrooms and crunchy bamboo shoots; sautéing them all in a gingery scallion oil built lots of flavor quickly. After simmering the rice for 10 minutes, we laid fresh cod fillets on top, ensuring the fish and rice would finish at the same time. We prepared a supersimple red coconut curry sauce in the microwave and drizzled some over the cod to infuse the fish while it cooked. The fish's natural juices flavored the rice from above, marrying all the flavors of the dish. A bright squeeze of lime and sprinkle of scallions, plus some extra sauce, tied everything together before serving. You will need a 12-inch nonstick skillet with a tight-fitting lid for this recipe.

serves 4
total time: 45 minutes

1 tablespoon vegetable oil

1½ cups long-grain white rice

8 ounces white mushrooms, trimmed and sliced thin

1 (8-ounce) can sliced bamboo shoots, rinsed

2 teaspoons grated fresh ginger

3 scallions, white and green parts separated and sliced thin

2¼ cups water

Salt and pepper

¾ cup canned coconut milk

3 tablespoons red curry paste

4 (6- to 8-ounce) skinless cod fillets, 1 to 1½ inches thick

Lime wedges

1. Heat oil in 12-inch nonstick skillet over medium heat until shimmering. Add rice, mushrooms, bamboo shoots, ginger, and scallion whites. Cook, stirring often, until edges of rice begin to turn translucent, about 2 minutes. Add water and ½ teaspoon salt and bring to boil. Cover, reduce heat to medium-low, and simmer for 10 minutes.

2. Whisk coconut milk and curry paste together in bowl. Pat cod dry with paper towels and season with salt and pepper. Lay fillets, skinned side down, on top of rice mixture and drizzle with one-third of coconut-curry sauce. Cover and cook until liquid is absorbed and cod flakes apart when gently prodded with paring knife and registers 140 degrees, 10 to 12 minutes.

3. Meanwhile, microwave remaining coconut-curry sauce mixture until warm, about 1 minute. Sprinkle scallion greens over fish and rice mixture. Serve with remaining coconut-curry sauce and lime wedges.

miso-glazed salmon

why this recipe works With just a few bold ingredients, this classic Japanese dish boasts salty, sweet, and rich-tasting salmon and a deeply caramelized, almost candy-like exterior. We found the perfect ratio of white miso, sugar, and sake that offered intense flavor and a texture thick enough that it clung nicely to our fillets. Fresh grated ginger, though not traditional, helped to brighten the dish. Authentic Japanese recipes call for marinating the salmon for up to two days, but we found that a minimum of 5 hours gave the salmon plenty of time to absorb the flavors. Broiling was the best way to achieve the caramelized crust we were after; in less than 10 minutes, our salmon was perfectly done. A sprinkle of minced cilantro contributed fresh, grassy notes that offset the richness of the fish. When removing the salmon from the marinade, do not wipe away any excess marinade clinging to the fish; the excess marinade will turn into a sweet-salty crust during cooking. Use center-cut salmon fillets of similar thickness so that they cook at the same rate. The best way to ensure uniformity is to buy a 1½-pound whole center-cut fillet and cut it into 4 pieces. Be sure to buy white miso, but do not buy light or low-sodium white miso; these will not work in this recipe. Note that you'll have to read the label carefully to know if the miso is light or low-sodium. Serve with Sesame Sushi Rice.

serves 4
total time: 20 minutes
(plus 5 hours for marinating)

1 cup white miso

½ cup sugar

½ cup sake

1½ teaspoons grated fresh ginger

4 (6-ounce) center-cut skin-on salmon fillets

2 tablespoons minced fresh cilantro

1. Whisk miso, sugar, sake, and ginger together in medium bowl to dissolve sugar and miso. Place fillets in a 1-gallon zipper-lock bag and pour marinade evenly into bag. Seal bag, pressing out as much air as possible, and refrigerate at least 5 hours or up to 24 hours, flipping bag occasionally to ensure fish marinates evenly.

2. Adjust oven rack 6 inches from broiler element and heat broiler. Line broiler pan bottom with aluminum foil and top with slotted broiler pan top. Remove fish from marinade and lay on broiler pan top, skin side down. Spoon 1 tablespoon marinade over each fillet; discard extra marinade.

3. Broil salmon until center is still translucent when checked with tip of paring knife and registers 125 degrees (for medium-rare), 7 to 10 minutes. Transfer salmon to platter or individual plates, sprinkle with cilantro, and serve.

sesame sushi rice
serves 4 to 6

2½ cups water

2 cups sushi or short-grain white rice

2 teaspoons seasoned rice vinegar

1 teaspoon salt

2 scallions, sliced thin

2 tablespoons toasted sesame oil

1 tablespoon sesame seeds, toasted

Bring water, rice, vinegar, and salt to boil in medium saucepan over high heat. Cover, reduce heat to low, and cook until liquid is absorbed, 14 to 16 minutes. Remove rice from heat and let sit, covered, until tender, about 15 minutes. Fluff rice with fork, stir in scallions, oil, and sesame seeds, and serve.

argentine steaks with chimichurri sauce

why this recipe works There's something about summer that calls for Sunday evenings spent outside around the grill. For an impressive steak dinner that would feed a crowd, we scaled down an Argentine favorite: 2-pound steaks grilled over a hardwood fire, boasting plenty of smokiness and a thick, flavorful browned crust. To translate their method to smaller American steaks, we rubbed our steaks with salt and used the freezer as a dehydrator to evaporate all the surface moisture; this helped develop a substantial crust on the grill. Rubbing the dried steaks with cornstarch enhanced browning even more. Covering the grill for the first few minutes of cooking helped jump-start the flavoring process. A fresh, herb-packed chimichurri sauce complemented the richness of the meat. Serve with Garlic Mashed Potatoes (page 11).

serves 6 to 8
total time: 1 hour 30 minutes
(plus 30 minutes for salting)

sauce
¼ cup hot tap water

2 teaspoons dried oregano

1 teaspoon salt

1⅓ cups fresh parsley leaves

⅔ cup fresh cilantro leaves

6 garlic cloves, minced

½ teaspoon red pepper flakes

¼ cup red wine vinegar

½ cup extra-virgin olive oil

steaks
1 tablespoon cornstarch

1½ teaspoons salt

4 (1-pound) boneless strip steaks, 1½ inches thick, trimmed

4 medium wood chunks, unsoaked

1 (9-inch) disposable aluminum pie plate (if using gas)

Pepper

1. for the sauce Combine water, oregano, and salt in small bowl and let sit until oregano is softened, about 15 minutes. Pulse parsley, cilantro, garlic, and pepper flakes in food processor until coarsely chopped, about 10 pulses. Add water mixture and vinegar and pulse to combine. Transfer mixture to bowl and slowly whisk in oil until emulsified. Cover and let sit at room temperature for 1 hour.

2. for the steaks Meanwhile, combine cornstarch and salt in bowl. Pat steaks dry with paper towels and place on wire rack set in rimmed baking sheet. Rub entire surface of steaks with cornstarch mixture and place steaks, uncovered, in freezer until very firm, about 30 minutes.

3a. for a charcoal grill Open bottom vent halfway. Light large chimney starter filled with charcoal briquettes (6 quarts). When top coals are partially covered with ash, pour evenly over grill. Using tongs, place wood chunks directly on top of coals, spacing them evenly around perimeter of grill. Set cooking grate in place, cover, and open lid vent halfway. Heat grill until hot and wood chunks are smoking, about 5 minutes.

3b. for a gas grill Turn all burners to high, cover, and heat grill until hot, about 15 minutes. Leave all burners on high. Place wood chunks in disposable aluminum pie plate and set on cooking grate. Close lid and heat until wood chunks begin to smoke, about 5 minutes.

4. Clean and oil cooking grate. Season steaks with pepper. Place steaks on grill, cover, and cook until beginning to brown on both sides, 4 to 6 minutes, flipping halfway through cooking.

5. Flip steaks and cook, uncovered, until well browned on first side, 2 to 4 minutes. Flip steaks and continue to cook until meat registers 115 to 120 degrees (for rare) or 120 to 125 degrees (for medium-rare), 2 to 6 minutes longer.

6. Transfer steaks to carving board, tent with aluminum foil, and let rest for 10 minutes. Slice each steak ¼ inch thick. Serve, passing sauce separately.

to make ahead
Chimichurri sauce can be refrigerated for up to 3 days.

japanese-style stir-fried noodles with beef

why this recipe works For a home cook–friendly version of this Japanese stir-fry, we isolated the best supermarket alternatives to hard-to-find Japanese ingredients. Undercooking lo mein noodles mimicked the chew of *yakisoba* noodles. Garnish with pickled ginger and our Sesame-Orange Spice Blend.

serves 4 to 6
total time: 1 hour 15 minutes

⅛ teaspoon baking soda

12 ounces flank steak, trimmed, sliced lengthwise into 2- to 2½-inch strips, each strip sliced crosswise ¼ inch thick

¼ cup ketchup

¼ cup soy sauce

2 tablespoons Worcestershire sauce

1½ tablespoons packed brown sugar

3 garlic cloves, minced

3 anchovy fillets, rinsed, patted dry, and minced

1 teaspoon rice vinegar

1 pound fresh or 8 ounces dried lo mein noodles

1 tablespoon vegetable oil

6 ounces shiitake mushrooms, stemmed and sliced ¼ inch thick

1 carrot, peeled and sliced ⅛ inch thick on bias

¾ cup chicken broth

6 cups napa cabbage, sliced crosswise into ½-inch strips

7 scallions, cut on bias into 1-inch lengths

Salt

1. Combine 1 tablespoon water and baking soda in medium bowl. Add beef and toss to coat. Let sit at room temperature for 5 minutes.

2. Whisk ketchup, soy sauce, Worcestershire, sugar, garlic, anchovies, and vinegar together in second bowl. Stir 2 tablespoons sauce into beef mixture and set aside remaining sauce.

3. Bring 4 quarts water to boil in large pot. Add noodles and cook, stirring often, until almost tender (center should still be firm with slightly opaque dot), 3 to 10 minutes (cooking times will vary depending on whether you are using fresh or dry noodles). Drain noodles and rinse under cold running water until water runs clear. Drain well and set aside.

4. Heat ½ teaspoon oil in 12-inch nonstick skillet over high heat until just smoking. Add mushrooms and carrot and cook, stirring occasionally, until vegetables are spotty brown, 2 to 3 minutes. Add ¼ cup broth and cook until all liquid has evaporated and vegetables are tender, about 30 seconds. Transfer vegetables to bowl.

5. Return skillet to high heat, add ½ teaspoon oil, and heat until beginning to smoke. Add cabbage and scallions and cook, without stirring, for 30 seconds. Cook, stirring occasionally, until cabbage and scallions are spotty brown and crisp-tender, 2 to 3 minutes. Transfer to bowl with mushrooms and carrot.

6. Return skillet to high heat, add 1 teaspoon oil, and heat until beginning to smoke. Add half of beef

in single layer. Cook, without stirring, for 30 seconds. Cook, stirring occasionally, until beef is spotty brown, 1 to 2 minutes. Transfer to bowl with vegetables. Repeat with remaining 1 teaspoon oil and remaining beef.

7. Return skillet to high heat; add reserved sauce, remaining ½ cup broth, and noodles. Cook, scraping up any browned bits, until noodles are warmed through, about 1 minute. Transfer noodles to bowl with vegetables and beef and toss to combine. Season with salt to taste, and serve immediately.

sesame-orange spice blend
makes ¼ cup
Store in an airtight container for up to one week.

¾ teaspoon grated orange zest

2 teaspoons sesame seeds

1½ teaspoons paprika

1 teaspoon pepper

¼ teaspoon garlic powder

¼ teaspoon ground ginger

⅛ teaspoon cayenne pepper

Place orange zest in small bowl and microwave, stirring every 20 seconds, until zest is dry and no longer clumping together, 1 minute 30 seconds to 2 minutes 30 seconds. Stir in sesame seeds, paprika, pepper, garlic powder, ginger, and cayenne.

panang beef curry

why this recipe works With its tender chunks of meat and hallmark sauce just waiting to be absorbed by fluffy rice, panang curry will bring the flavors and aromas of Thailand into your home. Made with an orange-red paste that usually includes ground peanuts, this dish is a sweeter, more unctuous derivative of red curry. For a meaty, rich panang curry, we started by using a traditional technique of simmering a tougher cut of beef in water before adding it to the quick-cooking sauce. We cut boneless beef short ribs into ¼-inch slices, so they cooked up ultratender in just an hour. Store-bought red curry paste made for a quick and flavorful base, while coconut milk, fish sauce, and sugar turned it into a creamy, well-balanced sauce. Kaffir lime leaves and a Thai red chile lent brightness and heat while a final sprinkling of finely chopped peanuts gave the dish its characteristic nutty flavor. Because red curry pastes vary in spiciness from brand to brand, start by adding 2 tablespoons of paste. Then taste the sauce and add up to 2 more tablespoons to suit your taste. We highly recommend seeking out kaffir lime leaves for this dish. If you cannot find them, substitute three 3-inch strips each of lemon and lime zest and add to the sauce along with the beef in step 2 (remove the strips before serving). Do not substitute light coconut milk. Serve with Foolproof Baked White Rice (page 10).

serves 6
total time: 1 hour 45 minutes

2 pounds boneless beef short ribs, trimmed

2 tablespoons vegetable oil

2–4 tablespoons red curry paste

1 (14-ounce) can unsweetened coconut milk

4 teaspoons fish sauce

2 teaspoons sugar

1 Thai red chile, halved lengthwise (optional)

6 kaffir lime leaves, middle vein removed, thinly sliced

⅓ cup unsalted dry-roasted peanuts, chopped fine

1. Cut each short rib crosswise, with grain, into 3 equal pieces. Slice each piece, against grain, into ¼-inch thick slices. Place beef in large saucepan and add water to cover. Bring to boil over high heat. Cover, reduce heat to low, and cook until meat is fork tender, 1 to 1¼ hours. Using slotted spoon, transfer beef to bowl; discard water. (Beef can be cooked up to 2 hours in advance.)

2. Heat vegetable oil in 12-inch nonstick skillet over medium heat until shimmering. Add 2 tablespoons curry paste and cook, stirring frequently, until paste is fragrant and darkens in color to brick red, 5 to 8 minutes. Add coconut milk, fish sauce, sugar, and chile (if using) and stir to combine and dissolve sugar. Taste sauce and add up to 2 more tablespoons red curry paste to suit desired spiciness. Add beef and stir to coat with sauce, and bring to simmer.

3. Vigorously simmer, stirring occasionally, until liquid is thickened, reduced by half, and coats beef, 12 to 15 minutes. (Sauce should be quite thick and streaks of oil will appear. Sauce will continue to thicken as it cools.) Add kaffir lime leaves and simmer until aromatic, 1 to 2 minutes. Transfer to serving platter, sprinkle with peanuts, and serve.

cuban braised shredded beef (ropa vieja)

why this recipe works A comforting Cuban dish of braised and shredded beef, sliced peppers and onions, chopped green olives, and a brothy sauce, ropa vieja is as hearty as it is rustic. Traditionally, the dish requires making a beef stock and then using the meat and some of the liquid to make a separate sauté with onion, pepper, and spices. To simplify, we combined the two cooking methods into the ease of a Dutch oven braise, which also meant that all of the beef's juices ended up in the final dish. We eschewed traditional flank steak in favor of brisket, which contains the right mix of beefy flavor and collagen to guarantee tender, flavorful, juicy shreds. We cut the brisket ahead of time into 2-inch-wide strips, which sped up cooking and made shredding a breeze. To mimic the meatiness that commonly comes from an MSG-spiked seasoning blend, we chose to sear the meat before braising, and we added glutamate-rich anchovies to the mix. We found that slowly caramelizing the onion and pepper strips mimicked the deep flavor of a traditional sofrito without requiring an extra step. The final addition of briny chopped green olives and a splash of white vinegar brought all the flavors into sharp focus. Look for a brisket that is 1½ to 2½ inches thick. Serve with Foolproof Baked White Rice (page 10).

serves 6 to 8
total time: 3 hours

1 (2-pound) beef brisket, fat trimmed to ¼ inch

Salt and pepper

5 tablespoons vegetable oil

2 onions, halved and sliced thin

2 red bell peppers, stemmed, seeded, and sliced into ¼-inch-wide strips

2 anchovy fillets, rinsed, patted dry, and minced

4 garlic cloves, minced

2 teaspoons ground cumin

1½ teaspoons dried oregano

½ cup dry white wine

2 cups chicken broth

1 (8-ounce) can tomato sauce

2 bay leaves

¾ cup pitted green olives, chopped coarse

¾ teaspoon white wine vinegar, plus extra for seasoning

1. Adjust oven rack to middle position and heat oven to 300 degrees. Cut brisket against grain into 2-inch-wide strips. Cut any strips longer than 5 inches in half crosswise. Season beef on all sides with salt and pepper.

2. Heat 4 tablespoons oil in Dutch oven over medium-high heat until just smoking. Brown beef on all sides, 7 to 10 minutes; transfer to large plate and set aside. Add onions and bell peppers and cook until softened and pan bottom develops fond, 10 to 15 minutes. Transfer vegetables to bowl and set aside.

3. Add remaining 1 tablespoon oil to now-empty pot, then add anchovies, garlic, cumin, and oregano and cook until fragrant, about 30 seconds. Stir in wine, scraping up any browned bits, and cook until mostly evaporated, about 1 minute. Stir in broth, tomato sauce, and bay leaves. Return beef and any accumulated juices to pot and bring to simmer over high heat. Transfer to oven and cook, covered, until beef is just tender, 2 to 2¼ hours, flipping meat halfway through cooking.

4. Transfer beef to cutting board; when cool enough to handle, shred into ¼-inch-thick pieces. Meanwhile, add olives and reserved vegetables to pot and bring to boil over medium-high heat; simmer until thickened and measures 4 cups, 5 to 7 minutes. Stir in beef. Add vinegar. Season with salt, pepper, and extra vinegar to taste; serve.

moroccan braised white beans with lamb

why this recipe works A dish of stewed white beans, *loubia* is well loved in Morocco—and for good reason, as the beans are cooked in a warm-spiced, tomatoey base that's enhanced by a lamb shank and makes for a comforting, cozy weekend meal. *Khlii*, a Moroccan preserved meat, is often used as a flavorful seasoning, leaving the beans to take center stage. But khlii is difficult to find in the United States, so we decided to use more easily accessible lamb shank to infuse meaty flavor into the dish. We seared and then slowly braised the lamb in the oven with the beans. A healthy dose of Moroccan-inspired spices gave the dish a deeply flavorful backbone, and some white wine provided acidity. A combination of mostly chicken broth and a little water gave the dish some savory depth without making it too salty. We chose dried beans over canned so that the beans would cook at the same rate as the lamb shank, leaving us with creamy, richly flavored beans and melt-in-your-mouth tender pieces of lamb. You can substitute 1 pound of lamb shoulder chops (blade or round bone), 1 to 1½ inches thick, trimmed and halved, for the lamb shank; reduce the browning time in step 2 to 8 minutes. Serve with Classic Couscous (page 9).

serves 6 to 8
total time: 2 hours 30 minutes
(plus 8 hours for soaking beans)

Salt and pepper

1 pound (2½ cups) dried great Northern beans, picked over and rinsed

1 (12- to 16-ounce) lamb shank

1 tablespoon extra-virgin olive oil, plus extra for serving

1 onion, chopped

1 red bell pepper, stemmed, seeded, and chopped fine

2 tablespoons tomato paste

3 garlic cloves, minced

2 teaspoons paprika

2 teaspoons ground cumin

1½ teaspoons ground ginger

¼ teaspoon cayenne pepper

½ cup dry white wine

4 cups chicken broth

2 tablespoons minced fresh parsley

1. Dissolve 3 tablespoons salt in 4 quarts cold water in large container. Add beans and soak at room temperature for at least 8 hours or up to 24 hours. Drain and rinse well.

2. Adjust oven rack to lower-middle position and heat oven to 350 degrees. Pat lamb dry with paper towels and season with salt and pepper. Heat oil in Dutch oven over medium-high heat until just smoking. Brown lamb on all sides, 10 to 15 minutes; transfer to plate. Pour off all but 2 tablespoons fat from pot.

3. Add onion and bell pepper to fat left in pot and cook over medium heat until softened and lightly browned, 5 to 7 minutes. Stir in tomato paste, garlic, paprika, cumin, ginger, cayenne, and ⅛ teaspoon pepper and cook until fragrant, about 30 seconds. Stir in wine, scraping up any browned bits. Stir in broth, 1 cup water, and beans and bring to boil.

4. Nestle lamb into beans along with any accumulated juices. Cover, transfer pot to oven, and cook until fork slips easily in and out of lamb and beans are tender, 1½ to 1¾ hours, stirring every 30 minutes.

5. Transfer lamb to cutting board, let cool slightly, then shred into bite-size pieces using 2 forks; discard excess fat and bone. Stir shredded lamb and parsley into beans and season with salt and pepper to taste. Adjust consistency with extra hot water as needed. Serve, drizzling individual portions with extra oil.

meatless sundays

mushroom bolognese

why this recipe works Pasta with Bolognese is a cozy Sunday favorite, but we wanted to create a vegetarian pasta sauce that mimicked its rich, long-cooked flavor and hearty texture. Traditional Bolognese sauce gets its rich flavor from a combination of several types of meat, so we turned to two types of mushrooms to replicate that complexity: Dried porcini delivered depth of flavor while fresh cremini gave the sauce a satisfying, substantial texture. To boost the sauce's savory flavor, we added two umami-rich ingredients: soy sauce and tomato paste. To make prep easy, we used the food processor both to chop the cremini roughly and then to finely chop the onion and carrot. Pulsing whole canned tomatoes in the food processor allowed us to get just the right texture. We also used red wine to lend richness and depth and a little sugar for some balancing sweetness. A dash of heavy cream at the end rounded out the sauce and gave it a decadent silkiness. Cremini mushrooms are also known as baby bella mushrooms.

serves 8 to 10
total time: 1 hour

2 pounds cremini mushrooms, trimmed and quartered

1 carrot, peeled and chopped

1 small onion, chopped

1 (28-ounce) can whole peeled tomatoes

3 tablespoons unsalted butter

½ ounce dried porcini mushrooms, rinsed and minced

3 garlic cloves, minced

1 teaspoon sugar

2 tablespoons tomato paste

1 cup dry red wine

½ cup vegetable broth

1 tablespoon soy sauce

Salt and pepper

3 tablespoons heavy cream

1 pound fettuccine or linguine

Grated Parmesan cheese

1. Working in batches, pulse cremini mushrooms in food processor until pieces are no larger than ½ inch, 5 to 7 pulses; transfer to large bowl. Pulse carrot and onion in now-empty processor until finely chopped, 5 to 7 pulses; transfer to bowl with mushrooms. Pulse tomatoes and their juice in now-empty processor until finely chopped, 6 to 8 pulses; set aside separately.

2. Melt butter in Dutch oven over medium heat. Add processed vegetables and porcini mushrooms, cover, and cook, stirring occasionally, until they release their liquid, about 5 minutes. Uncover, increase heat to medium-high, and cook until liquid has evaporated and vegetables begin to brown, 12 to 15 minutes.

3. Stir in garlic and sugar and cook until fragrant, about 30 seconds. Stir in tomato paste and cook for 1 minute. Stir in wine and simmer until nearly evaporated, about 5 minutes.

4. Stir in processed tomatoes, broth, soy sauce, ½ teaspoon salt, and ¼ teaspoon pepper and bring to simmer. Reduce heat to medium-low and simmer until sauce has thickened but is still moist, 8 to 10 minutes. Off heat, stir in cream.

5. Meanwhile, bring 4 quarts water to boil in large pot. Add pasta and 1 tablespoon salt and cook, stirring often, until al dente. Reserve ½ cup cooking water, then drain pasta and return it to pot. Add sauce and toss to combine. Season with salt and pepper to taste, and adjust consistency with reserved cooking water as needed. Serve with Parmesan.

to make ahead
Sauce, prepared through step 4, can be refrigerated for up to 3 days or frozen for up to 1 month; if frozen, thaw completely in refrigerator. To reheat, bring sauce, covered, to gentle simmer, stirring often, and continue with step 5.

campanelle with roasted cauliflower, garlic, and walnuts

why this recipe works Going meatless doesn't mean your Sunday pasta dinner has to be dull; we transformed a standard garlicky pasta into an exceptional, rustic dish with bold flavors and hearty textures. When done right, high-heat roasting can turn cauliflower from a mild-mannered vegetable into an intensely flavored, sweet, nutty foil for pasta. To achieve a golden exterior, we sliced the cauliflower into wedges to create maximum surface area while leaving the core and florets intact. Tossing the cauliflower with a little sugar jump-started the browning; preheating the baking sheet also helped to develop as much flavor as possible. We found that cream-based sauces muted the nutty cauliflower flavor and pestos overwhelmed it, so we focused on a simple lemony dressing with mashed garlic that we roasted in the oven until tender and sweet. We rounded out the sauce with fresh parsley and some Parmesan and topped each serving with a handful of toasted walnuts to add a pleasing crunch. If campanelle is unavailable, farfalle or fusilli make a good substitute.

serves 4 to 6
total time: 1 hour 15 minutes

2 garlic heads, top quarter cut off to expose garlic cloves

6 tablespoons plus 1 teaspoon extra-virgin olive oil

1 head cauliflower (2 pounds)

Salt and pepper

¼ teaspoon sugar

2 tablespoons lemon juice, plus extra as needed

¼ teaspoon red pepper flakes

1 pound campanelle

1 ounce Parmesan cheese, grated (½ cup), plus extra for serving

1 tablespoon chopped fresh parsley

¼ cup walnuts, toasted and chopped coarse

1. Adjust oven rack to middle position, place large rimmed baking sheet on rack, and heat oven to 500 degrees. Place garlic heads, cut side up, in center of 12-inch square of aluminum foil. Drizzle each with ½ teaspoon oil and wrap securely. Place packet on oven rack next to baking sheet and roast until garlic is very tender, about 40 minutes.

2. Meanwhile, remove outer leaves from cauliflower and cut stalk flush with bottom. Cut head from pole to pole into 8 equal wedges. Toss cauliflower with 2 tablespoons oil, 1 teaspoon salt, ¼ teaspoon pepper, and sugar in bowl. Remove baking sheet from oven. Carefully lay cauliflower wedges cut side down on hot baking sheet. Roast cauliflower until well browned and tender, 20 to 25 minutes.

3. Transfer cauliflower to cutting board, let cool slightly, then cut into ½-inch pieces. Transfer garlic packet to cutting board, let cool for 10 minutes, then unwrap garlic. Gently squeeze to remove cloves from skin, transfer to small bowl, and mash smooth with fork. Stir in lemon juice and pepper flakes, then slowly whisk in remaining ¼ cup oil.

4. Bring 4 quarts water to boil in large pot. Add pasta and 1 tablespoon salt and cook, stirring often, until al dente. Reserve 1 cup cooking water, then drain pasta and return it to pot. Add chopped cauliflower, garlic sauce, Parmesan, parsley, and ¼ cup reserved cooking water, and toss to combine. Season with salt, pepper, and extra lemon juice to taste. Add reserved cooking water as needed to adjust consistency. Sprinkle individual portions with walnuts and serve with extra Parmesan.

eggplant parmesan

why this recipe works Eggplant Parmesan is an Italian favorite among vegetarians and meat-lovers alike. But frying the eggplant is time-consuming and can make the dish heavy. In the hope of eliminating most of the grease as well as some of the prep time, we opted to cook the breaded eggplant in the oven. To keep its excess moisture from turning the eggplant soggy, we salted and drained the slices before baking. Leaving the top layer of eggplant mostly unsauced ensured that it would crisp up nicely in the oven.

serves 6 to 8
total time: 1 hour 45 minutes

eggplant
2 pounds eggplant, sliced into ¼-inch-thick rounds

Kosher salt and pepper

8 slices hearty white sandwich bread, torn into quarters

2 ounces Parmesan cheese, grated (1 cup)

1 cup all-purpose flour

4 large eggs

6 tablespoons vegetable oil

sauce
3 (14.5-ounce) cans diced tomatoes

2 tablespoons extra-virgin olive oil

4 garlic cloves, minced

¼ teaspoon red pepper flakes

¼ cup chopped fresh basil

Kosher salt and pepper

8 ounces mozzarella, shredded (2 cups)

1 ounce Parmesan cheese, grated (½ cup)

10 fresh basil leaves, roughly torn

1. for the eggplant Toss eggplant with 1½ teaspoons salt and let drain in colander until eggplant releases about 2 tablespoons liquid, 30 to 45 minutes. Wipe excess salt from eggplant, then spread out over baking sheet lined with paper towels and thoroughly pat dry with more paper towels to remove as much liquid as possible.

2. Meanwhile, adjust oven racks to upper-middle and lower-middle positions, place rimmed baking sheet on each rack, and heat oven to 425 degrees. Pulse bread in food processor to fine, even crumbs, about 15 pulses (you should have about 4 cups). Transfer crumbs to shallow dish and stir in Parmesan and ½ teaspoon pepper. Wipe out food processor bowl.

3. Combine flour and 1 teaspoon pepper in large zipper-lock bag and shake to combine. Beat eggs in second shallow dish. Working with 8 to 10 eggplant slices at a time, add eggplant to bag with flour mixture and shake to coat. Shake off excess flour, dip eggplant in eggs, then coat with bread-crumb mixture; transfer to wire rack set in separate rimmed baking sheet.

4. Remove preheated baking sheets from oven. Add 3 tablespoons oil to each sheet, tilting to coat pan evenly. Place breaded eggplant on baking sheets in single layer and bake until well browned and crisp, about 30 minutes, switching and rotating baking sheets after 10 minutes, and flipping eggplant slices after 20 minutes. Do not turn off oven.

5. for the sauce Process 2 cans diced tomatoes and their juice in now-empty food processor until almost smooth, about 5 seconds. Heat oil, garlic, and pepper flakes in large saucepan over medium-high heat, stirring occasionally, until fragrant and garlic is light golden, about 3 minutes. Stir in processed tomatoes and remaining can diced tomatoes and their juice, and bring to boil. Reduce heat to simmer and cook until slightly thickened and reduced to 4 cups, about 15 minutes. Off heat, stir in basil and season with salt and pepper to taste.

6. Spread 1 cup tomato sauce over bottom of 13 by 9-inch baking dish. Layer half of eggplant slices into dish, overlapping slices to fit. Top evenly with 1 cup sauce and sprinkle with 1 cup mozzarella. Layer remaining eggplant into dish, then dot with 1 cup sauce, leaving majority of eggplant exposed so it will remain crisp. Sprinkle with Parmesan and remaining 1 cup mozzarella. Bake until sauce is bubbling and cheese is browned, 13 to 15 minutes. Let cool for 10 minutes, then sprinkle with basil and serve with remaining sauce.

hearty vegetable lasagna

why this recipe works For a hearty vegetable lasagna with bold flavors that won't leave you missing traditional beef lasagna, we used a mix of zucchini, yellow squash, and eggplant. Instead of using ricotta, we made a cream sauce with cottage cheese, heavy cream, and Parmesan. Avoid preshredded cheese, as it does not melt well. If using table salt, reduce all salt amounts by half.

serves 8 to 10
total time: 2 hours 30 minutes

tomato sauce
1 (28-ounce) can crushed tomatoes

¼ cup chopped fresh basil

2 tablespoons extra-virgin olive oil

2 garlic cloves, minced

1 teaspoon kosher salt

¼ teaspoon red pepper flakes

cream sauce
8 ounces (1 cup) whole-milk cottage cheese

1 cup heavy cream

4 ounces Parmesan cheese, grated (2 cups)

2 garlic cloves, minced

1 teaspoon cornstarch

½ teaspoon kosher salt

½ teaspoon pepper

lasagna
1½ pounds eggplant, peeled and cut into ½-inch pieces

Kosher salt and pepper

1 pound zucchini, cut into ½-inch pieces

1 pound yellow squash, cut into ½-inch pieces

5 tablespoons plus 1 teaspoon extra-virgin olive oil

4 garlic cloves, minced

1 tablespoon minced fresh thyme

12 ounces (12 cups) baby spinach

12 no-boil lasagna noodles

½ cup pitted kalamata olives, minced

12 ounces whole-milk mozzarella cheese, shredded (3 cups)

2 tablespoons chopped fresh basil

1. for the tomato sauce Whisk all ingredients together in bowl. (Sauce can be refrigerated for up to 1 day.)

2. for the cream sauce Whisk all ingredients together in bowl. (Sauce can be refrigerated for up to 1 day.)

3. for the lasagna Adjust oven rack to middle position and heat oven to 375 degrees. Line large plate with double layer of coffee filters and spray with vegetable oil spray. Toss eggplant with 1 teaspoon salt and spread evenly over coffee filters. Microwave eggplant, uncovered, until dry to touch and slightly shriveled, about 10 minutes, tossing halfway through microwaving. Let eggplant cool slightly, then toss with zucchini and yellow squash.

4. Combine 1 tablespoon oil, garlic, and thyme in small bowl. Heat 2 tablespoons oil in 12-inch non-stick skillet over medium-high heat until shimmering. Add half of eggplant-squash mixture, ¼ teaspoon salt, and ¼ teaspoon pepper, and cook, stirring occasionally, until vegetables are lightly browned, about 7 minutes. Clear center of skillet, add half of garlic mixture, and cook, mashing with spatula,

until fragrant, about 30 seconds. Stir garlic mixture into vegetables and transfer to medium bowl. Repeat with remaining eggplant mixture, 2 tablespoons oil, and remaining garlic mixture; transfer to bowl.

5. Heat remaining 1 teaspoon oil in now-empty skillet over medium-high heat until shimmering. Add spinach and cook, stirring frequently, until wilted, about 3 minutes. Transfer spinach to paper towel–lined plate and drain for 2 minutes. Stir into eggplant mixture. (Cooked vegetables can be refrigerated for up to 1 day.)

6. Grease 13 by 9-inch baking dish. Spread 1 cup tomato sauce evenly over bottom of dish. Arrange 4 noodles on top of sauce (noodles will overlap). Spread half of vegetable mixture over noodles, followed by half of olives. Spoon half of cream sauce over top, and sprinkle with 1 cup mozzarella. Repeat layering with 4 noodles, 1 cup tomato sauce, remaining vegetables, remaining olives, remaining cream sauce, and 1 cup mozzarella. For final layer, arrange remaining 4 noodles on top and cover completely with remaining tomato sauce. Sprinkle with remaining 1 cup mozzarella.

7. Cover dish tightly with aluminum foil that has been sprayed with oil spray, and bake until edges are just bubbling, about 35 minutes, rotating dish halfway through baking. Let lasagna cool for 25 minutes, then sprinkle with basil and serve.

farro bowl with tofu, mushrooms, and spinach

why this recipe works Vegetable-and-grain bowls give you the freedom to mix things up—literally and stylistically—at dinnertime. This bowl is a shining example of that. The base of this bowl, hearty, nutty farro, is traditionally associated with Italy and flavor profiles of the western Mediterranean. We wanted to prove that farro need not be typecast, and we thought it would stand up well to bold Asian ingredients. For toppings, we chose crispy seared tofu planks, along with a simple sauté of mushrooms, shallot, and spinach. We partnered these easy-to-prepare toppings with our Miso-Ginger Sauce, which is enhanced with a little mayo for body. We prefer the flavor and texture of whole-grain farro; pearled farro can be used, but the texture may be softer. We found a wide range of cooking times among various brands of farro, so start checking for doneness after 10 minutes. Do not use quick-cooking farro in this recipe.

serves 4 to 6
total time: 1 hour

1½ cups whole farro

Salt and pepper

2 teaspoons toasted sesame oil

1 teaspoon sherry vinegar

14 ounces firm tofu, sliced crosswise into 8 equal slabs

⅓ cup cornstarch

¼ cup vegetable oil, plus extra as needed

10 ounces cremini mushrooms, trimmed and chopped coarse

1 shallot, minced

2 tablespoons dry sherry

10 ounces (10 cups) baby spinach

1 recipe Miso-Ginger Sauce

2 scallions, sliced thin

1. Bring 4 quarts water to boil in Dutch oven. Stir in farro and 1 tablespoon salt, return to boil, and cook until grains are tender with slight chew, 15 to 30 minutes. Drain farro and return to now-empty pot. Drizzle with sesame oil and vinegar, toss to coat, and cover to keep warm.

2. While farro cooks, spread tofu on paper towel–lined baking sheet and let drain for 20 minutes. Gently press dry with paper towels and season with salt and pepper.

3. Spread cornstarch in shallow dish. Coat tofu thoroughly in cornstarch, pressing gently to adhere; transfer to plate. Heat 1 tablespoon oil in 12-inch nonstick skillet over medium-high heat until just smoking. Add tofu and cook until both sides are crisp and browned, about 4 minutes per side, adding more oil as necessary to prevent charring. Transfer to paper towel–lined plate to drain and tent with aluminum foil.

4. In now-empty skillet, heat 2 tablespoons oil over medium-high heat until shimmering. Stir in mushrooms, shallot, and ⅛ teaspoon salt and cook until vegetables begin to brown, 5 to 8 minutes. Stir in sherry and cook, scraping up any browned bits, until skillet is nearly dry, about 1 minute; transfer to bowl.

5. In now-empty skillet, heat remaining 1 tablespoon oil over medium-high heat until shimmering. Add spinach, 1 handful at a time, and cook until just wilted, about 1 minute.

6. Divide farro among individual serving bowls, then top each bowl with tofu, mushrooms, and spinach. Drizzle with Miso-Ginger Sauce, sprinkle with scallions, and serve.

miso-ginger sauce
makes about ¾ cup

¼ cup mayonnaise

3 tablespoons red miso

2 tablespoons water

1 tablespoon maple syrup

1 tablespoon sesame oil

1½ teaspoons sherry vinegar

1½ teaspoons grated fresh ginger

Whisk all ingredients in bowl until well combined.

ultimate vegetarian chili

why this recipe works We wanted to develop a vegetarian version of classic chili so flavorful, savory, and satisfying that even meat lovers would enjoy it on its own merits. We incorporated two kinds of beans, plus bulgur, to bulk up the chili, giving it a substantial texture. A combination of umami-rich ingredients—soy sauce, dried shiitake mushrooms, and tomatoes—added deep, savory flavor. Walnuts, also high in flavor-boosting glutamates, contributed even more richness and body. Sautéing the spices in oil helped to bloom their flavors. We chose a combination of dried ancho and New Mexican chiles, toasted them in the oven until fragrant, and then ground them and added them in. To substitute chili powder for the dried chiles, grind the shiitakes and oregano and add them to the pot with ¼ cup of chili powder in step 4. We recommend a mix of at least two types of beans, one creamy (such as cannellini or navy) and one earthy (such as pinto, black, or red kidney). For a spicier chili, use both jalapeños. Serve with your favorite chili toppings.

serves 6 to 8
total time: 4 hours
(plus 8 hours for soaking beans)

Salt

1 pound (2½ cups) assorted dried beans, picked over and rinsed

2 dried ancho chiles

2 dried New Mexican chiles

½ ounce dried shiitake mushrooms, chopped coarse

4 teaspoons dried oregano

½ cup walnuts, toasted

1 (28-ounce) can diced tomatoes, drained with juice reserved

3 tablespoons tomato paste

1–2 jalapeño chiles, stemmed and chopped coarse

6 garlic cloves, minced

3 tablespoons soy sauce

¼ cup vegetable oil

2 pounds onions, chopped fine

1 tablespoon ground cumin

7 cups water

⅔ cup medium-grind bulgur

¼ cup minced fresh cilantro

1. Dissolve 3 tablespoons salt in 4 quarts cold water in large container. Add beans and soak at room temperature for at least 8 hours or up to 24 hours. Drain and rinse well.

2. Adjust oven rack to middle position and heat oven to 300 degrees. Arrange anchos and New Mexican chiles on rimmed baking sheet and toast until fragrant and puffed, about 8 minutes. Transfer to plate, let cool for 5 minutes, then remove stems and seeds. Working in batches, grind toasted chiles, mushrooms, and oregano in spice grinder (or with mortar and pestle) until finely ground.

3. Process walnuts in food processor until finely ground, about 30 seconds; transfer to bowl. Process drained tomatoes, tomato paste, jalapeño(s), garlic, and soy sauce in now-empty food processor until tomatoes are finely chopped, about 45 seconds. Set aside.

4. Heat oil in Dutch oven over medium-high heat until shimmering. Add onions and 1¼ teaspoons salt and cook, stirring occasionally, until onions begin to brown, 8 to 10 minutes. Reduce heat to medium, add ground chile mixture and cumin, and cook, stirring constantly, until fragrant, about 1 minute. Stir in rinsed beans and water and bring to boil. Cover pot, transfer to oven, and cook for 45 minutes.

5. Stir in bulgur, ground walnuts, tomato mixture, and reserved tomato juice and continue to cook in oven, covered, until beans are fully tender, about 2 hours.

6. Remove pot from oven, stir well, and let stand, uncovered, for 20 minutes. Stir in cilantro before serving.

stir-fried eggplant with garlic-basil sauce

why this recipe works Eggplant is the perfect base for Asian-inspired stir-fries, as it soaks up the flavor-packed sauce and softens to a melt-in-your-mouth consistency. We wanted to achieve a great Thai-style eggplant stir-fry without having to take the extra effort to salt or pretreat the eggplant before cooking (after all, stir-fries are supposed to come together quickly, not involve a lot of additional work). We started by cooking the eggplant for about 10 minutes. In that time we were able to drive off the excess moisture and brown the eggplant, all in one 12-inch skillet. To complement the earthy eggplant, we also added a sweet red bell pepper to the skillet. We tested adding additional vegetables, but anything more felt superfluous and hid the great flavor and texture of the sautéed eggplant. For the Thai-style sauce, we used a combination of water and fish sauce substitute flavored with brown sugar, lime, and red pepper flakes. Stirring in a generous amount of basil and scallions before serving added some last-minute freshness and a pop of color. Do not peel the eggplant; leaving the skin on helps it hold together during cooking.

serves 4
total time: 30 minutes

sauce
½ cup water

¼ cup fish sauce substitute

2 tablespoons packed brown sugar

2 teaspoons grated lime zest plus 1 tablespoon juice

2 teaspoons cornstarch

⅛ teaspoon red pepper flakes

vegetables
2 tablespoons plus 1 teaspoon vegetable oil

6 garlic cloves, minced

1 tablespoon grated fresh ginger

1 pound eggplant, cut into ¾-inch pieces

1 red bell pepper, stemmed, seeded, and cut into ¼-inch pieces

½ cup fresh basil leaves, torn into rough ½-inch pieces

2 scallions, sliced thin

1. for the sauce Whisk all ingredients together in bowl.

2. for the vegetables Combine 1 teaspoon oil, garlic, and ginger in bowl. Heat remaining 2 tablespoons oil in 12-inch nonstick skillet over high heat until shimmering. Add eggplant and bell pepper and cook, stirring often, until well browned and tender, 8 to 10 minutes.

3. Clear center of skillet, add garlic mixture, and cook, mashing mixture into skillet, until fragrant, about 30 seconds. Stir garlic mixture into vegetables. Whisk sauce to recombine, then add to skillet. Cook, stirring constantly, until sauce is thickened, about 30 seconds. Off heat, stir in basil and scallions and serve.

fish sauce substitute
makes about 1¼ cups
Use this as a vegetarian/vegan substitute for fish sauce.

3 cups water

3 tablespoons salt

2 tablespoons soy sauce

¼ ounce dried sliced shiitake mushrooms

Simmer all ingredients in large saucepan over medium heat until mixture is reduced by half, 20 to 30 minutes. Strain liquid through fine-mesh strainer and let cool completely.

to make ahead
Fish Sauce Substitute can be refrigerated for up to 2 months.

stewed chickpeas with eggplant and tomatoes

why this recipe works In Greece, fresh eggplant and dried chickpeas are cooked together for hours to create a hearty stew with deep flavor; the silky, luxurious texture of the eggplant is complemented by the firm-tender chickpeas. These stewed chickpeas are able to achieve an impressive depth of savory flavor without using any meat, making them perfect for a comforting, vegetarian-friendly supper. For a streamlined version of this dish, we started with canned chickpeas, which hold up well even during long cooking. We chopped canned whole tomatoes to give the dish a rustic texture and a tomatoey backbone. We found that a combination of stovetop and oven cooking created the texture we were after. To jump-start the cooking process, we sautéed onions, bell pepper, garlic, oregano, and bay leaves to create an aromatic base. We added our chickpeas, tomatoes, and eggplant (cut into 1-inch pieces to ensure that it softened but didn't completely break down) and transferred the pot to the oven. Baking the mixture uncovered concentrated the flavors and allowed any unwanted liquid to evaporate, eliminating the need to pretreat the eggplant. Stirring a couple of times during cooking ensured that the top layer didn't dry out. Some fresh oregano, added at the end, gave this savory dish a welcome burst of herbaceous flavor. This versatile dish tastes equally good when served warm or at room temperature. Serve with Classic Couscous (page 9).

serves 6

total time: 1 hour 15 minutes

¼ cup extra-virgin olive oil

2 onions, chopped

1 green bell pepper, stemmed, seeded, and chopped fine

Salt and pepper

3 garlic cloves, minced

1 tablespoon minced fresh oregano or 1 teaspoon dried

2 bay leaves

1 pound eggplant, cut into 1-inch pieces

1 (28-ounce) can whole peeled tomatoes, drained with juice reserved, chopped coarse

2 (15-ounce) cans chickpeas, drained with 1 cup liquid reserved

1. Adjust oven rack to lower-middle position and heat oven to 400 degrees. Heat oil in Dutch oven over medium heat until shimmering. Add onions, bell pepper, ½ teaspoon salt, and ¼ teaspoon pepper and cook until softened, about 5 minutes. Stir in garlic, 1 teaspoon oregano, and bay leaves and cook until fragrant, about 30 seconds.

2. Stir in eggplant, tomatoes and reserved juice, and chickpeas and reserved liquid and bring to boil. Transfer pot to oven and cook, uncovered, until eggplant is very tender, 45 minutes to 1 hour, stirring twice during cooking.

3. Discard bay leaves. Stir in remaining 2 teaspoons oregano and season with salt and pepper to taste. Serve.

potato vindaloo

why this recipe works Vindaloo is a complex, spicy dish that blends Portuguese and Indian cuisines into a potent braise featuring warm spices, chiles, wine vinegar, tomatoes, onions, garlic, and mustard seeds. We set out to translate its comfort food appeal into a hearty vegetarian Sunday supper. Centering the dish around potatoes seemed right, as it required low and slow cooking to develop complex flavors, and a combination of red and sweet potatoes elevated the stew's flavor even further. Because cooking potatoes in an acidic environment can prevent them from becoming tender, we cooked the potatoes until tender before adding the tomatoes and vinegar. To give our vindaloo exceptionally deep flavor, we used a mix of Indian spices plus bay leaves and mustard seeds, and simmered them with the potatoes, which soaked up the flavors as they cooked. Serve over Foolproof Baked White Rice (page 10) and with a dollop of yogurt.

serves 6
total time: 1 hour 15 minutes

2 tablespoons vegetable oil

2 onions, chopped fine

1 pound red potatoes, unpeeled, cut into ½-inch pieces

1 pound sweet potatoes, peeled and cut into ½-inch pieces

Salt and pepper

10 garlic cloves, minced

4 teaspoons paprika

1 teaspoon ground cumin

¾ teaspoon ground cardamom

½ teaspoon cayenne pepper

¼ teaspoon ground cloves

2½ cups water

2 bay leaves

1 tablespoon mustard seeds

1 (28-ounce) can diced tomatoes

2½ tablespoons red wine vinegar

¼ cup minced fresh cilantro

1. Heat oil in Dutch oven over medium heat until shimmering. Add onions, red potatoes, sweet potatoes, and ½ teaspoon salt and cook, stirring occasionally, until onions are softened and potatoes begin to soften at edges, 10 to 12 minutes.

2. Stir in garlic, paprika, cumin, cardamom, cayenne, and cloves and cook until fragrant and vegetables are well coated, about 2 minutes. Gradually stir in water, scraping up any browned bits. Stir in bay leaves, mustard seeds, and 1 teaspoon salt and bring to simmer. Cover, reduce heat to medium-low, and cook until potatoes are tender, 15 to 20 minutes.

3. Stir in tomatoes and their juice and vinegar and continue to simmer, uncovered, until flavors are blended and sauce has thickened slightly, about 15 minutes. Discard bay leaves, stir in cilantro, and season with salt and pepper to taste. Serve.

thai vegetable green curry
with jasmine rice cakes

why this recipe works Herbaceous and aromatic, green curry is a bright-tasting alternative to the red variety. Making your own requires a laundry list of ingredients, not to mention a fair amount of time, so to ensure you don't spend most of your Sunday in the kitchen, we looked to the grocery store for a convenient ready-made version. We used just a few tablespoons of green curry paste as the base for our sauce and added a whole can of coconut milk for richness and depth. To soak up all the extra sauce, we made jasmine rice cakes to go along with our vegetable curry. Pulsing some of the cooked rice in a food processor helped to create a sticky base so the cakes wouldn't crumble apart when served. We loved the combination of bamboo shoots and green beans for the vegetables, but the real key was finishing the dish with chopped radishes and fresh cilantro to bring some color and fresh flavor to the dish. You can use store-bought precooked jasmine rice. Basmati or long-grain white rice can be substituted for the jasmine rice; however, the cakes will be slightly less flavorful.

serves 4
total time: 45 minutes

4 cups cooked jasmine rice

1 large egg, lightly beaten

2 tablespoons all-purpose flour

Salt and pepper

3 tablespoons vegetable oil

1 (13.5-ounce) can coconut milk

3 tablespoons Thai green curry paste

2 tablespoons fish sauce substitute (see page 160)

1 tablespoon packed brown sugar

12 ounces green beans, trimmed and cut into 2-inch lengths

1 (8-ounce) can sliced bamboo shoots, rinsed

1 tablespoon lime juice

2 radishes, trimmed and chopped fine

2 tablespoons minced fresh cilantro

1. Adjust oven rack to middle position and heat oven to 200 degrees. Microwave rice in covered bowl until hot, about 90 seconds. Pulse half of rice in food processor until coarsely ground, about 10 pulses. Return processed rice to bowl with unprocessed rice, let cool, then stir in egg, flour, ¾ teaspoon salt, and ½ teaspoon pepper. Using your wet hands, pack rice mixture into eight 3-inch-wide cakes and place on baking sheet.

2. Set wire rack in rimmed baking sheet. Heat 1 tablespoon oil in 12-inch nonstick skillet over medium-high heat until shimmering. Gently lay cakes in skillet and cook until golden brown and crisp on both sides, about 6 minutes, turning gently halfway through cooking. Transfer cakes to prepared rack and keep warm in oven.

3. Whisk coconut milk, curry paste, fish sauce substitute, and sugar together in bowl. Wipe out now-empty skillet with paper towels, add remaining 2 tablespoons oil, and heat over medium-high heat until shimmering. Add green beans and cook, stirring occasionally, until tender, about 5 minutes.

4. Stir in coconut milk mixture and bamboo shoots and simmer until sauce is slightly thickened, about 4 minutes. Off heat, stir in lime juice and season with salt and pepper to taste. Sprinkle with radishes and cilantro and serve with rice cakes.

cheesy stuffed poblanos

why this recipe works Inspired by the Mexican dish *chiles rellenos*, we set out to make a recipe for cheesy stuffed poblano peppers, a fun, casual meal that would bring everyone to the table. Chiles rellenos are traditionally poblano peppers that are stuffed with cheese and then battered and fried. We felt the bright, vegetal flavor of the pepper was lost during frying (not to mention we didn't want to contend with the mess that frying created); instead, we decided to roast the stuffed peppers to deepen their flavor and tenderize the peppers. Stuffing raw poblanos without tearing them was tricky, but after a quick trip to the microwave, they were more pliable. To improve our filling's flavor and to anchor the cheese in the peppers during roasting, we added a couple of cans of pinto beans (half of which we mashed), corn, garlic, onion, and spices to a combination of Monterey Jack and cheddar cheeses. A quick fresh tomato salsa nicely balanced the rich, cheesy peppers.

serves 4 to 6
total time: 1 hour 15 minutes

2 (15-ounce) cans pinto beans, rinsed

1 cup water

1 tablespoon vegetable oil

1 onion, chopped fine

4 garlic cloves, minced

1 tablespoon ground cumin

1 tablespoon minced fresh oregano or 1 teaspoon dried

1 teaspoon chili powder

1 teaspoon grated lime zest plus 1 tablespoon juice

Salt and pepper

⅛ teaspoon cayenne pepper

2 cups frozen corn

4 ounces Monterey Jack cheese, shredded (1 cup)

4 ounces sharp cheddar cheese, shredded (1 cup)

¼ cup minced fresh cilantro

8 poblano chiles

1 recipe Easy Cherry Tomato Salsa

1. Adjust oven racks to upper-middle and lower-middle positions and heat oven to 425 degrees. Line 2 rimmed baking sheets with aluminum foil and set wire rack in each. Using potato masher, mash half of beans and water together in bowl until mostly smooth.

2. Heat oil in 12-inch nonstick skillet over medium heat until shimmering. Add onion and cook until softened, about 5 minutes. Stir in garlic, cumin, oregano, chili powder, lime zest, ½ teaspoon salt, and cayenne and cook until fragrant, about 30 seconds. Stir in mashed bean mixture and cook, stirring constantly, until nearly all liquid has evaporated, 3 to 5 minutes. Stir in remaining beans and corn and cook until warmed through, about 2 minutes. Off heat, stir in Monterey Jack, cheddar, cilantro, and lime juice. Season with salt and pepper to taste.

3. Leaving stem intact, cut slit lengthwise down 1 side of each poblano. Microwave poblanos in covered bowl until just pliable, about 2½ minutes. Gently pry open poblanos, remove seeds, and stuff evenly with bean-cheese mixture.

4. Lay poblanos, stuffed side up, on prepared sheets. Bake until tender, switching and rotating sheets halfway through baking, 30 to 40 minutes. Serve with salsa.

easy cherry tomato salsa
makes about 1 cup

6 ounces cherry tomatoes, quartered

1 tablespoon extra-virgin olive oil

1 tablespoon minced fresh cilantro

1½ teaspoons lime juice

Salt and pepper

Combine all ingredients in bowl and season with salt and pepper to taste. (Salsa can be refrigerated for up to 1 day.)

to make ahead
Stuffed poblanos, prepared through step 3, can be refrigerated for up to 24 hours. To bake, continue with step 4.

quinoa and vegetable stew

why this recipe works Quinoa stews are common in many South American regions, but authentic recipes call for obscure ingredients. We set out to make a traditional quinoa stew with an easy-to-navigate ingredient list that would make your Sunday meal prep a breeze. We found that paprika has a similar flavor profile to traditional annatto powder; we rounded it out with cumin and coriander. As for the vegetables, we chose red bell pepper, tomatoes, red potatoes, sweet corn, and frozen peas. We added the quinoa after the potatoes had softened and cooked it until it released starch to help give body to the stew. Finally, we added the traditional garnishes: avocado and cilantro. We like the convenience of prewashed quinoa. If you buy unwashed quinoa (or if you are unsure whether it's washed), be sure to rinse it before cooking to remove its bitter protective coating (called saponin). This stew tends to thicken as it sits; add additional warm vegetable broth as needed before serving to loosen. Do not omit the garnishes; they are important to the flavor of the stew.

serves 6 to 8
total time: 1 hour

2 tablespoons vegetable oil

1 onion, chopped

1 red bell pepper, stemmed, seeded, and cut into ½-inch pieces

5 garlic cloves, minced

1 tablespoon paprika

2 teaspoons ground coriander

1½ teaspoons ground cumin

6 cups vegetable broth

1 pound red potatoes, unpeeled, cut into ½-inch pieces

1 cup prewashed white quinoa

1 cup fresh or frozen corn

2 tomatoes, cored and chopped coarse

1 cup frozen peas

Salt and pepper

8 ounces queso fresco or feta cheese, crumbled (2 cups) (optional)

1 avocado, halved, pitted, and diced

½ cup minced fresh cilantro

1. Heat oil in Dutch oven over medium heat until shimmering. Add onion and bell pepper and cook until softened, 5 to 7 minutes. Stir in garlic, paprika, coriander, and cumin and cook until fragrant, about 30 seconds. Stir in broth and potatoes and bring to boil over high heat. Reduce heat to medium-low and simmer gently for 10 minutes.

2. Stir in quinoa and simmer for 8 minutes. Stir in corn and simmer until potatoes and quinoa are just tender, 5 to 7 minutes. Stir in tomatoes and peas and let heat through, about 2 minutes.

3. Off heat, season with salt and pepper to taste. Sprinkle portions with queso fresco, if using; avocado; and cilantro before serving.

variation
quinoa and vegetable stew with eggs
Serving this stew with a cooked egg on top is a common practice in Peru.

Crack 6 large eggs evenly over top of stew after removing from heat and seasoning with salt and pepper in step 3; cover and let eggs poach off heat until whites have set but yolks are still soft, about 4 minutes. To serve, carefully scoop cooked egg and stew from pot with large spoon.

conversions and equivalents

Some say cooking is a science and an art. We would say that geography has a hand in it, too. Flours and sugars manufactured in the United Kingdom and elsewhere will feel and taste different from those manufactured in the United States. So we cannot promise that the pie crust you bake in Canada or England will taste the same as a pie crust baked in the States, but we can offer guidelines for converting weights and measures. We also recommend that you rely on your instincts when making our recipes. Refer to the visual cues provided. If the pie dough hasn't "come together," as described, you may need to add more water—even if the recipe doesn't tell you to. You be the judge.

The recipes in this book were developed using standard U.S. measures following U.S. government guidelines. The charts below offer equivalents for U.S. and metric measures. All conversions are approximate and have been rounded up or down to the nearest whole number. For example:

1 teaspoon = 4.9292 milliliters, rounded up to 5 milliliters
1 ounce = 28.3495 grams, rounded down to 28 grams

volume conversions

u.s.	metric
1 teaspoon	5 milliliters
2 teaspoons	10 milliliters
1 tablespoon	15 milliliters
2 tablespoons	30 milliliters
1/4 cup	59 milliliters
1/3 cup	79 milliliters
1/2 cup	118 milliliters
3/4 cup	177 milliliters
1 cup	237 milliliters
1 1/4 cups	296 milliliters
1 1/2 cups	355 milliliters
2 cups (1 pint)	473 milliliters
2 1/2 cups	591 milliliters
3 cups	710 milliliters
4 cups (1 quart)	0.946 liter
1.06 quarts	1 liter
4 quarts (1 gallon)	3.8 liters

weight conversions

ounces	grams
1/2	14
3/4	21
1	28
1 1/2	43
2	57
2 1/2	71
3	85
3 1/2	99
4	113
4 1/2	128
5	142
6	170
7	198
8	227
9	255
10	283
12	340
16 (1 pound)	454

conversion for common baking ingredients

Baking is an exacting science. Because measuring by weight is far more accurate than measuring by volume, and thus more likely to produce reliable results, in our recipes we provide ounce measures in addition to cup measures for many ingredients. Refer to the chart below to convert these measures into grams.

ingredient	ounces	grams
flour		
1 cup all-purpose flour*	5	142
1 cup cake flour	4	113
1 cup whole-wheat flour	5½	156
sugar		
1 cup granulated (white) sugar	7	198
1 cup packed brown sugar (light or dark)	7	198
1 cup confectioners' sugar	4	113
cocoa powder		
1 cup cocoa powder	3	85
butter†		
4 tablespoons (½ stick, or ¼ cup)	2	57
8 tablespoons (1 stick, or ½ cup)	4	113
16 tablespoons (2 sticks, or 1 cup)	8	227

* *U.S. all-purpose flour, the most frequently used flour in this book, does not contain leaveners, as some European flours do. These leavened flours are called self-rising or self-raising. If you are using self-rising flour, take this into consideration before adding leavening to a recipe.*

† *In the United States, butter is sold both salted and unsalted. We generally recommend unsalted butter. If you are using salted butter, take this into consideration before adding salt to a recipe.*

oven temperatures

fahrenheit	celsius	gas mark
225	105	¼
250	120	½
275	135	1
300	150	2
325	165	3
350	180	4
375	190	5
400	200	6
425	220	7
450	230	8
475	245	9

converting temperatures from an instant-read thermometer

We include doneness temperatures in many of the recipes in this book. We recommend an instant-read thermometer for the job. Refer to the table at left to convert Fahrenheit degrees to Celsius. Or, for temperatures not represented in the chart, use this simple formula:

Subtract 32 degrees from the Fahrenheit reading, then divide the result by 1.8 to find the Celsius reading. For example: "Roast chicken until thighs register 175 degrees."

To convert
$175°F - 32 = 143°$
$143° ÷ 1.8 = 79.44°C$, rounded down to 79°C

index

C